ARCTIC EMP

Book One of the Talus 3 Series

Peter Sandor

Arctic EMP, 1st Edition.

06-05-25, Rev. 12

ISBN 978-1-7772782-1-2

Read other books by Peter Sandor

Dedication

This is dedicated to my wife, Jane. Without her critical eye and loving inspiration, this would not have been possible.

Contents

Chapter 1: St. Petersburg

Jim Roberts was startled by a glow from behind him. He turned and saw the light and its rusted, metal cover, hanging from a wrought-iron arm attached to the corner of the building. It swayed from the slight breeze coming in from Neva Bay. The light came on as dusk settled over Gorskaya, a small industrial area just northwest of St. Petersburg, Russia. Jim considered *industrial* wasn't the right term, but the closest he could come up with for this area smelling of oil, burnt metal and acrid chemicals. Establishments such as the concrete factory and the scrap metal plant, seemed to be expelled to this location, by default, by city officials who just wanted the resulting contamination absent from their home districts. Jim smirked as the concept reminded him of a storm sewer where all the shit and garbage tended to get caught at the exit.

Ironically, Chao Yang, sitting opposite to Jim, was looking in the other direction, directly towards Neva Bay and beyond it to the larger Gulf of Finland. He lifted the glass of ice-cold beer to his lips as he viewed the darkness not having completely chased away the sunlight. Still remaining was a curved line of amber sky in the distance above the low dam separating the bay from the gulf. As he lowered the glass, his lips curled up into a wry grin since he enjoyed the resemblance of this area to the smog-filled, industrialized cities of his Chinese homeland.

Jim drew Chao's attention back as he spoke. "Has the money been arranged?"

Chao tilted his head towards the beer in front of Jim. "Take a few moments and relax. Russian beer is actually quite good."

With his fingers shaking, Jim curled them around the base of the glass. He looked again towards the white-washed, concrete wall of the seedy bar they were sitting in front of. There was a monstrous beer bottle crudely painted below the sign hanging across the top of the building, and beside the bottle was a large window covered with thick, iron bars. Each day a simple patio pattern of four plastic tables with matching chairs were set up for patrons who thought the risk too great to actually go inside. The comical patio was completed with sections of portable wrought iron fence, and hanging from them at intervals were long flower pots filled with small stones. Sticking out from these stones were fake, lime-green plants, supporting red and blue plastic flowers fluttering in the breeze—the breeze, now carrying a chill as the thin line of sunlight that had been in the distance was completely chased away.

Chao took another drink of beer, then pulled his cell phone from its case. He glanced at it and said, "Janco, we still have a few minutes before the money is to be transferred."

As Jim was lifting his beer glass to his lips, he froze with his mouth gapped open and his eyebrows raised. He stammered, "Your organization only knows me as Jim. How do you know my name is really Janco?"

Chao's chest expanded underneath the black leather jacket he wore while his matching, black eyes shone from the reflected light. "Your name is Janco Devos. Although you claim to be British, you were born in Cape Town, South Africa. You attended the University of South Africa in Pretoria for four years, earning a degree in Economic Studies. Your marks were quite good, but not great. However, with the help of your father and his influence as one of the most successful ranchers in South Africa, owning vast plots of land handed down to him from his Boer forefathers, he managed to have you accepted at the Swiss Polytechnical Institute in Zurich. There, you found your calling, excelling at computer science studies, resulting in your master's and doctorate degrees. You returned to South Africa and worked for the government for two years before you realized, even though there was interest in the work, the level of pay was not so interesting. The lure of significantly increased compensation from several renowned companies, resulted in your employment at Morrison Security Services in London." Chao paused to take another long drink of beer.

Still leaning forward with his glass hanging from his fingers and his jaw gapped open, a chill went up Janco's spine. Maybe it was a mistake to deal with the Chinese Ministry of State Security, but he was fully committed, so there was no turning back. He regained his composure, leaning back in the plastic patio chair and emptied half the beer from his glass.

Chao enjoyed having leverage on people. He enjoyed the control it gave him, just as he enjoyed the scared shitless look Janco just had on his face. "You were happy working at Morrison's for a short time with a six-figure-salary and interesting work, but it just wetted your appetite for more—especially more money. It is that greed that has resulted in the two of us sitting here today, drinking this fine beer."

Now, Janco was getting even more nervous, and his eyes darted from side to side. He knew he was at the mercy of the Chinese agent.

"Where is the memory stick?" Chao asked.

Janco licked his lips before he answered. "You'll get the memory stick with the information you require on it once the money has been transferred to my account." He took his phone out and opened his banking app to check for the transfer.

Angling his own phone up, Chao's facial recognition kicked in. "It will only be a few more minutes before you see the 500 thousand American dollars in your account. You have verified the emails from Universal Mining's vice-president are on the memory stick?"

Janco nodded in the affirmative.

"Did you check the emails? Is there evidence Universal Mining is working with the Angolan government?"

Talking was making Janco feel more comfortable, so he continued. "I checked enough of them to ensure your associates in the Chinese secret service will not be disappointed." Janco leaned back once again in the patio chair. "It's clear Universal's researchers found a large deposit of uranium in northeast Angola, but unfortunately, there are still rebel remnants, not satisfied with the result of their 27-year civil war, who have a significant presence in that area. The British mining company has asked for the Angolan government's help in removing the insurgents, but of course, the Angolan government wants two things—money and armaments."

Chao's eyebrows lowered under his crop of jet-black hair. "So far this is not new information."

After a smart-assed grin, Janco continued. "Of course, things get much more interesting. The British government have their fingers in the pot. There are ministers of parliament being paid by the mining company to help secure the rights, just as there are Chinese government officials also being bribed to ensure the illegal sale of military supplies goes through without opposition. That's why you're here willing to pay me 500 thousand dollars. You want the names of the Chinese government officials."

Chao provided his own grin, giving his face a younger appearance than his 40 years. "Such information leading to the identification of such Chinese officials could have several results. On the one hand, they might be considered traitors, or the leverage provided could allow others to blackmail these officials for completely unrelated goals." He chuckled. "You are right, it can be very complicated."

The phone in front of Chao emitted an electronic *beep*. He looked down as the screen lit up, then his gaze rose to Janco. "The money transfer has started."

Before Chao finished his sentence, Janco swept his finger across the screen of his phone. A green bar was progressing across the screen, verifying the transfer was in progress.

Anyone watching the two men sitting outside the seedy bar would be amused as they were both intently looking down at their phones, obsessed with the progress of the transfer bar. Even more amusing would be when the synchronized bars completed their race across the screen to the 100 per cent mark, triggering them both to raise their faces to look at each other in unison.

"You have your money." Chao said what Janco already knew. "Now, the memory stick." He held his hand out indicating it was more than a friendly request.

Janco put his phone in its holster hanging off his belt, then leaned towards the fake flower pot hanging off the railing beside their table. He dug his hand into the small rocks between two fake plants and retrieved the memory stick wrapped in black electrical tape. He shook off the dirt that had collected and lifted himself off the chair as he reached towards Chao's hand.

Chao was startled by a recognizable *whiz* as the left side of Janco's head exploded outwards from the force of the bullet, and the memory stick dropped conveniently into Chao's palm. He watched as Janco's blue eyes opened wide in surprise before they froze that way as his lifeless body fell away from the chair. Even before his body hit the ground, Chao had sprung to his feet, sending the plastic chair flying backwards. With his extensive training and athletic ability, he easily hopped the railing and was speeding towards the Jeep parked 50 metres down the pot-hole-filled, narrow roadway. He was almost there when a flurry of bullets smashed into the side of the vehicle, throwing out shards of sharp metal.

Chao skidded to a stop on the gravel as he saw two of the tires flattened. Instantly, he changed direction. As he ran across the road, he thought, *who the fuck has ambushed us?* His one foot slammed into the murky water at the bottom of the opposite culvert, sending up a splash of stinking, wet mud. Just before he disappeared into the line of spruce trees, two bullets hit into the ground, just centimetres from his foot.

"Easy Ringo. That was a little fucking close." The electronic message came from the headset microphone of Tony Edmonds, better known as *Bossman.* He was laying prone on the roof of the concrete factory, a half kilometre to the south of the seedy café. As leader of the British Special Air Service squad, he required and had full view for several clicks around his position through the scope of his assault rifle.

There was a crackle over the airway before Ringo responded, "No bother mate." You could discern the thick, cockney accent through the whisper.

Bossman rotated his weapon, following Chao as he dodged between the sparse trees. "He's coming your way, *Ace.*"

Ace peered through the opening of the balaclava, looking for Chao. He heard him before he saw him as the Chinese national's footsteps crashed through the crisp, brown leaves having fallen early, in this the third week of September. Ace rested the barrel of his weapon on the large rock he hid behind and fired a shot into the ground behind the Chinese agent.

Chao jumped a half metre into the air as his fingers grasped the chain links of the fence protecting the scrap yard. He threw himself over and nimbly landed on his feet. The two small clouds of dust created were swept away as he propelled himself back into his headlong sprint. He dodged between old cars and racks filled with rusty, metal parts as bullets continued to fly around him. He didn't know who infiltrated their intelligence and ambushed them. Right now, the only thing important was to get to *Plan B* and finish the mission.

He grunted as he flipped himself over the opposite fence of the scrap yard and was now on the road paralleling the small Gorskaya harbour. The harbour was man-made in the shape of a square with a narrow row of dirt and rock, topped with short trees and gangly brush, on the other three sides of the corralled water. At the north end was an opening, allowing small ships and boats to enter and exit.

However, Chao turned in the opposite direction and once again continued his flight. As the moon came out from behind a cloud, a quarter kilometre away he could see the small peninsula jutting out into the harbour. Another bullet slammed into the ground near his ankle as he pulled out his phone. He managed to hit his *emergency contact* icon, and after he heard a response, he yelled into the phone, "I'm coming in hot!"

Chao continued down the gravel roadway and turned up the small peninsula where a ten-metre express cruiser was waiting with its twin engines humming. As soon as Chao jumped into the back, the pilot pushed the throttle lever all the way forward. The sleek, grey boat jumped forward and sped off towards the opening to the larger harbour.

"He's all yours, *Chuck*," Bossman said into the small microphone.

Along the outside break wall of the harbour, another engine roared to life, and the dim running lights revealed another boat. Chuck grasped the wheel with one hand and gave the two Mercury outboard engines full power as he directed the large pontoon boat after the cruiser.

"Not to close, Chuck. Keep him moving, but we need to give him room," Bossman directed.

Chao whipped his fingers through his hair, wet from the spray sent up by the cruiser. He saw the pursuing boat and judged their speed to at least match their own. "Make for the Neva River! We'll lose them in St. Petersburg!"

The cruiser pilot veered the boat east towards the beautifully lit city and hopefully, their escape.

"Is the laptop in the cabin?" Chao asked.

Without losing his focus on the direction ahead, the pilot nodded his head up and down.

Bossman thought, *so far things have gone as planned.* "Chex, is the transmission sent?"

Chex was seated on a rock on the northwest side of Neva Bay, beside Chav who was down on one knee with the loaded GS-777 rocket launcher resting over his knee. Looking at the screen of his own laptop connected to the small radar disc pointed out towards the bay, Chex replied, "Nothing yet."

"Chav, the target should be in your sight now. Lock on."

The deadly rocket launcher was lifted to Chav's shoulder as he saw the spray of the cruiser 200 metres in the distance, and he could see their trajectory would cross the speeding boat in front of his position.

Chao found the laptop in the small cabin of the cruiser, and he whooped out a resounding Chinese curse his forefathers would be proud of when he saw he had an internet signal. Luckily, the bay was relatively calm, but it still took some expertise to engage the memory stick into the USB port. It was even more difficult to hit the correct keys to initiate the transmission, but he finally accomplished this. He all but smashed his index finger into the *enter* key, and the solid bar began to slowly move across the screen.

Chex's screen, latched onto Chao's, showed the same progress bar as the cruiser sped past Chex's location. Chav followed the boat's path with the scope on the RPG and the automatic tracking system within the eyepiece. He whispered, "Better give me the go ahead soon, or he'll be out of range." The boat was now 100 metres past their position.

"What do you have, Chex?" Bossman's voice was strained.

"I can't make it go faster! It needs a few more seconds," Chex answered.

"Fuck," Bossman whispered as he followed the cruiser with his weapon's eyepiece. The vessel was now 600 metres away and increasing the distance from Chav's position.

Chao was sweating as he watched the bar on the laptop screen almost finish. Finally, the message, *100%*, flashed on the screen. He raised a fist in the air as he knew, even if he did not escape, the information was in the cloud and accessible by his organization.

Chex also saw the *100%* message and in the coolest, calmest voice, confirmed, "Transmission complete and verified."

"Fire!" Bossman hissed.

There was a puff of smoke at Chav's shoulder, and the rocket launched from the muzzle of the weapon. It took less that two seconds for the ordinance to travel the 800 metres to the cruiser. Chao's arm, still held in the air, blew off as the cruiser exploded into a thousand small pieces at the base of a 30-metre ball of flame.

The RAF, British Aerospace 146 accelerated down the runway. Once it reached its specified rotational velocity, the pilot pulled back on the stick and the small, four engine cargo plane lifted from the airfield at Utti, Finland. Bossman looked out the small window back towards Russia in the distance.

Sitting beside him, Chex tapped on Bossman's shoulder. As Bossman turned with a *why are you bothering me* frown, Chex asked, "Have you ever been on a weirder mission?"

Bossman slouched back in his seat, closing his eyes. "It was just a mission. You were briefed just as I was. There's not much else to worry about." The last words were said in a firm tone. He hoped that, along with his closed eyes, it would send Chex the message he wasn't interested in banter.

However, Chex wouldn't leave it alone. "Sure, I know all about the background. I know about the uranium in Angola and the British mining company, along with the Angolan government and the Chinese, all working on who can screw the other before they get it in their own ass. The Chinese got their emails with names of corrupt Chinese officials. Word will get back to the mining company who will panic and contact their people in the British government. Of course, MI5 is waiting, and we will find out about our own corrupt officials, but we're all ignoring the elephant in the room."

Opening one eye, Bossman replied, "What the fuck elephants are you talking about?"

"Russian elephants."

"For a smart bloke with two degrees, you're daft, Chex."

Chex just couldn't let it go. "Listen, I know what we and the Chinese got out of the operation, but what about the Russians?"

Bossman snickered. "You mean the Russian elephants."

Poking Bossman in the shoulder, Chex said, "Fuck off already. The Russians just looked the other way as we killed a Chinese agent on their soil. Three hours ago, when we crossed the border into Finland, the Russian security officers barely looked at our papers and just waved us through."

"It sounds like there was an arrangement made ahead of time," Bossman offered.

"I can feel my asshole tightening up because you know they'll want something in return. We just don't know what it is yet," Chex concluded.

Bossman turned his face towards the window and muttered, "There'll come a day when the Russians remind us of this favour, and I have a feeling we might as well pull our pants down and get ready, because it's going to be painful."

Chapter 2: Enhanced Solutions

"Alexa, shut the fuck up!" Natalie yelled.

It was 5:45 a.m. and the small speaker across the room played a song at a loud volume, cutting through the blackness of her bedroom. Her iPad played a different song each morning, and today's was "Thunderstruck" by AC/DC. The opening guitar riff was just joined by the words from the lead singer, "Thunder! Thunder!"

Natalie slammed her palm into the mattress and yelled out again, "Alexa, enough already!"

There was no response, so Natalie threw the blankets off and thrust her shapely legs off the side of the bed. Her feet hit the floor hard before she stomped over to the dresser across the room, where she went through the motions on her iPad to turn off the music. She stretched her five-foot-seven-inch frame upwards, reaching even higher with her hands, while tilting her feet up onto her tip toes.

There was no *Alexa*. Her yelling at the music, asking a non-existent home monitoring system to shut off the music so she could slide back under the covers, was a ritual she performed every morning. The alarm on her iPad required her to physically get up and turn it off, assuring she would never be late for work.

On the night stand, a fancy clock threw the time, in large red letters, on the far wall. She scratched her fingers back and forth through her hair as she saw the time change to 5:51. *One minute late,* she thought as she made her way to the bathroom.

After a quick ten-minute shower, she wiped the condensation off the mirror and had a good look at herself. Her auburn hair was cut short and rolled stylishly to the left across the top of her head. The cut was longer at the top and shortened quickly at the back and each side, so there were only short bristles surrounding the top of each ear. It looked very ordinary until you noticed the two lines of shocking pink, starting at the part and coming across the slope of hair, then down through her side-swept bangs. She could not help but grin at her reflection, enjoying the vivid pink lines that confused people who would have difficulty believing she was forty, rebellious years old.

It took only a few minutes to apply a discrete amount of makeup—discrete until she applied a brilliant coat of red to her lips. She combed her hair, then went to her closet to choose an outfit for the day. She remembered there was an important meeting later this morning, followed by an interview, so after she slid open the closet door, she searched for a sharp, eye-catching outfit. The skirt she selected was tight-fitting with a short slit up the back. The colour looked black, but as she walked, if the right angle of light reflected off it, the dark-purple shimmer would be revealed. To match, she selected a simple, white blouse. The simplicity would draw people's attention to the low-cut cleavage. She quickly put these on as well as a pair of black, three-inch high heels to complete her ensemble.

After a glass of orange juice and toast, she was on her way to the parking garage of the condo complex where her white BMW awaited her. Her job as a director for a very successful company gave her the salary to afford the higher end and more expensive BMW 7 model. The vehicle roared to life, and almost subconsciously, she navigated the three turns she had made every morning for six years, finally exiting up to ground level and the city of Toronto, Canada.

To be more specific, Natalie lived along the shore of Lake Ontario in Etobicoke which is technically an area of West Toronto. From the 30-story condo she lived in, she could get into the night life of downtown Toronto in 20 minutes, but her office building was an arduous 45-minute drive in the opposite direction each and every morning. This Wednesday morning was like every other morning. As she took the on ramp to the highway heading west, she merged into the crowd of cars going no where near the speed limit. Just like most other rush hour drivers, she tightened her grip on the steering wheel and took on her aggressive driver persona.

This area of Southern Ontario, bounding the north side of Lake Ontario, is one of the most heavily populated areas in North America, and the most populous place in Canada. As she drove, crossing from one congested lane to the other, supposedly saving seconds of valuable time, the BMW seamlessly passed from city to city as one merged into the other without any noticeable break in the urban landscape. Etobicoke changed to Cooksville, then Port Credit and the remainder of the Mississauga region. By now, Natalie's palms were sweaty, caused by the tight grip on the steering wheel as the ordeal continued through Oakville, and finally, she reached Burlington. She expelled a sigh of relief as she veered her vehicle onto the offramp.

Ten minutes later, she turned into the driveway splitting the well-manicured lawn dotted with tall oak trees, surrounding her office building. Almost immediately, she passed a large, white sign with striking red letters.

It read, *Enhanced Solutions*. Natalie grinned as she continued up the long driveway, thinking the name of the company was vague enough that most people wouldn't know what type of services they really offered. Upper management liked keeping prying eyes away.

Two hundred metres along the winding driveway, Natalie arrived at the guardhouse. Running in each direction, as far as she could see, was a two-metre-high, wrought-iron fence with red-brick columns every fifteen metres. From the road, the complex looked complacent, but when anyone reached this point, the high security hidden from the street was very evident.

Natalie held her hand out the window holding her company identification. "Hi, Jack. How's you're morning going?"

The uniformed guard who moved from the guardhouse towards the car smiled. "I haven't had to shoot anyone yet this morning, Miss Lowe." He glanced at the identification and gave a slight nod of his chin. His gaze searched out the inside of the vehicle as he mumbled to her, "You don't have any terrorists hidden in your trunk, do you?"

Natalie tilted her chin up and covered her eyes with her hand to block the blinding, morning sunlight just clearing the treeline. She smiled sweetly and replied, "Now Jack, I'm mortified, but even more so, I'm deeply hurt. To make amends can you please ask Nabil to—open the fucking gate."

Jack laughed and turned to Nabil in the guardhouse and, with his hand, made a circling motion over his head. In response, the heavy gate creaked and slowly slid open.

Just before she pressed her foot to the gas pedal, Natalie said, "Have a great day, guys."

It was a short drive to her private parking spot at the front of the building. She made her way through the front doors into the atrium where a larger red-lettered sign with the name, *Enhanced Solutions*, faced her.

Enhanced Solutions employed only 90 people. They were a highly sought after and successful marketing company. Their specialty was customer surveys they sold for top dollar to companies who wanted to know the likes, dislikes and quirks of buying customers. A simplistic view of the company would find two sides. One side did research into what things merchandising companies wanted to know, such as which companies should they target, and what information would they pay for? This included everything from automotive trends, to companies making furniture or even something as simple as hand-mixers.

The other side of the company dealt with doing the actual surveys of customers and analyzing the results. The sales department was also included in this half of the company, and this was where the money was made. Convincing, for example, a large ceramic tile manufacturer what patterns people really wanted, or what colour preferences were popular, was a much sought-after and profitable skill.

The atrium was four stories high, taking up the entire height of the building. Natalie took the elevator to the second floor and said, "hello," to several early starters until she reached the door to her office. The sign on it read, *Natalie Lowe, Director North American Corporate Research*. Her office was not large, but felt much larger since the wall between her office and the main office area was made of glass. Her furniture was modern, and there was a door on the wall opposite her desk leading to a conference room. On the other side of that, through an adjoining door, was an office similar to hers, but it was occupied by Cheryl Jameson. She was the *Director of European Corporate Research*.

Her mornings were typically repetitive with a brief staff meeting after checking her emails. The meeting was dreaded by her subordinates as Natalie never forgot an assignment due to her simple but effective filing system. She came to her staff meeting with three files. The first, was titled, *To Do* and was filled with assignments she took responsibility for personally. The second file, and the one that was the dreaded one, was titled, *Assigned To*. These were tasks she gave to her subordinates. This file, along with the list of these assignments in her planner, ensured no task assigned was ever forgotten.

The end of her staff meeting always ended the same way. Her subordinates cringed as she turned to the back of her planner, and they knew she would ask for an update on each and every assignment. Natalie enjoyed this time, knowing there were more assignments assigned to each person than what they could ever accomplish in a reasonable time frame. She particularly enjoyed watching them improvise responses, where she took careful note of how well they prioritised their time. This ability to think on their feet, was a major factor she used when assessing their performance.

However, the third file was the one that served her the best over the years. It was a last piece of advice from her predecessor before he retired. Her third file was called the *Bullshit file*. It could have been called the *Buffer file*, but ultimately, *Bullshit* was more apropos. In almost any job, you have subordinates and you have a boss. The boss also has superiors in the chain of command. There are times when the superior, distanced from the working level of an organization, feels a need to directly interject an assignment into the working level. Of course, he gives the assignment to your boss, who often, while stating what a good idea it is, thinks, *what a fucking moron*. The boss, nevertheless, is compelled to give the person, in this case Natalie, the assignment—well, because it came from his superior.

Natalie, with a few years of experience with this process, knows to put these types of asinine assignments into the *Bullshit file*, while realizing there's a very high probability the superior will forget all about it. Although not as high, there is still a good probability the superior *and* her boss will forget about the assignment. If a given assignment is in her *Bullshit file* for a month, she transfers it to the recycling bin. If her boss asks about the assignment within the month, she moves it to the *To Do* file or the *Assign To* file. The process is near perfect. The only thing that would make it absolutely perfect, is if her boss had his own *Bullshit file*.

She tried to keep the meeting to 30 minutes, and then she usually worked on some of her assignments. Of course, her phone would ring constantly as one of her employees or a company she deals with, would call with an emergency. These calls could drastically change the course of her day.

This morning there were only two such calls, and her time was moving quickly when Cheryl poked her head into Natalie's office. "It's 9:50. We better head to Philip's office for our meeting." Philip, their boss, was not as anal as Natalie and only had his staff meetings every Monday, Wednesday and Friday.

Slipping her high heels, that she always kicked off when seated behind her desk, back on, she picked up her planner and followed Cheryl down the aisle to the elevator. They took it up to the fourth floor and exited onto what they all called, *Executive Row*. There were three offices along the far wall that was faced with solid oak paneling, and in front of each office was an assistant. *Secretary* was no longer an acceptable term, with *assistant* providing a less sexist persona. Natalie grinned as she thought of this while very well knowing each assistant was, in fact, female.

The door to the office on the far right was open. Cheryl and Natalie said, "hello," to Jenny as they walked by her and into the expansive office on the other side. Philip was the Vice-President of Research and enjoyed his comforts, but then he deserved them. He was a workaholic and often would not go home for days at a time. As such, in front of the window that covered the entire wall, was a complete living room set. This included a western-style, brown, faded, leather couch with oversized nail-head trim. There were two matching armchairs, and between them was a large coffee table. Natalie knew the French provincial style dresser in the far corner contained blankets, pillows and a change of clothes to support Philip's marathon work sessions.

When the two women came into the office, Philip stood up from his desk and came over to them with a wide smile. Natalie thought Philip was good looking, and he looked even better when he smiled, but there was a drawback. She worked for Philip for six years now and learned, in spite of the great smile, when he was just talking, his teeth looked weird—like they were too big for his mouth. She knew it was a small thing overshadowed by his general great looks, distinguished-looking hair with grey peppered through the brown, and a six-foot-two-inch physique he kept in wonderful shape.

Philip had a habit of shaking everyone's hand the first time he saw them in the day, so he did so and led the two women over to the large conference table on the opposite wall from the windows.

By now John, Alejandro and Singh, respectively the Director's of Research for the African, South American and Asia/Pacific regions, joined them at the conference table. Philip followed a format, and Wednesday's meeting was an opportunity for each director to give a summary of progress in their regions. The update was to include breakthroughs but also shortfalls, so Philip had the opportunity to do his job.

Natalie was the last to give her update in a meeting that had so far been quite sedate, but she was about to understand, not for the first time, what it meant when Philip took the opportunity to *do his job*. She did notice as she was giving her update, Philip's face turned a bit pink, and the hue changed to a deeper shade of red when she announced she had finished.

Philip took a deep breath and straightened himself in his chair. He was trying to stay calm while running the fingers of both hands back through his hair. Cheryl's face snapped towards Natalie in an instant. Natalie gazed back and swallowed hard. Both women had seen a semblance of this before. Pushing the fingers of one hand back through his hair was a sign Philip was irritated, but she wasn't sure she'd ever seen him use both hands. *She was about to get fucked over*, Natalie thought.

Philip raised his face and looked directly at Natalie, and in a voice just above a whisper, said, "What about the Genuine Apparel case?"

Natalie gulped and said, "I'm not ready to give you an update as we're having some minor issues."

Philip's voice increased in volume. He looked at all his directors now. "Do you think I ask you to come in here every couple of days to just hear how wonderful things are?"

There was no response, and they were all looking down into their laps.

Philip rose and began to pace around the table. He pointed to his door. "Remember, I used to work out there! I know what it's like. I know there are problems. I have more experience than all of you put together, so you better not ever treat me like I don't need to know about problems. I really only have one job—well two, and in a way, they really are one. Part of it is to keep my asshole boss, who sits in the other corner office, off your backs. The second part of my job is to help you get your job done. To be clear, it's not to do your job for you, but to make sure you have the right resources to get it done!"

Singh raised his gaze and said, "We understand, Sir. We'll do better."

Natalie narrowed her gaze as she looked at Singh. *God damn, suck-up wimp*, she thought

Philip froze. He put his fists onto his hips and said, "Singh, you god damn, suck-up wimp!" He waited a few seconds to see if anyone else wanted to comment, but there was only silence. "Everyone, get out!"

The five directors shot up from their chairs, then walked as fast as they could to the door while trying not to look like their pace was panicked. Natalie was almost at the door when she heard Philip say, "Not you, Natalie. We need to talk about the Genuine Apparel account. Have a seat on the chair by the window."

Natalie almost got away, but she turned and dropped herself in one of the leather armchairs. Philip went to the door, closed it and turned the lock, ensuring they wouldn't be disturbed. Philip liked his privacy and enjoyed the fact there were no windows on the inside wall. He and Natalie were very much alone. He walked across the room and stood by the armchair with his arms crossed.

Natalie began to explain. "Let me tell you about the issues with the account."

"I don't give a shit about the account," Philip admitted.

"What…"

"Stand up and take off your panties."

Natalie's face instantly went white, and an odd noise came from her lips. It was like a yell held back in a hushed tone. "Philip!"

His strong fingers reached down under her arm, and he pulled her up to her feet. Philip was her boss, and in her state of shock, she resisted but not enough to stop his coaxing. She stumbled slightly as he led her over to the huge picture window.

"Philip, what are you doing?"

His hand came up behind her neck and he bent her forward towards the window. Her hands came up just in time and slapped into the glass. Philip's foot came forward and kicked her feet further apart.

"You can't be serious! Oh my god!"

The words came as Philip reached up into the slit at the back of her skirt. He grabbed her panties with his fingers and roughly dragged them down to mid-thigh. He must have worked his fly down at the same time because the next thing Natalie felt was a thrust. Philip groaned at the moment he filled her.

She whimpered, "Oh my god," but this time it was in a deeper, sultry tone.

Philip moved his hips in a hard rhythm as he took her. Her fingers, pressed against the glass, curling as they tried unsuccessfully to grip onto something—anything. She tried to stop her passion as it swept over her, but she failed as her eyes half closed. She pushed back into him each time he thrust forward. She didn't want to, but she couldn't stop. Her excitement built as she thought how decadent this was.

Then, her eyes shot open. *The gardener*, she thought. They had a fellow come by every Wednesday to cut the grass and manicure the few gardens on the ten-acre grounds. No one ever came to this side of the building except him. He was a young guy—good looking, and even though it was September and the growing cycle had slowed, he would certainly come. He would easily see them!

Philip continued to move against her, and even though the idea of being seen horrified her, it added to her level of excitement. Her legs began to shake as she mumbled, "Gardener." Her one hand lifted off the glass and made a feeble slap on it.

Philip paid her no attention. His arm slid around and under her waist as her thighs shook.

"Cutting grass," she muttered through her moans.

She couldn't hold back any longer, and she bit her lip to keep herself from screaming. She pressed back hard against him as her passion overwhelmed her. Her eyes rolled back, and for several moments, she forgot where she was while not even feeling Philip's own passion release.

Ten minutes later, Natalie had composed herself in the small, private bathroom adjacent to Philip's office. Her legs were once again under her as she walked over to Philip who sat on the couch, one leg crossed over the other. She sat down beside him and asked, "What the hell was that?"

Philip chuckled. "I would say *that* was great. The whole situation made it very exciting."

"I don't think my passion has ever been so intense." Natalie raised an eyebrow as she gazed at Philip. "You planned this whole thing, didn't you? You even did the *I'm really pissed* act to get you and I alone."

"I am a little upset about the Genuine Apparel account, but we can talk about that tomorrow."

"You took a big chance. The guy who cuts the grass must have decided to wait until the afternoon to do this side of the building," Natalie concluded.

"Nothing was left to chance," Philip said through a sly grin. "I made arrangements to ensure he didn't come today. He'll be back around tomorrow."

"You're pure evil," Natalie said as she laughed. She and Philip had been having a sexual relationship for two years. For even more years, Natalie avoided boyfriends and really any kind of romantic relationship. She and Philip had an understanding. It was just about sex. There were no flowers, no Valentine's Day, no birthday cards and no going out on dates. Usually once a week, either at her place or his, they would have sex. There were no sleep overs. Once the sex was over, sometimes there was some polite conversation and a drink, but when the glass was empty, they would part. That was the unwritten rule.

Sex at work was a surprise. It was the first time. She was happy with it, but sensed perhaps it was the beginning of the end. It was a sign he needed more, and she had also enjoyed it immensely. The bigger implication of *more*, was not what she wanted, so she realized they could go on for a time, but soon she would end it.

She rose to her feet. "I better get back to work."

As she walked across the room, he said, "Make sure you look angry. They think I just gave you pure shit."

Waving her hand above her, indicating she understood, she opened the door and stepped out. The assistant didn't turn her head, but she jumped when Natalie slammed the door behind her. *Gave me shit—you've got to be kidding,* she thought.

On her way down in the elevator, her cell phone buzzed. She looked at the text from Cheryl. It read, *Remember our interview. He's here.*

Natalie texted back, *On my way.*

Once in her office, she continued into the conference room where Cheryl was sitting across from a handsome, young man. When he saw Natalie, he rose to his feet and smiled. As he held out his hand, he said, "Hi. I'm Jason

Moore."

Natalie noticed he was lean with a muscular build. He had a nicely-trimmed, black moustache and beard, and his hair flowed back like it was wind-blown. Her eyes glanced to Cheryl who sat behind Jason. Cheryl made an adolescent face and mouthed the word, *hunk*. Natalie's gaze came back to the 28-year-old man and she said, "Natalie Lowe. Nice to meet you."

The two women interviewed Jason for a good 45 minutes. His master's degree in marketing impressed them, but not as much as the answers he gave. They were looking for a junior research analyst, and he fit the bill perfectly. At the end of the interview, Cheryl said they were impressed, and they would be in touch after they made a decision. With the interview concluded, Natalie left the room for a moment and brought in another analyst to take Jason back out to the lobby.

After Jason left, Cheryl slid back in the chair, fanning herself. "He was so hot."

Natalie laughed. "I thought you were going to ask *me* to leave the room. Too bad we can't hire him."

"That really sucks since he would have been perfect for the job."

Natalie opened her planner and read the names. "You know why we can't hire him. He was the fifth candidate we interviewed. I'll make sure we send out letters to each of them, indicating they were considered, but another person filled the position."

Cheryl frowned, but only for a moment. "When is Jacklin McDonald starting the job?"

"She's flying in from Heathrow in late October. It would be great if you could pick her up and get her settled in her apartment. You do that, and I'll do the orientation when she gets here," Natalie suggested.

"Fair enough," Cheryl agreed.

Natalie smiled. Cheryl was so easy to work with. "Have you talked to her?"

"Not a word." Cheryl shrugged. "We're told she has the job, so she has the job. No questions asked."

Natalie nodded. "It's probably better that way."

Cheryl sighed. "Why can't we hire Jason for something? There must be something he could do."

"Like what?"

"I don't know. Maybe he can cut the grass."

"Fuck off, Cheryl."

Cheryl's eyebrows rose in a look showing her lack of understanding, and she thought, *Wow. I think she needs to get laid.*

Chapter 3: The Library

Natalie was looking at her feet under the desk. She wasn't sure if she liked the dark-red nail polish she had used on her toes. She used the same colour on her finger nails, and they looked great, but for some reason, she wasn't happy with how the colour looked on her toes. *Maybe it was the lack of light under her desk*, she thought.

"Are you listening to anything I'm telling you?" Steve asked.

Natalie lifted her gaze across the desk while she swiped her bangs back off her forehead. She hoped the motion would hide the slight blush coming over her face. "Of course. This is important stuff." She hated lying to Steve since he was a great data analyst and an even better supervisor, but he had given Natalie the information she requested at the beginning of their discussion. After that, since Steve loved to talk, he did just that, and it was about everything and anything that really was of no value to the real details of his report, or anything else Natalie could be remotely interested in. Once Steve began his ongoing words that quickly turned into an obnoxious drone, Natalie couldn't help but zone him out. She tried to keep focused, just as she tried many times before, but once again, she failed.

"Maybe you're tired," Steve offered.

Natalie snapped her fingers and slid her shoes on. "I think you're right. I'm going home."

Steve laughed. "It's only 2:00 in the afternoon. You can't be going home."

Natalie pushed up onto her feet and smirked. "Watch me. It's Friday, and I think I've done my fair share of work this week."

Steve also rose to his feet and said, "What about me? I worked hard."

"You certainly have, Steve." She picked up her cell phone and small, black purse, then waited at the door for Steve to exit ahead of her. "If you stay until 4:00 and perform your supervisory duties and take on my responsibilities for the next two hours, then I think you'll have worked just as hard as I have today. Feel free to go home then," she offered with a satisfied grin.

As Steve walked by Natalie and out the door, he shook his head and mumbled, "You can be such a bitch."

The smirk that hadn't left Natalie's face, grew wider, and she replied,

"Why thank you Steve." She locked her door and made a hasty exit before anyone could call her back for help on a problem they should be able to take care of themselves.

Since she was leaving work early, even though it was Friday, the traffic was lighter than normal. Upon arriving at her building, she took the elevator up from the parking garage, but rather than going to her condo on the 12th floor, she got off at the main lobby. She headed out onto the main street and took a deep breath of fresh air—at least as fresh as it could be in a big metropolis. Still, it did have a fresher feel one always felt when they snuck out of work early.

When she left, it hadn't been a random act. She knew early in her day she wanted to get out early, so she attacked her tasks accordingly. It was all working out until Steve made an impromptu entrance into her office late in the day. Ultimately, Steve only cost her a few minutes, and her plan was now coming to fruition as she headed east towards the public library. It was a nice, late-September day, and there were quite a few people out enjoying it as much as she was. It was only two blocks until she arrived at the old, brown-brick building.

Natalie liked reading, so she liked going to the library, but she really enjoyed going to *this* library. The building used to be a gun factory in the early 1900's. There were three floors, and each still had the original, maple, plank floors while some of the interior, brick walls survived the years as well. She crossed the road, entering through the double, glass doors, and instantly she could feel her heartbeat relax. Taking a deep breath, she smelled the paper, but the scent held a tinge of gun-metal time had infused into the 100-year-old building. She felt like she just walked into an old, western novel.

She said hello to a couple of the librarians she had come to know through her numerous visits, before taking the wide, central staircase to the second floor. The fiction books were up here, and the specific section she was looking for was in the back, right in front of a well-hidden and cozy seating area. Natalie scoured the books in this section, pulling several out, reading a few pages of each. Most she put back, but there was one she retained. After another twenty minutes of searching, she now carried three books. She could have easily taken more, but these would fill her allocated reading time for the next two weeks. With two books under her arm, she was glancing through the third book, following a line of text with her finger. As she reached the end of the aisle, she stepped out and turned right. There was a *thump*, and all three books went flying. She stumbled backwards, and one high heel caught in the planking. Her momentum sent her backwards, landing her on her ass.

"Shit!" Natalie yelled out. Since the outcome was easy to foresee and inevitable, the word came out even before her ass made contact. Her brow furrowed, and her lips pinched together in a wide grimace as she looked up at the man who was, by now, squatted down on his haunches, looking quizzically at her. His brown eyes were open wide and filled with concern.

He held out his hand and said, "I'm so sorry. Let me help you up."

Natalie was angry, probably more at herself for burying her face in the book, but when she looked up at his warm eyes and general good looks, her face softened, and she replied, "Thanks." Natalie placed her hand in his, and he pulled her up to her feet. When she placed her full weight on her feet, she stumbled forward. Her hand came up and pressed on his chest, stopping herself from fully pressing against him.

The man grasped her shoulders, and the concern in his eyes grew. "You're not okay."

Natalie pulled back and shifted her weight from one foot to the other several times. "I think I twisted my right ankle when my heel got caught in the floor board, but it already feels better."

He gently grasped her arm behind her elbow and coaxed her forward. "You better sit down for a minute," he said as he led her to the well-padded couch in the seating area by the large windows.

After he made sure she was comfortable, he hurried back and picked up the three scattered books and brought them over. As he sat down beside her, Natalie took even more notice of his appearance. He was about six-foot-two inches tall with a slender build, but far from skinny. He was clean-shaven with neatly-trimmed, light-brown hair, a nose that seemed too big for his face and a mouth also seeming a bit out of place. Natalie thought all of this was odd as, to her, he seemed to fit the mold some men have where the individual elements were not pretty, but somehow, when you put them all together, they provided a ruggedly handsome appearance.

The man took off his brown, leather jacket and placed it down beside him. "You should sit for a few minutes and make sure that ankle is okay."

"I'll be fine," Natalie responded as she felt a bit foolish about the whole misadventure. She reached for the three books he held.

He reached out, and as he did so, he read the title of the top book and grinned. "Harlequin Romances." He glanced up at the two lines of pink in her auburn hair. "First appearances would not have told me you were a fan."

Natalie hastily grabbed the books and smiled innocently at him. "Can I tell you a secret?"

"Sure."

"In this section of the library, and especially in the Harlequin Romance books, it's the only place you can find well written porn."

He laughed. "I'm not sure if that was a pass, or you are trying to scare me away."

She cracked a smile, and it gave her face a playful appearance. "I don't think I'd make a pass at a man wearing a man-purse." She pointed at the valise he had been carrying and was now laid down beside him.

"It seems we are both making assumptions about each other," he replied. "Why don't I buy you a coffee. I feel real bad running into you the way I did."

Natalie always went into the coffee shop next door after getting her books, in any case, so why not let him pay for it. "Sure, it's on my way home."

He held out his hand and said, "My name's Josh Harris."

She took his hand, and she rose to her feet. "I'm Natalie."

They walked down the stairs, and Natalie signed out her books. When she left the counter, she realized her ankle felt absolutely fine, but in spite of it, she put on a slight limp. Josh saw it and put his arm around her waist. She smiled and thought, *so predictable*. After they exited the library, she stopped the limp and said she was fine. Josh politely slipped his arm away from her. The wind had picked up, so it was cooler, and as a result, they hastened their walk to the coffee shop next door. Once inside, they found a booth, removed their coats and settled into the soft, cushioned benches.

The waitress attended to them quickly, and they both ordered a large coffee. Natalie said, "Wait a second," then turned to Josh. "You do want a large coffee, right?"

Josh shrugged and answered, "Sure."

"Bring the coffees in cups to go," she said to the waitress. When she left, Natalie explained, "You only get a large coffee when you order take out. Otherwise, they give you a regular cup, and they'll refill it, but it's not exactly large."

"Thanks for the tip."

The coffees came quickly. Natalie topped up with sugar and cream while Josh left his black.

"This is really a pretty small coffee," Josh said.

"Ah, you're an American," she replied.

"And you're very observant," he concluded.

"I spent a lot of time in the States. In fact, I went to school there. I learned very quickly that Americans like everything supersized. After all, they invented the term *Big Gulp*," Natalie chided.

Josh smiled and leaned back in the bench seat. "You *really* are very observant. I am visiting from New York—not the city, but the State. I have a place in the Adirondack mountains. It's quiet—just the way I like it."

"Mmm, a mountain man. I'm not sure I would have figured that."

"I only spend about three or four months a year there. It's my escape from the more difficult work of being a second mate," Josh added.

Natalie leaned forward. "Like on a ship?"

"Yup. I contract myself out and am gone for six to eight months at a time. I'm 43 years old, and this old body needs the time off in a quiet place to recover. That's the reason for the place in the mountains."

"Now, I could see you on a ship—absolutely. I could picture your head topped with one of those wool, dome caps sailors wear. It makes them look like they're up to no good," she explained.

Josh took another long drink from the cup. "I am really pretty harmless."

"I'm not too sure about that, Josh."

Through an involuntary frown, Josh said, "What do you mean?"

Natalie put down her cup and intertwined her fingers on top of the table. "It's odd. You're here in Toronto from New York in late September, when there really isn't anything exciting happening in the city. It's not tourist season. Even if it was, Etobicoke isn't the place to be. You're a burly ship mate, yet somehow, you're in the romance novel section of a library, even though, as a foreigner, you can't sign out books. And then, it's just by chance you bump into me—literally."

Josh was already blushing. "Okay—Okay. I think you've caught me red-handed. William said you had a sharp mind."

"William?"

"Do you remember William Johnson from Boston?" Josh asked.

Natalie took a drink of coffee as she thought back on a name that was vaguely familiar.

"He worked at MIT," Josh added.

Natalie's eyes widened. "He was the superintendent of the residency apartment I was staying in when I was attending the Massachusetts Institute of Technology. He was a nice old man, but when I knew him twelve years ago, he was already having issues with his memory. Why would he send you here?"

"Because I am desperate." Josh's chin sagged and he suddenly looked older. "I have a problem I need help with, and he told me, 'If anyone could help me, you could.'"

"Jesus! William's ex-wife was taking him to the cleaners and siphoning money out of his bank account. I investigated, and sure, I used some advanced resources I had access to at MIT to help solve his problem."

"It sounds like he has not forgotten about you. He said you had some special contacts at the FBI," Josh said. "When you left so quickly, and you asked him to clean out your apartment for you, he did. He found some paperwork indicating you were transferring to the CSIS."

"Josh, your story is way out of control." Natalie pushed the bangs off her forehead and continued. "I went to school at MIT and obtained my undergrad degree and my master's. I did work at the FBI for two years as an intern as part of my education in advanced data analysis. Then, I went back to MIT and obtained my doctorate degree. Now, I work for a very successful marketing company, and what the hell is the CSIS?"

Josh paused for a moment. Maybe he got this all wrong, but he was desperate, so he continued. "The CSIS is the Canadian Security Intelligence Service. It's your countries version of the CIA."

Natalie slid her ass off the bench seat and rose to her feet. "You seem like a nice guy Josh, but this discussion is way over my head, and I have nothing to do with the CSIS."

Josh curled his fingers around her wrist. "I really do need help. It seems I am on a wild goose chase, but you are sharp, and you at least used to have good investigative skills. Would you at least listen to me for two minutes, and give me your opinion? It's fair trade for the coffee I bought you."

Natalie paused for a moment as there was a sense of honesty mixed with the desperation in his voice. *She could at least listen to him for two minutes.* As he released his grip, she slid back onto the bench.

Josh smiled and his face lit up. He reached down, pulled the valise up onto the table and unzipped it. Once he opened it, a stack of different colour papers was visible. He was prepared, and now he looked up at Natalie. "I have a 23-year-old son who has been missing for two months."

Natalie's brow lowered with concern. "Did he run away?"

Josh rubbed his chin. "I really wish that was the case, but it is more complicated. You see, my son, Hendrix, joined the marines when he was 20. He was doing really well, but a year ago he was critically injured in a training accident. He took a massive hit to his head, and the doctors said he should have died. Instead, he survived, if that is what you call being in a coma on life support."

"I'm sorry to hear this, but in his condition, how could he be missing?"

"Exactly. That is the question." Josh emphasized. "Two months ago, I received a call from the long-term care facility in Saratoga Springs, and they told me Hendrix had disappeared. Of course, I drove there immediately and met the home's security people and the police. They have closed circuit cameras and they showed nothing at all."

"How can that be?" Natalie asked.

"There was some kind of very strange electromagnetic interference on the tape during the time when he went missing. The police have no idea how to even begin an investigation like this. How do you search for a guy in a coma? Needless to say, they have not found him or any useful information on what seems to be a kidnapping." Josh ran his fingers back through his hair, adding to the frustration etched on his face.

There was compassion in Natalie's olive-green eyes. Josh appeared vulnerable, and it was drawing her closer to him. She caught herself and said, "I understand what you're telling me, but from it, I can tell you missing persons and kidnapping fall under the jurisdiction of the FBI. You need to see them."

"Don't you think I have been there? Of course, I have," Josh explained with a higher pitch of desperation in his voice. He realized this and lowered it back to a whisper. "The local police said the same thing, but the FBI is perplexed, especially after I told them about the others."

"Others?" Natalie questioned as a chill ran through her.

"Yes, the others," Josh repeated. He turned his valise around so it faced her. He sorted through it and pulled out several pages with a picture on each. "No one was doing anything, so I did some of my own research. Here is a picture of Frank Dale. He is another young military guy, but he was in the army. He had a seizure and was also in a coma. He disappeared from a hospital in Virginia a week before my son did." He pulled out another page. "This is Jeremy Kline. He has advanced Parkinson's and was in a long-term care facility near Buffalo. He was in a chronic state, no longer being able to walk or talk. He has also gone missing." He paused and slowly said, "He was 85 years old."

Natalie looked at the pages and she was confused. Josh didn't stop as he showed her two more files of elderly, infirmed people who had also, inexplicably and impossibly, vanished from their care facilities. She pushed the valise back towards Josh as she said, "I wish there was something I could do to help you. This really is a job for the FBI."

Josh leaned in and panned back and forth with his eyes before he whispered, "Is there someone else at the CSIS who can help me? There is something really weird going on here."

Natalie smiled warmly as she really was just starting to like Josh. "I know nothing about the CSIS, Josh. Please go to the FBI."

Josh took a deep breath and sat up straight, thinking, *perhaps I just made a fool of myself.* He pulled out a pen and a small pad from his valise. He scribbled on it, then ripped off the top slip, placing it in front of Natalie. "Here is my cell number. I'll probably be in town for another few days. If you have any second thoughts or ideas, give me a call." He now returned Natalie's warm smile. "If you just want to have another coffee, I would like that as well." Josh pushed all his papers back into the valise and zipped it up. He slid out of the booth and said, "Thanks anyways." After pausing for a few seconds and gazing down at her, he gave her a last hopeful smile, then turned and left the coffee shop.

Natalie sipped her coffee for another fifteen minutes as she stared down at the little piece of paper. For some reason, she couldn't forget the vision of his ruggedly-handsome look, or the deep tone he had in his voice. At the same time, she thought of the wild tale he told, and she questioned his sanity—and even hers for listening for so long. Certainly, any further communication with Josh was going to be nothing but trouble.

She slid out of the booth and smiled at the waitress as she walked by the counter before heading to the garbage and recycling station near the door. The cup was in one hand and she threw it in the paper recycling slot. The small scrap of paper with the phone number on it was between two fingers of her other hand. She flicked it towards the recycling opening, but it didn't release. Her fingers had involuntarily tightened on it, and now she looked down at the numbers he wrote. She pictured his face again and frowned for a moment, knowing this was going to be a big mistake. She jammed the paper into her pocket and took a deep breath. Her face now had a smug *what the fuck* look on it as she walked out the door, thinking, *yup, this is going to be very bad.*

Chapter 4: The Grand Tour

Natalie enjoyed many aspects of her career, but waking up and making her way into the office on Monday morning wasn't one of them. She unlocked the door to her office and set herself down on her comfortable office chair. She put her cell phone on her desk and checked the time. It was 6:45 a.m. so she was right on time.

Having 15 minutes before the rush of associates who always arrived five minutes before the whistle, she kicked off her shoes under her desk and opened the laptop. She quickly printed off her agenda and tasks for the day, then retrieved them from the printer by the window. Once back in her chair, she reviewed the document and added some notes by hand.

As she finished, there was a knock on the open door leading through the conference room. Cheryl smiled and asked, "Are you ready?"

"Sure. C'mon in," she replied.

Cheryl entered followed by a tall, young, attractive Asian woman with shoulder-length jet-black hair. As they came to the desk, Natalie rose to her feet and smiled at the newcomer.

Cheryl said, "This is Jacklin McDonald."

Natalie's smile widened. "I've heard a lot about you. I'm Natalie Lowe."

All three women sat down and Cheryl said, "Natalie and I are directors of different global zones. Although you'll work for one of our supervisors, we're both very hands on and will be involved with you on a regular basis."

Jacklin nodded. "That sounds great."

Natalie said, "This morning I'll show you around and answer your questions. Cheryl and I cover for each other, so she'll keep an eye on things for me while I'm with you." She pushed her agenda printout across to Cheryl.

Cheryl reviewed the list and concluded, "I don't see anything worrisome."

Natalie slipped her shoes back on and said, "Great. Let's get going."

The three women all rose to their feet. Cheryl headed back to her office while the other two women exited the office and headed down the aisle towards the elevators. As they walked along, Natalie said, "You look good in blue." It might have seemed an odd comment to Jacklin, but to Natalie, who wore a very similar black pant suit, it was spot on.

"What…"

Natalie laughed and said, "Relax. I know it's your first day. I was just admiring your outfit. The slacks and matching blazer look great in blue. Is that royal blue?"

"Yes, Mum."

Natalie just grinned. "That's very English—both the colour and the wording, but you best call me Natalie. Mum would age me more years than I would like."

"Of course—Natalie."

Natalie pressed the elevator button, and a minute later they were exiting on the first floor. Halfway down an interior hallway, there was a set of metal double-doors. Natalie led and passed her identification over the scanner. Jacklin did the same, and the doors swung open. Here, in front of a row of three elevators, was a man and a woman in black suits with their jacket buttons smartly done up, giving them a very professional look. The communication earpieces they wore added a dangerous and efficient edge to their appearance.

The man moved closer to them, and the two women both showed their identification to him. Even though he knew Natalie very well, he took a moment to compare the picture to her face, and he did the same for Jacklin. Satisfied, he stepped aside, allowing Natalie to press the elevator button.

Once inside, Natalie pointed to the buttons inside the elevator and explained, "There are five underground floors. *U1* is just below us, and *U5* would be the deepest underground."

Jacklin nodded her understanding as Natalie pressed *U3*.

A moment later the doors opened onto a very large room. As they stepped out of the elevator, Jacklin saw the room was painted a light-green colour, and the many overhanging fluorescent lights gave the room an appearance of anything but a basement. On the right wall was a row of glass offices and conference rooms. The rest of the large room was filled with sixty cubicles, and half of them were occupied.

Jacklin spun around and looked back at the elevators where two more daunting looking security guards stood. Above the elevators, in small letters, it read,

Communications Security Establishment, Echelon Group.

Natalie interrupted Jacklin's moment of awe and said, "This way."

Jacklin followed Natalie along the aisle around the cubicles towards the glass-walled offices. She noticed the floors were all grey, painted concrete, and she correctly assumed this was for more efficient maintenance. Natalie led her into an empty conference room and offered Jacklin a seat before closing the door and taking a seat herself.

Natalie began the orientation with a few questions. "How long were you with MI6?"

"Two years in total. There was one year of training, and then one year of field service," Jacklin replied.

There was a file that Natalie's supervisor, Steve, had left on the table for her, and she opened it now. After a minute of reading, she said, "I see you're on an exchange program. You're set to be here with us at the CSE for three years, and we've sent one of our young recruits to MI6 for the same time period."

"That's the plan, but there's one point that has me confused. Can I ask a question?"

"Sure," Natalie answered.

Jacklin extended her body and peered outside at the sign above the elevator. "I clearly see this is a Communications Security Establishment office. When I was briefed on this in England, my superiors talked about the CSE and the Canadian Security Intelligence Service interchangeably. Can you explain the difference to me?"

Natalie leaned back in the chair. "Sure. In many ways we're the same service and work together. The CSIS reviews and reports on intelligence reports, including human interactions. Here, at the CSE, we provide those reports through our surveillance of various communication systems." Natalie pointed to the cubicles outside. "Most of the people you see are CSE analysts, but there are at least five who are CSIS employees taking information back to their organization as required."

Jacklin was getting more comfortable, so she began asking more questions. "You have an office upstairs, and you spend time down here as well. Can I ask what you do here in the lower floors?"

Natalie leaned on the table with her elbows and intertwined her fingers. "These five underground floors are a high security CSE operation. However, if the sign out front read, CSE, then it wouldn't be so secret or secure. Even if there was no sign, it would draw the attention of many prying eyes. As a cover operation, *Enhanced Solutions* is a very real marketing company. We make excellent profits, and that makes the cover even better. Down here I'm a Senior Data Scientist, and upstairs I'm a Director of Research."

Jacklin's eyes narrowed a bit as a line formed on her brow, showing her confusion. "How do you do both jobs?"

"You recall Cheryl from upstairs?" Natalie asked.

"Of course."

"She's what you call—my twin. We do similar jobs, so when I come down here, she covers for me upstairs. It works the same in reverse, so if she received a call down here, I would cover for her. Soon, you'll also be assigned a twin," Natalie added.

A flash of colour on the far wall caught Jacklin's attention. A large map of Britain was displayed on a screen while two men were in discussion in front of it. She turned to Natalie. "Britain? I don't get it?"

"I guess they didn't tell you as much at MI6 as I thought." Natalie shrugged and then pointed to the sign above the elevator. "It's really wrong to have *Echelon* posted there as it implies Echelon is this department and the people in it. Echelon is the actual hardware and software that stores the huge amount of information from our spying activities. That hardware takes up half of the fourth floor."

Wanting to show she was not altogether daft, Jacklin offered, "I do understand this office, similar to MI6, spies on people by accessing their computers, satellite communications and even underwater fibre optic cables, but why Britain?"

With a smug look on her face, Natalie explained, "You don't think countries spy on themselves, do you?"

"Well…" Jacklin's face drooped in defeat. "I have no idea."

The door opened. Steve walked in and sat himself down.

Natalie made a hasty introduction. "Jacklin, this is Steve. Steve is your supervisor. Don't shake hands. Steve, don't open your mouth until I tell you to."

Steve looked at Jacklin and shrugged.

Natalie continued as if the interruption never happened. "I'm sure you know about *Five Eyes?*"

"Of course."

"Then you know Five Eyes is a higher-level security organization consisting of the CSIS, CIA and MI6. Australia and New Zealand make up the remaining two security services. We all share information and work together. That's why you're here, but really the trust is at arms length."

"I can understand that."

"The kicker is we don't spy on ourselves," Natalie divulged. "I mean, how would it look if MI6 got caught hacking into British people's computers? People would be fuming, and there would be all hell to pay. However, if another country gets caught hacking British citizens, well, it's called a breach. There'll be a bit of political turmoil, but it would go away quickly."

Jacklin's eyes widened. "So, you spy on each other."

Natalie grinned. "Yes, and then we share the pertinent information with each other. It's how we keep ahead of threats and terrorists."

Pointing at the British map, Jacklin said, "Let me guess. You spy on British interests."

"I think you have it," Natalie concluded. "And MI6 spies on Canadians. The CIA spies on Australia and New Zealand, and collectively, Australia and New Zealand work together spying on Americans."

What tasks will I be given here?" Natalie asked.

"I'll answer that in a minute, but to see where you fit in, you must understand how Echelon works." Natalie pointed to the cubicles outside the conference room. "Since we cover Britain, we divide the land mass up geographically. There are different CSE offices around this country assigned to these areas. This office is assigned to London and its metropolitan area. If we consider only emails, do you know how many are sent in or out of London every day?"

"I wouldn't even hazard a guess."

"There are just under nine million people in London proper, and if you consider the surrounding metropolitan area, the population grows to almost 14 million. These people, each day, send an average of 1.5 million emails."

"That's unbelievable! How do you manage that?" Natalie's eyes grew in size as she considered the daunting challenge.

"There's no way we can look at every piece of communication, so we have to prioritize the data, leaving only the high-risk ones for us to physically evaluate. First, we subdivide the information. We know there are high risk targets in London. This includes suspected terrorists, criminals and arms dealers, to give only a few examples. Half of the Echelon organization focuses on communications from these targeted people." She pointed at the cubicles outside the glass wall. "The other half of the analysts are tasked with the remaining volume of random communication occurring every day."

Natalie shook her head. "That's still a huge amount of data to filter through."

Natalie smiled. She liked knowing more than other people. "You're correct. If we left it there, this room would need to be the size of many soccer fields—sorry—football fields. This is where our Echelon computers take over. We provide a list of key words that would indicate a possible threat. These would include words such as, *terrorist, bomb, explosive,* and *kill.* These are just a few examples. We have several hundred similar key words, and each has a ranking. Our computers review all the communications and look for the words and combinations of words. Each communication then gets a ranking."

Jacklin was excited, learning how the spy world works and interrupted. "So, you have a prioritized list of possible threats."

Natalie winked at Jacklin, appreciating her ability to learn quickly. "About half of the analysts review approximately one thousand pieces of communication a day. You won't be in this group."

Jacklin's face sagged with disappointment.

Natalie continued. "The other half of the analysts monitor the efficiency of the keywords and the results the computer software provides based on them. The list is critical with even the order of the words in the search making a huge difference. We adjust and tune the keyword list almost daily. I have the ultimate lead and authority on keywords. That's my job. Steve works for me, and you'll work for him."

Jacklin's frown changed quickly into a wide smile. "That's awesome. I certainly won't let you down."

Natalie gave Jacklin the stare down—the same stare down she gave every new employee. Her eyes narrowed, seeming to bore into the woman sitting opposite to her. "That's correct. You won't. We sit here in a level of comfort, and some lose sight of the fact our jobs result in lives being saved. Sometimes many lives depend on us."

Jacklin pressed her lips tightly together and swallowed hard. The slight nod of her head told Natalie she understood the important task at hand.

Rising to her feet, Natalie stretched upwards. "We've been sitting for too long. Let's go for a tour of the rest of the facility."

Steve and Jacklin both rose to their feet, following Natalie from the conference room towards the elevators. Steve had complied with Natalie's request for silence, but as they waited for the elevator, he blurted out, "Natalie, do you need me for this? I was in the middle of a study…"

"Sure. Go do your thing," Natalie agreed. "We'll be back in no time, and I'll leave her in your capable hands."

Steve walked away, but after a few steps, Natalie said, "Steve, wait one second."

As Steve turned, Natalie walked over to him. She moved close and, in a hushed voice, said, "I need you to do something for me, and it needs to be done very discretely. Can you do that for me?"

This was only the third time in the three years he worked for her that Natalie asked a task that he now knew would take him out of normal CSE protocols, but then, to obtain results, their organization had the leeway and discretion to stretch the guidelines. He also knew Natalie had his back and helped him many times with tasks when he was having difficulty. He trusted her. "Sure. Ask away," he whispered while his eyes glanced back and forth around the room to ensure no one was listening, or focused on them in any way.

"There's a man named William Johnson who works at the MIT complex in Boston. He's between 75 and 85 years old and is the superintendent of a residency apartment within the complex. I want you to do a level one scan of his electronics. If there are other people assisting him in his job, or if there's anyone living with him, I want the level one scan extended to them— all computers, cell phones, tablets—everything. Any documents or correspondence with the key labels, *CSE, CSIS, FBI,* or my name, is to be erased. Understood?"

Steve knew better than to ask questions. "I'll do it this afternoon."

Natalie appreciated Steve's loyalty to her more than he knew. This is why she tolerated the obnoxiously lengthy dialogue he sometimes expelled. She smiled while brushing the bangs back from her forehead. "Thanks, Steve."

Natalie returned to Jacklin who'd been waiting by the elevators. The two women entered and Natalie pressed *U5.* "Let's start at the bottom and work our way back up."

The discussion with Steve reminded her of Josh Harris. For a moment, the image of his handsome face crossed her mind. She didn't like lying to him at the library, but technically, she didn't. He implied she worked at a

CSIS office, but in fact, she worked at the CSE. She frowned and thought, *why's this even bothering me?*

The bump as the elevator doors closed interrupted Natalie's mini-daydream. The elevators weren't set up very well, and even though there were very few floors, there was a lurch, leaving Jacklin's stomach in her chest. Just as quickly, it shifted as her gut was pushed down until the doors opened. Natalie led them out into a room the same size as the one she just left on the third floor, but the configuration was different. Here, there were similar glass-walled offices on their right but only three rows of cubicles. On their left, there was a large open area with a huge screen mounted on the wall.

Natalie gave a description of the room as she led them down the central aisle towards the back. "Notice the walls here are light-blue, and the room we left was light-green."

"Of course."

Each floor has a different bright colour and bright lights. Since there are no windows, we do as much as we can to provide a basement that doesn't feel like a basement. There are scientific studies indicating a darker, underground environment leads people to depression and suicide."

Jacklin asked, "Does the bright paint work?"

Natalie smirked. "No one blew their head off last week."

Jacklin stopped, grasping Natalie's elbow. "Before that?"

Natalie's smirk turned into a laugh. "Relax. I'm just pulling your leg."

A nervous laugh came from Jacklin as Natalie pointed to a set of double-doors on the back wall of the room. In front of it stood two more guards in black suits. Jacklin did a double take as she turned her gaze back to the elevators, and saw a similar set of double-doors there.

"The doors at the front lead to an emergency set of stairs in case the elevators fail, or if there is a fire, whereby the elevators shouldn't be used," Natalie explained.

Turning her gaze to the back wall, Jacklin asked, "And these doors?"

Natalie moved to a position directly facing the younger woman and put her hand on her shoulder. "I can't stress enough the importance of what I'm telling you." She paused for a few moments, to make sure she had Jacklin's full attention. "The world and the Canadian people know CSE monitors communications, and many understand why we do it, but there are very few people in the world who understand the extent of our invasive activities. It wouldn't be good if the public knew how deeply we subvert their rights each and every day."

"I myself am a little flabbergasted at how deep the penetration goes," Jacklin admitted.

"That's understandable, but criminals and terrorists don't abide by constitutions and charters of rights. You'll come to see the need for our methods, but for now, what's most important is the requirement for this facility and what we do, to be an absolute secret."

Jacklin was getting uncomfortable with the hand on her shoulder and shifted, so she faced the doors at the back of the room. "What does this have to do with the doors?"

"Our work and the secrets we keep would be very valuable to other countries and groups who might want to minimize our effectiveness. This means there's always the risk of an attack."

"An attack! We're just analysts!"

Natalie ignored Jacklin's comment. "If we're ever attacked, as you see, we have security guards to protect us, and an attack would come from above us." She pointed her finger upwards. "These back doors lead to another set of stairs leading up to the second floor. There's a tunnel there leading to a building 200 metres away. From the surface, it has the appearance of an electrical transformer station, but in reality, it's an emergency exit. There are monthly drills."

Jacklin had heard enough about the possible danger of the job, so she deflected the discussion. She waved her arm towards the people in the cubicles. "What do the people down here do?"

Natalie pressed her hand to the small of Jacklin's back, coaxing her back towards the elevator. "The far row of cubicles is for security personnel. The other two rows are another arm of our surveillance system. Its officially code named *Geoint* which is short for Geospatial Intelligence."
"That's a mouthful," Jacklin muttered.

"You're right. That's why we tend to refer to them simply as *Geo*. In the same way we monitor emails and other forms of communication, they monitor visual satellite fields," Natalie elaborated. "There are hundreds of satellites orbiting the earth. Some are owned by companies and some by the military. Geo hacks into the feeds and monitors what they see. They also hack into closed circuit cameras if the need arises."

As Natalie pressed the elevator *up* button, she pointed her chin at the large screen. "As you now would have likely guessed, the screen is to review pertinent videos or slides."

Jacklin said, "Yes, Ma'am," as she followed Natalie into the elevator.

Their next stop was at *U4*. They both exited, but stayed near the elevators. From behind them they heard a deep voice. "Good morning, Ms. Lowe."

Natalie turned and saw an awkward smile on the handsome face of the guard. He had his fingers intertwined in front of him as he shifted his weight from foot to foot. When Natalie turned to face him, her face went pink. She managed to say, "Hello, Paul. Nice to see you." After the abrupt hello, she turned back to the room a little too quickly.

Jacklin had taken psychology as her major in university, but she didn't need that background to realize these two people had a romantic relationship—something that wasn't allowed within the organization. She decided to keep the tidbit of information to herself for now.

"Again, this is another similar room," Natalie offered.

"The walls here are grey, so not as bright as the other floors," Jacklin replied.

"The people in the cubicles on the right are the programmers for all the systems we have here," Natalie explained. "They're on their computers for long hours, and the darker colour and lower light level, gives them less reflection off their screens. The left side of the room is filled with the servers and other computers that run all our software and store all of the data we collect.

"What about the depression and suicide?" Jacklin asked.

Shrugging, Natalie confessed. "They're computer programmers. These are the people who play video games all night and day, but they are the best of the best and also the craziest of the crazies."

"So, crazy people are immune to depression," Jacklin chided, tongue in cheek.

"The record would appear to substantiate that." Natalie pulled out her phone and looked at the time. "We better move on."

The pair continued their upward tour and exited out onto *U2*. Once out of the elevator, Jacklin did a double take to the sign above the elevators. This floor looked almost identical to *U3*, but the wording she read was, *Communications Security Establishment, Prism Group*, and of course, she realized the wall colour was different.

Jacklin asked, "What's the Prism group?"

Natalie replied, "This department is set up the same as Echelon. The difference is the walls are yellow, and these people monitor and work with larger communication and social media companies."

"Like Facebook?"

"Facebook, Instagram and Twitter to name a few," Natalie clarified.

"But they have nondisclosure agreements with their customers." Jacklin offered.

"Most of the information Prism monitors are public posts, looking for the same key words Echelon does, but we do also review subscriber's personal information."

"Isn't that illegal?"

"Jacklin, by now, I would've thought you realized most of what we do here is illegal," Natalie admonished. "However, in most cases, we obtain a court order from a judge, citing national security, and the service gives us the information we need. Of course, the Facebook's of the world don't admit they provide the information, just as we don't say we obtain such court orders."

"You seem to have everything covered," Jacklin commented.

"Most of the time," Natalie corrected. "Sometimes the legal process gets bogged down, and when we need the information truly for national security, we hack the files we need."

Jacklin knew when to leave a topic alone. She raised an eyebrow. "I have to ask, why is it called *Prism?*"

"That's what this department of the CSE is called. For some reason, every department seems to have some kind of a James-Bond-type code name," Natalie suggested through a grin.

Jacklin replied, "I was wondering if one of the floors would reveal *Spectre,* or if you were going to introduce me to Pussy Galore."

"On that note, we have one more floor to go." Natalie extended her arm to the elevator, urging Jacklin towards it.

The elevator doors opened at *U1,* and they exited onto the nicest of the floors Jacklin had visited. She noted, "The walls are bright white, and there's modern art on the walls."

As they walked forward towards a set of double, oak doors, Natalie explained, "We don't have a lot of visitors, but from time to time, we do receive senior CSE personnel and even high-ranking government officials.

We bring them here, and we call this the *War Room*." She opened the heavy, oak door, and inside was a large theater much like a university lecture hall. "Occasionally, we're invited to town hall meetings here as well."

They walked back out of the War Room, after which Natalie led the way down a hallway towards the back wall of floor *U1*. Tucked behind the war room was a group of 30 cubicles. Natalie explained, "This is a small, but very important group. They look after logistics."

"Like transportation?"

"Not quite, but close," Natalie corrected. "These people coordinate the information that goes to and from other Five Eyes organizations. This could include tips or even movements of people of interest. In addition, remember MI6 monitors Canadians, so they send information to us through the Logistics group. Even within our CSE branch offices, information is shared through the Logistics group. As you can see, they have a very important function."

"There you are!"

Both women turned towards the hallway and a man, who just uttered the words, was briskly walking towards them. "Natalie, I've been looking for you everywhere. Is your phone on?"

Philip had creases on his face, indicating there was something wrong, and it instantly put Natalie on alert. As she pulled her cell phone from its holster, she said, "Of course, I have it on—oh shit. I had it on mute for the earlier part of the orientation, and I forgot to turn the volume back on."

Philip hadn't met Jacklin yet, but there was no time for introductions. "Please excuse us for a few minutes."

"Of course. I will wait by the elevators." As she finished her words, she quickly moved down the hallway.

Natalie whispered, "What's going on?"

"The people upstairs have been trying to get a hold of you all morning."

There was an urgent, quick pace to Philip's words that caused Natalie's heart rate to accelerate. "Why?"

In a low, comforting voice, Philip asked, "Your father's name is Edward—Edward Lowe, right?"

Natalie stood frozen, not sure what to think. The nod of her head was barely perceptible. Then, it began slowly, but her heart suddenly felt like it was going to burst from her chest. Expecting the worse, she braced herself with her hand on Philip's arm.

By her action, Philip knew the answer. He didn't want to provide the news, but there was no choice. He whispered, "He's missing."

Chapter 5: Moscow

Moscow, in late fall, before the imminent snowfalls, was a dreary vision. Most leaves had already fallen from the many oak and birch trees, but those that hadn't were crisp and brown. Even the larches had lost their needles, giving the appearance of forests of dead trees.

The silver Range Rover left the British Embassy near the center of Moscow, crossed over the Moscow river and now, ten minutes later, was speeding along the highway towards the southern district of Yasenevo. The British ambassador to Russia and his newly arrived consular officer, were in the back seat of the vehicle as it passed one such forest of larches.

James Gilmour looked out the rear seat, passenger-side window and asked the ambassador, "What's with all the dead trees?"

Ambassador Roger Smithers was 62 years old and near the end of his career with the British foreign service. He had been assigned to Russia six years ago and understood his younger associate's confusion. "Larch trees look like coniferous trees because of their needles, but they're actually one of the few deciduous trees having them, and as deciduous trees, the needles fall off in late autumn," the ambassador explained.

James really wasn't overly concerned about the trees. He'd only been assigned to the Moscow embassy three weeks ago, and this was his second trip with the ambassador. His comment on the trees was his effort at making small talk, and he tried again. "Have you been invited to the Russian foreign intelligence service offices before?"

"That's a mouthful," the ambassador replied. "Their shorter designation is the SVR RF, and we shorten it even more to the SVR. To answer your question, no. I've never been to their head office before."

Their vehicle was making a wide sweep while turning south. Another similar embassy vehicle with four armed security personnel in it, was one quarter kilometre behind them. Ambassador Smithers received the call from an SVR contact only the day before. He was told it would be necessary for him to clear his schedule as a prompt meeting with the Russian officials was critical.

"Since we're meeting with the SVR, who look after issues external to Russia, it's probable they want something from us," Smithers forecasted. "Now, if we were meeting with the FSB, which is Russia's answer to the

FBI in America, or our own MI5, then they would be discussing an internal, national issue."

James laughed. "You mean, in that case, they would have a complaint."

Smithers turned his face to the younger man and smiled. "You're new to my organization, but you seem to have a grasp of how the game is played. However, once we're in the meeting, although you have a grasp, I am the expert. You'll only speak at the introduction and when I ask you to. Is that understood?"

"Of course, Sir."

The Range Rover first left the bustle of the city center and now the suburbs. They were driving along the edge of a large forest of oak trees, with a few white-birches mixed in. The driver flicked the indicator lever, and a moment later, the vehicle was turning right, into the wooded area.

"I never would've thought the SVR complex was in the middle of a forest," James noted.

"As would any people not from Moscow, but trust me. Every person native to Moscow knows exactly what is within this park-like setting," the ambassador added.

As the vehicle followed the serpentine, long driveway, James said, "That reminds me of a funny story. A few years back, my wife and I were looking for a house, and there was one that interested us. The advert said it was in a park-like setting."

Smithers raised his eyebrow. "And?"

"It backed onto a fucking cemetery." James laughed as he concluded the story.

Ambassador Smithers lowered his head and looked out the window— first one side, then the other. "Maybe not in this era, but in past years, I suspect there were people killed here. In fact, I know there were, so your definition of a park-like setting possibly being a cemetery, might hold true here."

The ambassador's Range Rover, now followed closely by the chase car, popped out of the forest. Almost immediately they arrived at a guardhouse, and five armed guards in military uniforms surrounded the lead car. Their driver lowered his window and announced the two occupants to the guard who lowered his face to window level. The guard looked at both of the occupants for a moment. "Credentials please," he said in English with a thick accent.

Each of the three occupants pulled out their British foreign service cards held in leather wallets, then gave them to the security guard. He took them and returned to the guardhouse where he could be seen making a phone call.

After a minute, he returned and handed back the wallets. "The other car will need to wait here, and can you please open the trunk?"

"It's called a liftgate or even a boot," their driver corrected.

The guard smiled. "The boot then. Please open."

Their driver pressed the button, and as a second guard moved over for the inspection, their driver phoned his counterpart in the second car and said, "Wait here for us."

As he put his phone down, the driver heard the boot being closed. The first guard lowered his face one more time. "Follow the jeep in the compound to your destination."

Their driver nodded as the metal gate was opened. A second later, another guard came out of the guardhouse and jumped into the green, military jeep. The engine roared to life and the jeep careened up the narrow road. The ambassador's vehicle followed, and three minutes later, they pulled in front of a six-story building. James exited the vehicle first. He surveyed the complex, seeing three more large buildings and many smaller ones. Once satisfied, he said to the ambassador, "We're good to go."

The ambassador directed the driver, "Wait here," then exited the vehicle and followed James towards the glass doors at the end of a short run of stairs. Once inside, another person with a stoic demeanour, wearing a grey suit, reviewed their credentials for a second time before leading them up to the sixth floor. By now, the two Englishmen determined this building looked very much like an institution, with hospital-green walls and a white, polished floor. After walking almost all the way down a long hallway, the Russian attendant opened a heavy, wooden door and waved the two visitors into the room, before closing the door behind them.

This anteroom was much different with oak wainscoting half way up the walls and a plush, red carpet. A pretty secretary on the other side of a black, lacquered desk rose to her feet and said, "Welcome," again in broken English. She scooted out from the desk and opened an inner door. "The director is waiting for you."

Ambassador Smithers leaned over and whispered in James's ear, "This must be important for the director to see us personally." Before waiting for a response, he walked through the door, followed closely by James. Once inside, the ambassador was surprised to see two men, one sitting on either side of a huge desk at the far end of the long room. They both rose and walked towards the visitors.

Both the ambassador and his subordinate took a moment to review the office they were in. If the anteroom was opulent, this room was closer to palatial. The red carpet continued into this room, but here there were intricately added, silk patterns hand-sewn into the weave, in colours of gold and mint-green. The room was 15 metres long and four metres wide. In the middle was a large, oak meeting table surrounded by matching chairs. The oak theme continued to the walls covered in paneling and hand-carved moldings.

The older Russian had a round, red face with thick black eyebrows that seemed to match his thick, oak-tree-type body frame. He held out his large, gnarled hand to the ambassador and said, "Good morning. I am Victor Annenkov, director of the SVR." As they shook hands, Victor added, "This is Boris Lipin. He holds the same position I do except he heads the FSB."

Boris was younger with fine, blonde hair that was visibly receding. Notwithstanding this, he didn't look a day over 30. Smithers thought, *something big is going on to have both security heads here.* He introduced James as his consulate officer, and then they were led, by Victor, to the large meeting table. As soon as they sat down, Victor pressed a button on the intercom.

"Yes Mr. Annenkov." The secretary responded almost immediately.

"Please send in Mr. Belov," Victor directed.

"Of course."

Victor Annenkov leaned back in his chair, and looked at Ambassador Smithers. "How long have you been at the embassy in Moscow?"

"It's been six years now. This is probably my last assignment before I retire," the ambassador responded. However, inside he was suspicious. He thought, *what the fuck is going on here.*

The far door opened, and a man in a stylish, navy-blue suit entered the room. Right away, he looked different from the two seated Russians who had older-style, dark suits on. The blue suit on the newly arrived gentleman was the latest style, made of a shiny material, and it suited his six-foot-tall, lean frame.

As the man walked over to the table, Victor said, "This is Leonid Belov."

Leonid's black hair was neatly combed to the side, matching the perfectly trimmed, van dyke-style moustache and beard. He arrived at the table, shook hands with both Englishmen, and then he took a seat beside Boris, opposite the British officials. He took the folder he had been carrying under his arm and pushed it across the table to Victor.

Victor leaned forward intertwining his fingers above the folder. "Can I get anyone a drink—water or perhaps something stronger." Everyone said, "No thank you," allowing the SVR director to continue. "I know you both are very busy men, as we are, so I won't waste much of your time. I hope we all understand this instance of the directors of the SVR and the FSB meeting with you together, underlies the importance of this meeting."

"Yes, it certainly is unusual," Ambassador Smithers agreed.

Director Annenkov smiled. "Thank you." He opened the file and perused the single piece of paper within it, after which he promptly closed it and brought his gaze up to the ambassador's. "There are five names in this folder. They are Canadian nationals who are also persons of interest to us. We politely ask you to provide a detailed personnel file on these people to us—everything you have."

James wondered if the Russians noticed his eye sockets opened wide enough for his eye balls to fall out. Ambassador Smithers, with more years of experience, only had a slight twitch at the corner of his right eye to indicate his surprise at the request.

The ambassador, as he was trained many years ago to do, kept his words slow and calm in response. "Canadians? Why on Earth would we have information on Canadian nationals?"

Boris leaned forward, and he lifted a finger indicating he had something to say.

James smirked, wondering if this was a *good cop—bad cop* routine.

Boris said, "My friend Victor indicated, with both of us being here, that this was a reflection of the importance of this meeting. Let's not play games."

James thought, *nope. It's bad cop—bad cop.*

The ambassador was about to reply, when Victor interrupted. "Before you answer, it should be obvious to you that we all know about Five Eyes. For the most part, you can read all about it on *Wikipedia.*"

Smithers shrunk back in his chair.

"We know within Five Eyes, the British spy on the Canadians. If you don't have files on these people, we know you can obtain them very quickly through your surveillance systems. If that falls short, you do have some MI6 people within the Canadian agencies who, I am sure, can help."

Even though he was told not to speak, James shook his head and blurted,

"Why should we give you information on our allies in Five Eyes?"

Boris said, "Since I am in charge of Russian national security, let me answer that. Five weeks ago, we approved a SAS operation in St. Petersburg. The SAS assault squad killed a South African who worked for a British company and a Chinese secret service agent."

James leaned over the table, "Are you kidding me?"

Ambassador Smithers curled his fingers on James's wrist, then turned to Boris. "Yes, I know of the operation, and as you said yourself, 'you approved it.'"

"And now we request a favour in return," Boris clarified. "We would not ask for the information about these people if it was not important, not only to Russia, but also Britain and Canada as well."

Smithers hoped the slight lowering of his jaw did not give away his utter confusion from the last comment. He needed time. "I'll take your request back to London, and we can give you an answer in two weeks."

Boris said, "The Chinese have been investigating the death of their agent. They are getting very close to finding out about the SAS operation. We are doing everything in our power to deflect them, but we aren't sure how long we can hold them off. It would be terrible if they found out their agent was killed by a British, military kill-squad. I'm not sure what would be worse— that, or the British and South African people finding out their civilian was killed by the same group. In some parts of the world this would be called *terrorism*."

The threat was not very well veiled. Smithers insisted, "One week for an answer. That's the best we can do."

There was a *buzzing* sound that, thankfully, broke the tension in the room. Leonid pulled his phone from his pocket and read the text message. The fingers of his other hand played over the van-dyke style moustache and beard combination adorning his hawk-like face. He pointed to the file in front of Victor and said, "Please hand that back for a moment."

Victor complied and Leonid opened the file. He took a pen from his jacket pocket and scribbled at the bottom of the list. He slapped the file closed, and as he pushed it back to Victor, clarified, "There are now six names on the list."

James lifted his hand and pointed to Leonid. "Who the fuck is this guy?"

"You have his name," Victor chided. His voice had an edge to it now. "That is all you need to know."

Smithers waved his hand in front of himself. "Five names or six names—it does not matter. We still need time for such a delicate investigation. We need to involve MI6."

"Mr. Smithers. MI6 is sitting right beside you." Victor offered.

"James—He's my consular official."

"I hope neither of you take this personally, but you are very mistaken," Victor scolded. "Do you think we don't know James is a senior MI6 agent? I am sure he can help fast track the request."

The ambassador shook his head from side to side and was about to speak when Victor interrupted. "We were going to give you until this afternoon for the files, but since we have added another name to the list, we will expect the files back here at 10:00 a.m. tomorrow morning."

James blurted, "That's impossible!"

Boris smiled politely. "In our world, impossible just means it will take a bit longer, and we have extended our deadline to tomorrow. It should be—How do you say it in your country—easy peasy."

"But..."

Victor cut off the ambassador again. "At this point, I believe your time would be better spent in the task at hand, rather than continuing to explain your inefficiencies."

As Victor pushed the file across to Smithers, Boris rose to his feet and said, "I will show you out."

Ten minutes later, the embassy Range Rover was released from the guard house. As they passed their chase car, it made a U turn and followed them down the long driveway, through the somber terrain that seemed colder on this, the return leg.

James waited until their vehicle made a left turn off the SVR property before he commented on the morning discussion. "Can you believe the Russian balls on those three—telling us what to do?"

"They know they have us over a barrel on this one," the ambassador confessed.

James sat forward and leaned over to look more directly into the older man's face. "You're not thinking of agreeing to this request, are you?"

"More than likely, we will." Smithers rubbed his chin. "First, we need to find out who these six people on the list are—especially the sixth name added on the fly." He looked at his watch. It was 12:05 p.m. "We have 22 hours to get the information to them."

"It's going to be a late night," James mumbled.

An hour later, the ambassador commandeered a conference room in the British embassy. He told his assistant he would need the phone line encrypted for all calls through the following day. After asking his assistant to bring in a pot of tea and two cups, he said to James, "We're going to call your boss, the Director of MI6, and explain the request to him."

James dialed the secure line, and a MI6 screening operator asked the purpose of the call. The ambassador pressed the speaker button and said, "This is Ambassador Smithers, heading the Moscow embassy. It is imperative Mr. Gilmour and I speak with Director Walker right away."

The operator replied, "I will let the director know. Will you both be on this phone number when he calls back?"

"We are not hanging up!" James yelled. "Get the director! This is a matter of national security, and we will wait."

The response came back, and the operator's voice had a sense of urgency now. "Of course, Sir. Right away!"

They heard the *click* putting them on hold, and ten minutes later they heard a second *click,* followed by a voice with a thick, East London accent. "This is Director Walker. Is that you Roger?"

The ambassador cleared his voice and said, "Yes, it is, and I am here with one of your officers. His name is James Gilmour."

"You sound like you have an emergency."

"Indeed," Roger agreed. "Remember the St. Petersburg mission five weeks ago?"

"Sure," the MI6 director replied.

Roger moved his face closer to the speaker. "The Russians are going to share the information with the Chinese, the Angolans—even the British population who will not understand our activities."

"Who the hell do they think they are threatening us?" Walker demanded.

"Victor Annenkov, Director of the SVR," Smithers replied.

"Annenkov—you're kidding?" The MI6 director's voice shook slightly.

"And Boris Lipin as well," the ambassador added.

There was a pause for a few seconds as the names sunk into Walker. "You're telling me the two of you were in the same room with the two most powerful men in Russia, next to the president?"

"Yes."

Walker was still having trouble. "They were there at the same time?"

"Yes. Now you understand why we escalated this to you," Smithers clarified.

Sean Walker was showing himself as a man of few words, and in the present circumstances, this was beneficial. "What do they want?"

"It's a strange request," Smithers admitted. "There's a list of six names with social insurance numbers, and they want a full dossier on these people. It looks like they want a thorough workup including detailed information on any close relatives and friends."

"Fuck," Walker hissed.

The ambassador continued, "The kicker is they're all Canadians. They know we monitor the Canadian public and have the means to get them the information they are requesting."

"Read me off the names and identification numbers," Walker ordered.

James took this as his cue, and he read off the requested information.

"Stay by this phone. I don't know how long this will take, but any which way, you have a long night ahead of you." There was a *click* indicating the conversation was over. Smither's assistant, seeing this, knocked on the glass door before entering with a tray of hot tea.

"Thank god for that," Smithers muttered.

It wasn't until 8:00 p.m. Moscow time, when the phone in the conference room rang. James was the only one in the room and pressed the connect button. "This is Gilmour."

"Get the ambassador," Walker demanded.

James rose, but the ambassador heard the voices and came in from his office next door. The ambassador said, "Relax Sean. I'm here."

"I have the files almost complete for the first five names on the list. I don't see any type of security risk with these people, but there's something very odd," Walker revealed.

Smithers put his palms down on the edge of the table and leaned in. "What's that?"

"I'm not going to tell you until I see the file on the last name," Walker said.

"Is there an issue with the sixth name?" James asked.

"Fucking right there is!" Over the speaker, the two men heard a loud bang that sounded like Walker slamming his hand on the table at his end. "We tried to pull the information on the sixth name. As soon as we did, all kinds of restricted red flags started to pop up. It seems I don't have the security clearance required."

"The last name will be a deal breaker. It came into play, real time, during our meeting with the Russians. It must have significant importance for them to add it last minute," Smithers explained.

"I'll have to go to the foreign secretary for him to give me higher-level access," Walker admitted. "I've had this job for eight years and never had to do that." They heard the same slap on the table for the second time.

"The foreign secretary approved the SAS raid in St. Petersburg. In fact, he pushed for it. What goes around, comes around," Smithers offered.

"I'll call you back when I have more information. Don't go home." There was a *click* as Director Walker hung up his phone.

"Jarvis! Come in here!" Smithers yelled out.

The ambassador's young assistant rushed in. "Yes, Sir."

"Go down and get us some food from the kitchen, Jarvis."

Jarvis's eyes started to blink rapidly. "The kitchen closed long ago. They've all gone home."

Smithers was irritated at being at the embassy for so long. "Jarvis, if you know how to cook, you better make us some dinner. If you don't, you better learn quick, and make us some dinner."

Jarvis opened his mouth, but his response was cut off by the ambassador. "Just go and do it."

Fortunately, Jarvis could cook. He found three meat pies and cooked some potatoes to go with them. The three men ate, and Jarvis cleared away the dishes, but still, there was no phone call from London. The two men were getting increasingly nervous as the hours passed—midnight—2:00 a.m.—and 4:00 a.m. Finally, at 4:35 a.m. the phone rang.

James pressed the speaker button before the first ring finished. Smithers said, "We're here."

Walker sounded tired. "It took some convincing, but the foreign secretary gave me clearance to obtain the information we need on the sixth person on the list."

"What…"

Walker interrupted Smithers. "This is one of the strangest things I've seen, and it boggles my mind thinking about what the Russians could possibly have to do with this."

"This is the odd pattern you talked of earlier?" James asked.

"Listen closely to this," the MI6 director chirped. "Three of the people on the list are between the ages of 20 and 25. They are young. The other three are quite old, with ages between 78 and 86. There's no real connection there, but the unusual fact is all six of them were institutionalized."

"That is odd," James commented.

Walker added, "No, that's not the odd part. You see, all six of them have a debilitating condition whereby all were in a coma or an unresponsive state within those institutions."

James scratched his head. "Okay—that's really screwed up."

"You're almost there, Mr. Gilmour, but the key phrase I said was, 'They *were* institutionalized.' Over the past seven weeks, all six of those people, incapacitated as they are, went missing. The last one, which was your sixth man on the list and the one who raised all the red flags, went missing only two days ago."

"Are we giving the information to the Russians?" James asked.

Walker admitted, "We have no choice. Once I told the foreign secretary the request came personally from Annenkov and Lipin, he flipped out. He said, 'Fuck the Canadians and give the Russians what they want.' We have reviewed all the information, and there really isn't anything there that's anywhere near a security risk. Even that sixth name having the red flags all over it, didn't have anything visible as a security risk. There is obviously something there—some type of association to someone important, but if we can't find it, the Russians won't be able to either. The files are being transmitted to you via a secure line as we speak."

The lack of sleep and now confusion over the odd list of names put three creases across Smither's brow. "The sixth name—the one seeming so important to the Russians, and the one that put up all the red flags—what is it?"

Walker paused a few seconds, then said, "Lowe. Mr. Edward Lowe."

Chapter 6: Kingston

Natalie's eyes were red and moist from the tears she held back. Once she heard the news of her father's disappearance, she had a brief discussion with Philip. He told her to take all the time off she needed. He gave her a quick hug, and she sped back to her condo. She packed a travel bag and considered taking the Smith and Wesson firearm she kept stored in a gun safe in her bedroom closet. Although the general public considered both CSE and CSIS jobs to be performed at a desk, there were occasional tasks out in the field, and sometimes there was an element of danger. In this specific case, she didn't think danger would be involved, so she left the weapon at home.

Her tension eased somewhat as she completed navigating the gauntlet of cars and trucks across Toronto, and now the traffic eased. She relaxed her grip on the steering wheel and set the cruise control on the BMW. She called her father's retirement home, and it was redirected to the facility manager. He gave his profuse apologies, and he didn't have any further explanation other than when the nurse did a bed check at 3:00 a.m. he was missing from his room. Her continued questions brought up the same answer, repeatedly. "You'll need to contact Steve Drumm of the Kingston police department."

She tried several times to make contact, but between dodging traffic and being passed through the police department's phone answering system, there were several failed attempts. Finally, she connected with a real person who was able to verify Detective Drumm was leading the investigation into the disappearance of her father. She was also told he was not available, but he would return her call shortly.

That was where things were left. Now, as she was an hour into her trip, with another two hours to travel, there was nothing to do but listen to the music on the radio and keep the wheels in between the white lines—that and watch the scenery go by. But even this was made more difficult as large, fluffy snow flakes began to fall. It was unusual to have a snowfall this soon in the season, but it certainly was not rare. It began as a light snowfall, but became heavier, requiring her increased concentration on her driving.

It was difficult to not think about the issues at hand, and that meant her thoughts went to her father. He was 78 years old and was raised in Kingston. He had been a very successful electrical engineer—successful enough for him to be recruited into a military role in a Canadian scientific group. He retired when he was 65, but the military kept him on as a consultant until he was 72. He was well respected, but his memory began to fail him shortly after he began consulting. It wasn't a significant amount, but it was enough that he noticed it. After several medical evaluations it was determined he had early stage dementia.

Initially, others didn't notice, but the slight regression in the sharpness of his mind bothered her father greatly. He mulled it over, but decided to retire entirely from military work or work of any type. In his opinion, if he was not 100 per cent, then he would not continue the challenge.

Two years later, Natalie's mother died of a stroke. By this time her father's dementia was more noticeable, and without his wife, he needed to be moved to an assisted-living environment. The result was his agreement to take up residence in the Clarington retirement home in Kingston. Without his wife beside him, Edward lost much of the fight left in him, and the disease progressed much more quickly.

Now, four years later, he was in advanced stage six dementia. Natalie would visit him at least every second weekend and saw the deterioration. For the last year, her father would not move out of bed unless urged to do so, and it was only occasionally that he recognized who the people around him were. To Natalie's distress, that included her.

The phone rang, bringing her full attention back to the road in front of her, although her vision was still interrupted by the intermittent snowflakes. She pushed the *accept* button on the video monitor and said, "Hello."

The car's Bluetooth system allowed the response to come through the car's speakers. "Hi. Is this Natalie Lowe?"

"Yes," Natalie replied.

"This is Detective Steve Drumm. I'm leading the investigation into your father's disappearance."

"Thanks for getting back. Is there an update?" Natalie asked.

"Nothing yet. We're making inquiries at all local nursing homes and hospitals. I really need to talk to you in person. It would help if I knew more about your father," Drumm explained.

"What do you need to know? He has advanced dementia, can barely walk without help and doesn't know where the fuck he is most of the time! How could knowing more about him help? Obviously, someone took him," Natalie snapped.

"I'm sorry your father is missing, Ms. Lowe. What little I know is your father was a military scientist. The only thing that makes any sense, is he knows something, or has a skill someone else needs."

"Actually, that doesn't make any sense at all, seeing as he can barely talk!" Natalie blurted.

"Still, can you come to the police station when you get to town?"

Natalie calmed herself, and the tone of her voice lowered. She needed help from the detective, so she knew better than to push him away. "I'm going right to the retirement home. I want to personally see what happened and what the people there know. I will be there in 90 minutes. Please be there to meet me."

Detective Drumm began to answer, but was cut off as Natalie's finger pressed the *End Call* icon on the screen. The snow had stopped, and she could better see the familiar landscape she'd passed so many times before. Kingston was her home town, and it had been convenient for her to complete her degree in computer science at Queen's University, located in the same city. Her marks were high—high enough so that, near the end of her last semester, a man visited her and her parents at their home. He introduced himself as a member of a Canadian education lobbying group, and they had taken notice of Natalie. They would be willing to provide a full scholarship for Natalie to continue her studies towards a master's and PhD degree.

Natalie's father was sharp and knew there was likely a catch. At least in part, that became evident when the mysterious benefactor indicated they would only fund the education if Natalie went to the best school, and that was MIT in Boston. The other catch was the requirement for Natalie to work in Canada once her education was complete. This work was to be, at a minimum, for five years in government service.

It took Natalie and her parents some time, but not a lot, to realize this was the opportunity of a lifetime, and they eagerly agreed. The two years to successfully complete her master's degree in computer science was successful, but then the problem began. She decided she wanted to switch and conduct her PhD research in numerical analysis of medical applications.

Since the initial meeting with her mysterious benefactor, there had been only occasional follow-up meetings, and they were, at the best, informal. However, she didn't realize she was being monitored so closely. The day after she talked to her professor about the change in direction, the mysterious man was at the door of her residency apartment. Their discussion that day had a much more serious tone—one that indicated the man's empathy, but held an overriding threat. He told Natalie the decision was hers, but he wasn't sure he could convince his superiors to continue the funding unless the curriculum was one better benefiting Canada.

Now more wary of the motives of the mysterious lobbying group, especially when their representative told her he was certain if she continued in numerical methods and data analysis, the funding would continue, Natalie was cautious. Since she really wanted to achieve the PhD degree, she agreed to maintain the course recommended. It was years later when she realized, ever since that first meeting with the mysterious benefactor during her last year at Queen's, she was being groomed and manipulated for her eventual recruitment into the CSE. They viewed her as a valuable commodity then, and an even more valuable asset now.

Although she would remember and be irritated from time to time, she didn't mind so much because she enjoyed the work she did, and the government had a heavy investment in her. As such, she had leverage. She hadn't used it yet, but one day it might be valuable.

She was distracted by a slight glare from the instrument panel. The yellow, *low gas* light had illuminated. "Oh shit," she muttered. When she lifted her gaze up, she saw the green sign and read, *Napanee 2 kilometres*. She exhaled in relief and prepared for the turnoff.

Five minutes later, her BMW was parked in front of a gas pump at the Flying J super station. She filled up the car with gas, then parked in front of the main entrance to the small complex before entering. She frowned for a moment as she passed the gift shop. She would stop here often on her way to visit her father, where she would buy him a shirt or a hat—anything to hopefully get a spark from him, or even a glint of recognition. This time, there was no point, and she just went to the coffee stand for a large cup of java.

It was a quick stop before she was back on the highway heading east. It was only another 30 minutes to Kingston, and her thoughts changed. The way Philip told her about her father's disappearance bothered her. There was nothing wrong with the words, or even the hug he gave her, but it was cold and clinical. It served a purpose, just like their sex, but there was no warmth or real compassion there. She definitely knew their more intimate relationship was over.

She shook her head, finding it odd that as soon as she thought about warmth and compassion, the image of Josh Harris's face popped into her mind. It upset her that a man she barely knew would intrude on her emergency. Nonetheless, the image and now the sound of his voice, didn't go away. She thought it an odd coincidence Josh was looking for a missing son with talk of a conspiracy of missing persons, and here she was in the same dilemma with her father. Her eyes narrowed. She pushed back the bangs from her forehead, wondering if this was some kind of perverted CSE plot, and her mysterious benefactor would be waiting for her at the retirement home. The thought crossed her mind, *maybe she should have brought her gun.*

Now that Natalie was getting closer to her destination, it seemed to take longer and longer. The anticipation of hopefully discovering the background of what could only be considered a kidnapping, was gnawing at her. The first exit to the city of Kingston couldn't come soon enough, and four turns later, she was pulling into the driveway of the retirement home.

She had been here numerous times visiting her father, so she knew her way to the reception desk. As she walked towards it, a young man with a scraggly beard, blue jeans and a grey windbreaker walked towards her. Natalie knew the nurse behind the desk and greeted her as the man said, "Are you Ms. Lowe?"

Without looking behind her, Natalie thrust up her hand towards the man, indicating he needed to wait his turn. She said to the nurse, "I'm looking for Detective Drumm."

The nurse pointed over Natalie's shoulder. "He's right behind you."

Natalie turned and looked Detective Drumm up and down. She was expecting an older more seasoned officer, and the last time she looked, detectives wore suits. This man, in addition to the jeans, had a plain red t-shirt on under the windbreaker. She tried to keep the surprise out of her voice. "You're Steve Drumm?"

The young man removed a small leather wallet from the inside pocket of his jacket and flipped it open so Natalie could see the badge. "Yes, I'm in charge of the investigation regarding your missing father."

"Don't you mean, *kidnapped* father?"

"I understand how you feel, Ms. Lowe, but we don't have any evidence of an official kidnapping," Detective Drumm offered.

Natalie placed both hands on her hips. "I'm sure you know my father's condition, so you know he didn't just walk out of here. I'm his only family, and he's not here with me, so kidnapping should be obvious to you."

Detective Drumm opened his arm towards a table and chairs against the far wall of the foyer. "It'll be more private if we sit down."

They walked over to the chairs and sat down. Natalie leaned forward and said, "How old are you?"

Detective Drumm chuckled with the knowledge he was asked that question often. His long, brown hair, tied back in a ponytail added to people's skepticism of his official capacity. "I'm 28, and yes—I admit I look a little young for my age."

"You would look older if you wore a suit."

"I think I'd just look stupid in a suit," Drumm responded as he also leaned forward. "There are three other detectives in our police department, and they're all older. Two of them even wear suits. They'd never heard of anything like this missing person report before, and they thought a fresher and younger set of eyes might do better."

"What do you have so far," Natalie asked.

"Not much," Drumm admitted. "I have a helper who's going around to all the local nursing homes, senior's homes and hospitals with a picture of your father. So far, no one has seen him."

"I'd like to see his room," Natalie requested.

"Sure." Detective Drumm rose to his feet and began walking to one of the hallways at the back of the front foyer. Natalie rose and increased her pace to catch up to the detective. They went through one of the glass double-doors and turned to face the nursing station directly on the other side. Drumm said to the nurse sitting behind it, "We're going to Mr. Lowe's room for a few minutes."

Natalie's father's room was on the right side near the far end of the hallway. It was a large single room with a bathroom. Drumm gave Natalie a pair of nitrile gloves, and put on a pair himself. As they entered the room, Natalie surveyed it. Nothing was out of place, and the sheets on the bed were neatly folded as if no one had slept in the bed. "Why did they clean up the room?"

"That's an odd factor. No one from the retirement home did. Whoever helped or took your father, also took the time to clean up. The nurse on shift says the only thing missing, other than your father, is a small travel case and a few items of clothing."

Natalie walked slowly around the room, looking in the closet and several drawers. She mumbled, "It's odd that nothing is out of place."

Drumm added, "There's more. We dusted the entire room for fingerprints this morning, and there are none."

"So, they wiped down their prints. Why is that odd?" she asked.

"Because it's not only their prints that are missing. There are absolutely no prints in this room. You would think, with nurses and other workers coming in and out every day, there would be some residual prints somewhere, but there are none. Even if someone wiped and sanitized this room for a day, there would still be a print somewhere."

Natalie stopped her inspection and faced the young detective. "That sounds impossible."

"Almost as impossible as your father walking out of here," he replied.

"So, you *do* believe he was kidnapped."

"Of course," he admitted, "but notwithstanding the circumstances, we can't go to an official missing person case for three days, and even with the dubious situation we see here, we cannot report it as a kidnapping for seven days. Right now, we are at day two."

"What now? We do nothing?"

Drumm smiled. "I think that's why they assigned me on the case. Between the other detectives having no idea what to do and the case presently not being official, they put me on it—sort of washing their hands of it."

"Then, you're all we have," Natalie said as the realization sank in.

Drumm walked over, directly in front of Natalie. "You're better off with me than them. They wouldn't have even given you the time of day. I have six more days to look into this, and then I'll call in the RCMP since kidnapping is a national crime."

Natalie brushed the bangs from her forehead as she walked by him and out into the hallway. He followed, and she asked him, "Where are the cameras?"

"From this point, I think it's best if you leave the police work to me," he replied.

She peered up and down the hallway several times as she explained, "After receiving my degrees at MIT, I worked for the FBI as an intern for two years, so I have some skills. You've been left on your own, so you could use some help," she insisted.

Drumm pointed to the back, glass door. "That's the emergency exit from this assisted-living wing. There's one surveillance camera outside. There are three other standard retirement living wings with a similar fire exit at the back. Each of those also has a monitoring camera. There is a camera monitoring the front entrance and two cameras viewing the parking lot."

"That's it?"

"There's also a service door on the east side for kitchen and maintenance deliveries. There's one camera there as well," Drumm added.

"I'd like to see the video from last night," she urged.

"I've gone through it all, but sure," he said

He led the way back out of the assisted-living wing and into the foyer. As they walked, he elaborated on what they had investigated so far. "The fire exits are always locked, and if anyone opens one up, the alarm will ring. There was no alarm activated last night. The front entry is locked after 9:00 p.m. and there's a nurse always manning the desk right next to it. I interviewed the nurse from last night, and she didn't see or hear anything. The night shift nurse started at 11:00 p.m. Her standard schedule is a room check at that time. Your father was asleep. The next room check was at 1:00 a.m. and your father was still sleeping. At 3:00 a.m.—that's when she found your father missing and the room in the exact condition you saw it."

"Let's see Orville," Natalie said.

"You know him?" Drumm asked with a raised eyebrow.

As Natalie headed to the security office door on the west wall of the foyer, she replied, "I've visited my father here at least every second weekend for the past four years. Of course, I know Orville and everyone else who works here."

She knocked on the door, and a deep voice replied from the other side, "Come in."

She pushed the door open, and she and Drumm faced an older, black man with a white beard. He wore glasses, and when he saw Natalie, he wished he could hide his face behind them. His face had many wrinkles, but still, his face noticeably sagged. He rose to his feet and said, "I'm so sorry, Ms. Lowe. We've never had anything like this happen before, and as the head of security, I'm working with Detective Drumm, doing everything I can to help find your father."

She and Drumm sat in the two chairs opposite to Orville. Natalie said, "It's okay, Orville. I would also like to help where I can. What's on the tapes from the video cameras?"

"I've spent hours going through them all, and when I was done, the detective did it again. The cameras at the maintenance entrance and the fire exits from the three wings your father was not in, worked normally and showed nothing at all."
She was getting anxious and interrupted, "What about the other ones?"

Orville nervously nodded his head up and down. "Sure, but first I'll tell you we have an outside company that comes in every month to check the cameras and the taping system. They were here just a week ago, and everything checked out fine."

Natalie leaned forward, "Was there something wrong with them last night?"

Orville rotated his chair around to face the video screen behind him. He ran his fingers over the keyboard below it until he found the file he wanted. He pressed the *enter* button, and a video began to play on the screen. He rotated the chair halfway back around, so he could see both the screen and Natalie. "This is the video from outside the fire exit to your father's wing. I set it so you are seeing what happened at 2:12 a.m."

After a few seconds, she asked, "What am I looking for?"

Orville didn't answer. He just pointed a finger into the air, indicating she needed to wait. It was, in fact, about a minute later that the screen began to flicker and then went to a static-filled, snowy condition. Orville turned to Natalie. "The main entry camera and the two parking-lot cameras have this exact same visual fault at the exact same time." He then turned back to his keyboard and skipped through most of the static. He pushed his chair around again and said, "Watch."

The picture suddenly returned, looking every bit the same as what they saw before the static event. Orville clarified, "What is just as strange as the four cameras going to static at the same moment, is they all went back to a normal picture at exactly the same time – 2:40 a.m."

"There must be something wrong with your system," Natalie suggested.

Detective Drumm cut in. "I had the video maintenance people come here this morning. They, along with our police video specialist, went over each camera, the computer—absolutely everything, with a fine-toothed comb. They couldn't find anything wrong. Their final conclusion was there had to be some type of outside interference."

Orville pushed his chair closer to the desk and said, "Ms. Lowe, I'm not an expert like the people who checked out the system, but in my younger years I worked for ten years in Kenya installing high-power, electrical lines. I'm not an electrical engineer either, but we spent a lot of time with the installations. We also checked to ensure the lines were high enough on the tower, so the electrical fields created were insignificant at ground level. I've seen thousands of signals checked, and what I can tell you, is the way the static signal on the video we just watched flickers every couple of seconds, is a clear indication the interference was from a strong electromagnetic field."

Something clicked in Natalie's brain, and she rose to her feet. "Thank you, Orville." She turned to Drumm and stated, "I need to go back to

Toronto. I'm going to call you every day for an update, but if you have even a shred of information, day or night, call me right away." The tone of her voice indicated it was a demand and not a request.

Natalie said goodbye to the nurse on her way out before heading to her car. During her time in the retirement home, she lost all track of time, but when she started the car and saw the time on the clock, it was 4:30 p.m. She waited a second for her cell phone to connect to the car's Bluetooth before she pushed her hand into her jacket pocket. Pulling out the piece of scrap paper, she unfolded it and viewed Josh's phone number. The talk of electromagnetic interference brought her mind to him, and now, she read the digits to the microphone of the phone system. She was tense and cleared her throat as the phone rang.

There was a click and then a familiar voice, "Hello."

Natalie replied, "Josh, this is Natalie."

"Natalie—Hi. I was hoping you would call. Coffee?"

A wave of relief went through her. She feared he'd not remember her at all, and say, "Natalie who?" After a deep exhale, a flood of words came out quickly. "Not a coffee. First, I need to apologize to you for a few things, but I'll save that until I see you. I do need to talk to you about your son and more. I'm in Kingston, but I can pick you up in the morning."

"King who?"

"Kingston," she corrected. "It's a small city about three hours east of Toronto. I'm exhausted, and I'm going to spend the night in a hotel. I want to miss the rush hour traffic in the morning, so I'll be up early. Can I pick you up at your hotel at 6:00 in the morning?"

"No problem. I'll be in the lobby of the Hampton Inn by the airport, waiting for you."

"Thanks Josh. I'll see you then." She hung up the phone and relaxed back into the car seat. Josh had also talked about an electromagnetic field causing camera interference, and here it was mentioned again. She was suspicious, thinking whether or not this was just a coincidence, or was there something else in play. Did all this somehow have to do with her father's previous military career, or was there a twist coming from the CSE?

She was surprised to find these thoughts were being pushed to the back of her mind. What came to the forefront, and it seemed to be fixated there, was she was going to see Josh again. She shook her head to try and clear the vision of his face, but it stuck there, and she thought again, *yup. This is going to be bad.*

Chapter 7: Ochokova

Leonid Belov sat in the living room of his small apartment located in western Moscow. His packed suitcase was by the door with his coat draped over it. The sparsely furnished apartment had been his home for the past two months while he worked with the Russians. He missed his home, but the mission he was on was more important than his comforts.

There was a beeping tone from beside him. He picked up his cell phone and said, "Hello."

There was a curt response. "I am downstairs. Come now."

Leonid walked over to the front hallway, pulled on his thigh-length, black overcoat, and put the cell phone in the interior pocket. He took one last look at the apartment, knowing he wouldn't be back for some time—if at all. He shrugged and thought, *he would not miss it.* He picked up his suitcase and was out the door without another thought.

He took the elevator down from the eighth floor and saw the copper-coloured Renault Duster idling in front of the ground-floor, glass doors. A few seconds later, he opened the rear door of the vehicle and placed his suitcase in the back seat area before he slid onto the front seat beside Victor Annenkov.

"Good evening, Victor," Leonid offered.

"It's cold," Victor replied. "When I was young, the severe temperature we see in Moscow was never a problem, but now, as I am getting older, even this slightly cold weather seems to sink into my bones with too much ease." He clapped his gloved hands together before shifting the SUV's transmission into gear, and they sped out of the driveway.

This was the first time Leonid saw Victor in civilian clothes. The SVR director was not wearing a uniform, but typically he would wear some item signifying his position. Leonid hadn't seen either the silver pin reflecting his military service, or the gold badge of the SVR. The double headed, gold eagle, with a blue globe in the forefront and a crossed sword and torch in the background, was almost always pinned to his lapel. However, tonight, he wore a dark-green, wool sweater and dark-brown slacks. Victor looked very ordinary, but then, that was his plan.

Leonid glanced at the car clock. It was 9:30 p.m. and the evening was dark with only a slit of a moon, poking its light between the intermittent clouds. They were driving south-east towards their rendezvous in the Ochokova district of Moscow. It was primarily an apartment-filled suburb of the larger city, where strangers would not visit because there was absolutely nothing of interest to see. It also made the area of the city a perfect location for a covert SVR location to be hidden.

Twenty minutes later, they arrived at a small, white, six-story apartment building that appeared ready to fall over. Leonid looked up the side wall of the building and saw many of the windows boarded up with plywood, and there were no lights on. The building looked deserted. Victor had told him the building was once fully occupied, but the owner had financial troubles. Consequently, the apartment deteriorated with disrepair, and many inhabitants moved out. The owner finally abandoned the property altogether whereby the government secretly took over ownership. To any others questioning the future of the building, they were notified it was abandoned and unsafe because of the lack of maintenance. It was not even cost-effective to tear it down.

The Renault SUV moved to the back of the decrepit apartment building where overgrown willow and maple trees made it impossible to see the lower levels. Victor drove the vehicle under the branches and turned down the ramp to the abandoned parking garage. There was a card reader stand where Victor pressed his identification card to it. After a *beep*, the garage door in front of them creeped up.

Once the Renault cleared the electric eye on the far side of the opening, the heavy, metal door rolled back down. There were very few lights in the parking garage, so the headlights stayed on to guide them. A moment later, the light revealed five other vehicles parked beside the elevator door.

Leonid hopped out of their vehicle after they parked alongside the line of cars, and he pulled his suitcase from the back seat. Leonid's footsteps echoed off the walls of the large underground level as he joined Victor, walking to the elevator door. There, Leonid saw Victor carried a briefcase as he once again pressed his access card to a reader, and the hum of the elevator's electric motor whined into life. A minute later, the pair of men were travelling upwards until the elevator door opened at the fourth floor. There were a few dimly lit bulbs in the hallway, revealing the many stains in the old, heavily-worn carpet that was the source of the heavy, musty smell surrounding them. Victor led the way until they reached apartment 410. Victor opened the door and led Leonid directly into the cramped living room.

The large window on the far wall was boarded up from the outside with plywood, so the only light in the room was from a table lamp. From the shadows on the far side of the room, three men revealed themselves and moved towards Victor. As is the European custom, the three men shook hands with Victor with the third man nodding a greeting as he said, "Director."

Leonid had never seen any of these men before, but he shook hands with each of them before Victor asked them all to be seated. At least this apartment was clean, and there was a long couch against the wall across from four cheap, wooden chairs. The men moved towards the wooden chairs, but Victor redirected them to the couch. After they were seated, Victor and Leonid sat in two of the wooden chairs facing them.

As Victor pulled the briefcase across his knees, he announced, "My apologies, but there won't be any formal introductions. Also, everyone needs to get right into character, so English only please." He popped the two small levers on the front of the briefcase before lifting the top half of it. "You are each getting a new identity for this mission." He pulled out a plastic pouch and threw it to the man who was sitting on the left side of the couch. He was shaved bald leaving the brown, squared-off beard as the only hair on his head. With his menacing look, Leonid was glad the man was on the team. As the man caught the pouch, Victor continued. "Inside the pouch you have a Canadian passport, a Canadian driver's license and an information packet about a small city named North Bay, Ontario. This is where the four of you now come from."

Victor pointed at the first man. "Your name is now Brian Selkirk."

He threw another plastic pouch to the man sitting in the middle of the couch. He had thick, black, curly hair, and even with the winter jacket on, you could tell he had a muscular physique. Victor said, "You are now Tony Messina."

The newly anointed Brian chuckled as he punched Tony in the shoulder. "It's a good Italian name, matching your appearance."

Victor ignored them as he threw another pouch to the man on the right side of the couch. "You are Nick Anderson."

Nick was tall. You could tell by how high his knees were off the ground as he sat on the couch. He had a chiselled, handsome face, topped with a neatly-trimmed head of short, blonde hair. He opened the zipper on the pouch and searched through the documents.

Finally, Victor tossed the last pouch to Leonid. "You are now Logan Russell."

Nick leaned forward and said, "Director Annenkov, the two men beside me, I've known for years and have been on many missions with them. I trust them with my life." He pointed at Logan. "Who is he?"

Victor slammed the briefcase closed and put it down beside him. He now had the full attention of all four men. "I am sure he has the same questions about you three, so I will explain the facts you need to know, and no more. Too much information could make you a liability."

Victor waited a moment to see if any would voice complaints, but there were none. He continued, "Good. Logan, these three men are agents of the SVR from Directorate S. They are from a specialized group that very few people know about. This group is very small, numbering 50, so they are known as the Spetsnaz 50. They specialize in infiltration assignments, and since you are going to Canada, they will be invaluable. Nick is the lead for the three agents, and he will also lead the team. Once you are in Canada, you two—" He pointed at Logan and Nick. "—will need to work together to lead the group. Nick has the tactical experience, and you have the critical information pertinent to this crucial mission." He now looked directly at the three men on the couch. "Just remember, Logan has my absolute trust, and when he speaks or gives direction, he speaks for me."

All three men nodded their acknowledgment, so Victor pointed at Logan, then continued, "Logan is with Roscosmos"

"Why do we need someone from the Russian space program?" Nick questioned.

The central portion of Victor's two eyebrows curled down with his irritation. "Because he is critically important to the success of the mission— a mission I have not yet explained, yet you already question!"

All three men on the couch squirmed as Nick gave his apologies.

Victor rose to his feet and paced back and forth across the room. "I will repeat, Logan is with Roscosmos, but he works for me as an agent of Directorate X," the director clarified.

Nick's eyes opened wide with surprise when he heard this. "I thought Directorate X was dissolved years ago."

"Most of the department was, but I have retained a small team that looks at scientific and technical risks from an intelligence standpoint at my discretion. Several weeks ago, Roscosmos found something in their space surveillance. They did not see it as a risk, but Logan did, and he brought it to my attention. I am not going to give you more details now since Logan has very reliable intelligence from a source we cannot reveal at this time. But know that Logan has all this information, and he will share it with you when the time is appropriate. Is that understood?" Victor turned to face the three men on the couch with his fingers clasped together behind his back.

All three men indicated their absolute agreement.

"You had your pre-briefing, Nick?" Director Annenkov asked.

"Yes, Sir. Travel arrangements have been made, and I have the names of our travel contacts. I also have the list of our operatives in Canada," Nick responded.

Director Annenkov added, "Logan has a list of six names with their associated and detailed information files. These Canadians are linked to the crucial event found at Roscosmos which could mean the end of us all. You need to find these people. Failure is not an option." Victor's voice was deeper, and he couldn't fully hide the fear his mind held.

Nick rose to his feet, followed by his two Spetsnaz colleagues. He heard every word Director Annenkov said, but he also knew every man in the room was an alpha male. There would be struggles for leadership, and he was taking the first step. "We've a long way to go. We better get to it." He clapped his hands together and his two fellow Spetsnaz 50 comrades instantly jumped to their feet.

Logan also rose, and showing his curiosity, an eyebrow was lifted. "Where are we going?"

Nick did not know Logan, but a member of Directorate X deserved some respect. He smirked and thought, *still he would need to earn it*. Nick responded, "We're going to Denmark."

Chapter 8: Word Search

The drive from Kingston had been uneventful. Thankfully, even though there were very few cars on the highway, there were quite a few large, noisy trucks to keep her sharp and awake. The night before, her sleep was fitful, and she estimated she managed, in total, four hours sleep before she started her car and headed back towards Toronto.

Now, she was turning off the main highway and heading south to the Hampton Inn. It was 6:15 in the morning when she pulled up to the entrance of the four-story hotel. A few seconds later, Josh came out the front doors and slipped into the BMW beside Natalie.

"Nice car," Josh offered.

She pulled away from the hotel and headed for the highway that would take them further south to Etobicoke and her home. "Thanks. Is everything okay?"

"It's all good," he replied. "I'm hungry though, and even more than that, I really need a coffee."

Natalie hadn't thought much about food for a while, and she realized she hadn't eaten anything since yesterday morning. Glancing down at her thin sweater and blue jeans, she confessed, "I've been wearing these same clothes for way too long, and I need a shower. I don't think I could sit in anywhere, but there's a good restaurant with a drive through near my condo. How about we pick up a coffee and a breakfast sandwich there?"

"That sounds great," Josh replied, but his voice lowered with concern. "It sounds like you've had a tough time since our coffee four days ago. What's been going on?"

Natalie brushed the hair from her brow and glanced at Josh. She felt more at ease with him there beside her. "There's much to be said. When we get to my condo, I'll explain it all."

As promised, Natalie took them to a local restaurant where they ordered their two large coffees and sandwiches. It was only a few more minutes, and they were walking down the hallway on the 12th floor towards her condo. She unlocked the door and turned on the hallway light as she entered. Her entire condo had a grey, engineered, laminate floor throughout, so she didn't bother to take off her shoes as she continued to her master bedroom.

Halfway to her bedroom door, she turned her face towards Josh and told him, "Just make yourself comfortable, and I'll be out in a moment." A curious grin crossed her face as she saw what he was doing. "You said you were American, right?"

Josh was leaned over as he untied the laces of his hiking boots. One was already off, and he was working on the second one as he tilted his face upwards. "Yes, New York State," he reminded her.

She shook her head and continued to the bedroom, closing the door behind her. Five minutes later, she came back out and saw Josh sitting at the kitchen table with the sandwiches on plates he found in the cupboard. Natalie had used the few minutes to change the clothes she had been in for two days, wash up, and she was in her silk pajamas covered with a fluffy, blue house coat.

Josh grinned and said, "That's a good look."

Although Natalie's frame was slight, there was a loud *thunk* as she dropped herself in the chair beside Josh. "Ya think," she replied just before she took a large bite from the sandwich.

Josh began eating as well, and between bites said, "I was serious. Most women you see out there are covered with makeup and fancy clothes. It's refreshing to see you without makeup and, let's say more comfortable, to find you look just as nice after driving for a few hours when most every other sane person would be sleeping."

As Josh talked, Natalie took a deep drink of coffee. She peered at him over the rim of the cup, then placed it on the table. "I think there was some type of compliment in there, so thanks for that."

He took another bite and then asked, "Why did you ask if I was American?"

After finishing another bite of the sandwich, she said, "I lived in the Boston area for four years while I was finishing my schooling, so I learned a lot about American customs. One of them I noticed was Americans almost never take their shoes off when they enter their house, or anyone else's." She took another drink of coffee before continuing. "In Canada, we always take our shoes off because it just makes sense to keep dirt out of where people live. It was curious that you did the Canadian thing in taking yours off, even after I didn't."

"When a woman you barely know invites you to her condo for the first time, I thought it best to be on my best behaviour."

She smiled warmly at him, and whispered, "Don't worry. You're doing just fine so far." Natalie stretched her arms up over her head and yawned. When her mouth closed, her hands came down and slapped the table. "We have some things to talk about, but even my ass is sore from so much driving the past two days. I need to find a more comfortable spot for it." Rising to her feet, she headed for the well-padded, dark-blue love seat in the living room. She lowered herself into it and threw her feet up on the ottoman. She tapped the seat beside her in offering. "There's things you need to know, Josh."

He slid onto the cushion beside her, making sure not to offend her by sitting too close. He put his feet on the ottoman beside hers and asked, "What's been going on the last few days?"

"Is there any news on your son?"

He sighed heavily. "No, absolutely nothing"

After waiting what she thought was a polite few seconds, she changed the subject. "My father has advanced dementia and is in a nursing home in Kingston. At least he *was* in the home. Monday morning, I received a call saying he was missing," Natalie explained.

Josh's eyes opened wider, showing his concern. "I'm sorry. Most people would say, 'I know what you're going through,' but they don't. In this case, I do. Do the police have any leads?"

She shrugged, "Nothing yet. One of the reasons I called you was because there are similarities to your son's disappearance and those others you told me of last Friday."

"Like what?" he asked.

"Mainly, the local video cameras in the home had some type of electromagnetic interference during the time of the abduction," she elaborated.

"Do they know it was an abduction?"

"My father couldn't walk on his own, talked very little other than incoherent phrases from time to time, and most of the time, he didn't recognize the people around him," she admitted.

"Again, I'm sorry."

Natalie leaned her head back on the cushion back. "No, Josh. I'm the one who's sorry. You asked for my help, and I lied to you and wouldn't help you." She placed her hand on top of his as she continued. "I don't work for the CSIS, so I technically didn't lie to you, but I did deceive you since I do work for the CSE—a sister group to the CSIS, and in fact, better equipped to help you than if I was with the CSIS. I feel horrible. Now, I need your help since my father has disappeared under the same circumstances as your son. I need to see your files again, and maybe now we can help each other."

Josh thought about Natalie's words for a few moments before responding. "Don't worry about what happened last Friday. You didn't know me at all, and even now, you don't know me much better. Maybe this is a good time for us to put that behind us, and help each other from this point on."

He didn't hear a reply, but a moment later, he felt a light thud on his shoulder. He looked down to see Natalie's head had shifted and landed there. Her mouth was cracked open, and she was fast asleep. He smiled and pushed his head back in the cushion and closed his own eyes.

Two hours later, when Natalie stirred, Josh's eyes opened, and he looked down to see Natalie had slid closer. Somehow, his arm had wrapped around her shoulder, and her face was nestled against his chest, as was her hand. She was lying on her side, cuddled into him when her eyes fluttered. Realizing where she was, she bolted upright, and her head turned from side to side like a criminal about to make a getaway. Her hands pushed on Josh's chest as she rose to her feet with her face holding a pink tinge.

"How long were we asleep?" she asked as she rubbed her eyes.

He pulled his phone from his pocket and said, "It's 9:30 a.m. so we have been sleeping for about two hours.

"We have a lot of work to do. Can you pull out those files you have?" she asked.

Josh rose to his feet and retrieved the valise from the hallway. When he returned, Natalie was in what should have been her dining room. Instead, there was a large glass-topped desk, and on it were two large glasses of orange juice she had just poured. She was sitting in her well-cushioned chair behind the desk and told Josh to pull up one of the kitchen chairs.

Josh moved the chair to the opposite side of her desk, but Natalie waved her hand back and forth. "Not there. Come and sit beside me, so we can do this together."

She scooted her chair over, and Josh put the other chair beside her. After unzipping the valise, he pushed it in front of her. She quickly flipped it open and began to organize the papers into piles—one for each missing person Josh had found. She also wrote out her father's basic information on a piece of paper and made a separate pile, creating six piles in total.

What now?" Josh asked.

Natalie's chair was on a swivel. She pushed her foot off the laminate floor and spun around to face the computer on the smaller desk in front of the picture window overlooking Lake Ontario. She tapped the space bar, and the computer came to life. As she put in her password, she said, "What now, is I'm going to do my thing. In the CSE, I'm one of the experts on data searches and data analysis. Right now, I'm going to go to a couple of search engines I have access to that might bring up some more names." She paused for a moment and looked at Josh. "It's hard to believe these six people are the only ones missing under these mysterious and seemingly impossible circumstances. There must be a link between them, and to find out what that is, we need to find more people missing under those same circumstances." She turned back to the computer and started hitting keys.

"That makes sense," he added. "I have looked at the five names I came up with, and I don't see a pattern. There are old people, young people, men and women, but I don't see any consistency."

Natalie muttered, "Your sample size isn't big enough." Her fingers now flew over the keyboard, and the screens on the monitor changed quickly. "First, I have access to a search engine that checks for similarities. You can put in up to twenty pieces of data, and the search will reveal any similar articles out there on the internet."

"That sounds like a plan."

"Read me off the six names we have so far," Natalie directed.

Josh leaned over the larger desk and read the names, and she typed them in. She double checked her typing before she hit *enter*. A new screen popped up asking for additional parameters that would prioritize the search. She put in *Kingston, Saratoga Springs*, and the key phrase *missing person*. She explained to Josh the search would take a couple of hours, searching from the location points entered and working outwards.

"It will look for similar articles?" Josh questioned.

She already opened up a new window as she answered, "Yes. While that works, we're going to search using some old school methods." She hit *enter* on the keyboard and the google search engine popped onto the screen.

Three hours later, after a creative and exhaustive google search, they filtered through the data provided by the similarity search engine. Unfortunately, they only uncovered two more missing person cases fitting the profile they were looking for. One was in Vancouver, British Columbia and the other was in Grand Rapids, Minnesota. Natalie printed off the information for each of these missing people and placed them on the larger glass-topped desk. There were now eight piles, but it was still not enough data to see a pattern.

Natalie was frustrated, but her deteriorating mood was broken by the ringing of a cell phone. She ran over to her purse on a small table in the hallway and retrieved her phone from it. "Hello."

"Ms. Lowe, this is Detective Drumm…"

"Have you found my father?" she interrupted.

"I'm sorry, Ms. Lowe, but no. As I told you, we checked local nursing homes and hospitals without any success. We then started checking local gas stations in case the people who took your father made a stop. Some had video surveillance systems, so we checked as many as we could," Drumm explained.

"And?"

"We weren't having any luck, but then we received a phone call from the company that services the cameras at your father's retirement home. They said they received a call from a service center located just before the on ramp to the main highway to Toronto. They had the same electromagnetic interference on their video system early Monday morning. This morning, we have been contacting video equipment maintenance companies between here and Toronto."

"And?"

"There is another service center in Oshawa, just this side of Toronto, that had the same type of video camera service call. If the people who have your father are causing these camera outages, then they're heading west," Detective Drumm concluded.

"Thanks detective. Let me know if anything else comes up." Natalie hung up the phone and explained the conversation to Josh.

"They don't have a lot," Josh commented.

"Their investigation is moving too slow," she mumbled. "We have to do more ourselves."

He turned and looked at Natalie's face, seeing there was a conflict there. "What are you suggesting?"

"I have access to the powerful computers used at my CSE office. I can run a remote search from here," she confided.

"Isn't that illegal?" His face was drawn with concern, matching hers.

She managed a smirk. "It certainly is, but we perform a lot of activities that test the line of legality. Trust me, I have quite a bit of expertise and can hide my tracks very well."

"I'm game—anything to help find your father and my son," he confessed.

As she turned on the chair's swivel, she reached down to a lower drawer in her desk. There was a small combination lock there which she opened and retrieved a laptop. She connected a power cord to the laptop and said to Josh, "You might not want to watch this, otherwise your future plausible denial defence won't exist."

He laughed. "You certainly have a way with words that builds my confidence, but seriously, we are in this together now."

As she fired up the laptop and logged in, she mumbled, "Well if that's the case, we might be working together for a while. We better get you out of your hotel. If you have a rent-a-car, we can return it, and you can stay in my guest room." She raised her chin, pointing it to a door beside her bedroom.

"That would be more convenient." He put his hand on her wrist. "I feel like you're doing a lot more for me than I'm doing for you."

She enjoyed the feel of his fingers on her. She knew he was incorrect on his assumption, but now was not the time to explain her feelings. She realized, with her father missing and having only a few friends, none of which were close enough to share in her emergency, she was utterly alone. She needed Josh, even though he was really nothing more than a stranger with a friendly face. Nevertheless, she didn't think she could get through this ordeal without someone, and he was the one who was here. She still hadn't moved her wrist, nor had he removed his hand.

He finally shifted his hand, but it was to grasp her own and hold it tight. Then, it was as if he knew what she was thinking. He whispered, "No worries. We are definitely in this together now."

She tilted her head and her olive-green eyes were soft as she gazed at him. If he was as intuitive about her eyes as what his mind seemed to be, then surely, even though she was still in her pajamas and housecoat, he knew she was feeling as naked as a baby and just as vulnerable.

Josh finally released her hand and pointed at the screen. "It wants your password."

She smiled an honest smile and continued with her entries. She said, "Don't say I didn't warn you. There are things you'll see now that are restricted access. That means, if you divulge this information to anyone else, well, I'll have to kill you."

He laughed, but after a few seconds, when she didn't and continued to type, he thought it better to just speak when spoken to.

As Natalie typed in characters at an alarming pace, she explained, "I'm setting up two searches. One is for Canada, and the other is for all the Northern United States. I'm putting in keywords and giving them a weighting factor towards the importance of the search." She turned her eyes away from the screen and towards Josh. "I need your input here to help with those keywords and the percentage weightings."

It took about an hour of discussion as they deliberated over the keywords. They came up with ten keyword phrases, and at the top of the list with a heavy weighting were, *missing person, kidnapping, military, retirement home, nursing home, electromagnetic* and *video camera malfunction*. She entered all ten phrases and requested a time period for each search from the date of the disappearance of Hendrix Harris to now.

"There," Natalie muttered. "It's all entered and encrypted. It needs to sit until tonight. That's when there'll be the least amount of scrutiny. I've checked the run log and there's a typically large search scheduled overnight, as well as two other searches. I can add in the two searches we've set up that'll take about three hours to run. At 3:30 a.m. I'll sign on and transfer the results to my laptop and erase any sign our two searches were run."

"What else can we do now?" he asked. "The time has passed quickly, and it's almost 6:00 p.m."

Natalie rose to her feet. "I need dinner and then some fresh air. I'm surprised you haven't heard my stomach growling."

Natalie went to her bedroom and changed into a pair of blue jeans and a bright, yellow sweater. She pulled her winter jacket overtop of it, and both of them headed out the door. It was already dark outside as they left the condo parking lot in the white Beamer. It took a few minutes to check out of his hotel room, and it was convenient to return his car since the rental office was in the lobby of the same building. Everything was all done in a matter of minutes before they headed south.

"Where to for dinner?" Josh asked.

"There's a little-known family restaurant close by that has great home-cooked meals. I think you'll like it," she offered.

The restaurant didn't disappoint as Josh ate every bit of his meal, leaving the plate as if it didn't even need to be washed. The waitress came over to the table to remove the empty plates, and she had a wide smile seeing they had finished every morsel.

Josh grinned and said, "I hated it."

All three of them laughed, and with the situations Josh and Natalie were in, they needed that.

As they were leaving, Josh moved to pay the bill, but Natalie would have none of that as she added her half to the money on the counter. It was a short drive back to the condo where, after parking the car, they walked out a back door into the cool air.

Natalie's condo was in a row of six condos along the lakeshore. Between the condos and the lake was a parkette where, in this season, the grass was faded-yellow and the many trees were devoid of leaves. Still, in the light of the moon, allowed by the cloudless sky, they enjoyed the fresh air and each other's company.

They walked slowly beside each other and Natalie asked, "Tell me about your son."

Josh pressed his hands into his coat pockets and replied, "Hendrix is a good kid. His mother raised him well, and she had to, seeing as I was gone much of the time on a ship going here or there for long periods. I wish I could've spent more time with him, but I made a vow to make the time I did spend with him, quality time. I think we did that."

She hoped she was not prying when she asked, "What happened to his mother?"

"His mother was my wife until she died of cancer five years ago. I think that's what drove him to the military."

"I'm sorry about your wife and your son's accident."

Josh was glad to tell her a bit about his history, but he wanted to know more about Natalie as well. "I know of your father. What about your mother?"

Natalie shivered from the cold and zipped her jacket all the way to the top. Josh, seeing this, wrapped his arm around her shoulder and pulled her close. She did not draw away as he made a meek effort to justify his action. "We'll both be warmer like this."

They walked for a few minutes, moving towards the waterline and the sound of the waves lapping up on the rocks there. Josh reminded her, "You were going to tell me about your mother."

She looked up at him, and there was a smile on her face. Josh thought it lit up her face more than the light of the moon reflecting off of it. Her face was more long than round, with high cheekbones and a longer nose—but not too long. Her eyes were wide and angled upwards at the outside edges. He was getting used to looking at the face he thought was beautiful, just as he was getting used to the two pink stripes in her hair.

Natalie said, "I had a good childhood. My mother also died, but five years ago. She had a stroke, so at that point, it was my father and I, and his health was failing rapidly. He's very important to me, and I have to find him."

They made a wide circle on the sidewalk through the parkette as they continued to talk. Thirty minutes later, they were back at her condo. When they entered the building, Josh removed his hand off her shoulder, and she was a bit disappointed. She enjoyed the feel of him close to her. They took the elevator up to her floor and were back in the condo apartment a few minutes after that.

Natalie led the way to the living room and asked him, "What time is it?"

"It's 9:30 p.m. We have some time before you load the programs to be run tonight," he said.

She scratched her fingers through her hair. "I'm going to have a shower—you remember, the one I said I was going to take this morning. You might want to do the same in the main bathroom." She pointed to a door beside the guest room.

He replied as he walked towards the main bath, "I think that's a good idea."

From behind him, he heard the word, "Wait." He turned around and she whispered, "Come here."

Josh walked towards her, and once there, put his hands on her waist while looking down into her pretty eyes.

She took a deep breath. "I feel it too. There's a heavy tension here between us, and there is nothing more I want than to have you follow me into my shower."

There was a slight up and down nod of his head. "Am I that easy to read?"

She grinned. "I think we both are, but a romance would set us back. This needs to wait. In the meantime, we'll be spending a lot of time together."

"You're right," he agreed. He loosened his grip on her waist, but as he was releasing her, he felt her hands slide to his arms.

"I do want one thing," she whispered. "As the song goes—just one kiss."

He had a confused look as he said, "Song…"

He was interrupted by the feel of one of Natalie's hands sliding up the back of his neck. She lifted up on her tip-toes and tilted her head to the side.

Once Josh felt her warm lips on his, his face tilted involuntarily to meet hers. His hands slid behind her back as he pulled her closer. The kiss was not sexual. Rather, it was warm and romantic. Their embrace was a vision that would fit well on the cover of one of the romance novels Natalie had on her night stand.

Neither one of them wanted the kiss to end, but it had to, so Josh's arms unwrapped her and settled her just a breath away. There were no words because there was no need. Everything that needed to be said was in their locked gaze.

Josh whispered, "Go have your shower."

"Come with me," she quietly urged.

He smiled and brushed the bangs off her forehead. "I'll have my own shower, albeit a cold one."

She grinned. "I thought I was going to be the sensible one."

"We'll pick this up another time, when our full attention can be given to each other."

Natalie backed up, and it took some effort to unlock from his gaze and turn towards her bedroom. Her heart was pounding as she thought of their entire day. Even though, her father was missing, she was happy, and she was happy because of him. She was not alone.

Chapter 9: Greenland

At 1:00 a.m. Moscow's airport was mostly devoid of people. There were very few flights travelling to or from Moscow at this time, but there was a late Aeroflot flight leaving for Copenhagen. Nick, Logan, Tony and Brian, the undercover Russians, travelled in pairs. Nick and Logan travelled together, sitting in the forward part of the cabin, while Tony and Brian took seats near the back of the plane. Their Canadian passports were not questioned. When asked about the purpose of their trip to Russia, Nick and Logan explained they were artists on a cultural tour. Tony and Brian passed themselves off as businessmen.

Once the Sukhoi Superjet 100 was in the air, it didn't take Nick long to impress his ownership of the mission. He leaned over to his travelling partner and said, "Logan, I know Annenkov directed our need to share the leadership of the mission, but I'm the expert on infiltration, so I'm in charge and will make sure you make it to Canada in one piece."

Logan heard Nick say his cover name and thought, *it will take a little time to get used to it, just as it had taken time to get used to Leonid.* He stroked his short van-dyke-style beard with his fingers and replied through a smug grin, "It did not take you long to challenge for position."

Nick shrugged. "It's obvious to me, but I wanted to make it clear to you. This makes sense."

"You are right," Logan confessed. "You are the expert on the logistics of our trip. However, once we get to Canada, we will discuss this again as I am the expert on the specific mission."

"Fair enough," Nick offered. "What details can you tell me of this mission?"

Logan paused for a few seconds before he retrieved his cell phone from his pocket. He put in a password to access a secure cloud file. As it was loading, he said, "I am loading the files of six people we need to track down in Canada. I will let you read the files as soon as they finish loading." A moment later, the access was complete, and he passed the phone to Nick.

Nick scrolled through the first person, then the second and third. He stopped and looked curiously at Logan. "These people are all in institutions where they were abducted. Why?"

Logan pointed to his phone. "Keep reading."

Nick turned his eyes back to the screen and read the other three files. "It's the same. All six people are incapacitated in some way, yet they were all kidnapped. It makes no sense."

Logan held his hand out, and Nick passed his phone back. Logan promptly deleted the temporary downloads and took a deep breath. "In the profession you are in, I suspect not much surprises you. Is that correct?"

"That's true. I've seen many unusual situations and people."

There was a bump of turbulence, and Nick's fingers tightened on the arm of the seat.

Logan, who barely noticed the bump, said, "You don't like flying."

Nick grinned. "I've flown so many times, but still I'm not used to it. Let's get back to the point, although your effort at deflection was commendable."

"You said you have experienced much," Logan repeated. "You also realize there are many governments that have secret organizations such as our SVR and the American CIA."

"Of course."

"It would not surprise you then to know there are other secret organizations, and they have advanced weapons, technology and science," Logan revealed.

Nick raised an eyebrow. "I think you're playing a joke on me since I told you I'm the leader of the mission."

Logan, with his lips barely open, chuckled. "I wish it was that simple. The Russian secret service has learned one of these organizations has such advancements, and they are taking advantage of these kidnapped people. Their agents are with them in Canada, and for the sake of all of us, we must stop them." Logan's voice had become stressed, and his face turned red as he spoke. "This other agency that has this advanced medical knowledge, also has advanced technical knowledge. For some of us, we have known of them for a long time, and we have been fighting them in the background in an ongoing, deadly war. It has become bitter, and for me and my organization, these agents are our sworn enemies."

Nick stared at Logan, inspecting his eyes, looking for some quirk or twitch to indicate the man was pulling his leg or outright lying, but there was nothing on the man's stone-cold face to indicate he was anything but truthful.

Logan leaned in and whispered, "It's best you consider these agents to also be your sworn enemy." His eyes narrowed as he continued, "These agents need to be terminated at all costs. If you understand that, the issue of leadership of our group and this mission will go much better for you."

Nick had been near his own death more than a few times, but being physically and mentally well trained, he hadn't felt total fear very often. However, now, he felt a chill run down his spine as Logan's dark eyes bored into his. He had seen dark eyes like this before, but only on cold, trained assassins, and he realized this man was not new to the concept. Nick realized he needed to carefully watch his step.

Logan broke the stare-down as he turned his face to look out the window. He saw darkness broken by a few lights from the coast, before the open water they were about to cross. He turned back to Nick who had relaxed back into his seat. "Why are we going to Denmark? Wouldn't it be easier to fly directly to Canada?"

Nick explained, "I asked Annenkov the same thing. He told me this mission was too important to get hung up in Customs. Only a month ago, one of our operatives was caught in Canadian Customs, known to be one of the most thorough services worldwide. In this case, we have a back-channel route we use that, although it's more cumbersome, will be more reliable."

"Denmark is more reliable?" Logan asked as he still did not understand.

"We fly to Copenhagen now. After a short layover, we fly to Greenland. Since it's a territory of Denmark, there's little to no customs security," Nick elaborated. "We'll get some rest there before we board a smaller plane that'll secretly fly us to Canada, bypassing Canadian Customs and Security."

It was just after 4 a.m. when the wheels of the plane touched down on the runway at Copenhagen. As they rolled up to the terminal, there was a light snow falling. Logan and Nick retrieved their luggage and went through Danish Customs without incident. When they exited through the automated sliding doors into the main terminal, they saw Tony and Brian waiting by a snack stand along the opposite wall. Nick and Logan ignored their comrades and walked along the wide hallway towards the tunnel leading to the hotels. A few minutes later a man with glasses and a blue toque walked by them. As he did so, the man's hand slid against Nick's.

With Brian and Tony 30 metres behind them, Nick and Logan entered into a book shop located just off the wide tunnel. Logan pulled out a magazine, opened it and placed the small note the stranger slipped him, in the center of the page. Nick read, *Hilton Hotel, room 423.*

Nick pushed the note into his pocket, and with Logan beside him, they continued their walk down the passageway with Brian and Tony following a short distance behind them. As they entered a lower entrance to the Hilton, Nick looked back down the hallway and lifted four fingers in the air beside his chest. Nick and Logan took the elevator to the fourth floor and waited in front of room 423. Once they saw Brian and Tony exit the elevator, Nick knocked on the door.

A few moments later, a young woman let them in with Brian and Tony just behind them. There were no introduction or greetings, just the woman pointing to the four piles of clothes on the two beds. Each pile had one of their names on it. She said, "Take the clothes out of your suitcases. Get changed into new clothes and pack the remainder of the new clothes in your suitcases.

Logan asked, "Why are we doing this?"

As Nick was removing his shirt, he replied, "We're Canadians now, and it would be odd for us to have Russian clothes with us. These are all Canadian or American stock."

They finished changing and packing, and Nick looked at the time on his cell phone. "We have one hour until our next flight to Greenland. We better get moving."

The young woman saw the cell phone and it reminded her. She snapped her fingers and said, "Give me your cell phones—all of you."

Each of the men complied, and as they did so, she replaced them with new ones. "These are similar phones, but they have Canadian data and phone services on them. They also have access to our cloud service if you need to message Moscow, or have files to transfer."

Nick asked, "Our tickets?"

The woman opened a drawer and pulled out the requested documents along with a small stack of Canadian and American cash for each of them.

Nick nodded his thanks, then placed his suitcase down on its rollers before leading the other three men back out of the hotel. They retraced their steps back into the main terminal, but this time, they didn't have to go through customs—only security. This was done without incident, and they waited at their gate with 30 minutes to spare.

It wasn't long before they boarded the Air Greenland, Airbus A330 plane. Not many travellers flew to Greenland, so this route was only flown once a week. Again, Nick and Logan sat together while Tony and Brian sat separately near the back of the three-quarter empty plane. All four of them knew, on a mission like this, there would be longer intervals of no sleep, so sleep when the opportunity presents itself. As such, all four men slept most of the five-hour flight.

When the message came over the intercom for the flight attendants to prepare everyone for landing, the men were somewhat refreshed. Although they wouldn't have seen it, most of the trip was flown in the darkness of night, but as Logan opened the window cover, he was disappointed to see the darkness hadn't lifted. It was 7 a.m. local time in Kangerlussuaq, one of the larger towns on the west coast of Greenland, and at this time of year, in early December, the sun rose at 8:30 am, lasting only seven hours before the darkness would envelope the tiny settlement once again.

The passengers disembarked via the stair truck, and as the Russians walked to the terminal, they saw their breaths heavily fogged from the cold temperature. The surrounding countryside, at least what they could see of it, was dominated by low rolling hills of smooth, wind-blown rock formations devoid of any trees. Logan was happy the clothes set aside for them included cold weather gear to cope with this cold, bleak environment.

There was a very superficial security check, and the four men exited out the doors of the small terminal building. There were three vehicles parked out front, where a man with an orange workman's jacket and a thick, scraggly beard, beside one of the vehicles, waved. Nick saw this, and they made their way over to him beside a large Chevy SUV. When they got closer, the man asked, "Nick, Logan—is that correct?"

Nick replied, "Yes, and Brian and Tony."

The man nodded, popped the rear hatch and said, "Bags in the back."

Once all the suitcases were loaded, they drove out of the airport parking area and headed for the only hotel in the small settlement consisting of a total of 15 buildings. In addition to the Tuttu hotel, there was a hostel, a small supermarket, a jail and a museum. It was only a three-minute drive and the four Russians were checked into two rooms where, again, Logan was paired with Nick. Once they were settled in, there was a knock on their door. Nick opened it to find Tony and Brian, along with the driver of the SUV who had introduced himself as Birger during their ride from the airport.

It didn't take Birger long to give them the quick rundown on the town, highlighting the restaurant which was the only place for visitors to eat. He told the Russians there were only three other visitors in town during this, their winter season. Birger told them to keep to the hotel as much as possible to minimize the number of people who might be curious why a group of men would come here when it's so cold and there is very little daylight.

The four men nodded their understanding, and Birger put his hand on the doorknob. "I'll pick you up at 11 p.m. Get some food and some rest until then." Birger reached into his pocket, pulled out a Ruger 9 mm pistol and handed it to Nick. "In case of an emergency," Birger said before he turned the knob and left the room.

Nick pushed the pistol into the back of his jeans. The gun was a reminder that death was a likely factor on this mission. He clapped his hands together, breaking the silence. "I'm starving! Let's go eat."

Casper Nielsen was just leaving the restaurant. He turned back and yelled, "goodbye," to the waitress. As he did so, he bumped into someone.

Tony said, "Excuse me," in perfect unaccented English before leading his three friends into the eating area.

Casper smiled and said, "No problem," as he instinctively brushed off the police coat before heading to his police cruiser. He thought, *that's odd. I wonder what they're up to.* He drove to the jailhouse where a trailer beside it served as his office.

Casper was the one and only police officer assigned to the town of Kangerlussuaq for the last three years. There were two more police officers in town, but they were exclusively assigned to the airport. Casper made regular rounds of the town and also down the only road leaving town, towards the scientific station at the end of it. His only real excitement was flying the police helicopter as he made surveillance rounds of the area, and occasionally travelled to nearby settlements.

After catching a few hours sleep, his evening was quiet as most evenings were. He yawned and realized he was having a difficult time keeping awake. He looked at the clock on the wall and decided to make his last round before retiring for the night. After boarding his Jeep Cherokee police vehicle, he fired up the engine and drove towards the hostel. That was always the first stop on his tour. As he did so, it was not hard to see Birger's Chevy Tahoe in front of the hotel, one road over. He thought, *that was odd at this hour.* His curiosity peaked as he saw the same four strangers from the restaurant, along with their luggage, pile into the SUV. There was also a sixth man who climbed into the front passenger seat compartment before the vehicle left the hotel compound.

Casper was curious and followed 100 metres behind, and as expected, the Chevy took the only road out of town towards the science station. He followed for a few minutes, wondering why he was bothering with this. Nothing exciting happened in Kangerlussuaq. The most excitement he had seen in his time here was taking drunks to the jail. He thought about turning around, but then remembered his duty as a police officer. Consequently, he sped up and turned on the police lights.

Birger saw the police lights in the rear-view mirror. "God damn it," he cursed. "What the hell does Casper want?"

Tony asked, "Is he a friend of yours you can get rid of?"

"He's not a friend, but I'll try and get rid of him," Birger replied as he pulled the Tahoe to the left side of the gravel road. Once Casper exited his cruiser and came to the driver's window, Birger lowered it. "What's up Casper—can't sleep?"

Casper smiled. "I was going to ask you the same thing. Who are your friends?" As he asked the question, he lowered his face trying to see in the back past the heavily blacked-out, rear windows. He could see the far side of the interior, but not Nick who was seated by the rear window on this side. Casper said, "Sir, can you please roll down the rear window?"

The window came down and Casper saw the muzzle of the Ruger pistol, then the blast. It was the last thing he ever saw as the bullet Nick fired hit Casper in the left side of the forehead, pushing him back, arms splayed out, into the snowbank.

The man in the front passenger seat, named Ardis, sneered, "We're fucked now!"

Birger got out of the SUV and kicked Casper's leg with his boot to verify he was dead. He turned back to the men in the vehicle and said with a shaky voice, "I'll get rid of him and his vehicle to a spot where they'll never find him." He looked at Ardis, thrusting a finger out at him. "You calm the fuck down! You and I are paid very well because we knew something like this might just happen, so relax and drive them to the gas tanks for their flight."

As Nick calmly fingered the Ruger, he asked, "Are you sure you have this under control, Birger?" Nick's face was tilted down, but he lifted his eyes in a questioning gaze.

"Birger hissed, "Don't worry I'll clean up your mess. Ardis, pick me up at Macgregor Point after these guys fly out."

Ardis had calmed down and replied, "sure," before he scampered around the vehicle and onto the driver's seat. He drove off, leaving Birger to the ugly task of disposing of Casper and his vehicle.

Ardis was sweating even though it was minus 11 degrees Celsius outside. His nervousness returned the more he thought of the murder just committed—*and a cop to make a bad matter even worse!*

The four Russians in the rear seats said nothing, and the silence was killing Ardis. He had to break it, and he did. "My partner's waiting at the plane, and we're only five minutes away. Normally, we maintain 11 oil and gas tank storage facilities across Western Greenland. Since the locations are wide spread and the roads are limited, we have the plane and a very simple runway at each location." He looked in the rear-view mirror, but he saw no reaction from any of the passengers. Ardis laughed nervously and continued. "That's my real job. Helping Birger with people coming through here, that's just a sideline for a little extra cash."

He was so distracted he almost missed the turnoff. He hit the brakes hard, and the SUV skidded along the icy road. When it almost stopped, he took his foot off the brake and turned the vehicle left down the long driveway between the two massive, round storage tanks. Once on the other side of them, all five men got out of the vehicle and retrieved the luggage. The wind had picked up, and even with their thick coats on, the men were cold.

As soon as the pilot caught sight of the SUV, he fired up the two Pratt and Whitney turboprop engines of the dark-blue Beechcraft Air King aircraft. Tony, Brian and Logan hopped up the two stairs and into the plane's cabin, before hoisting their luggage into the open area behind the seats. Nick had one foot on the lower step when he turned and faced Ardis. He pulled the gun out from underneath his jacket and pointed it at Ardis whose face, already white from the cold, turned even more bleak.

Nick smiled and spun the gun around, handing it to Ardis, butt first. "Please return this to Birger for me."

After Nick entered the plane, he secured the door and joined his three comrades in the passenger compartment. The pilot yelled, "Buckle up!" as he pushed the two throttle levers all the way forward. The plane reached its rotational velocity and the stick was pulled back. They shot up into the air and then leveled off at 300 metres.

Logan asked Nick, "Aren't we going higher?"

Nick said, "I've made this trip once before. We need to stay under one thousand feet to avoid radar."

The pilot overheard the question and answer and added, "Once we clear the Greenland coast, I'll get down to 60 metres. I suggest you keep your seat belts on in case I need to make some evasive manoeuvres."

"For what?" Tony asked.

The pilot laughed. "Icebergs!"

Tony muttered, "I fought in Afghanistan and Syria and survived. Now, here I am at risk of dying, flattened by an iceberg. We should call this plane the Titanic."

Normally, if the plane would have flown at a reasonable cruise altitude, the flight to Labrador would have taken four and one-half hours, but at this lower altitude, the time would be increased by at least an hour. The pilot only made three turns to avoid possible icebergs or ships, or as Tony thought, *maybe just to scare the shit out of him.*

The plane was equipped with jamming radar that was turned on when they came closer to the Canadian coast. The plane touched down at a rarely used runway at Davis Inlet, Labrador. With the one-hour time difference, it was 4:30 a.m. and they were in Canada. A helicopter was waiting for them, and very quickly, they were back in the air on their way to Goose Bay, the largest commercial airport in this remote part of Labrador.

By now, Logan was sick of flying and sick of seeing ice and snow, but they had one more flight to take. Once the helicopter arrived at the airport, they were met in the aircraft hanger by two Russian operatives and two vehicles.

Logan asked for Tony's phone and he transferred two files onto it. He said, "You and Brian are flying to Montreal. The two files I transferred— one man and one woman—went missing from the Montreal area. You need to find out, at all costs, what happened to them. Check the hospitals, their relatives—leave no clue without a thorough investigation. Understood?"

Both Tony and Brian nodded their understanding.

Logan added, "If you find out anything important, or for that matter, anything you don't understand, call me."

They both nodded again.

Nick saw they were done and pointed at the black SUV. "This man will drive you to the terminal. The tickets are in the vehicle, and you will be met at the Montreal airport by another operative."

Without another word, they departed, and Nick headed for the second black SUV. "C'mon, Logan. We have a flight to catch as well."

Ninety minutes later it was 9:00 a.m. and they were on another plane— this time a Boeing 737 headed for Ottawa. Logan muttered, "I'm sick of flying."

Nick smiled genuinely. He liked that, at times, Logan was assertive and took charge. They seemed to have a good sense of their lines of demarcation. "Hopefully, this is our last flight for a while—it is our last flight, isn't it?"

Nick had been made aware of all the travel arrangements up to and including this flight. The only other thing he knew was a car would be waiting for them at the Ottawa airport, and Logan would reveal their driving destination.

Logan saw Nick deep in thought and knew what he was thinking. "You weren't told about the final destination for security reasons, but now, I can tell you. We are going to Kingston. It's a small town two hours southwest of Ottawa. It is also the home of Edward Lowe, one of our missing persons. However, this person has added significance because, for reasons we don't yet know, his name raised red flags in the surveillance community."

"That's interesting. Hopefully we finally get some excitement."

Logan blurted, "You killed a police officer, and we just flew an obstacle course for six hours at low altitude, and you complain about a lack of excitement."

Nick leaned in close to Logan and whispered, "I don't like to kill people. You know I had no choice."

Logan knew Nick was right and said, "To be clear, as we jockey for the alpha male position of our mission, we don't kill anyone else unless it is absolutely necessary. Dead people get investigated in this country, and that's the last thing we need."

Nick leaned back in his seat and closed his eyes. "You've got it, Boss."

The remainder of their trip was made in silence. At 11:30 a.m. local time, after obtaining their luggage and clearing security in Ottawa, once again a man brushed by Nick and passed him something. This time it was a car key fob and a parking location ticket. The two Russian agents headed for the parking garage and, more specifically, the location identified on the ticket. Once there, Nick pressed the *key fob lock button,* resulting in a flash near the end of a row of cars. They moved quickly to the car and popped open the trunk of the black Chrysler 300. Within it were two assault rifles and two Ruger 9 mm pistols, and the two pistols both had shoulder harnesses.

Nick put one on and handed the other to Logan who hesitated. "You might need it. Like you said, we need to do whatever we have to, to complete this mission," Nick urged.

Logan put on the shoulder harness and took the gun from Nick. As Nick was about to close the trunk, Logan said, "Hold on a minute." Logan retrieved a silver briefcase and took it with him as he slid into the passenger seat compartment, but only after he threw his coat in the back.

Nick got in the driver's seat and asked, "Where to?"

Logan had the file open on his phone and was fumbling with the navigation system on the car's central screen.

After a couple of minutes, "Nick said, "Do you want me to do it!"

"Give me a minute. I've never used the system on this car before." Logan finally got the address of the Kingston retirement home into the GPS system, and a female voice began giving Nick instructions.

Nick drove out of the parking spot, paid at the gate and followed the verbal directions to the highway. They were finished with the flights, and it felt good to be driving—for both of them. As they did so, Logan opened the briefcase on his lap. There were several layers of items, neatly compartmentalized, and as Nick glanced over, he recognized very little, if anything.

"Since we're in this together, maybe you should share some of your toys," Nick suggested.

As Logan pulled a very small syringe from the briefcase and put it in his pocket, he replied, "All in good time."

Just before they got to Kingston, they stopped at a large service center and truck stop. There were changerooms, mainly meant for the truckers, Logan and Nick each used to change into dress pants, a pressed shirt and classy necktie. Each of them also pulled on an expensive-looking, thigh-length overcoat.

Once they got back in the car, Logan asked, "You're clear on the story—right? We are insurance investigators looking into the disappearance of Edward Lowe."

Nick smiled. "Yes—yes, and let you do all the talking. I got it. I'll just smile and look pretty."

Twenty minutes later, they pulled into the parking lot of the Clarington retirement home. Logan smiled at the nurse at reception and said, "We need to speak with whomever is in charge of security."

The nurse picked up the phone and dialed. Her face indicated her call was answered and she said, "Orville, there's a couple of men here to see you." There was a pause, and the nurse put her hand over the receiver. "Orville asked who you are?"

"We're with Great National Life Insurance. We're investigating the disappearance of Edward Lowe," Logan answered with the best smile he could manage.

The nurse relayed the message, nodded her head and hung up the phone. "Knock on the door over there." She pointed at the only closed door across the foyer.

The two agents crossed to the door and knocked. A voice from the other side urged them to enter, and they complied. Orville stood up and shook their hands, after which he offered them both a seat. Nick did sit down, but Logan leaned against the wall beside Orville's desk, complaining about having sat in the car for too long.

Logan asked many questions about the security system and what information they had about the disappearance. Quickly, Orville loaded the video with the suspicious electrical interference on it. Logan then asked about the room, and Orville explained how the room had been wiped completely clean of any prints. It was sterile.

By this time, something that was bugging Orville came further to the forefront of his mind. He frowned and said, "The police know all of this. Who did you talk to over there?"

Nick jumped in and said, "We called ahead and the officer at the front desk had a note for us with your name and address on it." As he talked, he casually slipped his hand inside his coat towards the handgun.

Orville's frown grew as did his suspicion. He started to rise to his feet and demanded, "Have you guys got some ID?"

Before Nick could reach his gun, Logan lurched at Orville. One hand covered his mouth while the other, having grasped the small syringe, pressed the needle into the side of Orville's neck. Almost immediately, the security guard slumped whereby Logan softly guided him back down onto his chair.

Nick leaned forward across the table and asked, "Is he dead?"

Logan was now rifling through the drawers of Orville's desk as he replied, "No. As I told you, there is technology and medical sciences you aren't aware of. The drug I injected him with will leave him unconscious for a month—long enough for us to finish our mission. The doctor's will be baffled, and the authorities will be distracted rather than looking for two killers."

Nick pressed his ear to the door and said, "We better not over stay our welcome."

By now Logan had finished with the desk and was searching the filing cabinet. He pulled out a file and muttered, "Got it." He walked over to Nick and said, "Time to go."

Nick opened the door and let Logan go first. He followed and closed the door behind them. As they walked out the main entrance, Nick smiled at the nurse, thinking this was his moment to look pretty, and said, "Thank you."

They drove out of the parking lot and Logan urged, "Head back to the highway."

"Okay. What did you get out of the interview?"

"Confirmation," Logan replied.

"Of what?"

"I told you the agents who abducted the missing people have advanced science, including a high level of expertise in utilizing electromagnetic fields," Logan elaborated. "It was such an electromagnetic field that created the interference you saw in the video. They also have scanners that can sterilize a room, resulting in what Orville described."

Nick said, "We're coming up to the highway. Which way?"

"We're going east," Logan directed.

"Why?"

As they veered onto the east bound ramp to the highway, Logan added, "We're going to Toronto. Mr. Lowe has a daughter who lives there. We will pay her a visit and see what she knows."

Chapter 10: Deep Shit

The early morning came quickly. Natalie opened her bedroom door and gave a large yawn as she walked into the kitchen area. It was 3:30 a.m. and she was surprised to see Josh already awake with a coffee in front of him at the kitchen table.

"There's more coffee in the pot," Josh offered.

Natalie scratched her head and mumbled, "I need to wake up quick." She poured herself a coffee and sat at the table beside Josh. "Did you get any sleep?" she asked.

"I got some, but then I got restless, so I started the coffee about 30 minutes ago," he said. "Speaking of sleep, who is Alexa, and why were you swearing at her?"

An impish, juvenile look crossed Natalie's face. She looked around from side to side and said, "Swearing—I didn't hear any swearing."

"Smartass," he chided through a sarcastic grin.

It was a good time to change the subject. Natalie rose to her feet and said, "The search programs should be done. I'm going to transfer the results and do the cleanup."

Josh took another drink of the hot coffee and offered, "This is your expertise, but if you need any help, let me know."

Sitting down at her desk, she unlocked her laptop and moved it to the top of her desk. It was dark outside, so the glow of the screen lit up her face. Josh smiled. He liked her look—that was until her eyes shot open and she jumped to her feet. It began as a whisper, but became louder each time as she cried, "Fuck, fuck, fucckkk!"

Josh jumped to his feet and joined her by the laptop. "What's wrong?"

Her mouth was wide open, and she pointed at the screen. No words came out as she seemed frozen in shock.

"What is it?" he asked again.

Her lips finally moved as she stuttered, "They're gone—my two search programs—are gone!"

"Maybe you didn't save them properly," he said.

Her eyes narrowed as she turned her face towards him. "Forgot to save them? You just said, and correctly so, 'this is my area of expertise.'" She turned her attention back to the laptop and completely rebooted it. The end result had her repeating the same words again. "Fuck, fuck, fucckkk!"

Josh knew better than to try and patronize her with a hug or even a touch, for fear of his life. Instead, he whispered, "Is there anything I can do?"

She flopped back into her chair, and the realization she was caught sunk in. "No, there's nothing you can do. I'm valuable to the CSE, so they won't fire me. The best case is a lengthy suspension. The worse case is they reassign me to some god-forsaken place."

Josh picked up her coffee with one hand and put his other hand under her arm, lifting her to her feet. He coaxed her back over to the kitchen table, thinking the greater distance to her laptop would be beneficial.

After she was seated, he sat beside her. The silence was getting awkward when she said, "There should be a call any minute, or a knock on the door."

Josh stayed silent as he nodded his head.

"I will have to go to the office, but just stay here, please. I likely won't be gone for long," she added.

"I will," he promised. "Can I make you something to eat?"

"My stomach is doing flips. I don't think I could eat anything," she admitted.

There was silence again for a few minutes, until there was a beeping from the bedroom. It wasn't loud, but it was enough for Natalie to jump to her feet once again. "That's my phone!"

The blood drained from her face as she looked to Josh for some sign of hope. He smiled and it did give her some assurance as she ran to the bedroom to take the call. The phone was still ringing when she came back to the kitchen table. She meant it when she agreed that the two of them were in this together. She sat down, pressed the *answer* button and said, "Hello."

There was a quiet voice on the other end of the call that, at first, she didn't recognize. "Natalie. You're awake."

It took a moment, but she did recognize the voice after a few seconds of thought. "Steve? Why are you calling me at this hour?" Steve was her subordinate supervisor at CSE, and he never called at this hour. In fact, he barely ever called her at all.

His voice remained low. "Why am I calling you? I'm calling you because

I saved your ass."

Natalie face was drawn and filled with confusion. "I don't know what you're talking about."

Steve's words came faster, showing his irritation. "You know we run programs every night just as you know, once a month, the department does an audit since very few people are here when the programs are running."

There was a pause, and then Natalie said, "I'm not sure how this involves me. I'm on a leave with the disappearance of my father and…"

Steve interrupted. "I know about your father and sorry. That's how I knew those two missing person search programs were yours!"

Natalie whispered, "What are you going to do?"

"You're lucky I was scheduled for the audit, and I found them instead of someone else. I erased all signs of the two programs."

"Shit," she cursed.

"Don't worry. I sent the results to your laptop first, including the listing of the top 500 results as well as a zip file with the associated detailed information file for each."

"You're the best, Steve!" she whooped.

"Yes, I am."

"And you know I love you to death," she added.

"Yes, you do."

There was a click as the connection was terminated. Natalie exhaled deeply as she slunk back in the chair. Then she started to giggle.

"What's so funny," Josh asked.

The giggling stopped and she pointed at him. Her mouth opened to speak, but the giggling started again, but much louder this time. She tried to stop, but each time she did, the giggles, which now turned into uproarious laughter, blurted out.

Josh had an annoyed look on his face as he crossed his arms across his chest and waited for Natalie's juvenile fit to finish. It finally did, but not until after many unsuccessful attempts. She was out of breath when she finally said, "I'm… I'm sorry." She took a drink of the cold coffee and dragged her hand down her face. "Okay. I'm good now. I have to warn you that once in a while I still do get the giggles. In this case, I'm not sure if it was the release of tension knowing I *wasn't* getting disciplined, or your face, looking like you just pooped yourself!" She started laughing hysterically once again.

Josh pushed himself to his feet. "I'm going to wash up. If I knew you better, I think I'd spank you," he scolded.

As he walked towards the bathroom, between her fits of laughter, he heard her say, "If I knew you better, I think I'd let you!"

Thirty minutes later, they were both washed up and dressed. Natalie gave Josh a kiss on his cheek and thanked him for sticking with her through a bad time. He suggested they go out for an early breakfast, but she offered to make them a nice breakfast as a way of making up for her fit of laughter. Of course, he agreed, and as the sun was rising through the large picture window, they had the greatest bacon and eggs breakfast.

After eating, Josh precleaned the dishes and set them in the dishwasher with Natalie as his helper. They didn't say so, but they both had the same thoughts. They were happy just spending time with each other, even in these mundane, domestic tasks.

Once this was done, they moved back over to the laptop, and together, they reviewed the 500 files Steve sent over. For the next three hours, they dissected each file, most of which were police reports google could not access, and they began to filter them. During their first cut, they removed any obviously unrelated files. These would include missing persons who were found or persons who had since died. That left them with 210 files requiring further review. Next, they inspected each remaining file in detail, keeping the ones where the person involved was incapacitated, so, supposedly unable to leave, but was still missing. They continued this process until the list was down to only 41 people on their list.

Included in the list, were the first eight names they came up with prior to the detailed search with the CSE program. Natalie printed off the fact sheet for each person and put the pile of papers on the desk. "What now?" she asked.

"The plan always was to see if we could find a pattern now that we have a larger sample size," he elaborated. "We can make the sorting easier, if you have some cue cards or something similar."

She opened the upper, right drawer of her desk and pulled out a stack of large post-it notes. Josh took them from her, and he pulled the top page from the stack of missing people. He took her pen and wrote on the first post-it note. "Just transfer the critical information such as age, race, gender, location and occupation."

He began on the second note as Natalie caught on. She copied his method, and soon there were numerous notes scattered on the desk. "Hold on," she said. "This might work better." She rose to her feet and began sticking the post-it notes to the large picture-window. Soon, between the efforts of both of them, there were 41 post-it notes on the window.

They both stood in front of the collage. Josh rubbed his chin, and before she could ask, "What now?" he said, "Look for a pattern."

After five minutes, Natalie said, "I don't see anything. I'm going to rerack them geographically." She began moving the post-it notes to locations as if a large map of Canada and the Northern States was on the glass. Josh caught on and helped, but when they were done, the post-it note locations were very random, with no pattern in particular.

"There's nothing there," Josh determined. "Let's do the same thing by age—younger on the left and older on the right."

Natalie nodded and the post-it notes moved for a second time. When they were done, it was obvious. There were 23 notes on the left side of the window and 18 on the far right with a huge gap in between them.

That's really odd," Natalie offered. "She pointed to a note on the left and said, "This group of 23 are all fairly young with the oldest being 32 years old. Your son, Hendrix, is in this group." She then shifted over to the right. "All the people here are in their '70s or '80s, and this includes my father."

Josh was already ahead of her with his nose close to the glass at the left-hand side notes. Then, he did the same at the right-hand side. He checked each and every one of the notes.

Natalie asked, "What are you seeing?"

Josh had a wide smile on his face as he stepped two paces away from the glass, next to Natalie. "What I am seeing is *what's not there.*"

"I don't follow you." She had a perplexed look on her face.

He pulled her over to a point in front of the right-hand notes. "Look at the occupations. There's nobody ordinary here. I don't see store clerks, garbagemen, car salesmen or factory workers. In fact, it's the opposite. These 18 older people were all very specialized scientists or engineers." He pointed to one tag after the other. "Look, here is an astrophysicist. Here is your father who was an electrical engineer. There are mechanical engineers, astronomers and the rest also have higher levels of education and knowledge."

"What about them?" Natalie asked as she pointed to the other group of notes.

Josh waggled his finger at the notes. "This is different, but there is a pattern. Once again, there aren't any mundane workers, or in this case— scientists. Every one of these young people either were in the military, or they excelled at sports. In other words, these people are all young and very fit, or at least they were before they had their accidents."

Natalie saw it now. "So, we have two groups. We have older, higher level scientists, and we have a group of young—" She searched for the right word, "—soldiers." Natalie was so focused on their revelation she didn't hear the beeping.

Josh shook her shoulder. "Your phone."

She retrieved her phone and said, "Hello."

"Ms. Lowe. This is Steve Drumm."

"Is there any good news?"

Detective Drumm replied, "We haven't found your father yet. I did manage to convince the RCMP to officially make this a kidnapping, so they're investigating."

Natalie thought about telling Drumm about the additional, similar kidnappings they had just discovered. Maybe it would help them, but she decided it was more likely to water down his specific search for her father. "Is there anything else noteworthy, Detective?"

"Yes, there is," he replied. "Do you remember the odd coincidences of the electromagnetic interferences we found? There was the retirement home, then the camera on the outskirts of Kingston and, finally, the camera at the service center in Oshawa."

Natalie knew there was more to come, so she kept silent and waited.

Drumm continued. "The RCMP has more resources than we have here in Kingston. They were able to expand the search for video equipment service companies who have received calls about electrical interference. From that, we have two more hits. One is at a service station in Sudbury, and the other is at a hotel in Sault Ste. Marie."

"They're travelling further west," Natalie deduced.

"It would appear so, but this lead might dry up. If they're going to Manitoba, they don't use a whole lot of video surveillance equipment there. Pictures of your father have been released to the authorities in Sault Ste. Marie and Sudbury as well as all the other police stations surrounding these smaller cities."

Natalie didn't have a lot of confidence in Detective Drumm or the RCMP for that matter, yet she was surprised the young Detective Drumm had found out as much information as he had. She didn't want to discourage him. "Good work, Detective," she replied. "Please keep me up to date." Then, she pressed the *disconnect* button on her phone.

Josh had moved into the living room, and Natalie sat down beside him. She explained the lack of overall results and also the interesting facts about the interference plaguing video cameras across Ontario.

Josh shook his head and said, "What we are finding is the strangest thing I have ever seen. Why in the world would anyone want to kidnap people who are incapacitated? We checked and it's not like these people have a lot of money, so ransom isn't a motive, and these people would just be a burden. It makes no sense at all."

Natalie put her hand on top of Josh's and curled her fingers down between his. "I'm at as much of a loss as you are. There's something going on here that we don't understand. As long as we keep searching, we'll find it."

"I hope so. We've made a good start, but as we find out more, it just makes even less sense," Josh confessed.

"It would make sense if the kidnapped people were fully active," she pondered. "In that case, you would have a group of great minds, and of course, a second group that would be well equipped to protect them."

"True enough, but they are not active—at all." Josh squeezed her fingers, and one eyebrow rose as he turned to her. "It's 2:00 p.m. How about a late lunch?"

She laughed and said, "You read my mind. I could use a good burger."

Josh rose to his feet and said, "I know just the place, but we'll have to drive a few minutes."

Natalie readily agreed, and a few minutes later they were heading back to the airport area in her white BMW. Josh gave directions and navigated them into the parking lot of an old-school burger joint. She looked up at the round, white and yellow sign and read, *Bela's*. They exited the vehicle, entered the restaurant, passing the dining area to the large, stainless-steel counter.

There, a man with thick, black, unkempt hair in a loose hair net, asked them for their orders. Josh had only been here once, finding this place by accident, but the discovery provided him with the best char-broiled burger he had ever eaten. Now, he smelled the cooked grease as the open flames licked at the metal gratings. Natalie smelled it as well, and they both ordered cheese burgers, fries and a coke to water everything down.

They were hungrier than they realized and ate both quickly and quietly. When they were finished, Natalie said, "I must have driven by this place a million times but never thought to stop here. Little did I know what I was missing."

Josh leaned in and whispered, "I'll tell you a little inside info. I've only eaten here once before, but thought enough of it so that I did some research on the internet. *Bela* is a Hungarian name. I'm not sure if people would like the burgers as much if they knew what *Bela* translates to."

Natalie rose to her feet and scooted out of the booth. As they walked out the door, she asked, "What does the name mean?"

As the door closed behind them, Josh replied, "Bela translates to *guts*."

Before they got in the car, Natalie slapped Josh on the shoulder and said, "That's a little too much information."

As they drove back to Natalie's condo, Josh asked, "What are we going to do next?"

She mumbled, "I'm not sure." She remained quiet for the rest of their drive as she thought. Even after parking the car and their subsequent stroll around the parkette, there was very little discussion until she said, "I think I know what we need to do."

Josh wrapped his arm around her. Even though the sun was bright in the sky, it was a cooler day and a light covering of snow was on the ground. "What are you thinking?"

"We have a good facial recognition program at CSE…"

Josh interrupted, "I know that's highly illegal, and you were already caught once."

Natalie smirked. "I told you before, much of what we do at the CSE is illegal. Besides, you didn't let me finish. I'm not going to use *our* facial recognition program. Our technology on this was the most advanced, so a few years ago, we shared it with our counterparts in Five Eyes."

Josh stopped and pulled her around to face him. "I'm confused."

Natalie had a sweet, innocent look on her face Josh was coming to find meant she was going to do something naughty. She said, "I'm not going to use the CSE software. I'm going to hack into *MI6's* facial recognition software."

Josh's mouth opened and a loud, "Holy Fuck!" blurted out.

Natalie turned and began walking back to the condo. Her fingers wrapped under his arm as she dragged him along.

Josh remained silent as long as he could, but after only a minute, asked, "You're serious?"

She turned to face him. The cold had given her cheeks a rosy sheen, but still there was that impish, evil look that gave him his answer.

Ten minutes later, they were back in her condo. Her CSE laptop was open and her fingers were dancing over the keys. Josh took up his place in a chair beside her in case she needed anything of him, but for the most part, he was bored and spent much of the time looking out the window at the lake and the few people in the parkette below them.

She had been working at her laptop for a good 90 minutes when she heard Josh mumble, "That's a big boat."

"Huh?"

Josh pointed out towards the lake. "There's a huge boat out there, covered with shipping containers."

Natalie turned for a moment and squinted her eyes. She saw the vessel and then, with a frown on her face, glared at Josh. "Some seaman you are. That's a ship, not a boat."

She spun the seat back to face the laptop to continue her work. She ignored Josh's response as he mumbled, "Ships go on the oceans. On lakes and rivers, they're called boats."

An hour later, when Natalie struck the *enter* key with finality, she said, "We're done for now. In an hour we can run the scan."

"Isn't that dangerous running it in the evening?"

She rotated her chair and pulled up her feet, crossing her ankles on his thigh. "You forget, there's a five-hour time difference to London where the server is located. There, in an hour, it'll be midnight."

With a raised eyebrow, he glanced down curiously at her feet, then back at her face. "You don't miss too much, do you?"

She laughed and jumped to her feet. As she walked by him, she kissed him on the forehead and chirped, "Not much."

Josh looked out the window, seeing another large boat off in the distance, visible only by its lights. He heard Natalie fumbling in the kitchen behind him. She said, "I'm still a little full, but I could use a snack, and since I don't like to eat alone…" She was back beside him, and a spoon was hanging from her fingers, offered to him. He took the spoon and watched her sit back down with her own spoon and a large tub of Maple Pecan ice cream. Her chair was on rollers, and she pushed herself close beside him. She helped herself to a large spoonful, and he followed suit. When the ice cream hit his mouth, he closed his eyes and pulled the spoon out slowly. A low groan came from his closed lips.

She chuckled. "Wow! One would think you never had ice cream before."

"Not Maple Pecan," he replied as he reached for another spoonful.

Forty-five minutes later, at what would have been 12:15 a.m. in London, she finished loading the pictures she had of her father and one Josh had provided of his son, into the search programs. The parameters for Hendrix's search was all of New York State. The search for her father was set for all of Ontario.

Once again, she hit the *enter* key with a heavy stroke. "There. That'll take a few hours to run. I'm going to check it at midnight, our time."

Josh rose to his feet and said, "I'm going to get a few hours sleep." He walked towards the guest room. Natalie quickly put away the ice cream and grasped his arm before he was halfway across the living room. She steered him towards the loveseat, bringing a smile to his face. He hunkered down in it while Natalie retrieved a blanket from her bedroom. She snuggled in beside him with her face against his chest just as it was the night before. He pulled up the blanket around her neck before he wrapped his arm around her shoulder. He fought the urge to kiss her or even do more. *That would complicate things*, he thought as he closed his eyes and tried to find the rest he needed.

For the last few days, Josh and Natalie had only found a few hours of sleep here and there, so once their eyes closed, they didn't wake again until 1:00 a.m. Natalie turned her head and looked at the time on the stove clock. She said, "Oh shit," and threw off the blanket. She ran to her laptop as Josh was in the middle of a huge yawn. Natalie was focused on the screen, and a minute later, she slouched back in her chair. By now, Josh had walked over to the desk, and he could tell by her body language the search had come up empty.

Josh admitted, "I'm sorry for both of us that the searches didn't work out."

"I need a shower, then some time to think," she said as she walked by him towards the bedroom.

He had a shower as well, and when they both came back into the living room, he sat down in the loveseat, while she loaded a movie into the DVD player. She sat down beside him and said, "I need to clear my mind, so I can think."

He nodded and thought better than to put his arm around her right now. She looked like she needed some space. One movie led to a second movie, and then her cell phone rang. "I hope that's not Steve again, getting used to calling me in the wee early hours."

Her phone was on the desk and she retrieved it, saying, "Hello."

"You need to get in here and see me now!"

Natalie's face went white. She answered, What's up?"

"Now!" came the response before the *click* indicating the connection was terminated.

Josh asked, "Was that Steve?"

She swallowed hard. "No, that was Philip, my boss. It seems, this time, I'm in deep shit."

Josh rose to his feet. "What can I do?"

"It'll be fine. We go back a long way," she replied.

She moved into the bedroom and dressed into something work appropriate, even though it was 5:00 in the morning. She gave Josh the best smile she could manage before heading out the door. Forty-five minutes later she was at her office building and immediately went to Philip's CSE office on level U3. Other than a few security people, she only saw two other people in the building and, of course, Philip.

She walked into his office and sat across the desk from him. He didn't say a thing as he rose and closed the office door. He sat back down, and Natalie thought his face looked calm. Then, it changed to red, and a stream of words spewed from between his lips. "What the hell are you doing? MI6? You hacked MI6's facial recognition program for a private investigation?"

She squirmed in the chair, "Technically, I hacked our program we loaned them."

He shook his head in disbelief and pounded the desk. "Natalie, I received a phone call at home 90 minutes ago from my boss when he was alerted to this."

"I'm sorry about that. I tried to be discrete."

Philip ignored her. "My call was because my boss was awoken 30 minutes before that by, do you know who?"

"Not a clue," she whispered.

"The Minister of National Defense, and that was because he got a call from the British ambassador," Philip blurted.

"That sounds bad," she confessed while innocently rolling her eyes.

"Bad? They all wanted you fired and thrown in jail for treason, but I convinced them we have a lot invested in you, and this adventure was a momentary mental disruption because of the issue with your missing father. In the end, they just wanted you out of the building on any kind of leave."

"I am already on leave," she reminded him.

"No, a longer leave," he stressed while giving her a stern look.

She whispered, "Ouch."

"What I am doing is giving you an assignment off site…"

She interrupted, "I don't have time for that right now. I need to find my father."

He raised his hand. "Let me finish." He had a curious look on his face, and his voice lowered. "Do you remember Lashkar Mann?"

She was confused by the change in direction. "Yes. I've talked to him several times, trying to recruit him to help us instead of working against the country."

"He's known as one of the most brilliant minds in the world, and he wastes it hacking into computer systems, supposedly for righteous causes. Unfortunately, that's landed him in custody, and that's where he's been for the last eight months." He pushed a folder towards Natalie. "There's a release order in here for Lashkar. I want him recruited."

Natalie opened the folder as she repeated, "I tried before, so trust me, he won't work with us." She stopped talking when she lifted the paper and saw another release order underneath it. "Who's this?"

"Subash Mann, Lashkar's father. He's in a federal prison near Edmonton. You do what you have to, but I want Lashkar recruited," Philip repeated.

"Why now?"

Philip lowered his tone even more as he lowered his head. "I have to *cancel* all your access to CSE computer systems. I'm sending you on an assignment to recruit Lashkar, who is a computer *expert*." He held that thought between them as his gaze bored into Natalie.

Natalie cocked her head to the side. She wondered, *why was Philip whispering? Why was he speaking so strangely, and why was he creeping me out with the full-on stare? What was he up to?* Suddenly, her eyes went wide. "Oh—Ohhh!"

He slapped the table with relief as she finally caught on. He rose to his feet, walked to the door and opened it. She rose as well, and as she was walking by him, he held her wrist. "You still have access to all other CSE resources, just no computer access." He smiled coyly.

It all made sense now. She knew and appreciated the risk he was taking for her, and she smiled back just as his hand slid down her wrist and slipped something into her palm. He whispered, "There was one hit on your facial recognition scan."

She bit her lip, or else she would have cried. She looked at him with affection. He hesitated but finally released her hand. He watched her walk to the elevators, realizing it was unlikely he would see her for a long, long time.

Natalie couldn't get home fast enough, knowing the memory stick Philip passed her had a hit of either Hendrix or her father. She sped home, slapping her hand on the steering wheel every time a car got in her way. The BMW screeched to a halt in her parking spot before she rushed upstairs. She burst open the door of the condo, surprising Josh as she ran to her laptop. He tried to speak, but she cut him off. "I'll explain everything in a minute. Come see this!"

Josh joined her as the laptop was fired up again, and the memory stick was pressed into the USB slot. She clicked on the only file on the stick and a video began to play. It showed a gas station where an older man in a grey overcoat was putting gas into a red minivan. He had white hair and glasses, but the video was low quality and fuzzy. The man walked briskly towards the station house, and the video changed to a different camera inside the store. The label across the top of the screen read, *Esso station, 342 Front street, Sudbury.*

There was no audio, but the man in the grey overcoat walked to the counter where he was met by the attendant. There must have been something funny said as the older man, at one point, threw his head back and laughed before he pulled out his wallet. He placed his credit card in the slot of the reader and processed the payment. He smiled at the attendant one more time, and they could read his lips saying, "Goodbye," before he walked out of the field of view. The camera changed again to the one outside, and the older man opened the heavy side door of the van, and all but jumped in before closing the door behind him. The van sped off, and the video concluded.

When the video had started, Natalie's jaw had gone slack, and as it played, her jaw dropped lower and lower. She steadied herself with her hands on the edge of the desk. She turned her face to Josh, and tears were streaming down her cheeks. She turned back to the blank screen, and finally words came to her. "That's impossible. That's my father!"

Chapter 11: Napanee

The black Chrysler 300 was speeding down the highway, heading east and away from Kingston. Logan glanced at the speedometer in front of Nick and warned, "You better slow down. If the authorities aren't already looking for us, they will be soon enough."

Nick glanced down at the number displayed in the center of the speedometer, and it read, *118 km/hr.* "The speed limit on the highway is 100, and in case you haven't noticed, most cars are passing us. If we were going 100, there'd be more risk of being noticed."

"You've been to Canada before?"

"Yes—a few years ago. It was a training mission. You're right though. We need to get off the highway," Nick suggested.

"I think we should keep going to Toronto. Let's not waste time," Logan urged.

"Listen, Logan. You have all the details about this mission, but it's my responsibility for the logistics. We haven't had much sleep, and the risk is great since they'll be looking for this car."

"What are you going to do about it?"

Nick pushed several buttons on the car's central monitor, and within seconds, via Bluetooth, a ringing came from the car's speakers. There was a *click* indicating the connection was made, but there was no verbal confirmation. After a pause, he said, "Nick Anderson – 510651."

There was an additional pause, then a response in a deep voice. "Good afternoon, Mr. Anderson. I hope everything is going well."

Nick replied, "Things are fine, but it's likely the authorities will be looking for us. We're 20 kilometres west of Kingston on highway 401. We need a place to stay for the night."

"One moment," came the response. After being on hold for two minutes, the voice returned. "Take the highway east to exit 579A at Napanee. Go north and in less than a kilometre, you'll see a Comfort Inn on the right side. You'll have reservations for one room with two queen beds."

Nick chuckled. "Get us two rooms, each with a queen bed." He winked at Logan. "I've been with this guy for 30 hours straight, and if I sleep in the same room with him, I'll begin feeling like we're married."

The person on the other end of the connection didn't seem to have much of a sense of humour. "Yes, Mr. Anderson. What else do you need?" he asked in a dry tone.

"We also need a new vehicle. Anything but black, with a company issue laptop in the trunk," Nick requested.

"Anything else?"

"Yes." Nick snapped his fingers a couple of times at Logan as he leaned towards him, whispering, "What's the address of Lowe's daughter?" He shifted away from Logan and continued in a louder voice, "I need you to stake out a location. Don't make contact—just follow her if she leaves."

"Of course," the voice responded over the phone.

Logan leaned forward and read from his phone, "Natalie Lowe. White female, 40 years old, brunette hair. I will send you a picture once we are off the phone." He continued with Natalie's address, the make of her car and the plate number.

The man said, "Okay, I have it…"

Nick interrupted, "We'll be in Toronto tomorrow, mid-morning. If anything important comes up, contact me." There was a *click* as he leaned forward and pressed the *disconnect* icon on the screen.

They'd been on the phone for more than a few minutes, so they were close to their exit. Fifteen minutes later, Nick veered the car onto the off ramp. Just north of the exit, they took note of the *Flying J* service center, seeing it contained a restaurant they would visit later. A half kilometre further on, they saw the blue sign high above the white post, reading, *Comfort Inn*.

They checked into their two rooms and re-parked their vehicle in a spot not visible from the road. After leaving his suitcase in his room, Logan knocked on Nick's door. The tall Russian was laying out some clothes on the bed to air out when he let Logan in. Logan sat in one of two uncomfortable looking chairs by a small round table in the corner of the room. After picking up the TV remote control, Nick joined Logan at the small table. Nick turned on the TV and muttered, "Let's see if we made the news."

Logan was barely listening as he inspected the room that looked just like his, except he thought he had an extra water stain on the ceiling, Nick didn't have in his room. The ceiling was white concrete, covered in stipple. The walls were beige except for the long wall with brown wallpaper, highlighted by a pattern of white and yellow circles of different sizes.

Logan's depressing mini-daydream was interrupted by Nick. "I think it's about time you tell me more about this mission."

"Why? Is this your play to lead?" Logan scoffed.

"Not at all. In fact, I've been impressed by you so far, and we seem to be doing fine sharing leadership."

"If it's going okay, why are you pushing it?" Logan pressed.

Nick exhaled deeply. "Listen, Logan. I'm here to keep you alive and get you where you need to go. If you keep me in the dark and keep me guessing instead of anticipating, not allowing me to be one step ahead of who—well that's the problem. I don't know who, *who,* is." He looked squarely at Logan's dark eyes. "You're limiting my abilities, and I don't want you to wind up dead because of that."

Logan thought on the tall, blonde Russian's words, and after a few moments, acquiesced. "You are right. I need to start trusting you more, but you need to trust me as well." Logan waggled a finger menacingly at Nick. "There is much that will be hard for you to believe. Just remember, when you hit that wall, you asked me to tell you."

Nick leaned forward with both elbows on the table. His interest was certainly piqued.

Logan was still wearing the necktie, so he took a moment to remove it and undid the top two buttons of his shirt before starting. "I told you already, there are other organizations out there very few in the world know of. I also told you these groups have superior knowledge of technology and medicine."

Nick nodded.

"Well, this specific group I have talked of, who we now know abducted these people who supposedly are incapacitated and of no value—" Logan searched Nick's eyes as he paused. "—they have the medical knowledge whereby they can wake up or revive these people into a normal state."

Nick's eyebrows shot up.

Logan gave a wry smile. "Remember, you asked me."

"That's hard to believe," Nick replied as he slouched back in the chair. "Where would they obtain this incredulous technology?"

Logan spoke slowly. "Not from here."

"I know that," Nick chirped. "Canada is advanced, but not that advanced."

Logan shrugged, and his gaze once again locked on his comrade's eyes. "I didn't mean this country."

Nick's eyes were filled with confusion. His mouth opened, but nothing came out.

Logan continued in a whisper. "I meant the technology is not from *this world*."

There was a pause for a few seconds. Nick's lips formed into a grin, and then he blurted through a loud laugh, "Fuck off!"

Logan waited for Nick's laugh to slow down to a simmer. "It's the truth. The people we search for are from another world, and so am I—just not the same world."

Nick slapped his thigh, and the uproarious laughter started once again.

Three creases formed on Logan's brow, showing his irritation as he drummed his fingers on the table while waiting for Nick to stop. Finally, he did and wiped the tear that spilled out of his eye, then Nick blurted, "Prove it!"

"You saw the serum I injected into the guard. Have you ever seen anything like that on this world?"

"No, nothing quite like that. It was hard to believe, but not in the category of being from a different planet!" Nick quipped.

"Do you have a knife on you?" Logan asked.

The confusion intensified on Nick's face. "Sure, but…"

"Give it to me."

Nick stammered, "I—I don't get…"

"Just give it to me!" Logan yelled.

A black-handled switch blade was produced, and Nick handed it across the table to Logan.

Logan stood up, mumbling, "Fucking people—fucking Russians," as he opened the switch blade. He slid the razor-sharp edge against the side of his finger before tossing the blade across the table back to Nick. A drop of blood formed, and then another. They dripped onto the table and formed a small pool.

Nick shot to his feet, toppling his chair on its side. "Your blood!"

Logan squeezed his finger and a few more drips of blood came out.

"It's blue! Your blood is fucking blue!" Nick exclaimed.

Logan turned his head from side to side, saw the door to the bathroom and retrieved a hand cloth to wrap around his finger. Upon his return, Nick was still staring down at the small pool of blue blood with his mouth gapped open.

Logan sat back down and Nick finally muttered, "It's turning clear."

Logan crossed one leg over the other and explained, "Your blood is a bright-red, but when oxygen hits it, it turns dark-red. My blood is blue, but when oxygen hits it, it turns clear."

Nick reached back and placed the chair under him before he fell back into it. He was in shock and whispered, "Unbelievable."

Logan shrugged. "Not really. You see your blood is iron based. The oxygen in your blood binds with iron molecules and that combination creates a red colour. On my world, our species evolved differently, and it is based on copper, not iron. In my veins, the oxygen combines with copper, creating a blue colour."

The look on Nick's face changed and resembled what it would look like if someone just saw a horrible car crash.

Logan gave Nick a twisted smile. "What? You have similar life on your world. Octopus, horseshoe crabs and even some spiders have blue blood."

Nick was still at a loss for words. All that came out, barely above a whisper was, "Octopus?"

Rising to his feet, Logan said, "Let's go."

Nick's eyes rolled as they followed Logan walking by him. Logan opened the door, and when there was no response from his partner, he yelled, "Come on! I'm hungry, and I need a band-aid!"

The two men put on their coats and walked the half kilometre to the Flying J. At the diner, they both had a hot meal with very little discussion. Nick seemed deep in thought the whole time and ate through instinct more than the hunger he felt earlier. When they finished their hot meal, Logan ordered a chocolate ice cream sundae.

With his head still spinning, Nick watched Logan take one large spoonful of ice cream after another. Finally, Nick could take no more and he blurted out, "You say you're from another world, yet you eat ice cream like you've been doing this all your life!"

"Shhh!" Logan replied as he leaned over the table top. He whispered, "Typically, species having copper-based, blue blood have such because, somewhere in their ancestry, there was a long period of evolution in a cold climate."

"Are there other differences?"

"Other than the colour of our blood, we are very similar to you," Logan explained. "However, our hearts are quite a bit larger than yours, and that again is due to the need for us to pump additional blood in our historically cold climate." There was playful misadventure in Logan's eyes as he added, "Oh, and we have much larger penises."

Nick ignored Logan's effort at a joke. He kept the questions coming faster. "This other alien species you've mentioned, do they also have blue blood, and why are we after them?" He thought for a second. "Even before that, why are they reviving these incapacitated people?"

Logan smiled. "Slow down. I know this is a lot at once. Their blood is red as they are almost identical to you, just much more advanced."

"Who else here knows about you and them?"

"On this world there is Annenkov and Lipin and only a handful of others. We came to them for help," Logan confessed.

Nick leaned back in the bench seat. "Why us? Why not the Americans?"

There was a laugh and then Logan answered. "Are you kidding? There's a crazy man in charge of America, and it seems just as the wind changes direction every day, so does he. The Chinese are no better, and that leaves the Russians who are similar to us in that they are logical to a fault."

Nick ran his fingers back through his short, blonde hair and thought, *I never thought Russian logic would be the factor to draw an alien alliance.* "So, what's the big deal? Why are we after them, and why are there abducted people?" He asked for a second time.

Logan's eyes grew darker. "I have told you much already and probably too much. That's enough for now. Just remember, Annenkov and Lipin are 200 per cent on board, and we all agree the Sholites are our collective, mortal enemies."

"Sholites?"

"The Sholites are the people we speak of from the planet, Shol. I am from the planet Kor, and both our worlds are several hundred light years away."

Nick began to ask another question when Logan slid out of the booth.

Before Logan headed for the exit, he said, "Your turn to pay."

Nick caught up to Logan just as they turned north to walk up the shoulder of the two-lane highway. When they turned into the motel parking lot, they walked around to the rear exit of the building. They saw the black 300 was gone and now, in its place, was a dark-blue Ford Mustang. They both walked through the building, back to the main office where the attendant said, "Your rental car guy was here about 30 minutes ago to swap out the vehicles. Here's the key."

Nick took the key, and as they walked down the hallway, they arrived at the door to Logan's room. He unlocked it and turned to Nick and rubbed his temple. "I need some rest. We have another busy day ahead of us tomorrow. My hope is that the Lowe woman has some information on her missing father."

Nick asked, "What happens if she has no answers?"

Logan replied, "Then, unfortunately, we will have no need for Natalie Lowe." Nick saw Logan's eyes go icy-cold and dark—a look he was becoming familiar with. Barely audible, Logan muttered, "And we have no need for loose ends."

Chapter 12: Edmonton

"Are you okay?" Josh asked.

Honestly, Natalie thought, *she wasn't sure.* Her father was alive and doing incredibly well, even though she knew that was impossible. However, the video was very clear, and there was no mistaking it was her father who was walking without any aid, smiling and conversing so easily. These were all things he hadn't been able to do for a few years now.

Natalie was in shock, and Josh recognized it. He wrapped his arms around her and drew her against him while kissing her forehead. They stood like this for a long time until she tilted her face up and gave him a light kiss on his lips before she whispered, "Thank you."

She slipped out of his arms and turned off the laptop. As she walked by him, her fingers intertwined in his, and she pulled him along towards the living room. They both sat in the loveseat that had been her own fortress of solitude—one that she now welcomed him into.

After a good ten minutes, she began to slowly come back to life and said, "You know what we saw there is impossible."

"It certainly is," he replied. "But we saw it is, in fact, a very wonderful impossibility. You should be happy."

She turned towards him and put her hand on his thigh. "I am! Seeing my father so healthy is wonderful, but the fact I still don't know where he is, is more than troubling."

"We are pretty sure he is going west—right?"

Natalie was deep in thought as she muttered, "Yes." Her brow was furrowed, then suddenly, the creases disappeared, and there was a decisive look on her face. "We know my father is safe. That's the most important thing. At the same time, I've been selfish in that we haven't found out anything more about your son's whereabouts. We need to shift our search in that direction."

Josh smiled and put his hand on top of hers. "We have done two searches for both my son and your father. It's not your fault only the search for your father gave us leads."

"Still, we need to shift our search," she insisted.

He shrugged. "Okay, what do you propose we do to find my son?"

She opened her mouth once, then a second time and a third. Each time nothing came out, and each time the cheeky grin on Josh's face grew wider and wider.

Finally, he laughed. "You see, the best clue we have to finding my son, is that the circumstances of his disappearance are identical to your father's. It would seem, the sooner we find your father, the sooner we will find my son."

Through a frown, she cursed, "You're so fucking logical!" Then her shoulders slumped. "But I think you're right, and we need to go west in any case."

"Why so?"

"My computer access to the CSE has been suspended, so I don't have access to that line of resources. However, Philip gave me an out, allowing us to continue on with our investigation," she explained.

"And that, for some reason, has us travelling west?"

"I have a release order for a prisoner being held for a long line of forgeries in a federal prison in Edmonton. He can help us," she elaborated.

"A forger—how is that going to help us?"

"Enough questions for now, Josh. We're going to get into activities that are well beyond the line of legality. The less you know, the more you increase your plausible denial in case we get caught." She rose to her feet and said, "We have a busy day ahead of us. I'm going to send an email to my neighbour to keep an eye on my place. We'll fly out later today, and we have a couple of errands to run before that."

As she headed back to her desk, Josh rose to his feet and stretched. "I'm going to have a shower and get packed."

She watched him walk into the guest bedroom before she spun her chair around to face her desktop computer. She logged in and accessed a Gmail address. Philip and Natalie had worked together for quite a while, and they planned and prepared for several contingencies. One of these was just such a case where secure CSE email communication was not available. The email address she just entered was a typical low security, Gmail address. They had agreed, in the case of an emergency, they'd use it in a unique way. Since they were experienced with surveillance methods, they knew *sent* emails and *stored* emails were heavily monitored. They also knew *draft* emails received very little to no attention.

She thought her discussion with Josh this morning was normal, and he was sweet for prioritizing her father's search, but at the same time, a little red flag went up in her mind. After a few minutes thought, she realized it was very odd he would not prioritize his son. It was possible he really considered the search for her father as the best way to find his son, but it was still odd to her. Her investigative side, where she questioned everything, had been stoked, and that's why she was writing the email:

Philip

I 'm going west, and I'll be travelling with a man I met who has a similar situation with a missing son. Everything seems fine with him, but as a precaution can you please check a few facts for me. They are listed below.

Josh Harris

Address is in Upper New York State.

Occupation is a second mate seaman.

He is a widower and has a son, Hendrix.

Son is, or was in an institution in Saratoga Springs, suffering from a long-term coma caused by a military accident.

I need this just as a precaution, so don't overly worry.

Natalie

Once she finished typing the email, she didn't send it. Rather, she closed it, knowing it would be saved in the *Drafts* folder. She sighed. Her feelings for Josh were growing quickly, and her stomach was tumbling because of her own insecurity. She closed the window and opened a text screen on her phone. She found Philip's phone number and typed in, *Chop chop*. This was the code words they came up with, long ago, to identify there was a note in the draft folders of the Gmail address.

Josh finished his shower. Natalie walked into the bedroom where he was packing his bag, with only a towel wrapped around his waist. She paused for a few seconds. He had the build of a seaman, or at least the build of someone who was not adverse to heavy lifting and work. Her gaze lingered and he must have sensed her fixation.

He tilted his head to face her. "What? Nothing better to do?" he chided.

"Pack light," she replied. "We'll go shopping for clothes when we get there."

An hour later, they finished a light breakfast. Natalie made one last round of the condo, making sure there wasn't anything out of place. She saw her secure laptop on the desk and muttered, "Oh shit." She walked over, retrieved it and placed it in her travel bag.

As they left the condo, Josh carried his duffle bag, while Natalie had the travel bag and a small suitcase. A few minutes later, these were all placed in the trunk of the BMW, and they were driving up the parking garage ramp into the city of Etobicoke.

Josh asked, "Are we taking the highway?"

"Yup."

She turned the car left out of the building, then made a quick right onto a busy road, from where they could see the large, green signs just before the highway. She kept to the right lane until they were on the bridge over the highway, and the extra lane to the westbound ramp, appeared.

She shifted the white BMW into the new lane when Josh cried, "No! Keep left!"

Natalie took a quick look right and saw what Josh did. Halfway down the ramp, the vehicles were stopped, and beyond that, the cars on all three lanes of the major highway were stopped dead. She veered back into the lane to their left, drawing the sound of a high-pitched horn from the car she just cut off. She frowned and instinctively looked in the rear-view mirror, seeing the driver behind her with his fist in the air. Just behind this car, she saw a dark-green Jeep Rubicon perform the same manoeuvre she just did as it pulled from the ramp lane to squeeze in behind the infuriated driver. She thought, *well, at least I'm not the only asshole driver out today.*

Josh raised an eyebrow. "Moving to *Plan B*, are we?"

She retorted, "Funny, funny man." She pressed her indicator lever down and forced her way left, one lane at a time, to the chagrin of Josh and the additional drivers who honked their horns. She finally made a left turn at a major intersection, then several more turns as they proceeded along this alternate route.

The light at the next intersection turned *yellow,* and Natalie pressed on the gas pedal to make the left turn before the *red.* Josh muttered, "Jesus," as his right hand grasped the header grab handle. Natalie laughed as she heard a horn sound behind her. She looked in the rear-view mirror, thinking it was for her, but, in fact, the dark-green Jeep Rubicon made the same left, but through a full red light. *That's odd,* she thought.

She made three more turns and saw the Jeep kept its distance, but it made the same turns she did. "I don't know what the fuck is going on," she cursed. "We're being followed."

"You're kidding," Josh replied as he spun his head around to look out the back window.

"It's the dark-green Jeep. Our situation is getting stranger by the minute."

"Can you lose them?"

"Of course." She made a left turn as did the driver of the Jeep about 50 metres behind them. She went straight until she reached a major crossroad with two lanes in each direction. She saw a pack of cars coming from her left, but she waited until they were almost right on top of them before she turned right, squealing out in front of the traffic.

The dark-green Jeep, having kept its distance, couldn't turn for quite some time. When their BMW sat at the front row of a mass of cars at a red light, Natalie saw the Jeep Rubicon five cars back. She leaned forward and glanced left, then right.

Josh said, "You're not seriously going..."

Once again, a squeal of tires was heard, and Josh's words were cut off as the BMW shot across the intersection against the red. Natalie glanced in the rear-view mirror, laughing as she saw the Jeep boxed in and unable to move. She made four more turns with no sign of the Jeep Rubicon.

"Where did you learn to drive like that?" Josh quipped.

Natalie laughed in response. "It's Toronto, and this is how we drive here!"

Fifteen minutes later, Natalie pulled into the parking lot of a large bank. She exited the car, and through the open door, said, "Wait here."

Josh saw she kept the car running, and asked, "What? Are you going to rob the place?"

"Very funny man," she said again before she closed the door.

After retrieving her travel bag, she entered the automatic door of the bank and asked the receptionist to see her safety deposit box. Natalie produced her identification and her key, whereby the receptionist took her back to the safety deposit box room. Natalie followed her past the first room and around a corner to a second, partially-hidden room at the end of the hallway.

The receptionist opened the door and let Natalie in. The woman pointed within and said, "There's a separate room where you can open your box in privacy."

Natalie thanked her and added, "Can you please close over the vault door?"

The woman complied, and Natalie was alone in the safety deposit box room. Both long walls were covered in larger, silver doors with a number and a key hole on each. Natalie took her key from her pocket and moved to box 324. She knew many of the boxes in this room were owned by the CSE. She turned the key and opened the door assigned to her. Pulling out the long box, she entered the small side room at the end of the long, narrow, main room. She opened the top of the box, searched through the contents and pulled out a passport. Natalie flipped through the pages and checked her picture. Just under it was the name, Susan Burns. Satisfied, she put this in her travelling bag along with a driver's license having the matching alternate name and address. After retrieving two credit cards, matching the same false name, and a stack of cash, she placed her laptop into the box.

In a small container within the box, she found a second safety deposit box key. When she was trained regarding this room and the emergency procedures associated with it, box number 285 was engrained into her memory. She took the second key and moved swiftly back to the main safety deposit box room. She bent over and ran her finger along the boxes until she found box 285. Unlocking it, Natalie pulled it out far enough so the back of the box was supported, but the lid could be opened. She did so and saw a multitude of small key boxes, and on top of them was a ledger.

Within the ledger, there was a listing of cities in Canada, and beside each was a key box number. When she flipped the pages, she ran her finger down each one until she came to, *Edmonton*. There were two entries – Edmonton East and Edmonton West. Not being sure and having no time to deliberate, she muttered, "what the fuck," and selected Edmonton East, for no reason other than it was first on the list. Beside the number was written, *Box 34*. There was a pen beside the ledger, and she wrote her name at the appropriate space along the line before slamming the ledger closed.

Natalie quickly found the small key box, labelled 34, and removed the key within it along with the card having an Edmonton address printed on it.

Finally having everything she needed, she retraced her steps, returning the two safety deposit boxes to their original locations. She pushed open the door to the room where she saw the banking employee was still waiting. Natalie smiled at her and said, "I'm all done," as she walked by her.

When she sat back in the car, Josh asked, "What did you need to do?"

Natalie brushed the bangs from her forehead and replied, "The list of strange occurrences we're seeing is growing, the most recent of which was the Jeep following us. I picked up an alternate ID and passport to keep whoever is following us off our trail."

As Natalie backed the car out of the parking lot, Josh asked, "What about…"

As she put the car in drive, Natalie cut him off. "Don't worry. Your ID is next."

A light snowfall had begun as Natalie turned out of the bank's parking lot. She continued north and then east for a few kilometres until she pressed the indicator lever down for a left turn. Josh looked over at the long strip mall with numerous shops in it. He thought, *this must be a Polish area of town as he had never seen so many shop names having an owner ending with 'ski.'* They parked in front of one of the small shops, and when Josh looked up, he read the sign. On the left side there was a fancy, calligraphed, *JJ*. On the right were the words, *Jaworski Jewellers*.

Josh followed Natalie into the store. She headed towards an old man resembling Albert Einstein, while Josh went to the glass counter to admire some rings. He heard Natalie whispering to the man, and a moment later, Josh saw him walk to the front door. He turned the lock and reversed the *Out to Lunch* sign.

As the old man walked by Josh, he urged, "Quickly—into the back."

Josh complied, and Natalie brought up the rear. They walked through the beaded curtain, then into a side office. This office had another door in the back they subsequently went through, finally entering a very large back room.

Once the door to this back room was closed by the old man, he asked Natalie, "What do you need?"

She looked around the room with bright-white walls and a black warehouse type roof with exposed ducts and pipes. "I don't need anything." She pointed at Josh. "He needs a passport and a driver's license."

There was a table in the room surrounded by four chairs. The old man pointed to it and said, "Take a seat. This will take about 90 minutes."

Josh accepted the offer, but Natalie followed the old man. She passed him her new passport and said to him, "His name is to be Joe Burns." The spelling of the last name is the same as mine." She pointed to her own name and then just under it. "Use the same address. We're married." Before she left him, she asked, "Do you have a computer?"

As the old man went to a green filing cabinet that looked just as old as he did, he said, "There's a computer on the desk next to the table. To unlock the screen, type in *bigboy*."

Natalie snickered when she heard the password, wondering if the old man had some surprises she just didn't want to know about. She pulled a chair in front of the computer while Josh slid his chair over beside her as she keyed in the password.

Josh had a silly grin on his face as he whispered close to her ear. "So, we're married, are we?"

Natalie frowned, thinking even the momentary brush of his warm breath against her ear, accelerated her heartbeat. "Relax. Whoever's following us is looking for a single woman, not a married couple. Small details could make a big difference."

He asked, "What are you doing?"

Natalie pulled one of the new credit cards from her travelling bag. "I'm going to book two tickets for the happy couple flying to Edmonton, and also a hotel room."

In the background, there was a shout from the old man. "Josh. I'm ready for you!"

Josh rose to his feet and said to Natalie, "I hope you know I think you're great."

Her fingers froze and she tilted her face up, but it was only to see his back as he walked away from her. If he would have turned around, he would have seen her slight blush and a huge smile.

Albert Einstein's double took two pictures with different cameras against different backgrounds. Josh realized this was not the first time the old man had been through this exercise. After examining both pictures on the computer, the old man mumbled, "Yes, these will work." He smiled at Josh and said, "It won't be much longer. Why don't you join your wife?"

Josh had a silly smile on his face as he walked to the table. This time, Natalie missed it as she was pulling everything out of her travelling bag. Before he sat down, she asked, "Could you get the bags from the car?" She slid the key fob across the table to him.

Josh shrugged and followed the direction. A few minutes later, he was back with her small suitcase and the strap of his duffle bag over his shoulder. He put both on the table and said, "Anything else?"

She twisted her neck to look around him and yelled across the room. "Where are the suitcases?"

Without lifting his head from the work at hand, the old man replied, "Behind the curtain at the back of the room."

Natalie turned her gaze back to Josh as she rose to her feet. "Come with me."

They walked over to the curtain that was gold with orange swirls through it. Josh muttered, "I feel like I'm in a time warp."

Natalie pulled back the curtain, revealing about thirty suitcases, purses and bags, lined up on three long rows of shelves. She explained, "These cases all have false, hidden compartments. I'll need one of these to hide my real documents." She searched along and found a dark-purple case about the same size as her own and pulled it off the shelf.

"What about me?"

"Don't worry," she said as she waved her hand. You can leave your original documents here."

"So, I don't need to swap my duffle bag?"

"Nope," she chirped.

He shifted to lean on one leg with a hand on his hip. "Just wondering—why did I bring my bag in?"

"I guess you didn't have to," she admitted with a sweet smile on her face. As the creases formed on Josh's brow, she added, "I think you're great too." The last word was followed by a soft kiss on his lips."

The creases were gone as he stood there somewhat dumbfounded.

She rolled her eyes, leaving an innocent look on her face. "Was that our first marital spat, Darling?"

Before he could answer, she walked by him, carrying the suitcase back to the table. When Josh joined her, she was searching the lining of the suitcase where, after a few minutes, she found a seam. She pressed her original passport, drivers license and one credit card into the sleeve that was hidden there. She then set about the task of transferring her clothes into the new case.

Josh leaned over and whispered, "Your little teasing kisses are getting dangerous. I'm not sure if I told you my background is Scandinavian."

She didn't look up as she asked, "What does that mean to me?"

"We have experience in these matters."

She was still focused on the luggage. "What matters?"

He whispered, "If it comes to raping and pillaging, we are experts."

She froze and without tilting her head, her gaze rolled up to him. He was stone faced. There was no smile, just the rugged, handsome look. *Was he kidding or serious*, she wondered until there was a quick one-eyed wink from him.

She turned her gaze back down and muttered, "You ass." Then she started to giggle.

He rolled his eyes and moaned, "Oh, don't start that again."

"I'm all done." The voice came from across the room.

Natalie snapped the suitcase closed and locked it. The remaining contents were put into the travelling bag. They walked over to the old man who handed Josh the passport and the drivers license. Josh inspected each and told the man he thought they were flawless.

Natalie asked for a spot where they could leave some personal belongings. The old man showed them to a counter with old-fashioned, oak cabinet doors under them, and behind the doors were four small safes. The old man turned the tumbler on one and pulled it open. Josh emptied his wallet into the safe and placed his old passport beside it. Natalie handed him half of the wad of cash before she put a few unnecessary items in beside Josh's belongings.

The old man closed the safe and spun the tumbler. Natalie and Josh thanked him, and then they exited the jewellery shop. Once they were on the road, Natalie said, "We're headed to the airport. I've booked two seats on a 6:00 p.m. WestJet flight to Edmonton."

The snow was still falling and beginning to accumulate on the ground. Josh looked up in the air through the side window. "It's not great flying weather, but a good time to get out of town." He turned his gaze back to her. For a moment he just stared. He thought she was good-looking, but with the light snowfall in the background, it surely made a beautiful vision—one he could easily get used to. As he cleared his throat, it brought him back to the issues at hand. "Do you have any idea who was following us this morning? Is there anything related to your work that could have someone's unwanted interest?"

"I can't see any reason for this to be work related. I have a feeling in my gut this is related to the 41 missing people, including my father and your son. If we find my father, we'll find your son and the mystery will be unravelled."

Josh nodded his agreement and hoped this was the case.

Natalie parked the car at the airport where, since they had time to kill, they ate a light meal at a nice restaurant. They talked quite a bit about their history—everything from their childhood to past relationships. The time seemed to fly by when Natalie looked at her phone and realized they needed to hurry to the gate now.

They did make the plane, and both of them snoozed for most of the four-hour flight. Natalie's head was leaning against his shoulder, and her hand was on his chest. It was a position becoming familiar and comfortable to her. Their slumber was interrupted by the *chirp* indicating their seatbelts needed to be fastened for landing. They landed without any issues, nor were there any issues going through security.

They were near the end of their journey and hopped into a cab towards an area on the east side of Edmonton called Sherwood Park. Natalie liked Hampton Inns, and she had made a reservation there for the two of them. After checking in, they went up to their third-floor room.

Once inside, Josh raised an eyebrow and said, "One king-size bed?"

She hoisted her suitcase onto the luggage rack and reminded him, "We need to act married."

He put his duffle bag beside her case. "We could act unhappily married."

Natalie chuckled. "Don't start again." She unlaced her dark-brown boots and yawned. "It's been another long day. I need a shower."

"I'm next after you," he responded.

Ten minutes later, she opened the bathroom door, allowing a wall of steam to enter the main room. Josh raised an eyebrow as she was naked except for the towel surrounding her, curled into a knot at her cleavage. His own shoes and shirt were already off when he walked into the bathroom and closed the door behind him. He looked around at her clothing strewn about the small room, thinking it reminded him of an archeological dig site.

The hot shower felt good. When he was done, he wrapped a towel around his waist, tying it at the front. Once he left the steamy bathroom, he was surprised to see Natalie standing in front of the bed, still in the towel.

She whispered, "I forgot my pajamas."

Josh let out a low growl. He had enough of the flirting and games. He moved to her and his hand was at the knot in the towel at her breasts. She didn't resist as he pulled on the knot, and the towel fell to the floor. He gazed at her slender form as his hands moved to her hips. He pulled her with his hands sliding behind her back.

Natalie shifted into him, pressing her breasts against his chest as she felt his lips lightly kiss her ear. His lips slid across her cheek and found her lips waiting. They pressed against hers, slightly open and their tongues danced together. She moaned as the kiss intensified with his hand coming up to cup her breast.

Sliding her hand down, it slid down and released the knot in the towel at his waist. The towel fell to the floor, and she shuddered, feeling him spring against her. He drew her over to the bed where they slid up the mattress. The motion didn't interrupt their kiss as their hands now joined in the exploration of each other. Their lips parted just a breath as they looked into each other's eyes, watching how they would close momentarily as one of them found a sensitive spot.

They were lying on their side, and he lifted his hips off the bed. It was like a dance, where they knew what the other wanted, and now, she did as she slid her leg under him. Her other leg wrapped around his thigh as she felt his breaths become heavier.

Then, something happened that had never happened to her before. He shifted his hips inwards and he slid inside her. As he did, her body began to shake, and her heel slid up behind his butt, drawing him in deeper. The shaking intensified as she bit lightly into his shoulder and the orgasm swept over her. It took a while for it to stop, but when he shifted, her body would jerk and another wave would storm over her.

This happened several times. After that, Josh kept still and let her body relax until he finally rolled her to her back. He kissed her softly on her lips, her neck and her breasts. They were warm, but not needy touches. He moved slowly at first, but as his fingers intertwined in hers and he pushed them stretched out above her head, his pace quickened. Her legs wrapped around him. She tried to pull him into her arms, but his locked arms held her hands against the bed.

His eyes were focused on hers, searching and watching her every reaction. For her, it had never been like this. He was in control, and she felt there was a message there. There was a level of ownership—an element of carnal need he was expressing, and for her, she wasn't embarrassed to find she liked it.

His movements became more urgent until, finally, his head was pressed back as he thrust his hips forward with his passion consuming him. She had no control as her back arched, her breasts pressed up into him, and her body shook uncontrollably. His face finally tilted down to find her beautiful eyes looking up at him. He saw happiness there, but also some fear, and he thought he understood that.

Josh rolled off of her, and as he moved onto his side, he kept her close in his arms. He reached down and pulled the blanket over them. He kissed her passionately again, and their breathing became heavy. However, he

123

stopped and kissed her forehead before whispering, "Let's get some sleep."

Quickly, she heard his breaths slow and become very deep as her face was leaning against his shoulder. Notwithstanding his calmness, she felt a sudden twinge of panic. This was something very new to her. With Philip and the few others she had been with, after the sex, the only urge she ever felt was for the man to go away so she could be alone. This was very different. She snuggled in closer to Josh, sliding her leg between his thighs. She didn't want him to go away. Her heart beat faster as an involuntary thought crossed her mind. *She never wanted him to leave!* Natalie's mind processed the purely emotional conclusion, and she smiled as her mind accepted it. She snuggled in even closer and the silly smile didn't leave her face as she fell asleep in his arms.

Chapter 13: Russian Arrival

Nick was dealing with the Toronto traffic as best he could. Their destination was a Russian safe house, the address for which had been put in the GPS, allowing the female voice to direct him along. He successfully negotiated the Allen Road exit, going south to Eglington Avenue. As directed, he turned east and was looking for Bathurst Street when the phone rang. Being unable to follow the GPS and answer the phone at the same time, he found a parking spot along the curb and pulled into it.

He pressed the *connect* icon and said, "Nick here."

"We lost her! I'm sorry, but we lost her!" the panting voice on the other end of the connection cried.

Nick slapped the steering wheel. "You idiots!"

"I'm sorry, Sir! The traffic was horrible, and she knew exactly what she was doing."

"She made your tail? She's a fucking marketing manager, not a trained driver, you imbecile. Where are you right now?" Nick asked.

"We're still searching this area of West Toronto since we lost them 30 minutes ago."

"We're going to the safe house. Don't return until you've found them." Nick raised his hand, again wishing he had an old-school phone, so he could smash it against something. Instead, he pressed his finger into the screen as hard as he dared to disconnect the call.

Nick reconnected the navigation system and the sweet voice said, "Continuing route."

As he pulled out into the road and continued east, Nick muttered, "You can't trust these *wannabe* Russians."

Logan had listened to the conversation from the passenger seat and asked, "Wannabe Russians?"

The navigation voice told Nick to turn south on Bathurst. When he finished the turn, he explained, "These guys we have here are locals." He made a twisted face like he just ate something bad and flicked one hand in the air. "They don't like the capitalist system, usually because they failed at it, so they attend protests and hug trees. Our recruiters find these guys to be easy pickings. We recruit them and train them, but they're not real Russians, just—" He emphasized the words "—want-to-be Russians."

Logan smirked. "Got it. If the wannabe Russians don't find the Lowe woman, what do we do next?"

Nick glanced at Logan, then the road, then Logan again. His face was in a dead-pan, stern countenance when he said "You're the leader of the mission. You tell me."

Logan's eyes opened wide, but only for a second, after which a smart-assed smirk formed on his lips.

Nick continued the sequence, watching the road, then glancing at Logan, then the road and then Logan again. Nick could hold it back no longer, and laughter burst from his lips. He looked directly at Logan, and the words rolled almost musically off his lips. "You're *not* the leader of the group!" He watched the road and laughed again. "You should've seen your face." Nick slapped his thigh. "You really thought I was going to let you lead?" Tears were flowing from his eyes, and Nick wiped them away while muttering, "Oh my fucking god—that was good."

"You missed your turn."

Nick was still trying to catch his breath. "What…"

Logan crossed his arms. "You're a moron—a native born, Russian moron, in fact. The voice told you to turn. You missed the message and the turn."

By now the GPS voice was saying, "Make a U turn," over and over.

Logan pointed at the navigation screen and, in a mocking tone, repeated, "Make a U turn. What do we know? We're just navigating. You're the fucking moron leader!"

As his chuckling subsided, Nick said, "Okay—okay. I'm sorry, and I take it back. As we agreed before, we're leading this together."

The GPS voice indicated a left turn, and a moment later they were heading west on Bloor Street. In this predominantly Russian district, there were restaurants and shops on both sides of the street, and for many of them, the signs were in both English and Russian. Three blocks down, Nick turned the dark-blue Mustang north into a subdivision of large, old homes. Many of them were three stories high with artistic brick work which is quite a few notches above what you see on today's cookie-cutter houses.

Five houses down, there was a double driveway on their left Nick directed the car into. He continued down the laneway to a large garage facing them. Just before the garage, Nick veered the vehicle right into the paved area between the garage and house.

They both exited the car and retrieved their bags. Nick pointed to the house on the other side of the laneway, stating, "Both these houses are Russian safe houses our operatives work out of. We'll be safe here until we decide what we do next."

Logan, still stone-faced, gave a barely perceptible nod of agreement.

Nick slowed and walked sideways beside Logan as he implored, "C'mon. I said *we*."

Logan pointed his chin towards the back door at the top of three concrete stairs. "Knock."

Nick rolled his eyes before bounding up the stairs. A face appeared in the window of the door just as he was about to knock. The door opened and a young man, appearing to be about 25 years old, stood in the doorway.

Nick said, "Nick Anderson and Logan Russell." He didn't want to deal with issues of who was in charge here, so he yelled at the wannabe Russian, "Move!"

The young man was startled, jumping out of the way, allowing Nick to walk by him. As Logan followed, making his own announcement of leadership, he handed him his suitcase and ordered, "Take care of this for me."

The back door led into a small mudroom and then to the kitchen. When Logan entered, Nick had his hands on his hips, staring at another young Russian. "Who the hell are you?" Nick chirped.

The second young man straightened and stuttered, "Roger—Sir."

"Well, Roger, in 30 minutes you're going to give us an operational readiness report. I want to know what vehicles, weapons and computer systems you have at our disposal. While you're getting your head out of your ass—" He glanced at the first young man "—Mr. No-name is going to show us to our rooms."

Roger continued to stutter, "Yes—yes—Sir."

On their way up the stairs, Mr. No-name managed to tell Logan and Nick his name was Don. On the second floor, they were each shown to a comfortable bedroom, where their bags were left. Logan told Nick he was going to take a one-hour power nap. Nick agreed and snickered, thinking of Roger, at the 30-minute mark, wondering what to do.

The one-hour mark arrived, and Logan and Nick retraced their steps back into the kitchen. Neither of the two young men were there, so they moved into the living area. There, Roger and Don were standing, side-by-side, in front of a comfortable-looking, grey, cloth couch with a red blanket draped over the back.

Before the men said anything, Nick moved between them, turned and placed one arm around each of their shoulders. In a low voice, he offered, "Guys, we've been pulling your legs, so relax. I'm sure you two are valuable assets, and we're going to need you." He gave each of them a reassuring slap on the shoulder before he slipped his arms free before settling into an arm chair facing the couch. Nick crossed his legs, one ankle resting on his knee and said, "Sit down," to the two men.

Logan sat down in an identical black-leather arm chair Nick had lowered into. He heard about this good-cop, bad-cop routine, and he considered Nick just became the good cop. The young men looked more relaxed, but they did need to be reminded, and Logan would oblige. "Now that we are all friends, that's good, but remember that applies as long as you two remember we are in charge."

The young men's smiles faded a bit, but they remained relaxed.

Nick clapped his hands together and said, "How about that report."

For the next 15 minutes, Roger and Don updated them on the four vehicles presently at the house, not including the dark-green Jeep Rubicon out searching for Natalie Lowe. Roger pulled a piece of paper from his pocket, reading off a lengthy list of weapons including ten handguns, eight assault rifles, 40 grenades and a rocket launcher.

Nick raised an eyebrow in admiration at the mention of a rocket launcher, but cautioned, "Hopefully we won't need that. How about residents and computers?"

Don piped in and said, "Other than the two of us, Jack and Emilio are on the road, as you know, and there are three more operatives in the house next door."

Roger added, "There's an office upstairs with two servers in it. There are four computers of varying capability, with one set up for encryption, allowing secure communication to Russia."

Logan nodded his approval while Nick asked, "Did you say—Emilio?"

Roger's voice vibrated nervously as he answered through a chuckle. "There's a large Italian-Canadian population in Toronto."

"They're running quite late," Logan offered.

"I am getting worried," Roger admitted.

Nick's lips twisted on an angle as he flashed a hand across his body. "Don't worry. I told them not to come back until they found that white BMW they weren't supposed to let out of their sight."

In fact, Jack and Emilio didn't come back for quite some time. The four men in the house had a late lunch, then dinner even later. They were all sitting in the living room at 1:00 in the morning, having a beer, when they heard the back door open. They also heard footsteps, and then two men with tired eyes walked into the room. They looked from Roger to Don with a questioning look, but they dared not speak. The two newcomers then glanced back and forth from Logan to Nick. It was an awkward moment.

Nick, figuring he let the moment go on long enough, raised the beer bottle in the air and said, "Well, finally and thank god!"

Both men were about 40 years old. The man, who now introduced himself as Jack, was black with a shaved head. Emilio wore dark sunglasses and had long, black hair in tight curls coated with shiny gel. His dark locks flowed over the shoulders of a black, leather jacket.

Nick looked from one man to the other, but finally focused on Emilio. "So, *Rock Star*, did you find them?"

Curious at Nick's use of words, Emilio lowered an eyebrow and replied, "We didn't find them, but we did find the car."

Logan slouched back in the chair, and let out a deep exhale of air. "This isn't going to be good. Where is the car?"

Emilio paused as he agreed with Logan, thinking, *this wasn't going to go over well at all.* "The white BMW is at a long-term parking lot by the airport."

Nick shifted forward and accidentally kicked the leg of the table in front of him. "The airport!" His stare bored into both men. "You're telling me they flew out of town?"

"Yes, it would seem so," Jack replied.

Slapping both hands down lightly, one on each knee, Nick said in a low voice, "Okay guys. What's done is done. Did you search the car?"

"Yes. It was clean."

"Who's your computer guy?" Logan asked.

Emilio, who seemed to be the leader of the group, pointed at Roger.

"How good are you?" Logan asked

"I can find anything," Roger replied with a boastful grin on his face.

"We'll see," Logan responded. "I want you to get on the computer in your office and check every flight that left the airport today. Check domestic and international flights. We want to find out where Natalie Lowe flew to."

Jack interjected, "There was a man with her in the car."

"What?" Nick asked.

Jack repeated the admission and added, "We don't know who he is. We didn't even get a good look at him—just a man."

Nick looked at Roger and modified Logan's request. "This should make it easier. You're looking for a couple, and one of them is Natalie Lowe."

Roger nodded and took the stairs, two at a time, up to the third-floor office.

Turning to Emilio, Nick ordered, "You two guys get some rest, but before you do, go next door and get two fresh guys to park themselves outside her condo apartment. You never know, the car at the airport could be a ruse. She might come back."

Once Jack and Emilio left, Nick turned to Don and indicated, "I guess that leaves you. We're going to sleep, so you need to stay up. Wake us if there's any news."

Don didn't have to wake up either of them as there was no news through the night. In fact, there was no news for the next three days. The stakeout at the condo achieved nothing, and Roger, who reported he could find anything, found nothing. On the second night, it was agreed Don, who apparently had excellent burglar skills, and Roger, broke into Natalie's condo dressed as Alarm Force security servicemen. When they reported back, their report wasn't helpful. During the break-in, they went through files, none of which were relevant. There was a safe they were able to open and within it was a handgun and ammunition.

That did, in fact, cause a few raised eyebrows amongst the Russians as they wondered why a Canadian marketing manager would have need of a weapon. There was only one locked drawer in the apartment and it was in the desk. They pried it open, but it was empty. That left only the desktop computer Roger thoroughly inspected. There were three email addresses used on the computer, and it was easy to see one was for family emails. One was for work, and there was nothing of interest unless you had an active interest for customer surveys. The third email was a Gmail address Roger thought was odd. It looked like it had only been recently set up, but outside of a few spam emails, there wasn't anything of note there. Roger checked the list of spam mails and even checked the sent folder, but there was nothing of value.

The Russian group seemed to be at an impasse with no new leads. Logan felt he had no choice but to move to the next level of the search, and that meant he needed to divulge more information to Nick. They were in the living room alone with a news channel on the TV. Logan had the remote and turned the volume higher, then leaned towards Nick and said, "Do you think this room is bugged?"

Nick made a *you-have-to-be-kidding* face, but then it changed to one filled with curiosity. "I'm not sure," he replied.

Logan peeked into the kitchen, then up the stairs, seeing if anyone was listening.

It was obvious to Nick that Logan had something he wanted to share privately. Nick suggested, "Let's go out and get some dinner. I'm hungry."

The two men donned their boots and coats and headed south down the suburban road towards Bloor Street. It had snowed on and off for the last few days, resulting in ten centimetres of snow on the ground. Thankfully, the sidewalk was clear, but it was cold as seen by their hands tucked deep in their pockets, and the fog created every time they exhaled a breath.

The restaurant wasn't fancy, but the sign on the window boasted good, Russian, homemade meals. They stopped in front of the glass door, looking through to the inside, seeing six small tables and an appropriate number of simple, red, leather-backed chairs.

"See, it's very simple, meaning the food must be very good," Nick concluded. He stretched out towards the door handle and pulled the door open for Logan.

As soon as they sat down, a man with fancy, black, leather shoes, black dress pants and an obviously mismatched, white t-shirt, moved from behind the counter at the back of the restaurant and came to the table. Nick looked at the menu signs posted behind the counter and said to Logan, "Hey, they have kvass. Do you want a glass?"

Logan's eyes lit up at the thought of the famous Russian beverage similar to a low alcohol content, fruit flavoured malt-beer. "Sure, and I see they have chicken pelmeni and potato and cabbage varenniki. Let's get an order of each, and we can share."

Both foods resembled stuffed perogies and were a favorite of Nick's. He agreed immediately, and the waiter scurried off to prepare their order.

The two glasses of kvass came quickly, and once the waiter left, Nick stared down into the brew as his fingers slowly turned the glass in a small circle. "Earlier, you had something you wanted to say?"

Just finishing a deep drink from the glass, Logan replied. "Yes." He placed the glass on the table and thought for a moment about the best way to put forth new information. He decided the easiest was to get right to the point. "The Sholites are building a large device. For it, they will need two materials that are not common, but available on Earth. They are mica and tantalum."

With his face still tilted down, Nick lifted his gaze from the glass to Logan. "How do you know this?"

There was no one else in the restaurant, but still, Logan double-checked the waiter was not within earshot. "You might have guessed that I am not the only Korian on Earth. In all, there are about 40 of us on the planet at any one time. With that said, at times, I do get intelligence from them."

"What do they need the materials for? Aren't they used in electrical boards and such?"

The waiter pushed open the hinged door with his ass and entered the main room with a large tray. He put the two plates of food in the middle of the table, with a large spoon on each one, while a clean plate was placed in front of each of the men. Nick said, "thank you," in Russian, bringing a wide smile to the waiter's face.

He snapped his fingers and offered, "More kvass?"

Both men said they were fine, and the waiter's smile dimmed a bit. He said, "Just yell if you need anything. I will be in the back," and off he went.

Each of the men spooned several morsels from each serving plate to their own and began eating. Between bites of the tasty meal, Logan continued, "You are correct. Mica and tantalum are used to make capacitors—devices used to hold a charge…"

Nick interrupted, "I know what capacitors are."

This brought a smile to Logan's face. "Of course. In that case, they are making several very large capacitors. Just to start, we estimate they will need 500 pounds of each material. This would be a very unusual order—one that you could have your surveillance people in Moscow monitor for. If we find such a large order of either, or both materials, it is likely we would find the Sholites behind it."

Nick had been chomping down mouthfuls of food as he listened. He picked up the napkin and wiped the corners of his mouth before replying. "I can do that, especially since we seem to have no other leads. What's this large device supposed to do?"

Leaning forward as far as he could, Logan twitched his head backwards, indicating Nick should lean in as well. Once his comrade was in close range, Logan whispered. "The Sholites home world is, or was, two light years away from Earth. It was decimated and no longer exists. Their remaining people travel the universe in huge ships, but the ships need supplies, so along the way, they find asteroids and planets that have minerals or water, which they harvest. In most cases, the worlds are not inhabited, but on a few, they have destroyed the populations to get what they want. This has been going on for over one thousand years."

"Was your world one of those destroyed?"

Surprise filled Logan's eyes for a moment before he responded, "Yes. That was many lifetimes ago, but our two civilizations continue the war as we travel through space. Now, the Sholites need supplies, and they plan on devastating this world, and when the carnage is complete, they will take the supplies they need."

"You're saying they have some type of planet killing device?"

"Not yet, but they have the technology to build such a device." Logan's eyes narrowed and became darker. "They are experts in electromagnetic technology, and your planet is really a large electromagnet. This device can overload the earth's magnetic field, causing the magnetic poles to reverse, resulting in unbelievable carnage and a massive loss of life."

"Now I understand why Annenkov was so insistent on the success of this mission at all costs," Nick admitted.

Anger could be seen in Logan's eyes, and little bits of spittle left his lips as he hissed, "Now you understand why the Sholites are *your* mortal enemy as well as mine. Every last one of them needs to be killed, or they will kill all of us."

The rest of the meal was eaten in silence. Logan paid the bill before they walked back to the house in the darkness now settled over Toronto.

Once inside, Nick said, "I'll send the message to Moscow to search for purchase orders for the materials we talked of."

Logan nodded. He still stayed silent as his mood was not good. He went to his bedroom on the second floor, and closed the door behind him. Lowering himself on the bed, he intertwined his fingers behind his head, on top of the pillow. His mind was troubled. As well as being his partner in the mission, Nick had become his friend. The only correct piece of information he just shared, was the Sholites needed materials to make a device. The rest was pure imagination and bullshit. He didn't like lying, but he needed Nick to have as much venom and hate for the Sholites as he did. If he had to lie to achieve that purpose, so be it. It didn't matter, as long as the Sholites were killed—every last one of them.

Chapter 14: Lashkar Mann

There was a knock at the door. Josh was still sound asleep, but the noise caused Natalie to stir and slide from his arms. She stretched her arms upwards, and her toes pointed to the bottom of the bed as she heard the knock a second time. This time the word, "Housekeeping!" followed the knock.

Natalie was still half asleep. Her fingers formed into fists as she rubbed them against her eyes. As she yawned, she heard a card key being pushed into the electronic lock and the subsequent metallic *clink* as the door pin caught on the safety catch.

Natalie yelled out, "Come back later!"

Josh shot up to a sitting position. His eyes were wide open, but still glazed over while his head turned from side to side.

Natalie chuckled as she looked at the small table clock. She said, "Relax. It's only 8:30 a.m."

He fell back into the pillow, and his eyes closed. She slid down against him before his arm wrapped her shoulder and drew her even closer. Her eyes closed as well, feeling the comfort in his arms. They lay like this for a long time, just enjoying the quiet, until it was quite unromantically broken by the sound from a vacuum cleaner outside their room.

Josh whispered, "We had better get up. Don't we have to get your convict today?"

She rolled over half on top of him, and her finger tapped on his stubble-covered chin. "My release order for Subash Mann isn't in effect until Monday, so we have the next three days free, for the most part."

Josh opened one eye and peered down at her smiling eyes. "For the most part?"

She kissed his chest, then returned her warm, green-eyed gaze back to his. "We have a few errands to run. It's nothing too strenuous." She stretched upwards, moving her lips to hover just above his. Josh closed his eyes, pursing his own lips in anticipation, but felt her soft lips place a kiss to his chin. She spun off of him to a sitting position on the edge of the bed and stretched her arms high over her head once again.

Josh rolled on his side and supported his head on his hand, propped up from his elbow. "That's it for a kiss after a romantic night?"

She turned her face back to him while she tussled her hair with her fingers. "The *good morning romantic kiss* only happens to the movie stars in the movies. For the rest of us, we need to brush our teeth before that first kiss. That's my next stop, then into the shower." Before he could respond, she was up on her feet, hurrying into the bathroom.

He grinned as he watched her with her dishevelled hair above her cat-like eyes. Inside his gut, there was a growl as he watched her cute butt shift from side to side below her narrow waist.

While Natalie was in the hot shower, she heard a noise from the other side of the shower curtain and poked her head around it to see Josh peeing into the toilet while a tooth brush hung from his mouth. *Typical male,* she thought as she pushed her head back under the stream of hot water.

As she massaged the shampoo into her hair with her eyes closed due to the suds dripping down her face, she felt a rush of cold air. A moment later, he was facing her with his grip on her wrists, bringing them down to her sides. His fingers replaced hers, stroking through her shampoo-filled hair, clamping on the short bits of hair at the base of her neck and tugging lightly. Her lips were forced up where his were waiting. They kissed softly, but quickly it changed to a passionate, needy touch.

Until that moment, Natalie had never made love in the shower, but now, she urged him on even though he needed none. As he took her, her mind was awhirl. He met Josh only a week ago, yet it seemed like she had known him forever. Their togetherness just seemed right, and it scared and fascinated her at the same time.

After the sex, their soapy caresses were also something new to Natalie, but with Josh, it seemed so natural. Natalie pulled herself from the shower first, combed her hair and then went into the bedroom. When Josh came out of the bathroom, with a towel tied around his waist, she was just hanging up the phone.

Josh asked, "Is everything okay?"

She was still completely naked, and she knew he wasn't looking at her eyes when he asked his question. She had a sneaky smile on her face as she turned to give him a better view. "I've arranged a car from a local CSE operative."

"I thought your privileges were suspended?"

"Only my computer access. There are many other resources still at my disposal." She batted her eyes playfully. "Anything else?"

He returned her look of innocence with a growl, thinking, *if she had an apple in her hand, he would know exactly the temptation Adam felt in the Garden of Eden.* He pushed the thought from his mind and replied, "You better get some clothes on, or we won't ever get to the car."

They both agreed on this conclusion and dressed, first pulling on jeans, and Josh pulled a dark-red sweater over his head while Natalie pulled on a blue, long-sleeved shirt. They went downstairs and had a casual breakfast in an area just off the main lobby. When they were almost finished, they saw a man come to the front counter and speak with the attendant there. He dropped a key fob into the hotel receptionist's hand and scurried back out the door.

"I think that's our vehicle," Natalie concluded, and she was right. They picked up the key on the way back up to their room. After locking their valuables in the safe, they retraced their steps back down to the lobby. Once they were out the door, Natalie pressed the key fob, resulting in flashing lights on a white Cadillac Escalade. She stopped for a second and peered speculatively at Josh. She threw him the key as she confessed, "I don't like driving vehicles that big."

Josh didn't have the same problem and was happy to drive. Natalie told him they had some shopping to do. Using the navigation system in the vehicle, she typed in, *West Edmonton Mall.* It took a little over 45 minutes to arrive at the Mall that is one of the largest in the world.

They both shopped for more relevant, thicker winter boots, appropriate for the amount of snow they now saw on the ground. A thick covering blanketed the city, and the plows had created two-metre-high berms of dirty salt and sand-filled snow along the sides of the roads. Natalie also showed Josh some bomber jackets. They were only waist length, but nevertheless, they were exceptionally warm. Josh selected a black one while Natalie picked a smaller woman's size in purple.

As they wandered through the Mall, they picked up a laptop, various other items they thought would come in handy and a few more items of clothing. As they shopped, they held hands, or walked with arms around one another. Natalie knew they were both in their '40s, but the time they spent together reminded her of her teenage years, when she spent too much time at a much smaller mall in Kingston. Then, it seemed there was a new boyfriend every month or two, and now, she had the same question as she glanced at Josh. Were they going steady? Were they a thing? She knew it was adolescent in nature—maybe even childish, but this was where Josh had taken her thoughts.

They stopped for some lunch at a little Bistro. Natalie was afraid she was talking too much as she told one story after the other from her past. Josh listened intently, showing his genuine interest in this woman who he had become so close too, so quickly. He shared some of his own stories, but he steered Natalie towards sharing more than listening.

After leaving the Bistro, Natalie looked at the time on her phone and said, "We better go since we have another stop to make."

Knowing Natalie would tell him more when he needed to know it, Josh nodded his head. They walked back to the Escalade, and after Josh started the engine, Natalie pulled a small card from her pocket. There was an address on it, and Natalie mumbled it aloud as she typed it into the navigation system.

Josh's eyes widened when he saw they were going to another bank. He shrugged and drove towards the main highway. Twenty-five minutes later, they were pulling into the parking lot of the bank made of large, textured concrete slabs, giving it a very modern look. Josh was surprised when she indicated, this time, he should come in with her.

Natalie asked for access to the safety deposit box room and showed the key she had retrieved from the safety deposit box in Toronto. The bank worker led them to a back vault, unlocked the door and held it open for them to enter.

He said, "We have a secure room next door that's private, where you can open your box."

Natalie replied, "Thanks. We'll be just one second, then we'll bring it there."

The young man walked along the length of the safety deposit box room where, a third of the way down, he announced, "Here it is." He pointed to *Box 34*, and when Natalie and Josh were in front of it, the young man moved to wait for them outside.

Unlocking the box, Natalie asked Josh, "Can you please carry it to the other room for me?"

Josh smiled and pulled the long box from its compartment. He led the way from the room where the young man was holding a door open to the room next door. Josh entered, followed by Natalie who shut the door behind them. There was a small, metal table within, and Josh placed the box down on it. Natalie opened the lid and, as she looked down at the two handguns with the appropriate shoulder holsters, asked, "Do you know how to use a gun?"

He retorted, "I'm American, so of course I do, but do you think we need them?"

Shrugging, she replied, "There are very strange events going on, and remember, there's someone following us. It's better for us to take precautions." She picked up one of the Glock 19, 9 mm handguns and handed it to Josh, along with the holster and three clips. As Josh checked the chamber, placed one clip in the gun and made sure the safety was on, she was satisfied he was comfortable with it. She did the same and placed the extra clips in her coat pocket.

They both put the shoulder holsters on under their new bomber jackets and zipped them up. A few minutes later, they were back in the Escalade.

Josh asked, "What now?"

She realized their tasks for the day were done. She suggested, "There's a light snow falling. It would be nice to just go for a drive."

Josh tilted his face, looked at her, and said, "When I bumped into you that day in your library, I wasn't too sure I liked the pink streaks in your hair. I have come to find I like it very much. It's quite exotic, matching your personality." In his mind, one thing led to another, and in a softer voice, he suggested, "I think we should go back to the hotel."

She returned his gaze and said, "What for..." but then she saw the glint in his eyes. She saw he wanted her, and it brought her own need to the surface so that her breaths were deeper. "Yes, let's go back to the hotel," she agreed.

The rest of their weekend followed the same pattern. Some might think their short excursions from the hotel were interrupted by interludes of passionate sex—others might, more appropriately, say their incessant sessions of passionate lovemaking were occasionally interrupted by short excursions from the hotel. Either way, they spent all their time together with a significant amount of it without the encumbrance of clothing. They explored every part of each other's bodies while finding every spot of pleasure, leaving nothing to the imagination.

It was a wonderful time for both of them, but they knew, come Monday morning, they needed to get back to work on their mission to find her father and, hopefully from that, his son. With the alarm on Natalie's phone signaling the time to awake, they both had mixed feelings when Monday did come.

Still lying in bed, Natalie confessed, "I don't want this to end, Josh. I've become very close to you." She looked up at his face and cupped his cheek with her hand, whispering, "I don't *ever* want this to end." For her, the admission was awkward. She wasn't comfortable letting someone see her feelings laid out so raw.

She tilted her eyes down, but Josh's strong fingers brought her chin back up, so their gaze was locked once again. He saw there was a tear in her eye, but he smiled. "I'm as happy as I've ever been, Natalie. No matter what happens from here, you have a place in my heart, and you always will. We have work to do now, but remember, even if the business at hand consumes us, I will always be thinking of, not you, but you and I together because that seems the way things have to be now. Never you. Never me. Always us." He tilted his head down and kissed her as passionately as he ever had.

When their lips parted, she smiled, and there were very few words to say that the kiss did not, so she whispered a simple, "thank you."

Their showers together had become ritualistic events, but this time, when they were done, they simply packed their bags. After checking out of the hotel, they loaded their bags into the back of the Escalade, and again, Josh took his position in the driver's seat. When Natalie sat beside him, she pulled a leather document case she had purchased on one of their shopping excursions, across her knees.

Josh, as had become customary, asked, "Where to now?"

Natalie pulled a file folder from the document case. She reviewed the top paper in it and typed an address into the navigation system. As she typed, she said, "We're going to the *Edmonton Institution*, as it's known. It's a federal penitentiary and the home of Subash Mann for the last three years."

As Josh drove, following the directions from the navigation system directing him out of the hotel lot, he responded, "You said this guy was a forger. How is he going to help us?"

"We don't really need him. We need his son, Lashkar Mann. Subash Mann is the leverage we'll have to convince Lashkar to help us."

Veering onto the highway heading north, Josh continued the questions. "Then, why do we need Lashkar, and more importantly, why wouldn't he just help us?"

Natalie turned on the music and found something modern to listen to. "Since you're going to find out soon in any case, here's the plan. Lashkar Mann is a computer and programming expert. However, since he uses those skills primarily for illegal activities, he's known as a hacker—likely one of the top five hackers in the world. Without having the use of computer systems for our investigation, we're dead in the water. We need him to…"

"Hack into the systems we need." Josh finished her sentence for her.

"Exactly." She pointed to the right. "We need to exit here."

A few turns later, they were driving along a service road at the back of the Institution. Josh looked through the high fence, topped with razor-wire, and exclaimed. "What is that?"

Natalie looked through the passenger window and saw the wooden boards. "That's a hockey rink set up inside the jail yard."

He laughed. "Seriously—prisoners playing hockey?"

"You have no idea," she explained. "In Canada, everyone plays hockey or wants to play hockey. Adding to that is, this is Edmonton, the adopted home of Wayne Gretzky."

"Wayne who?"

Natalie's eyes opened wide as she shifted, leaning her back against the passenger door, staring in dismay at Josh. "You're kidding—right?" She saw by his puzzled return stare, that he wasn't. "Many would say Wayne Gretzky is the most famous Canadian ever. He played for years for the Edmonton Oilers hockey team, leading them to multiple cup wins. He's like a living god."

Josh turned into the entrance to the prison as he quipped, "A hockey player is a god—really?"

"In Canada, absolutely," Natalie retorted. "Now, as for you, your lack of knowledge makes me wonder, what planet have you been living on?"

Putting the car in park, Josh exited the vehicle, followed by Natalie with her document case. Josh saw the brown-brick structure was three floors high. It was an older building, with three sections jutting out from the front of the larger structure.

Natalie suggested Josh wait in the car while she retrieved the prisoner. Josh nodded his understanding, but since he'd been sitting for a while, he decided to wait in the brisk, winter air.

Once Natalie went through the security check, she asked to see the warden who was expecting her. The older warden looked at her curiously as she produced the release order for Subash Mann who had six years left to serve on multiple forgery convictions.

Warden Miller had seen many unusual things over his 30 years in public service, so when he saw the release order signed by a senior official from the National Security and Intelligence Agency, he picked up his phone and spoke with his assistant. "Subash Mann is leaving us. Get him prepared and packed." Next, he opened his office door and motioned for a guard to come in. He said to the guard, "Show Ms. Lowe to Waiting Room Three."

Ninety minutes later, the door finally opened, and an older man was led into Waiting Room Three by the guard. Subash Mann darted his eyes from side to side in a confused state. He was wearing grey slacks with a blue and grey plaid shirt, and he was carrying a small duffle bag, hanging from his hands despite the handcuffed locking them together in front of him. Natalie motioned him to sit in the chair on the opposite side of the desk from her.

Subash placed the bag beside the table and lowered himself into the chair. The man was 52 years old with black, curly hair. However, the years had added as much grey to mix in with the black. Matching the hair on his head was a thick beard and moustache, coloured the same mix of black and grey. From behind his round spectacles, in a quiet voice, he said, "What's going on?"

Natalie crossed one leg over the other and casually replied, "My name is Natalie, and I've arranged for your release from prison."

His eyes vibrated nervously as he asked, "Why? I'm supposed to be here for six more years."

Natalie leaned in across the table. He sensed he should do the same, and when their faces were close, she said in a voice as low as the one he used, "I know you're a criminal, and you always will be. However, there's a need that allows me to use you for a higher purpose."

Subash frowned. "Is this about my son?"

Rising to her feet, Natalie warned, "We best get going. You never know when someone might change their mind."

Natalie walked out the door and down the hallway with Subash behind him and the guard bringing up the rear. They went through the security checkpoint where Natalie retrieved her gun. The guard gave Natalie the key for the handcuffs and told her, "Good luck."

When they arrived at the car, Josh was sitting inside with the engine running. Natalie made sure Subash was comfortable in the rear seat area with his seat belt secured, before she entered the front passenger seat compartment. Once settled, she said, "Subash, this is Josh. Josh—Subash."

Josh found himself asking the same question he always did. "Where to now?"

Natalie had her phone out and was searching for an address. She keyed it into the navigation system, and the route showed them going south while in the top left corner of the SUV's screen, it read the duration of the trip as two hours and 5 minutes.

Josh followed the directions that started coming from the navigation system. "What's in Blackfalds?" He had seen the town's name when she entered it in the navigation entry field.

"I'm hungry. Can I get some McDonalds?" The soft voice came from the back seat.

Turning around with her arm on the back of the seat, she looked at Subash. "Didn't they feed you this morning?"

Subash wobbled his head back and forth. His voice was louder, so now Natalie could hear the Indian accent. "Of course. They fed me the shit prison food—fake scrambled eggs, a processed meat patty and toast. It's not like the real processed food at McDonald's."

Natalie rolled her eyes as she considered Subash's misconceived thoughts of real and processed food. She looked out the front window and muttered, "We'll find a McDonald's along the highway as we go south."

As they turned onto the highway, Josh repeated, "Blackfalds?"

"Right," she replied while changing to a lower tone since what she was about to tell him was classified. "Blackfalds is a very small community just north of Red Deer. Within Red Deer, during the Second World War, there was an air force base – RCAF base Penhold. The primary base was in Red Deer, and there was a secondary landing site in Blackfalds."

"If you're trying to speak quietly, so I can't hear you, I can still hear you," Subash announced.

Turning her head, Natalie scowled at him.

Subash did the wobble with his head again and said, "Just saying."

Realizing it was silly to be whispering since, in two hours, they'd all be at the Penhold base, she continued explaining in a normal tone. "RCAF base Penhold was shut down after the war. The secondary base is isolated, surrounded on all sides by massive farms. It was considered a perfect location for the CSIS to set up a top-secret Five Eyes prison, so they did ten years ago."

"Why does it have to be top-secret?" Josh asked.

A voice piped up from the back seat. "Yes—I am also curious."

Natalie didn't need to turn around to know Subash was doing the head wobble.

"Many countries secret service organizations have to stretch the law for reasons of national security. High profile criminals and terrorists sometimes fall outside the purview of the law. Add to that the fact most of the world thinks the CIA are the bad boys on the block, and the Canadians are the meek ones. So where do you think Five Eyes puts their top targets when captured?"

There was a loud, "Aha!" from the back seat followed by, "RCAF base Penhold!"

Thankfully, Josh spotted a roadside service center advertising McDonalds take out. They went through the drive through where Subash ordered a breakfast meal, as did Josh and Natalie.

The terrain during the remainder of the drive was mundane. Each road sign they passed was the same as the one before. There were very few trees, and one farm began to look much like the next. A thought came to Josh, and he tilted his head back and asked Subash, "Did you play hockey at the prison?"

Subash's head wobbled back and forth as he was thinking, then his eyes lit up, knowing of what Josh spoke. "You are talking about the hockey rink at the back of the prison?"

"Yes," Josh answered.

Subash started to laugh. At first, Josh thought he would go into one of Natalie's now famous giggling fits, but he stopped and said, "Fucking Canadians can be stupid! They say the prisoners need exercise, so they give them skates and sticks to play hockey." He leaned forward and emphasized, "Don't they know skates are sharp and can be used as weapons?"

Natalie didn't think laughing at hockey was funny, but Josh did. He chuckled as Subash continued.

"So, the fucking, smart Canadians decide there'll be no more ice hockey in the winter. However, they will let the prisoners play road hockey in the summer. Don't they know the hockey sticks are weapons too? So, three years ago, they banned all hockey, yet the boards still stand as a symbol of their stupidity."

Subash's laughter increased and Josh joined him, that is until Natalie punched him in the shoulder, causing the reminder of the highway trip to be completed in silence.

An hour later, they were turning off at the Blackfalds exit, heading west. Another fifteen minutes later, after driving through the small community, they arrived at a barbed-wire fence with a gate. Every ten metres along the fence, a bright-yellow sign was posted with the words, *Warning. Hazardous Waste*. Looking through this fence, they could see a much higher steel fence surrounding a one-story, brown-brick building. Other than that, surrounding the compound, as far as the eye could see, was flat land covered in windswept snow. There wasn't a single tree to be seen.

Natalie took her cell and pressed in a phone number, after which she provided her name and an identification number. A small camera mounted on a post in front of them, scanned back and forth across the SUV. There was a pause followed by her giving Josh and Subash's names. When the gate began to slide open, she hung up the call.

One hundred metres down a gravel driveway, they came to the higher fence that had the same warning signs. Here again, a gate slid open, and Natalie directed Josh to drive the vehicle to the back of the building that they saw was really in the shape of a large U with the open end at the rear. There were a few cars parked in the U. Natalie held up her hand to block out the sun as she looked out the window, and then directed Josh to back into a spot ten metres away from a heavy, metal door.

As Josh exited the vehicle, Natalie told him to keep the vehicle running. She walked around to the rear door, directing Subash to scoot over. He complied and Natalie unlocked the handcuffs, only for them to be reconnected after the short chain was passed through the grab handle above the window. After tugging on his hands, she was assured he was unable to get free.

She closed the door and said to Josh, "You better come with me."

Josh and Natalie walked to the metal door as the wind swirled around them. She knocked on it, and a few seconds later, it was answered by a man with a second man behind him holding an assault rifle. She pulled out her CSE identification and showed it to the first soldier.

As he reviewed it, she informed him, "I need to see your commanding officer. He's expecting me."

The first man looked at Josh and Natalie suspiciously, but finally said to the man with the assault rifle, "Take them to the holding room."

The second armed man directed, "This way," as he pointed with his gun to a hallway on their left. At the same time, the first man was lost from sight into another wing of the building.

The room they were directed into looked like an old lunch room with two metal tables in it, and each was surrounded by wooden chairs, apparently left over from the '70s. The guard closed the door and waited outside.

As soon as they were alone, Josh stated, "This doesn't look like a prison."

She smirked and said, "That's the point. No one thinks there's anything important here. Everyone thinks the really bad people are at Guantanamo Bay, but they're not. The top 20 international risks, according to the intelligence communities, are here.

"And that includes this guy, Lashkar?"

"That it does. Don't be confused by this first impression. Below us are four floors of cells, offices and barracks, with the top floor being reserved for 30 hand-selected special forces personnel from the Five Eyes community."

They were interrupted by the door opening, and framed in the doorway was an older man with a squared-off, military haircut. He asked, "Ms. Lowe. Can I see you out here please?" Even though the words were in the form of a question, the tone clearly indicated it was not a request.

Natalie rose and pulled a document from her case. Once she was outside the door, she handed the paper to the older officer.

He glanced at the paperwork and muttered, "Yes, I was sent an email copy of this in advance." His eyes lifted and bored into her. "Are you armed?"

Natalie unzipped her bomber jacket and pulled one side back, revealing the Glock 19.

"And your partner?"

"He has the same," Natalie answered.

"Good."

Two muscular men were coming down the hallway, and just in front of them was a skinny man in handcuffs and leg irons. The leg irons were joined by a short chain, so the best he could do was a slow shuffle.

There was a table outside the room, and the officer asked Natalie and Josh to leave their firearms on it. They complied and then the prisoner, dressed in an orange jumpsuit, was led into the room.

Turning to the officer, Natalie said, "We'd like to speak with him alone."

With both fists pressed into his waist, the officer said, "My pay grade isn't high enough to understand what's really going on here, but I'm smart enough not to pry. However, I'm responsible for everyone's safety, so if you want to go back in that room, it's with one guard on the inside of the door."

By the look set on his face, Natalie knew this wasn't open for debate, so she acquiesced. "Very well," she mumbled before she strode back in.

Josh followed her, along with one guard, before the door was closed, leaving her facing Lashkar who was seated in a '70s chair by the table. The young man was only 25, so it was quite an accomplishment, of sorts, to be important enough to be housed in this facility. He resembled his father with the same curly hair, but it was jet black. He was clean shaven, and in her previous visits with him, found his smile to be his best attribute.

"Ms. Lowe, it's nice to see you back for a visit," Lashkar said through a wide smile.

Natalie didn't introduce Josh. Psychologically, it was better to keep Lashkar wondering. She sat down opposite the prisoner and said, "It's nice to see you as well. I think this is the third time in the last year."

There was a rattle as Lashkar placed his handcuffed wrists on the table. "As much as I like these visits, I hope you're not going to waste my time by again asking me to reform my ways and work for Five Eyes."

Natalie smiled. "I'm afraid I am, but this time, I have some added enticements."

Rolling his eyes, Lashkar grumbled, "You're wasting your time."

"I thought I would try," Natalie admitted. She closed her document case and looked like she was about to rise when she said, "Can you look out the window please?"

Lashkar was suspicious now. "Why?"

Pointing nonchalantly to the window, Natalie repeated the request. "Humour me."

The smile was gone from Lashkar's face as he rose to his feet. The room was quiet except for the sound of the leg irons dragging across the tiled floor as he shuffled to the window. It was fogged up, so he lifted both hands and wiped the inside of the glass. Through the metal bars on the other side, he saw several cars in the parking lot with the closest being a white Escalade. There was someone in the rear seat, and as he focused, the blood drained from his face.

Lashkar took a deep breath and returned to his seat. "You have my father."

"Your father is a free man right now," Natalie elaborated. He can remain free if you work for me. If you say no, it's only a two-hour drive to take him back to the federal prison, where he'll stay for the next six years."

There was anger in Lashkar's eyes as he hissed, "I won't work for Five Eyes."

Natalie kept her voice calm. "You won't have to. I'm asking you to work for *me*. There's an important investigation for which I need your computer skills. In many ways, it's a personal investigation."

Lashkar hesitated, and Natalie saw this. She added, "Tomorrow, your father could be in India with a 200-thousand-dollar bank account."

"My father has burned his bridges in India. The climate in Argentina would suit him better, along with 700-thousand-dollars."

Natalie knew she had him. "Buenos Aires and 500-thousand-dollars."

Lashkar let out a deep exhale. He was doing this for his father more than for his freedom. He looked at Josh and then Natalie. "I'll do it."

Chapter 15: The Credit Card Map

The guards at the Five Eyes prison couldn't have liked Lashkar very much. After being processed, the young man was given the clothes he came in with. The black cargo pants and blue t-shirt hadn't been washed during his 12-month incarceration. Natalie got a better idea of Lashkar's mindset as she saw the white letters, spelling out, *Screw You!* across the front of it. His running shoe footwear was not appropriate for the elements outside, but at least one of the guards brought him a thick, brown jacket.

The older military officer was waiting by the heavy, metal door. When the guard pulled it open, the older supervisor gave a nonchalant salute. "Adios," he said through the smirk on his face.

Natalie and Lashkar headed straight for the Escalade where Josh, who came out earlier, and Lashkar's father, waited. Josh had unlocked Subash's handcuffs, so when Lashkar entered the rear door, they locked in a tearful hug until the vehicle left the outer perimeter of the Five Eyes prison.

The father and son finally let go the embrace and chattered back and forth in a language neither Natalie or Josh understood. They had a lot to catch up on, so Natalie didn't interrupt them until they were a good 30 minutes along their approximate 90-minute drive to the Edmonton airport.

Natalie put her hand on top of the seat cushion as she turned to face the pair of men in the back seat. "Lashkar."

Lashkar continued to natter at his father.

"Lashkar!" Natalie yelled.

Both father and son stopped their conversation and turned towards her.

Natalie asked, "Have you told him of our arrangement?"

Nodding, Lashkar replied, "Yes, he knows he'll have 500 thousand dollars at his disposal."

Natalie noticed the wide smile that formed on Lashkar's face when he left the prison, was still there. He seemed genuinely happy and thankful. "Does he know he's going to Argentina?" Natalie questioned.

"He's fine with Argentina. He has several friends who live there. It couldn't be better," Lashkar admitted.

"I'm saying this to both of you now," Natalie said. "I want to make sure we have an understanding of our agreement." She turned her focus to the older man. "Subash, your son has agreed to help us on a mission that's personal to me, so not directly related to intelligence activities. In exchange, both of you have been freed, and you'll be given money and passage to Argentina. However, if your son fails to live up to his end of this bargain, I'll involve every Five Eyes country and make sure you're both back in jail— indefinitely. Do you understand? This is a yes-no answer, so just nod your head up and down, in which case, we continue to a hotel near the airport. If you make any other indication or feel the need to ask a question, we'll just keep going north right back to the federal prison."

There was no hesitation as Subash nodded his chin up and down.

Turning her focus to the younger man, Lashkar stopped the same question before it was asked. "I already gave you my promise when you asked me at the prison."

Natalie stared at Lashkar for a few seconds, contemplating the man. He was a criminal, somewhat of a free spirit and a rebel. She wondered if she could trust him.

It seemed as if Lashkar knew what she was thinking. He clarified, "What you read in your reports is all you know of me. Sure, I've done my share of illegal activities, but these were never done for a vain purpose or for my personal enrichment." He exhaled deeply and his eyes were wide: they were dark, but there was honesty in them. "Although we no longer religiously practice, both my father and I are from a long line of proud Sikhs. That means honour, not to be confused with legality, is important to us, as is our word that we'll do as we have said."

This gave Natalie a new found admiration for the young man. "I'll take both your words on that, and as such, you'll not be handcuffed or locked-in. You'll be given a long rope. Just don't take it for granted since that rope can just as easily be tied into a noose."

Before a response could be made, Natalie turned around and faced the front of the vehicle. They drove another 15 minutes through the generally flat, snow-covered terrain. Josh turned on the headlights since, by now, the day had flown past.

A question came from the back seat. Lashkar asked, "Will you give us a few days together before my father flies out?"

Natalie mumbled as she did some mental calculations. "Today is Monday, and we can't waste a lot of time since we need to get to finding my father." Her voice was louder as she concluded, "You can have tonight and all of tomorrow with your father, but then we'll get him a flight out by lunchtime on Wednesday."

Lashkar thought that no amount of time would be enough, but those thoughts quickly accelerated ahead in time. "When I finish working for you, what happens to me? Can I also go to Argentina?"

"I don't see why not. Your record has been expunged, so certainly, I will not stop you." Then she chuckled. "However, if you make it there, I'm not sure you'll be able to keep out of the kind of trouble that'll land you back in prison."

Thinking it better not to push his luck, Lashkar changed the subject. "I heard you say your father is missing. Is this what you need my help with?"

"It is. He's missing under very dubious circumstances—to the point where people have been following us," Natalie answered.

"Do you have any idea who the people following you are?" The young man continued the questioning.

"It'll take some time to explain, so it's better left for tomorrow." Natalie pointed to the green, roadside sign. "This exit is Airport Road. Go right, and there's a Hampton Inn a couple of kilometres away."

Josh grinned. "I should have assumed we're going to another Hampton."

Lashkar realized those were the first words the driver had spoken since the prison. Lashkar asked, "Who's he?"

"*He* would be Josh. His son is also missing and under the same circumstances we said we would discuss tomorrow," Natalie added before a wide yawn came over her face.

Once at the hotel, Natalie booked two rooms for a week. Josh and Natalie retrieved their baggage, and as they went up in the elevator, Natalie said to the just released convicts, "Tomorrow the two of you can go shopping for clothes, suitcases and whatever else you need. For tonight, you'll need to make do with what you have."

When they arrived at the first of their two rooms, Natalie handed Lashkar the key card. However, when he pulled on it, she held it even tighter. He looked up and saw a stern look on her face—one he would come to know. It was the look of, *I trust you, but only so far. Don't fuck with me.* She released the key and turned to Josh. She said, "I'm exhausted. Let's go to our room."

As Josh opened the door to their adjoining room, they heard Lashkar's door slam closed behind them. When their own door closed, they both had the same thought, but Josh said it. "I haven't kissed you all day." He dropped his duffle bag and roughly pulled her into his arms. Her lips were as needy as his as she pressed into him.

When she pulled her lips away, she had that adolescent grin on her face again. She whispered, "I'm not really that tired." His eyes lit up, but she added, "I'm having a shower first!"

She moved to the king-size bed and began to strip clothes from her, dropping them where she stood. Once naked, she turned, went to the shower and saw Josh was right behind her—and as naked as she was. They set the shower to a very hot setting, but it wasn't as hot as they were by the time they threw themselves onto the large bed, intertwined with each other.

The rooms were fairly thin-walled, so the chatter between Lashkar and his father could be heard in their room—that was if they weren't so engrossed with each other. After quite some time, once they rolled apart, above their heavy breaths, they now heard the chatter from the room next door. They tilted their faces to each other, realizing they both had the same dumb look on their faces.

Natalie burst out laughing before she covered her mouth.

Josh chuckled and admitted, "I sure hope they did not hear us the same way we can hear them."

Their laughter changed to smiles as they cuddled back together, and that's the way they fell asleep.

In the morning, the chatter from the room next door awoke Josh and Natalie. It was early, but Natalie realized Subash and Lashkar wanted to get an early start. After all, this was the last day they would spend together for a long time, and maybe even forever. After a quick shower, Natalie knocked on Lashkar's door, finding the two men waiting and ready to go. Josh joined them in the hallway before they took the elevator downstairs.

Natalie bypassed the hotel buffet as she stated, "Let's get a better breakfast on our way."

Twenty minutes north of the airport, they found a shopping mall. The sign out front boasted a family owned restaurant, and that's where the unlikely group of four found themselves at 9:00 in the morning. The waitress took their order, and while they waited, Lashkar asked, "Can you tell me about the work you need help with?"

Coffees arrived for all four of them. Natalie took a deep drink from the mug before she explained the mysterious circumstances of her father's disappearance. She didn't leave a single detail out, and included the Jeep Rubicon that followed them in Toronto. When she finished, Josh continued the explanation of his son and the similarities to the disappearance of

Natalie's father.

Their food arrived at their table. Between mouthfuls of pancakes, Lashkar said, "I can see why the intelligence community wouldn't readily support your problem. I also see where you think I can help you." Lashkar took another forkful of pancakes before adding, "I sincerely hope I can."

Josh sensed the same feeling Natalie had the day before. Lashkar seemed genuinely thankful for the release of both he and his father. It also seemed to extend to his willingness to help them. Natalie paid for the meal with one of her credit cards, then, she paused as she was about to put it back into her wallet. She smiled at Lashkar and flipped him the card.

Natalie flicked the bangs from her forehead and said to Lashkar, "I don't know how long we'll be together, but I don't plan on following you around the whole time. I'm going to trust your words about honour you stated yesterday, so you and your father can go shopping for what you need by yourself. Josh and I will be in the mall, but we have no plans to follow you around."

"I appreciate that," Lashkar replied. "How will we meet back up?"

Rising to her feet, Natalie offered, "Let's get you a cell phone first, then you two can go off on your own."

It didn't take them long to find several cell phone stores in the mall. Lashkar bought a pay-as-you-go phone similar to Josh's. As they were about to separate, Natalie reminded Lashkar to buy lots of cold weather gear, and both of them would need suitcases.

As Lashkar turned to leave with his father, Natalie called after them. "Lashkar, you will need computer gear, won't you?"

"Certainly," the young man responded. "But, it's not what you would think. I just need a good laptop and an external hard drive. If you don't mind, I will buy these items as we shop."

Natalie's brow furrowed since she couldn't understand how a basic laptop would support the systems she expected Lashkar to hack into, but again, she knew she needed to trust the man. "Go for it. Whatever you need."

For the next several hours, Josh and Natalie wandered around the mall. They bought a few more items of clothing. They had a light lunch in the same restaurant they visited in the morning, then they wandered the mall a bit more. When 1:00 in the afternoon came and went, Natalie began to worry. For all she knew, Lashkar and his father could be on a plane halfway to Argentina right now. She was relieved when her phone rang just before

2:00 p.m., and Lashkar told her they were waiting by the cell phone store.

As they sighted Lashkar and Subash sitting on a bench, they had numerous bags, a duffle bag and a suitcase, beside them. Lashkar handed the credit card back to Natalie before they all grabbed a few bags, and headed towards the Escalade in the parking lot. When they exited the mall doors, they saw a heavy snow was falling. They ran to the vehicle and hopped in before Josh roared the engine to life. Finally, they retraced their path down the highway, back to the hotel.

Once they were in the reception area of the hotel, Natalie, in a hushed voice, said to the two men, "This'll be your last evening together, so we'll leave you alone. There are several good restaurants within walking distance." She reached into her purse and counted out 200 dollars before handing it to Lashkar. "This should get you a good meal. I'm going to book Subash's flight, and I'll call you later this evening with the details, so have your phone on."

Stepping forward, Subash grasped Natalie's hand and shook it softly. His eyes were moist as he whispered, "Thank you for everything."

Natalie felt awkward. She realized she was helping the two of them, but it was all because she selfishly expected a significant amount of help from Lashkar. She pulled her hand from the old man's and replied, "Of course," and gave the best smile she could, knowing it wasn't altogether sincere.

Once Natalie and Josh were back in their room, Natalie opened the laptop and told him, "I'll be a little while on here. I need to find a flight for Subash.

Josh nodded as he turned on the TV and mindlessly hopped channels the way only men can.

Before Natalie looked for the flight, she logged into the Gmail account she and Philip shared, checking the *Drafts* folder. She was hesitant as she glanced at Josh, still hopping channels as he sat on the bed with his head propped up against the headboard. Her feelings for the man were very strong—admittedly stronger than she ever had for any man. She could tell he cared for her deeply in return. Their relationship was perfect, and she didn't want to ruin it by finding disturbing news in the folder. Her eyes came back to the screen as she re-evaluated that last thought. If Josh was the man she thought he was, then there was nothing to worry about. She pressed the *enter* key and the *Drafts* folder opened. It wasn't a surprise to see a note from Philip. It read,

Natalie

I hope everything is going okay. I checked out the name of the fellow

you are travelling with. All of the details you sent me have been verified. I dug further, and I cannot find anything of interest in his file—good or bad.

How is he connected to your missing father? Is there any news on his whereabouts?

Philip

Natalie was relieved. She felt bad about sending the request about Josh to Philip in the first place, but now, she felt even worse. She had a deep need to go over and kiss him passionately with the thought it would wipe away the deceit she also felt, but that would come after she found a flight for Subash.

That is exactly what she did. The flight was booked, and she rose from the chair and crawled up the bed where Josh had fallen asleep. His eyes pulled open when he felt her straddle him. She leaned down and kissed his smile until his lips parted and they were once again consumed with each other.

When 7:00 in the evening rolled around, Josh said, "I'm hungry. Let's go eat."

Natalie agreed as she hopped off the bed. She had tight jeans on and slipped into a pair of high heels instead of the winter boots she wore the last few days.

Josh gave out a low growl at the sight of her accentuated, slender legs, then offered. "If there's snow, your feet could get wet."

She was already on the way into the bathroom when her hand caught on the door jamb. She pulled her face back out and replied in a sultry voice. "The boots won't work. I want my man to take me somewhere nice."

As Josh heard the door close, he looked stunned. He thought, *she said, "my man."* The smile on his face grew wider, looking sort of silly since he was in the room alone. *Yes, I'm her man.*

When she came out of the bathroom, she had applied her makeup, including bright-pink lipstick. Josh watched as she removed her t-shirt and replaced it with a very low-cut black blouse.

Josh, who had changed into a nice pair of black slacks and a white, button down, long-sleeved shirt, liked her look but still offered, "Isn't the top kind of revealing?"

She walked over to him, looking quite the vixen with her eyes sparkling, and whispered, "Don't worry. These are all yours. I am all yours."

He leaned in and his lips barely brushed hers. They stayed only a breath away. "I hope you know how much I love those words."

Natalie's legs went weak as she leaned against her man. She thought, *Did I really just swoon.* Feeling his arms wrap around her, she knew, as she had forecast, she was in deep trouble with him, but it was the best trouble she ever had in her life, and she only wanted more of it.

They did find a small Italian restaurant with low levels of wall-hung lighting. The tables were in separate alcoves, and they all had white tablecloths. They were directed to a table in a corner that was secluded. It was, in fact, a curved booth in the shape of a horseshoe, and Natalie slid in first. Josh surprised her since he slid right beside her while moving his place setting next to hers.

The waiter asked, "Is this a special occasion?"

Josh replied, "Yes, this is our first-year anniversary."

Natalie had lifted a glass and, as she heard the exaggeration, almost spewed the mouthful of water back into it.

"Oh, Congratulations," the older waiter offered. "We will treat you extra special tonight," he added in his thick accent.

The waiter was not wrong as he provided fantastic service. There was a man with a violin and a woman playing the piano, in a corner of the restaurant. At one point, the waiter whispered in the man's ear, after which he came over to their table, giving the supposed one-year newlyweds a private serenade. Throughout the evening, as they listened to the soft music, or were eating the fine meal, Josh's hand would slide onto Natalie's lap underneath the tablecloth. It slid much higher than it should have, but Natalie didn't object.

At one point, later in the evening, Josh leaned over and whispered in Natalie's ear. "In case I failed to reply properly earlier, you are also my woman."

It was a wonderful evening, but Natalie thought, *would things change tomorrow? Subash will fly to Argentina, and we will need to shift gears with a heavy focus on finding her father and Josh's son.* So, it was with much reservation that Natalie rose from the table at the end of their meal. While in the car on the way back to the hotel, she called Lashkar and told him of her father's flight the following day at 1:00 pm.

The following morning, Natalie stayed at the hotel while Josh drove Lashkar and Subash to the airport. At 2:00 p.m. the two men returned to the hotel. Lashkar followed Josh into their room where Natalie was watching the news from the bed. Josh sat on the edge of the bed while Lashkar took the chair in front of the small desk.

Natalie leaned forward and explained again, "Our last sighting of my father was six days ago via a video surveillance system at a gas bar in Sudbury. We think they're travelling west."

"How did you find him there?" Lashkar asked.

"I hacked into a facial recognition program I no longer have access to," she answered.

"There are several facial recognition programs I can get into. Let me see what I can find." Lashkar rose to his feet before heading to his adjoining room.

Josh said, "Wait. Are you sure you can do that from your laptop?"

Through a laugh, Lashkar said, "Of course not, but the laptop is only for me to communicate with the computer systems I have elsewhere."

Both Josh and Natalie looked confused, so Lashkar elaborated, "I have a somewhat secluded storage locker I rent. In it are several computers and three servers. There's back up power, and I have a student—an apprentice of sorts, who makes sure everything is running properly."

Josh had a new found appreciation for the young man's foresight. He said, "Don't let us hold you back."

Over the next two days, Lashkar didn't leave his laptop. He was interrupted occasionally by Natalie or Josh asking for an update. Most of the time, Lashkar just waved them away, other than the few times he asked them to bring some food. Lashkar binged on the computer, and it wasn't until Friday evening that he knocked on the door of the adjoining room.

Natalie sprung to her feet and opened the door, followed by Lashkar saying, "I have something."

Josh followed Natalie and Lashkar into his room, where Lashkar took his seat in front of the laptop. The young man turned to Natalie and reported, "I went back to the time of the gas station in Sudbury and pulled the credit card transaction for your father's purchase. He's travelling under the name, Edward Ferguson. I also pulled the credit card file and reviewed the application. The address assigned to the card is bogus. I checked, and it's an abandoned farmhouse in southeast Ontario. However, I found it interesting they kept your father's actual birthdate on the card, so he's an older man with a *new* credit card application."

Lashkar turned back to the laptop and hit the spacebar. The screensaver flashed off revealing an unusual map of Canada. "There were little red *X's* at different locations. Two lines of *X's* seemed to go in an east to west direction, while three other lines of *X's* all wound north, towards or through Alberta.

"What does this represent, Lashkar?" Josh asked.

"I got to thinking," Lashkar explained. "Natalie's father's credit card was easy to flag because it was the *first ever* credit card assigned to an Edward Ferguson, aged 78. It's odd and very improbable that anyone aged 78 would be getting their *first* credit card. For whoever abducted your father and arranged his credit card, this was a mistake."

"I'm still not following you," Natalie confessed.

Lashkar continued. "I searched the databases of all the major credit card companies and found 12 other people who have the same odd combination of being over 70 and receiving their *first* credit card ever. The red *X's* are the location of these card usages over the last two months. Your father's card use is included as well as another hit for his card in Winnipeg, two days ago."

"So, he *is* going west!" she blurted.

Lashkar grinned. "Not only west but north." Lashkar pressed a couple of keys on the keyboard and the red *X's* turned into arrows and between them, lines formed.

As Josh watched, the pattern became clear. "They're all going to the same location." He pointed to the screen and asked, "Where is that?"

Zooming in on the spot where all the arrows and red lines converged onto, Natalie saw the point was close to the border between Alberta and British Colombia. She read the name of the town – "Grande Prairie," and muttered "What the fuck's in Grande Prairie?"

Josh and Natalie were stunned at the revelation, until Josh asked, "Was there anything found on my son?"

Lashkar snapped his fingers, "I almost forgot. Yes, his face was caught on a camera in a grocery store in Saint John's Newfoundland."

Josh's eyes opened wide. "Newfoundland!"

Natalie gripped his arm and, in an encouraging tone, said, "He's alive, Josh!"

"What's he doing in Newfoundland?" Josh mumbled.

"I don't know. He didn't use a credit card, but the video shows he was carrying a gun under his jacket," Lashkar elaborated. He spun on the chair and faced Josh and Natalie. "The question is, what do you want to do now?"

After some thought, Natalie said to Josh, "Maybe you should go east and look for your son."

"To Newfoundland? I don't have a lot to go on, and I still think, if we find your father, we can discover more about the whole conspiracy," Josh countered.

"I can't ask you to come with me," Natalie admitted.

Josh asked Lashkar, "How far is it to Grande Prairie?"

After a few keystrokes, Lashkar answered, "It's 450 kilometres so a four to five-hour drive."

Josh grasped Natalie by the shoulders and turned her to face him. "It's only four hours away, and we might find your father! Let's go to Grande Prairie, and if we don't find anything, then I will go to Newfoundland."

Natalie searched Josh's eyes and saw sincerity there. Turning to Lashkar, she indicated, "Get packed. We're going to Grande Prairie."

Josh and Natalie went back to their room to pack and left the adjoining door open. They hadn't been away from Lashkar for more than five minutes, when there was a yell from Lashkar's room. "Come back! Look at this!"

Natalie and Josh rushed back into the room where Lashkar was leaning over the laptop. Natalie asked, "What is it?"

Lashkar pointed to the screen and a smaller map of Alberta. A red dot was in the center of the screen. Lashkar's words came quickly in his excitement. "Your father's credit card was used not a minute ago in a motel right here." Lashkar's finger pointed to the red dot.

Natalie tilted her head and saw the location was slightly northwest of Edmonton. "How far?" she muttered.

Lashkar checked the map function and turned to look at Natalie. "Eighty kilometres! We can be there in an hour."

Chapter 16: The Drone

In the darkness, Logan heard the stark crack of breaking plastic along with the grinding crunch of metal. He instinctively ducked as pieces of the black drone slid down the wall and bounced, before settling into the alley behind the banquet hall. Shaking his head, he realized this had been a mistake that began 17 hours earlier as the team consumed a late breakfast in the kitchen of the safehouse.

Logan and Nick sat opposite to each other while Jack and Emilio sat in the other two chairs surrounding the table. Don was pre-cleaning the dishes before placing them in the dishwasher.

"Where's Roger?" Nick asked.

"He's checking the computer to see if there are any reports from Moscow," Emilio replied.

As it turned out, Emilio wasn't a bad guy at all despite his slick appearance, highlighted by the dark sunglasses riding on his nose, as they were right now.

Nick leaned back in his chair and cursed, "God damn shit! I can't believe the surveillance people in Russia haven't come up with anything on our requests to monitor large purchases of mica and tantalum."

"I'm frustrated as well," Logan confessed. "Does anyone have any other ideas we can follow up on?"

Emilio pushed the glasses up the bridge of his nose as he leaned in. "We've had someone outside the woman's apartment since she left, and she hasn't returned. Should we check her workplace?"

Logan and Nick glared at each other with frowns on their faces, thinking, *why didn't we thing of that?*

The sound of footsteps crashing down the stairs interrupted their thoughts. Roger came running into the kitchen before sliding the last metre. He shook a printout above his head and shouted, "We have a report from Moscow!"

Jolting to his feet, Nick snapped the paper from Roger's fingers. As he read, a smile formed, and the more he read the report, the wider the smile became. "There's been a purchase of 600 pounds of mica in Montreal by a company named *Modern Electric*." He strode towards Logan and dropped the report in front of him. "At least we have something to work from."

Logan tilted his face down as he read each line of the report carefully. Once complete, he raised his gaze and admitted, "This isn't going to help us."

As Nick's face turned red, he retorted, "What do you mean? You said we needed to find a purchase of mica over 500 pounds, and here it is!"

Pounding his finger into the report, Logan hissed, "Right here, it says 500 pounds of *powder* mica was purchased. We are looking for *sheet* mica, which is powder mica compressed with adhesive into large, thick sheets."

"It's the only lead we have," Nick qualified.

"It would be a better use of our resources to check Natalie's work location first. I think that was a good idea Emilio had," Logan offered.

"It won't take long for us to do a drive-by," Emilio indicated. "Where does she work?"

Logan pulled his phone from his holster and searched his files. "It's in a place called Burlington."

"That's only about 45 minutes away." Emilio looked at Don who had finished with the dishes, and said, "You get cleaned up, and we'll leave in five minutes."

Emilio walked to where Logan was sitting, copied the address into his phone and then asked, "What do they do at *Enhanced Solutions*?"

"Customer surveys," Logan responded. "They survey customers about topics affecting sales, then they sell the information to the companies that would be interested."

"That sounds stupid," Don interjected.

Nick placed his hands on his hips and scolded. "Okay, so they do stupid surveys." He stared at Don. "They might ask someone like you, 'what colour underwear do you like?' You tell them blue, and they sell Under Armour that piece of information for millions of dollars. As a result, Under Armour makes blue underwear and sells them for hundreds of millions of dollars. That's your capitalist system—right?"

Don was perplexed and blinked rapidly. "I don't care what colour my underwear is."

Nick clapped his hands together before pointing aggressively at the back door. "Then, get the fuck going!"

Don thought it better not to waste time washing up, so he picked his coat off the hanger before leaving the house. Emilio was right behind him, and a few minutes later, they were headed west to Burlington. Nick moved to the living room and turned on the TV while Logan went up to his bedroom. Roger liked watching TV, but suspecting Nick was still moody, he returned to the computer room. The house was quiet until two hours later when Emilio and Don came back from Burlington. They entered the living room, and since both Logan and Roger heard their return, they came down a minute later.

Nick said, "You're back early. What did you find out?"

"The place is curious," Emilio said.

"What the fuck does that mean?" Nick chirped.

"The company is in a large industrial park," Emilio elaborated. "From the road, you don't see much because there are many large trees surrounding it. It's in a park-like setting with a long driveway that's lost to sight once it winds into the trees."

"So far, it does not sound curious," Logan interrupted as he sat down in one of the armchairs.

Emilio raised a finger as he continued. "What also isn't curious for a marketing company, is there's no fence or cameras—so low security. We decided to go up the winding driveway where we found a guardhouse in front of the main building. There were two guards, and they were armed. We could also see three cameras. One pointed at the road, and the other two were pointed down each direction of the heavy, metal, shoulder-high, wrought-iron fence surrounding the building."

"That is curious," Nick now agreed. "Why would a marketing company need such tight security?"

"We told the guards we were looking for *Monochrome Plastics*, a company we saw three buildings down," Emilio explained. "You should have seen how agitated the guards became. They asked for our identification, but we reminded them about our Charter of Rights and told them to screw off. They weren't very happy when we backed up and turned around."

"So, that's all we know. How do we find out more information?" Logan asked.

Everyone was quiet. Emilio looked nervously at his feet when Roger blurted, "We can use the drone!"

All eyes turned to Roger as Emilio explained, "Roger purchased a drone and likes to tinker, so he upgraded it with both night vision cameras and recording cameras."

"Won't the rotors make a lot of noise?" Nick asked.

Roger shook his head from side to side. "Nope. I retrofitted the drone with these high-tech rotors similar to what is used on the stealth helicopters. You can barely hear it!"

So, the men in the room agreed that at 2:00 a.m. they would drive to a location near the industrial park from where they would launch the drone. Since there would only be room for four in the vehicle they would use to transport the drone, they decided Don and Jack would stay behind. The rest would try and get some sleep to prepare for the middle-of-the-night mission.

When they returned to the kitchen well after midnight, Roger carried a laptop and an iPad with him. He explained these were required to control the drone. Once 1:30 a.m. rolled around, Emilio went outside to bring the black pick-up to the back door. When Roger, Logan and Nick heard the honk of the horn indicating Emilio was waiting, they went outside to see him sitting high up in the Dodge two-ton, quad-cab pick-up. The night was exceptionally cold, and even in their warm jackets, the chill went into their bones, so it didn't take any extra urging for Logan and Roger to quickly slide into the backseat area, while Nick climbed up onto the front, passenger seat.

Once Nick closed the pick-up door, Emilio put the vehicle in gear, and they were on their way. Forty-five minutes later, Emilio was cruising slowly down one of Burlington's main roads about two kilometres from the industrial park. He was looking for a location for the launch, and when he saw the dark banquet hall, he decided it would work well. As he turned into the front parking lot, he turned off the lights and continued to the parking lot extension, curling around the back of the two-story-high building.

Once Emilio was certain the vehicle was well concealed between the building and the brick wall running around the perimeter of the grounds, the four men jumped out of the vehicle. Roger went directly to the back of the truck and opened the liftgate. There was a tarp, stretched tightly over the pick-up box, and Emilio pulled the two loops off the hooks on the left-hand side. He threw the tarp across the pick-up, revealing the dark-black drone in the bed.

Logan peered in, seeing the large drone taking up most of the bed and commented, "That's a lot bigger than I thought it would be."

With the aid of Nick, Roger pulled the drone from the bed and placed it on the ground beside the right-side of the vehicle. Roger snatched up the laptop and spun around to sit on the edge of the rear bench seat. With the door open, he had a good view of the drone, and he said to Nick, "There's a switch on the right side of the machine. Can you turn it to the *active* position?"

Finding it easily enough, Nick flicked it to the requested position before jumping out of the way. Roger reached around and snatched up the iPad. His fingers danced across it until a map of the area they were in was on the screen. He extended it towards Logan. "I need you to hold this in front of me."

Logan pulled the zipper for his coat higher and pulled his gloves on as well, realizing he would be in the elements for a while. He grasped the iPad and leaned against the quarter panel while holding the iPad where he and Roger could both see the screen.

Roger returned his focus to the laptop, and a few seconds later, he had a screen open with four black, square windows across the top. There were also a series of icons across the bottom with a red one on the left side. Roger pushed it, and the icon turned green while, at the same time, there was an electrical buzz from the drone. Roger looked around him and then asked Emilio, "There's a controller in the truck bed. Can you get it for me?"

Emilio found it and handed it to Roger who held the complicated-looking controller above the laptop. There was a four-way toggle switch that could interchange the live night camera between any of the four mounted on the drone. Between his manipulations on the joystick and the laptop, the four screens on the laptop lit up, filled with a view from each camera, one being on each side of the drone.

Pressing a second icon, the four rotors came to life. Logan was impressed as the rotors really were very quiet. Roger told everyone to stand clear as he pushed a lever on the controller forward, resulting in the large drone lifting three metres in the air. Logan looked at the screen where he could see the night vision was very effective.

The drone flew straight up until it altogether disappeared in the darkness. Roger focused intently on the laptop screen as he controlled a joystick, propelling the drone towards the industrial park. A small scale on the left side of the screen showed the altitude while a red, moving dot had appeared on the iPad map. As Roger pressed the lever to full power, the red dot was moving towards a blue dot, representing the Enhanced Solutions building.

The drone was flying at a 50-metre altitude, and there were two apartment buildings between it and their target, Roger easily manoeuvred the drone around them. It only took a couple of minutes for the drone to be over the industrial park, where Roger slowed the drone and dropped it to an altitude of 35 metres. He inched it closer until a fuzzy image of the Enhanced

Solutions building could be seen with the night vision. Lowering the altitude even further, he was skirting the drone between the branches of different trees, while it skimmed overtop of the shorter ones. At the last line of trees, Roger lowered the drone into a gap between two tall oak trees, ten metres above the ground.

Nick had moved into the back-seat area to peer over Roger's shoulder. He said, "What's that black object on the wall?"

Roger adjusted a setting and the front night vision camera zoomed in on the black box.

Nick squinted his eyes as the highly magnified image came into focus. "That's a very sophisticated motion sensor!" he exclaimed. "Why would they have a motion sensor?"

Roger expertly manoeuvred the drone around the building from one hiding spot to another. They found two motion sensors and two cameras on each side of the building. The mystery of why such high security was needed, was growing.

Nick asked, "Can you move the drone over the roof?"

"Sure, "Roger replied. "I'll have to go high to avoid the motion sensors, then come down directly on top."

Slapping him on the shoulder, Nick insisted, "Go for it."

Roger directed the drone straight up to 50 metres, then shot the machine across the distance to a hovering position above the center of the roof. He had all four cameras pointed down as the drone slowly lowered. At 40 metres, they could make out shapes on the roof, and at 30 metres, they could see a fenced off area with metal crates in it.

As the drone hit 20 metres, the image from all four cameras went bright-white.

Logan asked, "What happened? Did it break?"

Even though it was cold, a few beads of sweat appeared on Roger's brow. He hissed, "We've been made!" His fingers shook as he pushed the drone back up to 50 metres, but the white light followed. Even as he drove the drone horizontally at high speed, the light stayed with the drone. It was only when he dove the drone down towards the trees that the light could not keep up. Thankfully, Roger could now see where the drone was going, and the rear camera showed the bright, thin beam of light from the rooftop, trying to catch up with them.

Roger flew the drone at full speed between the branches, leaving the light behind, and when the drone zipped out of the trees, Roger maneuvered the drone around the apartments. It was fortunate indeed, seeing Roger's expert flying skills, that he spent a lot of time honing his aerobatic skills. It was also unfortunate he didn't spend as much time practicing landing procedures.

The recounting of the evening flashed through Logan's mind in the time it took for all the drone pieces to come to rest on the pavement after crashing into the back wall of the banquet hall.

Emilio started to pick up pieces and throw them in the back of the pick-up. He cried, "Help me gather the evidence!"

Roger's eyes were wide in shock, and he didn't move. Nick went to help as Logan shook his head while he entered the rear seat compartment beside Roger. With all the larger pieces returned to the bed, and the tarp secured overtop of it, they sped out of the banquet hall's parking lot and headed back to their safe house.

That was a waste," Emilio concluded.

"Not at all," Nick replied.

Even with Emilio wearing his sunglasses in the middle of the night, Nick could read the confusion on Emilio's face. Nick turned and asked Roger, "Something detected the drone. What could that be?"

Roger was still stunned by the accident to his pride and joy. He muttered, "Radar."

Nick had a smug grin on his face. "Obviously, a marketing company has no need for upward sensing radar." He slapped Emilio on the shoulder. "What buildings would need such radar?"

Emilio thought for a few seconds before responding. "Well, I can think of two—military or intelligence operations."

Snapping his fingers, Nick announced, "Exactly! However, a military building would have no need to hide. They would have a sign out front indicating it was a military facility."

"Then, *Enhanced Solutions* is actually an intelligence operation?" Logan suggested.

"Most certainly. Likely it's a CSIS or CSE operation—that's the Canadian version of fucking sneaky bastard spy people!" Nick said in an inflammatory, berating tone.

"You mean—like us," Logan coyly offered.

Nick uttered an indistinguishable response. Other than that, the remainder of their drive back to the house was a quiet one. Once in the rear parking area of the house, Roger and Emilio pulled the scraps of drone from the bed of the truck while both Logan and Nick realized how sleepy they were.

After the night of the drone, three more uneventful days went by. There was surveillance on the *Enhanced Solutions* building as well as Natalie's condo, but there were no new leads. There were also no new leads on the possible whereabouts of Ms. Lowe and her travelling companion. Finally, on the third day, Roger's stomping footsteps could be heard rushing down the stairs.

"Usually it's feast or famine, but this morning, it's feast, for sure. We have three hits on tantalum!" Roger whooped out the announcement.

Logan and Nick shot up from their seats in the kitchen. Roger strode over to the table and placed the three reports on the laminated surface. Nick and Logan shifted over beside the younger man and peered down at the papers.

Logan ran his finger down the first report and mumbled as he read. "Six hundred pounds of tantalum purchased in Minneapolis, Minnesota." He shifted his finger to the second report. "Nine hundred pounds purchased in Vancouver."

Nick's finger was tracing the lines on the third report. "This purchase is only 500 pounds in a place called Grande Prairie in Alberta."

Logan lifted his face and shifted his gaze from Roger to Emilio who had just entered the room. "Where is Grande Prairie?" Logan asked.

Emilio turned to Roger with a blank look on his face, so Roger shrugged as he looked at Logan. "I just know it's somewhere in Alberta, but there's a North American map on the wall in the computer room."

Nick led the way up, followed by Roger, Logan and Emilio. In the computer room there were wooden tables along three of the walls. On them, spread out, were four computers, a printer and a scanner. The walls were painted white, and as advertised, a large map covered half of one wall. Logan had brought the reports with him and tacked one report just under the city of Minneapolis, almost centrally located in America between the Pacific and Atlantic oceans, and a little over 600 kilometres south of the Canadian border.

The second report was tacked just under Vancouver, on the west coast of British Columbia. Logan held the third report as he searched the province of Alberta. Nick saw Logan having difficulty, so he joined him in the search.

After a minute, Nick said, "Here it is. It must be a small place because the letters on the map are tiny."

"How small is it?" Logan questioned.

"Roger!" Nick yelled out.

Already at the computer, Roger typed in, *Grande Prairie*. The screen advanced and Roger answered, "Grande Prairie has a population of 70 thousand people. It's small."

"How about Vancouver and Minneapolis?" Logan continued the questions.

Roger's fingers rattled over the keyboard, and, after a few seconds, he answered, "There are 2.5 million people in Vancouver and Minneapolis has a population of 440 thousand."

Clapping his hands together, Nick said, "Two of us can go to Vancouver and two to Minneapolis."

"Not so fast," Logan mumbled as he rubbed his chin.

Nick hesitated with his hands frozen, still in an *about-to-clap* position. "You can't seriously be thinking of going to this—Grande Prairie? It's a nothing place. Roger, what do people do there?"

Roger's fingers tapped across the keyboard, and he read from the screen. "There's some nearby forestry, and some of the people work further away at mines. It looks like some workers travel seasonally to oil sand mines."

Turning to Logan, Nick insisted, "We need to split up and go to Vancouver and Minneapolis. Roger has just verified there's nothing in Grande Prairie."

Logan blurted. "That's just it. You're looking at this the wrong way. You see, you're right that there is nothing in the little Alberta town, so why would anyone there be buying 500 pounds of tantalum?"

Nick opened his mouth to respond, but his mind stopped him from saying something stupid. He thought it was indeed odd for someone there to need a vast quantity of a rare metal. His indecision was interrupted by a beeping tone.

Logan pulled his phone from its holster and said to the group, "I'll be back." He walked out to the far end of the hallway. His voice was muted, so those in the room couldn't discern what he was saying. He was gone for five minutes, but when he returned, he only poked his head into the room. He pointed at Nick and said, "Let's go for a smoke outside."

Nick's eyebrows lowered with his confusion since Logan knew he didn't smoke. Then he shook his head as the realization came, Logan didn't smoke either. Finally, he understood Logan wanted to speak with him without the possibility of being overheard.

After retrieving their coats off the hangers in the mud room, they moved to a quiet spot outside beside the garage. Nick asked, "What's up?"

"I need to explain something to you," Logan confessed.

Rolling his eyes, Nick quipped, "I can see it coming—another piece of important information left out, but now you need something from me."

"Almost," Logan admitted. "However, I don't need anything from you, but I do have some added information that will end the debate we were having upstairs." Nick opened his mouth, but Logan waved him off. "I am sure it's not a surprise if I tell you I'm not the only Korian agent working on stopping the Sholites." Nick leaned against the siding of the garage, remaining silent, allowing Logan to finish. "There are several other agents around your world following leads. One of our agents in America has been tracking another group of awakened, missing people there. However, his tact is different since he has planted a spy in the group. It is difficult for the spy to contact him as none in the group are allowed phones, so the spy must use a calling card from a land line when he can sneak away for a few minutes."

"I take it he was able to find a few minutes just now."

"Yes," Logan answered in a low voice. "The spy called my fellow Korian agent, who just relayed some information to me. The spy is in Calgary, and from there, they are heading north."

"Where the fuck is Calgary?" Nick uttered. "Geography wasn't my best subject in spy school."

Logan slapped his comrade on the shoulder and smiled. "Let's have another look at the map."

The two men retraced their steps back up to the office. They didn't have to search for long as the name, *Calgary*, was in bold letters 700 kilometres south of Grande Prairie. Nick noted the indication of a major airport in Calgary, and then he traced his finger north towards Grande Prairie until he paused at the major airport located in Edmonton. He visually followed the remainder of the highway to Grande Prairie, but there were no more major airports.

Nick turned and gave direction to Emilio. "Logan and I will be travelling later today. Book us on the next flight to Edmonton."

Chapter 17: The Gunfight

With the news of Natalie's father's location only an hour away, Natalie, Josh and Lashkar packed and were on the road in record time. It had been dark for some time, but it didn't feel as cold as the day before. The slightly warmer temperature made the roads a mess, covered with a thin layer of snow, salt and sand—what the people of Canada, in a strange but loving endearment, call slush.

Nevertheless, Josh was driving the Escalade at a fast pace, skirting the populated areas of Edmonton. The course took them through localized forests and then plots of farmland. The pattern would repeat as they zigzagged west and north along the smaller highways towards the junction of highways 16 and 43. Once they turned north onto highway 43, Natalie adjusted the navigation system and stated, "Keep your eyes on the right side. There should be a Fas Gas station and a small motel right behind it, called the *South Onoway Inn.*

It was Lashkar who saw it first. Just above the trees, a neon sign showed the words, *Gas and Lodging.* He pointed, and Josh took his foot off the gas for the turn onto the service road. The driveway for the gas bar and motel was 100 metres further down. Josh took the turn and drove the Escalade through the trees where they came across the gas bar first. They continued slowly past it on the driveway, between a few more snow-covered trees, finally coming out onto a small two-story motel.

Natalie saw there were no vehicles out front, but she could see the edge of a van parked in the back. Advising caution, she directed Josh to park their vehicle in the back lot as well.

Natalie's excitement was pushing her fast. As she was about to jump out of the vehicle, Josh grasped her hand and suggested, "Take a deep breath, Natalie. Remember, someone in the motel took your father, so we need to be careful. Do you have your sidearm on you?"

Natalie was thankful for the words of reason. She replied, "Yes."

Josh released her hand as he said, "Me too."

They, along with Lashkar, exited the vehicle towards the double-glass front doors of the motel. Josh went in first, seeing a reception counter in front of them, and off to the right, was a sign that read, *Restaurant – This*

Way.

As Natalie followed Josh and Lashkar into the cramped entry area, an overweight, middle-aged man came from a back room behind the counter, and a wide smile formed. "Hi folks! Are you looking for rooms?"

Natalie smiled back and replied, "No, but we're hungry, so we'll visit your restaurant."

The man's smile faded slightly as he pointed to the sign. "If there's anything else you need, let me know."

Natalie led the way down the short hallway to the restaurant. It looked like it was still in the '70s with beige floor tiles and light blue wallpaper. The room was small as far as restaurants go, but likely appropriate for how many customers would normally visit. There was a long picture window facing out to the front parking lot, where a cantilevered roof covered the entry area for protected drop off and pick up of customers. There were four wide, brick-covered posts supporting the extended roof at the far side, and at it's base were several long, metre high, stone-faced flower boxes, presently filled with snow.

There were two tables in the middle of the restaurant, and along the back wall were four booths. The bench seats for each booth were dark-blue vinyl, matching the colour of the chairs around the tables. The tables were empty, in contrast to the booths, where three of them were filled with patrons. They seemed jovial enough with lots of discussion and laughter.

Natalie's hand came up to Josh's chest for support as she saw a group of older men in the far booth. A white-haired man in a grey shirt was in the middle of telling a story with his hands describing as much as his words. He seemed oblivious, but the others in the booths noticed the newcomers, until only the older man was speaking. Finally, he also noticed the quiet around him and looked over at the three newcomers by the entrance. The man with the grey shirt formed a wide smile on his face as he rose to his feet. Natalie's father raised a hand in the air and waved as he said, "Wow! Natalie—what a great surprise!"

Logan looked out the small window of the Boeing 737 and saw only darkness below them. He turned and asked Nick, "How much further to Edmonton?"

As Nick pulled his phone from its holster, the stewardess's voice came over the intercom. "We will be landing momentarily. Please put your tray in the locked position, and lift your seats to the upright position."

Putting his phone away, Nick said, "There you go. We'll be on the ground in 15 minutes."

The plane's rear wheels hit once and there was a slight bounce, but the second touch was perfect, allowing the front wheel to come down just before they heard the reverse thrusters come into play.

Nick and Logan had been on the plane for over four hours, so once they deboarded, they both switched their phones from airplane mode to regular service. Both their phones began to beep with the messages that were on hold during the flight. They stepped to the side of the wide airport aisle and checked.

Nick had one email and, after reading it, turned to his partner and said, "Okay—my operatives from Calgary are in town. Three of them are in a local hotel, and the fourth is outside waiting for us."

Logan looked at Nick with wide eyes, and his words were quick. Both indicating urgency. He grasped Nick's shoulder in a tight clench and uttered, "We need to leave quickly! The Lowe woman's father is only an hour away!"

They both headed for the far end of the terminal at a fast pace. Once they were at the baggage claim area, Logan urged, "We have no time. We'll come back for the luggage."

Nick agreed and kept walking towards the exit. "What was the message, exactly?"

Logan replied, "The Korian operative who has the spy, relayed the spy contacted him 45 minutes ago. They are at a motel northwest of the airport. Their group has merged with a second group and Adrian is with them!"

Between deep breaths, Nick asked, "Who's Adrian?"

"He is the leader of the Sholites," Logan quickly answered.

They were almost at the end of the terminal wing, where they saw four lines of departing passengers ahead of them. As each passenger was scrutinized by a security officer, many were passed through with only a random few stopped for questions. Luck was not with them as the security guard held his hand out in front of the two men.

The guard asked, "Where are you coming from?"

Nick answered, "Toronto."

Tilting his head first one way, then the other, the guard said, "Where's your bags?"

Nick was getting frustrated with the delay, as could be seen by his frown.

"We received an urgent call and have to leave right away. We'll come back for our bags later."

There was a chuckle from the guard. "Maybe if you were in Toronto, but that's not the way it works in Edmonton. Bags can't be left unattended, so best you go back and get them."

Logan blurted, "You have to be fucking kidding!"

The guard looked around the pair of men and demanded, "Please get out of the line, so the people behind you can pass."

Nick continued to protest, but the guard just ignored him. They left the line and were walking back to the baggage area when Nick said, "We can't wait. I'm going to send my team there."

"Tell your men to capture Adrian if they can, but if that is difficult, kill him," Logan clarified. "All the people travelling with Adrian need to be killed as well," he added as his eyes turned to narrow slits.

Nick had already keyed in the phone number of his operative waiting out front of the airport. As it rang, he said to Logan, "Show me the GPS location of the motel." Once the operative answered the call, Nick told him to send the three men at the hotel by the airport, to the motel. He read off the coordinates and gave him the mission direction, word for word as Logan told him. Hanging up the phone, Nick said, "That's set. Let's get our bags, and we'll be right behind them."

When Natalie saw her father alive and very healthy, her eyes filled with tears. She rushed across to him, and he met her halfway across the room, where her arms embraced him. At first, there were no words, but by now, the tears were streaming down her face to join the tears that were coming from her father's eyes. They embraced for some time before Natalie made a space between them.

Natalie sniffed and wiped her cheeks before she began to blurt out question after question. "What's going on, Dad? Why did you leave the retirement home? Why on Earth are you here in Edmonton?" Her eyes began to well up again. "I can't believe you are doing so well. How is this possible?"

"Is everything okay, Edward?" The gentle voice came from beside Natalie.

Natalie turned her face to the source and saw a lanky man of about 50 years old. He was handsome, with a slightly protruding chin, light-blue eyes and very light-blonde hair. It looked almost platinum in short, tight curls.

Natalie frowned and said, "Are you the man who kidnapped my father?"

Edward put one hand on his daughter's shoulder and the other on the blonde man's. "It's okay Natalie. This is my friend, Adrian." Turning to him, he said, "This is my daughter, Natalie."

"I don't care," Natalie uttered. She gave Adrian a suspicious stare, then turned to her father. "We need to leave here—*now*."

Adrian said to Edward, "It's great your daughter and her friends are here. I'll leave you to catch up on things, and you can explain to her why we're here."

Adrian moved to a table occupied by four young men. As Natalie and her father sat down, he turned to the young men and whispered, "I'm not sure how she found us, but they might have been followed. Be on high alert. It's also best you go back to the van and get your weapons."

After warning them, Adrian moved back to his table and sat down. He pulled out his cell phone and keyed in a number. After the call was answered, he whispered, "We might need backup, so make your way here." He hung up the call, then downed the remainder of his beer.

After Natalie sat down at one of the tables in the center of the room, she motioned for Josh and Lashkar to join them. Only very quick introductions were made since Natalie had so many questions. She reached across and held her father's hand, whispering, "Is everything okay, Dad?"

Edward softly tapped his other hand on top of his daughter's. "Everything's fine. I'm here of my own free will, and Adrian is a good man and my friend."

Her eyes began to tear up again as she asked, "How can you be so healthy?"

Edward did look very well and not a day over 60. A smile crossed his face before he admitted, "It's wonderful. Physically, I feel like I could run a marathon. Mentally, I feel as sharp as I was in my prime. All this is because of Adrian."

The four at the central table were so engrossed in their conversation they didn't notice the new locations of the four young men sent for weapons. Three were in heavy coats out front of the motel entrance, and the fourth was at the entrance to the restaurant. Everyone else in the restaurant had returned to their discussions until the waitress came into the main room.

She held up her cell phone and asked, "Does anyone else have reception? I don't seem to have any bars?"

A woman in one of the booths checked her phone and said, "I have nothing."

The young man by the entrance to the restaurant pulled out his phone and checked, as did Adrian. Adrian had zero bars, and when he looked at the young man, he could tell by the look on his face, he also didn't have a signal. Adrian rushed over to the entrance and whispered to the young man, "We're in trouble. Tell the others to be ready."

Nick was pissed. "I can't believe how fucking long it takes to get a few bags off the plane and onto that ramp." He pointed aggressively at the multitude of suitcases going around the baggage carousel, none of which were theirs.

Since Nick made the call to his operative, a good thirty minutes had gone by. It took another ten minutes before they saw their bags finally pop out of the chute. They quickly pulled them off and made a hasty exit from the airport under the sarcastic gaze of the security guard.

Their driver had been making loops around the pick-up area, so Nick and Logan had to wait a few more minutes before they were picked up. Once they were in the vehicle with Nick in the front and Logan in the back, Nick checked the time on the car clock, muttering, "We're 45 minutes behind the squad we sent."

Brandon, their driver, asked Nick, "Where are we going?"

Nick gave him the location of the motel and emphasized, "We need to get there fast. Do you have weapons in the car?"

The vehicle was a new, gold Subaru SUV. "I have some handguns in the back," Brandon replied.

As the vehicle left the pick-up area, Nick informed Brandon, "I hope you're ready for some action. Once we're off airport property, pull over so we can get the guns. We're going to need them."

Adrian stayed by the entrance to the restaurant with his man, when they heard the sound of tires crunching slush from the driveway. Both men ducked down as a silver pick-up sped into the front parking lot until the brakes were pressed hard, and the vehicle slid to a stop on the thin layer of slush and ice. Three men jumped from the vehicle, two on the far side and one from the passenger seat, who immediately pointed the barrel of the assault rifle at the entrance to the motel.

However, the first shot came from the motel, where one of Adrian's men saw the armed intruders. The man on this side of the pick-up turned and slid down the side of the pickup after the bullet hit the center of his chest. The two men on the other side of the pickup fired their automatic weapons in return. Lowering themselves behind the stone flowerpots in the driveway, Adrian's men returned fire. One of them came up from the cover for a little too long, and a bullet penetrated his forehead.

Adrian saw this and slapped the young man beside him in the shoulder, so he would replace the fallen man. Everyone else in the motel restaurant was flat on the ground except Josh and Natalie who tipped over a table and crouched behind it. They had their handguns drawn as they peeked out. Natalie took a moment to try her phone and still found no bars. Her CSE experience told her the attackers had a signal jammer in the pickup. No help would be coming.

The flurry of gunfire continued. There was the sound of windows breaking from the bullets, and *thuds* as they ricocheted off bricks or bored into wood trim. Adrian was down on one knee, peering out the window. No one paid much attention to the older woman behind him as she walked towards the front window in a bent position.

The woman yelled out, "Adrian!"

Adrian turned and was startled by the woman from his group, pointing a small caliber gun at him from three metres away. His eyes opened wide just before he threw himself to the side. There was a *pop* as the gun was fired and then a *grunt* from Adrian as the bullet hit him in the shoulder.

Turning onto his back, Adrian looked up to see the woman standing above him. The gun was pointed at his head, when she sneered, "You need to die, Sholite."

There was a louder *pop*, and the woman's eyes burst open just as a spittle of blood flew from her mouth. She fell to the ground, dead, and behind her, Adrian saw Natalie with her gun in her hand, still smoking at the barrel.

The gunfire continued outside as Edward and Lashkar rushed forward to help Adrian to a kneeling position. Josh came a second later with one of the tablecloths. He checked the wound and saw it was through and through and didn't appear to be a critical injury. Josh tied the tablecloth around the wounded shoulder, after which Adrian indicated he was okay.

By this time, Natalie took an accounting of the woman who shot Adrian. There was a lot of blood, but Natalie's mouth went slack as she saw it wasn't red. The dead woman's eyes were open, and from her mouth, there was a dribble of *blue* blood, while around her, a pool of *blue* blood was growing.

"What the fuck is that?" she exclaimed.

Adrian's eyes were soft as he said, "Thank you Natalie—truly. We have no time now, but please trust me as your father has. I'll explain everything when we're out of danger."

There was a loud, crunching crash of metal from the parking lot. Natalie thought, *Christ, what could be next.* She dropped to one knee to see out the picture window, the aftermath of a collision. A newly-arrived red vehicle had smashed into the far side of the silver pick-up. Both men on the other side of it were wiped away. A young man and woman jumped out of the red vehicle while Natalie lifted her gun into a menacing position.

Adrian lifted his one useable hand and pulled Natalie's arm down. "It's okay. They're with us."

The woman outside checked the first of the attackers, and he was dead. The second attacker must have still been alive until the bullet from the woman's gun finished him. After that, there was only quiet. Most everyone was in some semblance of shock, but the gunfight was over.

Natalie stood and flicked the bangs from her forehead as Edward helped Adrian to his feet. Adrian looked at his people as they were rising to their feet, and he said in a loud voice, "It's over, but there might be more trouble coming. I want everyone to go to their room and pack. You have five minutes to be back here."

The man and the woman from the red vehicle, as well as the three remaining young men who defended them, came into the restaurant. Adrian showed himself as a true leader, giving everyone direction in a time when most would have been panicked. He pointed to two of his men and asked, "Is Raymond dead?"

One of them nodded his head up and down.

"Put him in the back of one of our van's please. We must take him with us," Adrian directed. He then turned his focus to Natalie. "You and your friends must come with us—please."

"Since my father is not going anywhere without us, of course we're coming with you," Natalie assured him.

Adrian explained, "I know this is new to all of you, but I need your trust until we have a little time for explanations. We have a three-hour drive to a safe location. One of our vehicles is damaged, so we need to use yours for added transportation."

Josh replied, "That won't be a problem. It's a big vehicle."

Adrian's voice went lower as he whispered, "I must insist, since we know the road to our objective, one of my men should drive." He held his hand out to Josh.

Raising one eyebrow, Josh searched Natalie's face until she gave a slight affirmative nod. Josh pulled the vehicle key fob from his pocket and placed it in Adrian's palm.

Fifteen minutes later, three vehicles left the motel. There was a red van in the lead, followed by a blue one. The white Escalade brought up the rear as they turned onto the service road, then north onto the highway.

The temperature had become even more unusually warm, resulting in a thick fog having fallen over the area. Not ten minutes after the taillights of the Escalade were lost in the fog, a gold Subaru SUV turned into the driveway of the motel. They passed the gas bar and saw the red vehicle jammed against the silver pickup. Logan, Nick and Brandon pulled their weapons, exited the Subaru and inched forward. They saw the two dead men beside the accident, and even more carefully, they slowly sidestepped their way to the motel entrance. They saw no one behind the counter, so with their handguns at the ready, they entered the restaurant. There were three people sitting in chairs beside an overturned table, and they jumped in fright when they saw the handguns.

A middle-aged man yelled out, "Not again! Don't kill us!"

"Who are you?" Nick asked.

The man pointed at himself. "My name is Bill. I'm the owner." He had been holding his hands high in the air, but now, slowly, he lowered his hand and pointed at the young woman. "That's Elaine. She's the waitress." He pointed to the other man who wore a small, white hat and a grease-covered apron. "That's Rick. He's the cook."

Nick still held his gun pointed at the trio. "What happened?"

Bill answered. "We tried calling the police, but none of the phones work."

Brandon checked his phone and found zero bars of signal. He turned to Nick and offered, "The crew must have a signal jammer in the pick-up."

"Was there a man called Adrian here?" Logan interrupted.

"Why—yes," Elaine replied. "But he was shot."

Logan's eyes lit up with hope. "Is he dead?"

The woman shook her head from side to side. "No. He was hit in the shoulder, but she's dead." She pointed to the woman on the floor of the restaurant.

Logan and Nick walked over to the body where they saw the woman was lying in a pool of clear, somewhat thick fluid.

Nick leaned towards Logan and whispered, "Is that what I think it is…"

Logan completed the whisper. "Korian blood. She was one of us—our spy."

As Logan strode to the trio of motel people, he glanced at Brandon and said, "Put her in the back of our vehicle. We need to take her with us." As Brandon moved towards the dead woman, Logan glared at the three motel workers. "Where did they go?"

Bill exclaimed, "How would we know? Look at the fog out there."

"I need an accurate accounting of who was with Adrian," Logan added.

Elaine pipped up. "They left in three vehicles. First, there were the original red and blue vans. There were four young men, and one of them was killed. They took him away. There were five older men and the older woman who is now dead."

"You've only described two vehicles," Nick indicated. "What about the third vehicle?"

"I'm not sure of the make, but three more people showed up after dinner in a large, white SUV—two men and a woman, and I overheard the woman was the daughter of one of the older men," the woman explained.

Nick flicked the safety to his gun on and slapped it hard into the holster. "Fuck! That Lowe woman beat us here, and now she has two companions!" He glared at the three employees and said, "Once we leave, you'll find a transmitter in the glovebox of the pick-up outside. Disconnect it, and your phones will work. However, I'm asking nicely for you to wait 20 minutes before you call the police. The second thing I'm going to ask, is for you to tell the story as you told us, except leave out that we were ever here. Also leave out the woman's body we just took out. Understand?"

All three of them nodded their heads fervently up and down.

Before Nick turned around, he reminded them, "Because if you don't abide by these two requirements, we'll come back and kill you and your fucking families." The blood drained from the employees faces as Nick turned to leave.

At the entrance to the restaurant, Nick turned and said, "I know if we go south on the highway, we will get to Edmonton. What's north on the highway?"

Bill, still in shock, in a shaky voice, replied, "The next city is Grande Prairie. It's about a three-hour drive, but in the fog, it could take a lot longer."

As Nick heard, *Grande Prairie*, he smirked, then muttered, "Of course. Why am I not surprised?"

Chapter 18: The Farmhouse

Before Natalie and Josh entered the Escalade for their escape from the *South Onoway Motel*, Adrian kindly requested they remove their handguns. Since Adrian's men were well armed, there was no option but to agree. One of the young men drove Natalie's vehicle with Josh, Natalie and Lashkar in the rear seat area, while Edward sat in the front passenger compartment.

As they drove north through the pea-soup-like fog, Natalie started asking her father many questions. She looked at him and asked, "Do you trust this man, Adrian?"

Edward turned and his face appeared solemn. "Look at me, Natalie. He has given me a new life when my life was nothing. He has asked for my help in return, and although it has been only a week, he seems honourable, so I trust him."

Her father had never been one to make friends easily, so his words of acceptance meant a lot to her. Natalie leaned forward and put her hand on her father's shoulder. "How is your good health possible?"

"I can tell you, as Adrian has told me, he is from an advanced society. They have advanced science and medicine, including injections which have brought a new life to us."

The driver, who they learned was Jake, added, "Adrian is a straight-up guy, and he'll tell you most of the story when we arrive at our destination. I was also in an induced coma in a hospital when Adrian revived and saved me. He has told us bluntly that he has revived us to help him on a crucial mission. Maybe he's using us, but if it means we have a second chance at life, so be it."

As Natalie, Josh and Lashkar's mouths all seemed to open at the same time, to ask the obvious question about a mission, Edward waved his hand, cutting them off. "Enough talk of Adrian and the mission." He focused on his daughter and continued, "Tell me about you, and your new man." His eyes, once barren of emotion, flickered with mischief.

Natalie's face turned pink, and she brushed a stray hair from her forehead. "What do you mean, my man?"

Laughing, Edward prodded playfully as he pointed at the couple. "Even now, look at you and the way you're pressed up against him. I see the way you look at him even over this short time, and it's not half as obvious as the way he looks at you."

Josh grinned. "Mr. Lowe, it's awkward meeting this way, but you are correct. Although we have known each other only a short time, we've become very close."

Turning his gaze to his daughter, Edward said in a soft voice, "Are you happy?"

In an even lower hush, Natalie replied, "Yes, Dad."

The inquisitive look on the older man's face relaxed, highlighted by a wide smile. He said to Josh, "You can call me Edward." His gaze shifted to the other side of the rear seat. "And you, Mr. Lashkar—truly a man of mystery. What of you?"

Lashkar gave an uncomfortable grin. "I'm in an absorbing stage right now."

Laughter filled the Escalade as they continued north, and the further north they went, the fog lessened. Still, the darkness left very little to be seen. Discussion continued, but neither Edward nor Jake would reveal more information about Adrian or the mission. After two hours, the brake lights on the vans ahead of them lit, and all three vehicles pulled over onto the shoulder. One of the young men came from the first van to the rear window where Josh was seated. Josh opened the window and the man handed him three small, black sacks.

"Adrian offers his apologies, but he knows you'll understand. With only having met a couple of hours ago, our mutual trust is not complete. We have 30 minutes left to drive. Please put these sacks over your heads," the man directed.

Natalie's face was strained showing her protest, but when she saw her father give a brief nod, she grasped one of the sacks and pulled it over her head. Josh and Lashkar followed, after which the young man walked back to the first van.

With the loss of her vision, Natalie's other senses were heightened. She sensed the speed of the vehicle, and after ten minutes, she felt the side pressure as they veered along a long, shallow curve. They were now going west. It was only a few minutes later that they almost came to a stop, making a sharp, right turn where they went only five minutes north before they made a second sharp, right turn. Here, she could tell they were on a laneway from the sound the tires made on the mix of slush and gravel. The laneway wound along, and finally, their vehicle was parked.

Jake announced their arrival and said, "You can take off the hoods now."

The first thing the newcomers noticed once they exited the vehicle was the lack of wind. The moon had come out from behind a cloud, revealing their location was surrounded on three sides by thick groves of evergreen trees. The fourth side, to the east, was open, but as far as they could see, there were flat, snow covered fields.

In front of them was a regal house, and Natalie estimated it was a good 100 years old. The huge structure was made of square stones under a black, shingled roof. Surrounding the house was a wrap-around wooden porch, and, on this side, was a wide set of matching stairs. The driveway they were in was plowed, and as their vision followed to the cleared area behind the house, they saw three large barns. These were not old. Rather, the walls and roofs were made of new, sturdy aluminum siding.

Natalie had a keen eye and saw three guards in white snow gear, carrying rifles, at different points around the perimeter of the grounds. A tall woman with long, blonde hair threw open the front door of the house and skipped down the steps. She yelled to Adrian, "You're back!"

As she came closer and saw Adrian's arm in a sling, her tone changed and her bright eyes turned dark. "You're injured. Are you okay?"

"Yes," Adrian replied. "It needs to be properly cleaned, but it'll be fine."

By now, the woman's dark stare had turned to the newcomers. "Who are they?"

"Let's go inside, Rita, and I'll explain," Adrian offered. As he led the small group to the house, a man in a black parka came out and gave his greetings. Adrian said, "Frank, there are some other newcomers by the vans. Please set them up in the barracks." Without another word, Frank headed for the vans to welcome the new arrivals.

Adrian led them into the front foyer of the house which was wide and grand. It was highlighted by a wide, slowly curving stairway up to the second floor. Looking further up, the newcomers could see the stairs continued to a third floor.

Stopping at the bottom of the stairs, Adrian turned to address the group and Natalie in particular. He said, "Thank you again for what you did for me at the motel." He took a moment to explain the events at the motel to Rita and then returned his focus to Natalie. "You made a split-second decision, and seeing me being attacked, you chose to kill someone based on their act of aggression towards another. It tells me a lot about you."

"As thanks, maybe you could answer the many questions we have,"

Natalie requested.

Even through the pain in his shoulder, Adrian managed to smile, and Natalie thought it fit his reassuring, warm appearance. He said, "I don't know if you noticed, but it's well past midnight. I'm exhausted, and my injury needs to be addressed. Unfortunately, I need to delay your answers, but I promise, tomorrow, I'll answer them all." He put his hand on Rita's shoulder and said, "Rita is in charge of electronics and communications, and she's also my second in command. She'll show you to your rooms upstairs, and she'll arrange for your bags to be brought up."

Taking two steps towards what looked like a kitchen through a doorway at the end of the foyer, Adrian stopped and turned. "We are off to a very good start, my new friends, but we need to take precautions. I must apologize in advance because my people will search your bags before we bring them to you. There will also be an armed guard outside your room tonight. You will understand why, tomorrow, when I explain the nature of the critical work we're here to do."

Turning, indicating his words were not open for debate, Adrian shuffled into the kitchen area. Natalie, Edward, Lashkar and Josh were led up to the third floor where Rita pointed to one bedroom and said, "Natalie and Josh in here." Pointing across the hall, she added, "Edward and Lashkar in there."

Josh grasped Natalie's hand and suggested, "You stay with your father tonight. It's been a long time for the two of you." He smiled and said, "I'll stay with Lucky Lashkar!"

Lashkar rolled his eyes and threw himself down on one of the two twin beds in the room. Natalie and her father entered the other room, and both their doors were closed behind them. Josh and Lashkar fell asleep almost immediately. Natalie and her father were afraid to fall asleep, thinking maybe it was a dream, and they would awake alone. As such, they stayed up until the wee hours of the morning before they finally fell asleep.

When they did awake, it was from a loud knock on the door. Through it, a deep voice said, "You slept through breakfast, and you'll miss lunch if you don't get up now!"

Natalie and her father dressed, and along with Josh and Lashkar, fought for use of the bathroom in the hallway. Once they were all washed, the guard led them down through the large kitchen into an even larger dining room. They were famished, so they dove right into the fruit, breads, sandwich meat and cheeses, making up the grand country meal.

It wasn't until they were half done that Josh noticed the empty chair at the head of the table. "Where's Adrian?" he asked.

"His injury repair took a little more time than expected, and he's exhausted," Rita answered. "He gives his apologies, but says he'll be down before dinner to answer your questions."

Edward already knew those answers, but the trio of newcomers were disappointed. They were anxious to understand what they were involved in. After they finished their meal, Rita asked them to stay within the main house. Their guard directed them to a large living room where there was a fire roaring in the stone-faced fireplace.

Edward confessed, "There could be worse places to stay."

Natalie and Josh walked over to one of the large windows and looked out onto the parking area in front of the house. They didn't see it last night, but now, in the light of day, across from them, they saw a second large house. By the many windows, they suspected the wood-frame structure was a barracks. There were no less that 20 windows on the front, and they expected the same would be on the back.

As they watched, they saw many people moving from one building to the other, or around the corner to one of the three large barns. There were a few more vehicles in the parking area than the night before, where a man and woman jumped into a Jeep and sped off out the driveway. Josh concluded, "There's a lot of activity here."

Natalie agreed, and they watched for a few more minutes before joining Lashkar and Edward in comfortable chairs around the fireplace. The time passed slowly, even though there was a lot they discussed, and by the time Rita summoned them, they had a very good knowledge of each other.

It was 4:00 p.m. when Rita led them into the dining room, where a refreshed looking Adrian was seated at the head of the table. When they entered, Adrian took the time to shake each of their hands. He smiled and apologized to each of them for the delay. Introductions were made as there was a new face at the table. Adrian said, "This is Jeremy. He's my head of security."

They all took seats around the great table, and Adrian began. "I know you have questions, but I really need to know more about each of you first." He expected some protests, but there were none, so he asked, "How did you find us?"

Natalie answered, "I didn't find you. I found my father. Lashkar has extensive computer skills—unfortunately misguided computer skills that landed him in jail, until I had him released." She turned to Lashkar and asked him to explain the details.

He did, whereby Adrian and Jeremy had raised eyebrows of admiration.

Natalie was going to continue, when Adrian held his finger in the air. "One moment," he said as he leaned towards Jeremy. "When we're done here, have all the credit cards cancelled. Use new names, and use alternate birth dates that aren't so obvious."

He turned back to Lashkar, "That was quite clever. After we complete our discussion, you and your skills might want to join us."

Lashkar looked perplexed. "Join you at what?"

Ignoring the question, Adrian turned his gaze to Natalie. "How did you get him released from jail?"

Natalie opened her mouth to respond when her father cut her off. "Natalie is with the CSE, a branch of the Canadian security service. She also has superior skills," he proudly offered.

Adrian stared at Natalie for a few seconds. "I don't know much about the CSE, so I'm not sure how you can help us."

Edward answered for his daughter once again. "She has a high security clearance and access to lots of things."

Natalie grasped her father's wrist. "Dad! Enough!"

Adrian gave an honest laugh. "That's too cute," he muttered before turning to Josh. "What about you?"

Josh's hands were on the table, and he intertwined his fingers as he said, "It's a longer story. First, I will tell you I'm an American from New York State. I looked up Natalie, seeking help since my son went missing under the same circumstances as Edward." His jaw set firmly as he asked, "I want to know, where's my son?"

"Quite understandable," Adrian admitted. "Rita, can you bring in the manpower ledger?"

Rita jumped to her feet and left the room. A few minutes later, she returned with a large binder under her arm. As she sat down, Adrian asked Josh, "What's your son's name?"

Josh answered, "Hendrix. Hendrix Harris."

Rita opened the binder and began to flip pages. She scrolled down one page and announced, "Yes. Here he is. We revived him in Saratoga Springs four weeks ago." She lifted her gaze to Josh. "He's on a very important assignment in Greenland."

"Greenland!" Josh blurted as he rose to his feet.

Adrian waved his hand above his head. "Let's slow down." His calming voice was directed at Josh. "Most important, your son is alive and very well. That's more than we can say for the comatose state we found him in. Also know, he's a willing participant in the activities required of him. I can also tell you he'll be back here in two weeks."

Dropping back into the chair, Josh asked, "What activities? What mission? It's your turn to answer the questions."

Adrian rose to his feet and, with his hands behind his back, looked out the window. The sun was setting as he watched the people outside. "The majority of the people you see here are people like you, Edward, and Hendrix—even Jeremy who we have revived. There are 15 of us here, such as myself and Rita, who are *not* from this place."

Lashkar offered, "We didn't think you were from Canada."

Adrian turned, and the sunset framed him in the window opening. "I'm not talking about Canada. I'm saying we're not from this world."

There was an awkward pause until Lashkar burst out laughing. Josh chuckled and Natalie just had a *what-the-fuck* look on her face."

Adrian leaned back and half sat on the dark, wood stained window sill, waiting for the three newcomers to focus their attention back on him. Once they had, he offered. "The woman who was killed in the motel restaurant—you saw her blood was blue. Did you not wonder about that?" There was no response, so Adrian continued. "Natalie, you visited your father often, did you not?"

"Yes, often," she whispered.

"Then, you saw the state he was in. I'm sure the doctors told you he would likely die in the next six months."

She nodded her head up and down.

"You're well educated. Look at your father." Adrian pointed at Edward. "Do you know of any science or medicine on this world that would bring him to the state you see him in now?"

"Well, no," Natalie admitted. "What I see is considered a miracle."

Walking forward, Adrian placed his hand on Edward's shoulder. In a soft tone, he said, "A miracle is just an event we have no understanding of, such as the story I'm about to tell you."

Adrian sat back down in his chair and began. "About 200 light years from here are two inhabited worlds with species similar to humans. In fact, Rita and I are from one of those worlds named, Shol. Physically, we're almost exactly like you. The other world, about 70 million kilometres away from Shol, is called Kor, and their inhabitants are almost the same as you and I, except their blood is blue."

Lashkar interrupted, "You're saying the dead woman at the motel was from Kor?"

"Absolutely. There have been a handful of Sholites and Korians on Earth for some time, preparing for the event. Our intelligence services tell us the Korians have thrown in their lot with the Russians. I fear the other armed agents we saw at the motel were Russians."

A word stuck in Natalie's mind. "What event?"

Adrian shrugged as he frankly said, "A cataclysmic event that will destroy both my world and also yours. Everyone will die unless we complete our mission."

"Wait," Lashkar blurted. "How can a single event destroy our world and yours, 200 light years distant?"

"Let me start at the beginning." Adrian offered. "The two civilizations of Shol and Kor are about three thousand years older than yours. Our ways of life were not much different, first exploring our own worlds until space flight had us exploring our neighbouring planets and their moons. Shol was a planet, and Kor was a large moon in orbit around a huge planet called Talus."

Adrian paused a second to make sure no one was being left behind. "Of course, just as you're in the process of doing, we drained the resources of our planets and ran out of enemies to fight in our internal wars. Kor was much the same, except when they ran out of enemies, they attacked our planet. Our worlds fought for hundreds of years. It was bitter, and many people on both sides died.

There finally came a time when the living conditions on each planet became difficult and a truce was decided, but with terms."

"What terms?" Josh asked.

"As I said, Talus was a huge planet," Adrian elaborated. "Over many millennia, asteroids had collected in a ring around the planet, captured by the gravitational field. There were many, and it was agreed Shol would have the mining rights to those on one side of Talus, and the Korians would have rights to the other. The peace lasted for some time as each planet was able to restock resources.

At the same time, this didn't correct the poor living conditions on our planets. The Korians continued to develop exemplary space ships with more and more efficient propulsion systems. They sent out exploratory ventures to find new inhabitable worlds, but there was no success.

On Shol, we took a different tact. We mined large asteroids, some many kilometres in diameter, for our minerals. However, there were four in particular that had a perfect shape. As we mined, we were actually making massive caverns just under the surface of the asteroids. In secret, we continued the work for over a hundred years, while fitting the asteroids with our advanced, electromagnetic propulsion systems. Finally, over three years, five million Sholites were secretly moved to each of the four asteroid ships, appropriately named, Talus 1, 2, 3 and 4.

The plan was for all four ships to fire up their engines at the same time, and push our way into the opposite corners of our galaxy. However, the nature of the Korians came into play." Adrian laid his palms down flat on the table. "You see, the Sholite's culture is based on progress through logic and reason." Now, one of his hands curled into a fist. "The Korians, on the other hand, firmly believe progress is made through chaos. They had spies who alerted them once our Talus asteroid ships were underway. Their smaller, but faster ships caught up to all four Talus ships, destroying three of them. However, Talus 3 destroyed the attacking Korian ship and made their escape. Now, with the Korians living on or within their half dead planet, they have even more reason to consider us as their mortal enemies. As such, they follow us through the galaxies."

After a few moments, Natalie said, "The story is incredible. Even if it is true, what has any of this to do with us?"

Rising to his feet, Adrian replied, "It's best I show you." He turned to Jeremy and said, "Get Nancy and the two of you meet us in Building 2."

Adrian led the way out of the room, where they all donned coats and boots before going outside. By now, the darkness had overcome the day. Adrian led them around the back of the house and past the first large barn. Natalie noticed a guard outside it, as well as outside the second building as they approached it.

The guard opened the man-door, and Rita led them in before turning on the light. Once they were all inside, they saw a long, wide tube about half a metre in diameter, pointed at the roof. Hearing the door open behind them, Adrian said, "There you are Nancy." He introduced her to the rest of the group as the head of their science group. Adrian then made a request. "Can you please do a targeting for us, Nancy."

Nancy was a brunette with unusual darker skin and even darker eyes. Her nose was long and sharp, giving her a classic movie-star appearance. Of course," she replied before walking to a configuration of desks in the center of the room. She sat herself down in a chair and fired up one of several computers spread over the desks. Adrian waved his arm, urging the rest of them into a position behind Nancy. She pressed a button on the keyboard, and a grinding noise could be heard overhead.

Josh looked up and saw a huge section of the roof sliding sideways above the long, white tube. "It's a telescope!" he blurted.

Adrian chuckled. "You are not wrong."

Nancy rolled her chair across the cement floor to the second computer. Here, she pressed a flurry of buttons, and each time, a motor could be heard, and each time, the telescope moved in one of three directions.

She swivelled her chair around and said, "It's just coming into focus. Give it a few seconds." Then, she pressed the *enter* key on a third computer.

Here, the screen was much larger. It was black with a silver mass in the middle of it. A few seconds later, it focused, and they could see the silver mass was now grey, pockmarked with small areas of black. It could also now be seen as more cylindrical than round. After a few more seconds, they could see the object was slowly rotating along its center axis.

Natalie crossed her arms and asked, "So, what's that?"
Adrian was transfixed on the screen. His eyes were dark and certainly not as calm as they were in the house. "That's an object that passed Mars three weeks ago and is moving at 40 thousand kilometres per hour."

Shrugging, Natalie asked again, "So?"

Adrian pointed at the computer screen. "That's Talus 3. Its navigation motors were damaged in the Korian attack, and now, 200 years later, it's hurtling on a collision course with your Earth. In six weeks, unless we complete our mission, eight million Sholites on Talos 3, along with everyone on your Earth, will die."

Chapter 19: Whitecourt

"Are you sure they went north?" Logan asked.

With one hand on the steering wheel, Nick waved his other hand in the air. "We know they came from the south—at least that's what your fellow operative told you. I don't know why they'd go back to where they came from, and since this road only goes north and south, I'll assume they went north!" he bellowed.

Looking out into the thick fog, Logan lashed back. "You remember what you told me when we were leaving Russia? You told me you were the expert on infiltration, so you would take care of these aspects of the mission." His eyes bored into Nick. "So far you haven't taken care of anything very well."

Since they left the motel, Nick had been on edge. He needed to relax, so he told Brandon to sit in the back seat. He would handle the driving duties. Brandon, now interjected into the discussion. "You guys are on the same side, aren't you?" There was a pause before he continued. "Logan, you should be looking out the window for fresh tire tracks in case they turned off somewhere. Nick, this fog is so thick, if you don't focus on the driving, we're all going to die in a ditch."

It was quiet for several minutes before Nick broke the silence. "I'm sorry, Logan. Three of my operatives were killed at the motel. I take that as my responsibility." Logan's personality was different, and Nick thought, *maybe it's the way people are on Kor.* However, he was learning these quirks Logan had, and he knew, by his silence, Logan accepted Nick's apology.

From the rear seat, Brandon said, "It's three more hours of driving to Grande Prairie. I'm going to get some sleep."

"I've been thinking. I don't think we should go directly to Grande Prairie," Nick suggested.

Logan turned his gaze from the passenger window and the bleak, fog hiding the white, snow-covered fields he knew were beyond it. "What do you mean? We know the purchase of tantalum was in Grande Prairie. Grande Prairie is the only town of note on this highway. Why the hell wouldn't we go there?"

"First, the travellers from the motel are a larger group, most likely joining an even larger one. Grande Prairie is a smaller town, so they'd be very conspicuous. That's something they couldn't afford," Nick explained.

Brandon, sensing another argument about to begin, pried one eye open and added, "There's lots of farmland surrounding Grande Prairie that would be perfect for a larger group to hide out."

Logan turned to Brandon and asked, "What do you propose?"

Rubbing the short whiskers of his beard, he replied, "Let's just keep driving and I'll think of something."

Logan rolled his eyes and opened his mouth, but he was interrupted by Nick. "He's right. We have to come up with another option. The Sholites know we're now very close on their tail. They'll be watching for us, and the first place they'll look will be Grande Prairie."

There was very little discussion for the next hour before Brandon slapped the back of Nick's seat and said, "Turn off here!"

As they drove further north, the temperature lowered, and the fog was only a very thin mist. The green road sign they saw read, *Whitecourt, Next Two Exits*. Twenty metres behind the green sign, was a blue one, and on it were the words, *Flying J, This Exit*.

"I have an idea, but we need to get off here, so we can discuss it," Brandon urged.

"Thank god," Nick muttered. "I need a coffee."

Once they were off the highway, Nick drove directly to the Flying J and parked their vehicle. All three men stretched as soon as they exited and headed for the warmth of the building. It was after 9:00 p.m. but thankfully, the restaurant was open. After finding a quiet table in the corner, all three men ordered coffee and a meal.

After the waitress brought the drinks and food, Brandon leaned in and whispered the plan formulated in his mind. "As I mentioned earlier, there's a lot of farmland around Grande Prairie, but there's no farming being done. The cold weather drives many of the people south at this time of year. Arizona is a preferred spot."

"And?" Nick encouraged Brandon to get to the point.

"And, it's likely there are more than a few farmhouses that are empty." We could *borrow* one for a while."

The waitress had recommended their burgers, and they didn't disappoint. Logan hurried his chewing and after a huge swallow, chirped sarcastically, "So, we'll just go door to door, looking for empty houses, or maybe ask if we can use their home for a covert mission?"

"Yes," Brandon replied, "But not that simply. I can have a panel van painted professionally over the weekend. It'll look like a van from a gas company. We can go to the farmhouses doing inspections, but in reality, we'll be seeking a suitable command post."

"Do you think that'll work?" Nick asked.

"I'm not sure it's a great plan, but it's the only plan we have. I'm in," Logan offered.

Brandon replied, "Okay then—I'll leave first thing in the morning and be back with the van on Monday morning."

Nick thought about Brandon's timing for a few seconds before his eyes opened wide. "You're not leaving us in this shithole for the weekend without a vehicle!"

"Shhh!" Brandon responded. "I saw a Quality Inn across the road when we drove in. You can stay there overnight, and it's within walking distance."

When they finished their meal, they booked three rooms at the hotel and were quickly asleep. Early in the morning, Brandon left without waking his two comrades. He had a lot to do before his scheduled return Monday morning. Nick woke up at 9:00 a.m. and found Logan ready for the day. Logan was just hanging up the phone when he ushered his friend into his room. With little to do in the very small town, Logan suggested they go for a walk before getting a coffee at the Flying J.

Nick chuckled. "Your blue blood handles the cold better than mine, which doesn't make the walk enticing, but I've been sitting on my ass more than doing anything else lately. I'll pick up my gloves on the way out."

The temperature was cold, but there was little wind, and the sun was bright in the sky, making the walk quite pleasant. As they hiked along the side of the road, Nick asked, "Who were you calling?"

Logan's breaths could be seen in the cold air as he answered. "I think we are close to Adrian and his Sholites. I called my operative who was monitoring the spy who was killed at the motel. After giving him shit, I told him to be ready to come to Grande Prairie. I also told him to get seven other Korians to be ready to come with him." They had walked to the end of the main road through the town and now reversed their course. "There was something else," Logan added.

Nick kept quiet, knowing this was where Logan would add some important information, he should have been told long ago.

"It is obvious that the Sholites and Korians have space ships. Although the Sholites are a nasty race, they are ingenious, especially when it comes to electromagnetic energy. Their ships are driven by it, and they have the ability to conceal their ships with it as well."

"You mean like stealth mode?" Nick asked.

Logan grinned. "Much more than stealth. It cloaks their ship so that it is invisible to radar, but also to the human eye."

"No shit! That must make it difficult to find them," Nick offered.

"Yes, it does, but this ability has a weakness," Logan qualified. "You see, when they cloak their vessels with a combination of electromagnetic wavelengths that confuses the human eye, it does the same to their navigation instruments. In other words, just as we cannot see in, they cannot see out."

"That sounds suicidal."

They were almost back at the Flying J when Logan added, "If you think about it, they only need to be cloaked for short periods of time. During that time, if a receiver is on the ground, and they have a transmitter on their ship, they can send a tight band of ultraviolet waves to the receiver. The vessel can follow it much the way your planes, at times, use their instruments only landing systems."

Opening the glass door to the Flying J, Nick said, "It's a nice story, but why is this important?"

Logan pulled the hood off his head and replied, "Because, even though we cannot get through their cloak, we have a device that can track their ultraviolet landing signal. I have asked my operative to deliver one of these devices to us. Once we are seated, I will give you the address so Brandon can pick it up on his way here."

After they were seated in a booth in the restaurant with fresh coffee on the way, Nick asked, "So this device is alien technology?"

"Yes. Does that bother you?"

Nick's hands were still cold, and he rubbed them together. "That doesn't bother me. What does, is not knowing the big picture." He pointed at Logan. "Are the Korians in charge? Are we in charge? I don't know the whole story. Maybe even you don't. We seem to be similar in many ways, and I think that's why I like you. There isn't a lot of room for bullshit. The story you tell of the Sholites having a need to destroy this world is compelling, but in reality, I do what I do because my superiors tell me to do it."

The coffee they ordered arrived. Logan took a deep drink from the mug before stating, "It seems we are both good soldiers then."

The remainder of the day and the Sunday that followed were filled with pure boredom. They walked around the town where they found a hunting store. Perusing its products ate up a bit of time as did the farm equipment showroom. Other than that, they spent some time in their rooms, but made constant trips to the Flying J for a coffee or a meal.

On Sunday, during one of these walks back to the Flying J, the two men were arguing vehemently. Nick poked Logan in the shoulder and yelled, "Look at the symbol on the sign. It is a *J*. You can tell by the lower curl."

Logan grasped Nick by the shoulder and pointed at the same sign. "You idiot! That's not a *J*." Logan saw the symbol differently. Halfway up the leg of the *J*, there was a crossing line, and to him, it looked like airplane wings. "Look at the cross. Its sweptback wings are obvious, as is the plane fuselage it crosses. The *J* is actually a cleverly disguised *Jetliner*."

A horn blasted as a pick-up almost hit them while they crossed the road during their continuing argument.

Nick pressed on. "There's no way that's a tail of an aircraft. It curls like a letter *J*."

By now, they'd been in the restaurant so many times, they had a regular booth they went to. Logan added, "We are agreed then. We will ask the waitress about the name, *Flying J*. Whoever is wrong pays the bill for dinner, and that will be you."

As the waitress cleared the dinner plates, Logan was grumbling, what must have been obscenities, in a language Nick didn't understand. Logan's mutterings continued as he pulled a wad of cash from his pocket and counted out the money for the check.

Nick sat with a smug look on his face and his arms crossed. With his chin, he pointed at the table. "Don't forget the tip. She's nice so 15 per cent, at least."

Through clenched teeth, Logan implored, "How was I to know the founder and owner of the chain of truck stops is named *Jim*. There's too much vanity on your world, when the owner has to make his first name part of the god damn symbol!" he cursed.

Nick raised a finger in the air. "He has every right to name the company after himself, so there you go—*Flying J!*"

By the time they crossed the road to the hotel, they were both laughing at the same, meaningless name they argued about for a couple of hours. They both went to bed, knowing tomorrow their brief respite would be over.

Brandon didn't show in Whitecourt until 10:00 a.m. He knocked on Nick's door, and when it was answered, Brandon was excited. "You have to come and see this van!"

Nick slipped his boots on and knocked on Logan's door where he put on his own boots and followed them out to the parking area. There, parked on an angle to the painted lines, was a shiny, beige Ford transit van. It had double rear doors as well as a sliding side door, and there were no side or back windows. On each side, in large black letters, it read,

Harmon Fuel Inspections

Serving you for 40 years

Beside the lettering, at the rear of the vehicle, was the image of a clean-cut smiling repairman in a ball cap.

Logan said, "I'm beginning to think this might work."

"It's cold. Let's go back inside," Nick urged.

Once back in Nick's room, Brandon explained there was a toolbox in the van along with two tool belts. There were also two sets of orange coveralls, matching a thick, orange winter coat for each of them. Both coats had big, yellow, florescent *X's* on the front and back.

Nick finally realized something was wrong. "There's only two sets of work gear," he noted. "If Logan and I go to Grande Prairie in the van, how are you leaving here?"

"No worries. I have an associate picking me up in two hours. We'll go back and wait for your call in Edmonton," Brandon explained.

Logan interrupted. "I almost forgot. Did you pick up my shipment?"

"Of course. It's in the back of the van," Brandon responded.

Nick looked at Logan. "Let's get into the coveralls and check out of the hotel." He turned to Brandon and said with a smirk, "Come look out the window. See that *J* in the sign across the road. Do you know some people actually think it looks like a jetliner?"

"Enough already!" Logan yelled as he left Nick's room, slamming the door behind them.

It was a sunny day for the drive, although the wind, from the west, had picked up, blowing snow across the road. There was a wide curve they followed until they were travelling due west. The sign right after the long bend told them Grande Prairie was another 100 kilometres ahead.

An hour later, they slowly drove through Grande Prairie. There were very few trees and even fewer tall buildings. It appeared the town was built, in a way, to hunker under the inclement weather that was here much of the year. They decided to drive out the far side of town to begin their search.

Along the way from Whitecourt, they practiced their parts in the deception. Nick would do most of the talking, and Logan would pretend to write notes on the clipboard. Just in case, they both had their handguns in their shoulder holsters under their coats. After leaving the town, they turned north onto a country road and drove slowly while scanning the farmhouses on each side. Some were too close to neighbours while others were too much in the open.

Logan slapped Nick in the shoulder and pointed with his other hand at a red-brick farmhouse, barely visible beyond the trees. "Let's try that place."

Nick steered the van up the winding driveway. After they passed the treeline, Nick pointed and noted, "There's a propane tank just off the right side of the house."

They both exited the van, quickly skipping up the porch steps and rang the bell. A minute later, an older woman answered the door. As she said, "hello," a young boy, no older than three, hugged one of her legs while peering up at the two men.

Nick tipped his hat and said, "Hello, Ma'am. We're with Harmon Fuel Inspection, and we've been contracted by the Alberta government to conduct a random audit of propane users. It'll only take a couple of minutes, if you have time now."

A genuine smile came over the woman's face as she replied, "Of course. Come in and get out of the cold." As she waved them in the front door, she asked," Can I get you two a coffee, or a tea?"

They really wanted the coffee, but coming further in meant they would need to remove their coats and boots. Their guns would be revealed, so Nick said, "Thanks, Ma'am, but we have so many stops to make today, we just don't have time."

The woman leaned down and shooed away the boy. "Go play for a few minutes, Peter."

As the little boy waddled off, Nick asked the woman a few simple questions about the propane tank outside. As she was answering, Logan interrupted, "Ma'am, I'm sorry, but could I use your bathroom?"

The woman stopped, mid-answer, and said, "Sure." She pointed down the long hallway. "You'll find it at the back of the house, just off the kitchen."

As Nick continued the questions, Logan removed his boots and headed down the hallway. Once in the kitchen, he saw a door on the far left, down a short hallway. Seeing the sink on the far side of the door opening, he knew that was the bathroom. Just before the bathroom door, on the right, was another door leading to a rear covered porch. Logan entered the porch area and did a quick inspection. There were a few boxes, but more telling were several pairs of large, men's boots and two heavy winter coats, obviously sized for men.

Having seen enough, Logan retraced his steps into the front hall just as the woman made a comment to Nick. "My husband and son both work at the mill just up the road. They would be the best ones to answer some of your questions."

Behind the woman, Logan emphatically shook his head from side to side. He put his boots back on as Nick replied to the woman. "I think you did just fine answering the questions."

As the woman smiled proudly, Nick tipped his hat once again. They both left and got into the van. Once Nick fired up the vehicle, he summarized what they both saw and heard. "Along with her and the young boy, there are two men living there. That's exactly what we're *not* looking for."

For the remainder of the day, they went to ten more farmhouses with similar results. They didn't find any empty houses nor any seemingly easy targets. The sun had set when they made their way back to Grande Prairie and booked two rooms in a small motel for the night. Rather than raising suspicion, they ordered a pizza and a couple of drinks that sufficed as their dinner.

The next morning, based on their results of the previous day, they decided to leave the holsters in the van and keep their guns in their inside jacket pockets. Their day went in a similar manner, but they did manage coffee and biscuits at two of the farmhouses. Logan thought, *it was a shame someone might get hurt, but their mission was of paramount importance to all of them.*

Although, their bellies weren't empty, their efforts didn't achieve favourable results. Both men were getting very frustrated as they passed a short hill alongside the road. It was unusual since the landscape before this had been very flat. As they came to the end of the hill, Logan saw a barely visible driveway. Turning his head as they went by it, Logan saw two large barns and a large country home behind the hill.

"Stop!" Logan yelled. "There's a house back there we need to check."

Nick hit the brakes hard, and they skidded along the ice-covered road. He put the van in reverse, then turned into the driveway that cleverly wound behind the hill. He continued along behind it, then into a small parking area in front of the house.

The two disguised men strode up the steps, and seeing no bell, they knocked on the door. There was no answer. They knocked again, and Logan took a few steps along the porch, but he couldn't see any lights on in the house. Since there was a good 15 centimetres of snow on the porch, they were both optimistic no one was here.

Nick was about to knock a third time when the door creaked open. A thin man of at least 70 years stood in the doorway, wearing a grey shirt and green farm pants held up with green suspenders.

"Yeah. What do you want?"

Nick gave him the same introduction he'd given many times now, and waited to see the older man's response.

The old man narrowed his eyes and said, "Did you say you're from the government, because if you are, I'm not talking to you."

Nick waved his hand. "No, Sir. We have to give them a final report, but we work for Harmon Inspections."

"I guess that's okay then. You said you had some questions?"

Logan had an idea and interrupted. "We'd like to have a look at your propane tank. If you're not up to it, maybe your son could come out with us."

Frowning, the old man didn't like that Logan thought him not capable. He replied, "My son runs the farm, but he's gone south to Phoenix for the next month. I'll get my boots and coat and show it to you."

The old man pushed over the front door, leaving it open just a crack. Nick and Logan heard him slide on his boots and close the closet door. On the way out, he grabbed his coat from the hook. Pulling the door closed behind him, he said, "This way boys."

They walked, three in line, around the side of the house to the propane tank 20 metres behind it. Logan made the pretense of inspecting it while Nick said to the old man, "I'm surprised your son didn't take you to Arizona with him. You seem to be pretty sharp."

"Oh, I can hold my own. I go for a long walk every day and can do better than most on that *Jeopardy* show," the man answered. His eyes darted instinctively from side to side as he added, "It's my son's bitch wife. I can't stand her, so I love this time every year when I'm all alone, free of her nagging." He gave Nick a friendly nudge and whispered. "She wants to put me in a nursing home."

Nick and the man laughed as Logan rose to his feet. Logan reported, "Everything is looking good here."

Nick winked at Logan and said, "Yes, everything is very good."

The old man grabbed Nick's arm and said, "I have another propane tank beside the barns."

Logan replied, "Let's have a look—what's your name again?"

The man said, "Gord Crozier," before he walked towards the buildings across the field.

There were two barns. The first was made of wood with a heavy timber frame, and the propane tank was beside it. Again, Logan faked an inspection before rising to his feet and announcing all was well. Meanwhile, Nick and Gord had been talking and were becoming fast friends.

Nick asked him, "What's in the barn?"

"Come on. Let me show you." There was a large double-swinging door, and beside it, was a smaller man-door. Gord led the way through it and turned on a bank of overhead lights. He proudly described the farm equipment within and waited for the two visitor's admiration.

Logan pointed and said, "What's on the front of that tractor?"

Gord chuckled. "My son is pretty clever. He Macgyvered a large snow blower unit on the front of the tractor."

"What do you use that for?" Nick asked.

"Why, to clear the airfield," Gord stated.

Both Logan and Nick's eyes lit up, thinking, *this couldn't be getting any better.* "You have planes here?" Nick coyly asked.

Gord headed for the door as he waved his arm forward. "Let me show you."

They were walking across the short distance to the second barn as Gord described the property. "The airstrip is about 40 metres behind the house and runs down the length of this side of the acreage. You see, my son runs a modest cargo transportation business when he's home. Beyond the air strip is the farmland where I grow mainly corn. After that is Bear Lake. We're tucked in a great, secluded spot."

They reached the second barn which, in contrast to the first, was made of aluminum siding. It was also much taller than the first barn, and their curiosity grew as Logan and Nick were led in the man-door. Once the lights were turned on, they were shocked by what they saw. In front of them was a dust-covered, two-engine bush plane with dented panels and a missing door. They realized now the barn was in fact a hanger with two huge sliding doors in front of the neglected plane. As they walked down the length of the hanger, they saw a second set of large hanger doors. What they saw here was even more amazing.

Nick whispered, "Is that a Chinook helicopter?"

Gord smiled proudly. "That it is, and unlike the plane, it works fine, although it's only been flown maybe three times in the past six months. I used to fly it all the time, but my son is a worrywart, so only he takes it up these days."

It was huge with the capability of carrying at least 50 people, but Logan was not so impressed as he chirped, "It looks like an antique."

Gord winked at Nick before directing his response to Logan. "Some things that look old, work just fine."

Nick had his hand inside his coat, and he had an honest smile on his face. He said, "I like you Gord, so please don't take this personally."

"Huh?"

Nick pulled the gun out and pointed it at his new friend. "We need to borrow your farm and the airfield for a few days."

Wide-eyed, Gord slowly lifted his hands in the air. "Oh lordy. I guess you guys aren't from the gas company."

Chapter 20: Grande Prairie

For the next two days after they were shown Talus 3 through the telescope, Natalie, Josh and Lashkar didn't see Adrian. They were given free reign of the compound, and Rita or Jeremy would answer questions when they could, although those times were infrequent with their apparent hectic schedule of activities. The only stipulation given to them was to move together as a group, and in that way, an armed guard was never far from them.

They were shown the barracks where there was a large first-floor mess hall. There were also several bedrooms on this floor, and the second floor was filled with the same. The rooms were nice, but sparse with each having a rustic cottage atmosphere. Edward had been assigned to one of these rooms to share with an electrical engineer who had also been recently revived.

In the afternoon of their next day at the farmhouse compound, Rita showed the trio of newcomers the contents of the first large barn. It was filled with some equipment, but mainly vehicles and a vehicle repair area. There was a bus, a large truck, a plow and several cars, vans and SUV's.

The third barn was revealed next where inside was a very sterile manufacturing area. Natalie, Josh and Lashkar were asked to don lint-free coveralls, hair nets and masks, before they could go into the large, positive pressure room. Here, Natalie counted ten men and women in similar suits who were assembling components into a large polymer-walled box.

The unusual containers reminded Natalie of two nights earlier, when they looked through the telescope and saw Talus 3. At the time, Adrian briefly explained the unsettling disclosure that it was on a collision course with Earth. They didn't let Adrian leave it at that without some answer to the obvious question, "Okay, but what now?" Adrian had an assuring tone in his voice when he told them the Sholites had a plan to correct the situation. After all, that's why they were here.

That satisfied the newcomers for the time, but now, Natalie, suspecting the boxes being manufactured had something to do with the plan Adrian mentioned, asked, "What are they doing?"

Rita replied, "They're assembling what we call electrical storage units, or ESU's. Here, on Earth, they're called capacitors."

Lashkar had been listening with keen interest and blurted, "Those casings are almost two metres high! They must be the largest ESUs ever made."

As they watched, a man with a control pendant was moving an overhead crane hoisting a large square of hard, black material, to a position where he could lower the load into the casing. The block of material was over one-metre square and 150 mm thick.

Lashkar looked on with fascination, and mumbled, "That looks like an insulator."

Rita raised an eyebrow as she looked at Lashkar with more than a little surprise. "I see you're clever," she concluded. "That's a sheet of mica, and yes, we use those as insulators in the ESU. We use similar sheets of tantalum for the conductors." She pointed to a rack holding ten slabs similar to the mica, but these were shiny and silver in colour.

"What type of fluid do you use to cool the ESU?" Lashkar asked.

Close to the far wall of the insulated barn, was a large storage container beside what looked like seven completed ESU's. "In the storage container is a fluid we call sartolin. Before you scratch your heads, it's not found on Earth. Rather, it's created from a mineral we find in certain types of asteroids. The oil you use in your smaller capacitors just wouldn't be able to handle the heat load these will have."

Natalie interjected a question. "What are you using these for?"

Rita replied, "I'll leave Adrian to tell you the answer in more detail. Let it suffice for now that we're making a device to deflect Talus 3, and the ESU's are an integral part of that device."

"Thank god for that," Josh offered.

On their way back to the farmhouse, Rita took them into the second barn housing the telescope. Now, during the daytime, there were 15 more Sholites performing many tasks within the main room. With all the lights on, they could now see there were many more computers along the far wall, they didn't see two nights earlier.

Rita smiled proudly as she said, "What you see are our Sholites working hand in hand with the people of Earth we revived. None of them are held here against their will. They all know the importance of what they're doing."

Nancy, the Sholite who was introduced to them as the head of their science group, walked over to the visitors. After some greetings and pleasantries, Rita offered, "Nancy, Lashkar has shown a keen interest and an even stronger aptitude for the science of what we're doing. He's also, purportedly, one of the best programmers on this planet."

Clapping her hands together, Nancy exclaimed, "For me?"

Through a chuckle, Rita answered to the group, "Nancy always gets so excited when a new recruit is available." She turned to Lashkar. "If you want to work with our science group, I'm sure we could use your help."

That wide smile Natalie and Josh had become familiar with, formed on Lashkar's face. "Would I? Of course!"

As Lashkar and Nancy walked away, jabbering like long-lost friends, Natalie thought, *well, I think we just lost him.* It was probably just as well, since their agreement was Lashkar's release from prison, in return for his help finding Natalie's father. Since they did find Edward, Lashkar's debt was paid.

That evening, their sleeping arrangements changed. Edward was in the barracks while Lashkar was teamed up with one of the Sholite computer experts—a woman. It appeared the Sholites didn't have the same culture as most Earth populations, where new acquaintances of the opposite sex sharing a room would be inappropriate.

This adjustment allowed Josh to move into the same room as Natalie. The first thing they did was push the two twin beds together. They still had unanswered questions, but put those to the back of their minds. After dinner, they both feigned their weariness and went to bed early. They hadn't been intimate for a few days, so when they closed the door to their room, their clothes were quickly stripped from their bodies, and finally they were in each other's arms. Their hunger for each other was renewed and much like their first night together. Josh felt a need to show his claim on his woman—to remind her both, how much he cared for her, and how much he needed for her to be his.

They didn't get to sleep until late, so Natalie had to work to pry her eyes open in the morning when she heard the knock on her door. She wrapped a blanket around her naked body and then pulled the door open a crack.

Adrian was on the other side, with a wide smile, hoping it would hide the embarrassment he felt. "I'm sorry to bother you so early, but I'm going off compound for a few hours and was hoping you could join me."

By now, Josh was behind Natalie, and he pulled the door wider open. He held a pillow over his groin as he looked at Adrian with a frown.

"Josh, I would like to take Natalie into Grande Prairie this morning. I would take you as well, but three of us in one car might draw suspicion. I hope you understand."

"How long will you be?" Josh asked in an aggressive tone.

Natalie turned and put her hand on his chest. "It's okay. Things will be fine."

"If it makes you feel better, Josh, I'll be armed, and I'm giving Natalie her handgun as well." Adrian's blue eyes were warm and his face was apologetic. "I've been told all three of you have been on your best behaviour. It's time we started trusting each other more."

Both Adrian's appearance and his words, made Josh more at ease. He gave a slight nod of agreement Adrian appreciated before Natalie closed the door.

They ate breakfast together in the large dining room in the barracks, before one of Adrian's young soldiers brought a white SUV from the equipment barn to the house. He threw the keys to Adrian, and after Natalie was in the vehicle, they were on their way to Grande Prairie. The 30-minute drive was comfortable since the sun was bright and the sky was cloudless. However, the temperature was frigid, so Natalie hoped they'd not be spending too much time outside.

During the drive, their discussion was light, but mostly it consisted of Adrian asking questions about the compound and what Natalie had seen. She was honest with her answers, but careful since she still had questions of her own to be answered.

Once they reached the Grande Prairie city limits, Adrian made sure not to speed or perform driving manoeuvres that might draw attention to them. They wound their way through town until Adrian guided the SUV into the parking lot of a small restaurant. "Let's get a coffee," he offered.

Needless to say, there were very few fast-food establishments in the town of 70 thousand people. The smaller, family-owned diners, like the one they just entered, were more common. They took a seat by the front window and ordered their coffees."

"I'm confused," Natalie stated. "Why're we here?"

"I've been told you still have some questions, so I'll answer them now."

"But why here?" Natalie pressed.

Tilting his head slightly towards the window, Adrian peered down the road. He muttered, "The reason is coming right now." He straightened his head and said, "Don't turn around, but there's a black pick-up that'll drive by. Tell me what you see."

As Natalie took a drink of coffee, her eyes peeked over the top of the rim and to the left as the vehicle drove by. As it continued slowly down the street, Natalie said, "There are two men in the vehicle."

Adrian smiled, "Let's leave it at that for a moment. Please ask the questions you have been hounding Rita about."

For a moment, Natalie lowered her brow in confusion, but it cleared once the first question came to her mind. "You and Rita have told us you have a plan to stop the collision of Talus 3 into the Earth. What is it?"

"An excellent first question." Adrian put both his hands around the coffee mug to warm them. "Our Sholite science is much more advanced than yours. Don't take that as a slight. You see, our civilization is so much older, so this aspect comes with it. Specifically, we have a vast knowledge and expertise with electromagnetic fields. The machine we're building is a device that'll send a massive electromagnetic pulse from Earth to Talus 3. It'll bump the asteroid-ship ever so slightly, but it'll be just enough to shift its trajectory to avoid the collision."

"Don't you need a really big magnet?" Natalie questioned.

Chuckling, Adrian replied. "We have one, of course. Your planet is a *really big magnet* with a *really big* electromagnetic field. Our device will just focus it into a pulse and give that pulse a direction."

Her jaw was slack, and her mouth was open as she considered the enormity of the science, when a black spot at the end of the road caught her attention. The spot got bigger until Natalie whispered, "I think that black pick-up is coming back."

Adrian shrugged and preferred to take a drink of his coffee rather than provide more information.

After the vehicle drove by, she clarified, "It's the same vehicle with the same two men in it. What're they doing?"

"Probably looking for us," he offered.

Natalie's eyes widened. "Shouldn't we get out of here?"

"Not yet. I'm sure you have more questions." He pulled open the menu lying on the table and mumbled, "Are you hungry? You Canadians love your donuts, and I've fallen into that group." He pointed his finger at the menu. "Look—double chocolate!"

Natalie pushed the menu back down to the table. "Why don't you tell our government or any other government about the collision? They have a vested interest."

"It's a difficult question. Let me ask you, with the nut voted in as American president, would you tell him?"

"Well, no."

"Any other government we tell would be obnoxiously overwhelmed by the Americans, considering the way they have to be in the center of things. How about the Chinese? Would you ask for their help?"

Natalie considered the question and also the recent past of the secretive and still oppressive Chinese government. She shook her head from side to side. "That wouldn't go well, likely causing even greater issues across our world."

Leaning back in his chair, Adrian added, "That leaves only the Russians, and the Korians have thrown their lot in with them." He tilted his head towards the window once again. "Speak of the devil…"

Natalie didn't turn her head, but she saw the same black pick-up with the same two occupants, pass by from the initial direction. She grasped Adrian's wrist across the table. "Okay, tell me, why are they patrolling the street?"

"The Russians are in town," Adrian explained, "along with the Korians. They're close on our heels after the debacle at the motel. They know we're somewhere close by, but we know *exactly* where they are. He boasted, "Sholites are always at least three steps ahead of Korians."

Natalie saw Adrian's face, usually a spectre of calmness, unfold a sinister smile as he mentioned the Korians. However, it was only momentary, and he continued the explanation. "It seems anyone we would contact about the collision would also cause severe panic, first at the confirmation of alien races, then at the thought of their planet being blown into a million pieces of space rock."

The topic was bouncing back and forth, and Natalie was trying to keep up. "Why are the Russians on this specific road?"

With a twitch of his head towards the window, Adrian drew Natalie's attention there. "About four buildings down, on the far side of the road, do you see an electrical shop?"

Natalie squinted and said, "*Jensen Electric.* I see that."

"Nancy, who's in charge of our science team, purchased our basic electrical supplies from that shop. She got to know the owner pretty well— in fact, well enough to come to a business relationship with him. We needed some unusual, and unusually large, supplies for the device we're making. We were paying him well as the middle man to obtain the materials we needed. The Korians have obviously found out and are here in the expectation we'll come back."

Natalie shook her head and said, "This is so much information at once. My brain feels like it's on overload."

Adrian reached across the table, settling his hand on top of hers, and in a soft but still direct voice, said, "It's not easy, but this is a critical time. Unfortunately, this isn't the time for indecision. I need to know, will you work with us knowing this operation must remain secret and also knowing the Korian-Russian alliance will be trying to kill us at every turn? We can surely use your knowledge and skills. What do you say?"

There was a deep breath and an exhale as she looked into Adrian's soft eyes. "I love my country, and this world. I promise to work towards saving the planet with you, but I can't speak for Josh or Lashkar."

A wide, toothy smile crossed Adrian's face as he pulled his phone from his pocket. He pressed a speed dial number and waited for an answer. After a few seconds he said, "Were they asked? What did they say? Both of them?" There was a few more seconds of silence, then he chuckled. "His love for her is obvious. I figured his answer would be as much."

Disconnecting the call, Adrian was satisfied as he relayed what he heard. "Lashkar is an eager member of our team, and honestly, he'll help us immensely. I'm not sure where Josh fits in. He seems very physically capable, so for protection, we can use him. When he was asked to join our team, he said, 'If you were on the team, he was on the team.'"

Their drive back to the farmhouse compound was a quiet one. Natalie was putting together all her thoughts. Even though she pledged herself to the cause, she was very specific with the wording. She pledged to save the planet, not necessarily Talus 3, and she didn't promise to do so under the express direction of Adrian at all times. She left herself an out, if it would become necessary to use it.

There was one thought that came to the forefront of her mind, and she wanted to discuss it with Lashkar and Josh before she confronted Adrian with it. The question that was beginning to smolder in her mind was, *if this huge electromagnetic pulse would be sent from the Earth to nudge Talus 3, what collateral damage would this cause on Earth?*

Chapter 21: Gordie's Place

Nick stood with his arm around the shoulder of Gord Crozier as they looked out from the barn. It was a sunny afternoon, but it was deceiving since the brisk wind was howling across the flat panorama in front of them. Behind them was the remaining farm equipment after the machines that could handle the elements were moved outside. The extra room inside was needed for their vehicles with still more to come to the Crozier farm.

In Russia, Nick had been trained in various methods of coercion and subterfuge. He utilized one of them now as he spoke in a soft, persuasive tone. "Gord, I need to be sure you really understand how important our mission is, and how important you are to it."

Gord had a thick wool coat on with the collar turned up, covering his neck. His head was covered with a hunter style hat with a large bill and fur-covered pads, hanging down over his ears. "You've told me once, so I think I've got it."

Nick gave Gord's shoulder a reassuring shake. "I know we can count on you. If the information about our manpower buildup here was leaked, many of us would die."

"Don't you worry," Gord replied in a squeaky voice. "I can't believe there are Russians out there trying to brainwash good Canadians for their communist purposes. Thank god you Canadian intelligence guys showed up to take care of them."

"That's when we find them," Nick clarified. "I'm sorry we originally deceived you with the gas company uniforms, but we just couldn't be sure how far the Russian infiltration had gone."

"Don't worry. This is the most excitement I've had in a long time," Gord offered through a sly smile.

Nick pulled his gloved hands in front of him and rubbed them together to gain some warmth. "Remember—no phone calls. Don't answer your house phone. You told us you call your son every Wednesday, so that will continue with our coaching. We can't let him know what's going on. The less people who know about our operation, the safer it is for all of us."

"I won't put any of your agents in harms way," Gord confirmed. "For me, everything will be business as usual." He turned his head and gave Nick a reassuring wink.

"Do you think things will go okay with Emma Wilkins?" Nick asked.

"Oh, she'll be fine. Her and I were a thing 60 years ago, but she went off to Calgary for school. That was the end of our relationship, until ten years ago when her husband died. Now, once a month, we go out for dinner and get a room in a Grande Prairie hotel for the night," Gord explained, leaving too much of a visual in Nick's mind.

Nick held back the dry heave and said, "Your next senior citizen date night is in two weeks. Is that correct?" After Gord nodded, Nick continued. "You can't tell her anything about our operation. If the Russians find out about you helping us, and your relationship with her, it is beyond words what they might do to her." Blood drained from Gord's face as Nick added, "Of course we would try and protect her, but often collateral damage is an inevitability we cannot avoid."

Gord's eyes were thin slits as he hissed, "Don't you worry. I won't let those Commie bastards get my girl. My lips are sealed!"

Two SUV's, one red and one black, drove into the cleared area between the house and the barns, while kicking up a spray of snow. Nick said, "Those are the last seven of our Canadian agents. They had a long drive from Vancouver, and I need to greet them." He slapped Gord on the back, and before he walked away, said, "I really appreciate your patriotism. Your country thanks you."

Hearing the words, Gord straightened and clicked his heels together as he watched Nick leave.

Veering left, Nick walked by Brandon, who'd been loitering by the other side of the open barn doors. In a voice loud enough for Brandon to hear him over the wind, but low enough for Gord not to, Nick said, "I'm going to tell the Vancouver comrades to park here in the barn. Don't let the old man out of your sight, and don't let him near a phone." Nick continued across the cleared area, pushing his hands in his pocket as he shook his head. He couldn't seem to clear the unpleasant image of Gord and his girl trying to have sex on a squeaky bed in a seedy hotel.

After a quick greeting for the new arrivals, he jogged to the house, removed his coat and boots, then he headed straight for the fireplace in the living room. He held his palms to the roaring fire and said to Logan, who was sitting on the cozy couch, "Can you gather all your people. The last of the Russian agents are here, so let's get our stories straight with your Korians first."

Fifteen minutes later, when Nick considered Logan and the additional

Korians who arrived in the last two days, he couldn't see anything visibly different about the aliens. After Nick closed the wooden pocket doors of the parlor, Logan began. "Nick and I are co-leading this operation. That means if he gives you an order, you will follow it, just as you would follow mine. Is that understood?"

A mixed chorus of "Yes, Sir," followed and then Nick continued the discussion. "The last of my Russian agents are here. Including me, we have 26 Russian agents, and with Logan, there are eight Korians. I'm the only Russian who knows you're aliens. I'm the only one who knows the danger to the world the Sholites offer. That's the way we're going to keep it."

Some of the Korians looked confused.

"The Russians are goal oriented and don't need a lot of details," Nick elaborated. "If any of the Russians ask about you, say you're from Directorate X."

One of the Korians asked, "What if they press for details?"

Nick chirped, "If they do, tell them you could give them the details, but then you'd have to kill them." After a pause, Nick lifted a finger. "Make sure you laugh after you tell them that."

The confusion on the Korians faces didn't recede, so Logan jumped in. "We've had these types of missions before. Reveal as little information as possible. That keeps it simple."

"We just want to make sure we all have the same direction before we meet with the Russians here in ten minutes," Nick said just before he opened the parlor doors.

Brandon and Gord had also come back to the house, and Nick found them in the kitchen. He whispered to Brandon, "We're having a meeting with everyone in the parlor. I'll update you later because I need you to keep Gord occupied here, well away from the meeting."

Word spread there was a meeting in the parlor. It was a large room, but now there were 26 men and eight women in it, making it feel cramped. The lucky ones took seats as the group faced Logan and Nick at the front of the room.

Since the majority in the room were Russian agents, Nick started. "You all know me, but there are newcomers who just arrived from Vancouver." He pointed to Logan. "This is Logan and he's from Directorate X along with seven of his agents." There was a murmur that went through the group as Nick added, "I'll let Logan speak first about our general goals."

Logan cleared his throat before he said, "There are a group of foreign agents near this location that we need to find. No, I won't tell you which country they are from, because it is not pertinent. What is important is they have their own mission, and if they complete it, Russia and the world will be horribly changed forever. They have already killed four of our agents near Edmonton."

Logan paused and glared at the agents occupying the room—first one, then another, then a third. His voice dropped in tone and his words came slower. "Look around the room. Some of you are going to die. These foreign agents we are after are ruthless and efficient. Our goal is to stop them, and to do that, the direction is simple. Kill them before they kill us."

There was another pause when Nick was about to speak, but Logan raised a finger in the air. "One last thing. We will do whatever it takes to complete our mission, but do not kill bystanders indiscriminately. We are all professionals, but we aren't animals."

Confusion set in on a few faces, but Nick brought them out of it. He clapped his hands above his head and, in a loud voice, said, "The guys from Vancouver who just got here—I heard two of you know aircraft, and one specifically knows helicopters."

Two hands in the group shot up in the air.

"There's a Chinook helicopter in the hanger behind the house. Make sure it's operational and fire it up. There's also a truck load of fuel on the way, so make sure it's ready to go at a moment's notice."

One of them asked, "Who's going to fly it?"

"Gord, the old man who lives here, says he used to fly it often and still can." Nick offered.

There was a laugh and then one of the men said, "You mean the very senior citizen who we've seen stumbling about?"

Nick glared at the group. "Yes, the fucking senior citizen. If he can't fly it, then you better figure out how to! And, Gord thinks we're Canadian agents, and the agents we are after are Russian. So, play the part! Like Logan said, 'We're not going to kill people like him unless it's absolutely necessary.'"

Nick pointed to six Russian agents and gave them their assignment. "You'll continue to search for the foreign agents who are likely on a farm just as we are. There's only the lake west of us, so work every side road east of here."

Pointing to the Vancouver guys, he asked, "Did you bring the food as requested?"

A voice came back, "It's all in the SUV's, and we'll bring it to the kitchen."

Nick nodded, then turned his gaze to Brian and Tony. The two agents who had flown to Greenland with them and then to Montreal, were now here. "You two have been watching Jensen Electric in Grande Prairie. Any leads?"

Brian replied, "Nothing."

Waggling a finger at the two Russians, Nick said. "It looks like their agents aren't going back there, so it's time to pick up the owner and let's see what he knows."

Brian and Tony immediately headed for the door of the parlour, when Nick yelled after them, "Make sure he doesn't see you, so put a sack over his head!"

Two hours later, Brian and Tony returned with Rick Jensen squirming in the back seat. The sun had set and old man Crozier was having a nap in his favorite chair in front of the fireplace. It was best for Crozier not to come face to face with a hooded and bound Jensen, who, as for all the Russians knew, might be his best friend. They snuck Jensen in the back door, where stairs led down to the basement. As Nick had indicated, the large finished basement, now filled with cots, looked more like an army barracks. Jensen was dragged past these and into the cold storage cellar where he was pushed roughly down onto a wooden chair.

While Tony watched Jensen, Brian notified Logan and Nick that the shop owner was ready for questioning. They followed Tony down into the cold cement-block room, lit by a single bulb hanging from a cord in the center of the ceiling.

Jensen was squirming on the chair, and the sack was sucked in every time he took a breath, always followed by it billowing out with an exhale. He turned his head from side to side in a futile, panicked effort to see those around him. When Nick turned to Logan and whispered, "What do you think?" Jensen's face snapped towards the direction of the voice while the sack sucked in even further.

"I don't think he's smart enough to talk," Logan offered as he rubbed his chin.

"I'm very smart!" Jensen cried in a muffled voice.

Nick waited a few seconds before responding. "He might be smart to tell us what he knows, but I don't think he would be smart enough to keep his mouth shut afterwards."

"I won't tell anyone about this!" Jensen exclaimed.

"So, are you saying we should kill him?" Logan asked.

"No—no! I'll tell you whatever you want to know, and after, I'll have a complete memory loss. Heck, I don't remember shit at the best of times!" Jensen's voice came through panting breaths, and the top of the sack was wet with sweat from his brow.

"You made large purchases of tantalum. What was it for?" Nick asked.

"Tantalum—why tantalum?" Jensen muttered.

Nick had moved his handgun beside Jensen's ear, and when he pulled back the hammer, Jensen almost jumped out of his skin.

"I'm remembering now! Tantalum—yes. There were several orders over the last few months."

Nick whispered into Jensen's ear, "What was the tantalum for?"

"It wasn't for me," the bound man replied. "I was just the middle man. The people who took the deliveries paid in cash. It was good money for me. That's all it was!"

As Logan spoke, Jensen's head snapped to the new voice. Logan asked, "Where were the deliveries made to?"

Now, as Jensen spoke, a few words were directed to Logan and a few to Nick as his head snapped back and forth. "I didn't deliver the tantalum. They always picked it up and paid cash. They had a big, white truck."

"There must be more about the truck," Logan urged.

"I don't remember," Jensen mumbled.

"Think!" Nick yelled in Jensen's ear at close range.

"Okay!" Jensen yelled back. "It was white. The truck was a 20-footer, and yes, now I remember. It had black front fenders."

"Tell us about the people who came for the pickup," Nick demanded.

"There were always two young men, but not always the same men. The woman who came was always the same. She was the one who paid me." Jensen could not blurt the words out fast enough.

"What were their names?" Logan pressed.

"I told you, the men were always different. It was just the woman. Once, I heard one of the men slip and call her *Nancy*."

"That's all?" Nick asked.

"I'm not sure what else you want!" Jensen cried. "The woman said our business arrangement must be kept secret. She didn't come right out and say it, but I felt like my life was at stake. You guys have to protect me now!"

Nick admitted, "We've been watching you for over a week. If they come back, we'll still be watching, and they'll all be killed. Just keep out of the line of fire, and you'll survive."

"I don't think we'll get anything else out of him," Logan concluded. "Look, he just pissed his pants."

Tony interjected, "Should we kill him now?"

"No—no!" Jensen screamed. "I'll help you. If they come back, I'll let you know!"

Jensen still had a coat on, and the beads of sweat rolling down his neck were visible above the thick collar. Finally, Nick said, "Take him back to his shop." Then, he directed his voice at Jensen and hissed, "Don't forget your promise. You will not say a word about any of this to anyone, otherwise you'll be killed. If you tell your wife, then you and your wife will be killed."

Logan left the cold cellar, and as Nick followed, he turned back to Tony. "Take him away."

Logan whispered to Nick, "Let's go for a smoke," which by now Nick understood to mean he wanted to talk in private. They both put on their coats and boots and went out into the cold night. In actuality, Logan didn't have much to say. This time, he really did want to just get some air and look up at the stars.

Seeing something was not quite right, Nick said, "You don't seem yourself tonight. What's up?"

Logan shrugged. "I'm not sure. Maybe I am homesick. Maybe I want this all to be over with now."

Nick thought of his own sacrifices, having never married, and his only friends being fellow members of Russian intelligence. "We've all made sacrifices, but one day, when we die, hopefully we can say it was for the betterment of my world, and yours."

Not wanting to belabour it, Logan deflected the discussion. "Look over there." He pointed to four of his Korian operatives doing some work in the darkness on the far side of the airfield.

As they both walked towards them, Nick asked, "What are they doing?"

Logan delayed the answer until they were beside the four men. Logan slapped one of them on the back and said, "Are you making progress?"

The men were assembling a device. At the bottom, staked into the frozen earth was a large box. Out the top of it, protruded a long 40 mm diameter tube. It extended a good 20 centimetres above their heads, where a small, square radar array was attached. The man Logan slapped on the back, leaned over and opened a flap on top of the box. He flipped a switch within, and the radar array began to slowly rotate. Each time it made one revolution, a green light at the very top, blinked.

The man raised himself up to his full height and reported to Logan, "It's operational. We just have to run the cable to the monitor in the house."

"Excellent, Jay. Excellent," Logan offered as he slapped Jay on the back for a second time. Logan grasped Nick's arm and pulled him back towards the house. "The Sholites have the tantalum they need for their device. It is likely they also have their mica, but there is a third material they will need that is not available on Earth."

"What does that have to do with this machine just assembled?"

"The third material is something they have to deliver with one of their ships," Logan explained. "Remember, I told you, they will cloak their vessel when they come and use an ultraviolet beam to guide them. The device behind you is a sensor we have developed that will sense such an ultraviolet beam."

"That's very good," Nick interjected. "We shall need to have a strike team always ready."

"That is correct," Logan affirmed in a deep voice that told much about his hatred for the Sholites. "We will find them, Nick, and we will kill them— every last one."

Chapter 22: Fort Nelson

Natalie, hand in hand with Josh, walked around the perimeter of the farmhouse. They had been here for two weeks now while the site was a hub of activity. Only one more load of materials was received, and the focus was now on completing the assembly of the ESUs. The thick tantalum and mica sheets were set in place, and the space between and surrounding them was filled with the mysterious alien fluid held in the large vats in the barn. But there was a problem. As the final shells were going to be filled, there was no remaining fluid for the last four.

Consequently, as they met with Adrian in front of a white truck, the last four ESUs were being loaded without the fluid. Natalie asked Adrian, "Where are the ESUs being shipped? I've seen a full truck leave every couple of days for the last week."

Adrian, hearing the voice from behind him, turned and replied, "Oh, It's you Natalie and Josh." He had a wide smile on his face. "We're nearing the end of our mission. The ESUs are being shipped to the final site where we'll control the electromagnetic pulse."

"Many of your people have also left. Are they going to the same site?" Josh asked.

"Yes. Tomorrow, we'll be the last to leave and the farmhouse will be empty, having served its purpose very well," Adrian responded.

True to his word, the next day vehicles began leaving at two hour increments so as not to draw suspicion. Adrian had told Natalie and Josh the new site was a seven-hour drive, and a wagon train through mostly remote territory, would be too obvious. The last vestiges of equipment were loaded into the vehicles. No more than two people were allowed in a vehicle to allay any possible suspicions on the road. As such, the vehicles made several trips over the past week, until finally, their final exodus was underway.

Natalie, Josh and Lashkar were watching through the picture window of the house. As far as they knew, they were the last three, along with Nancy and Adrian, who waved to the people in the last SUV as it left. Suddenly, Lashkar realized, they were still here, but the last vehicle just left. He crashed open the front door and yelled at Adrian, "What about us?"

Adrian, with that warm, wide smile on his face, broke into laughter.

"What about you?"

For a moment, Lashkar thought they were being left behind, but then, as Adrian pointed into the sky, Lashkar heard the unmistakeable sound of rotor blades breaking through the thin, cold air at high speed. Two minutes later, he saw the dark-grey helicopter land in the center of the parking area beside the farmhouse. Once the rotor blades came to a stop, the pilot and co-pilot jumped from the door of the Bell 525 machine. They shook hands with Adrian, and then Adrian walked towards a gawking Lashkar.

Adrian slapped Lashkar on the shoulder as he walked by him, bringing him out of his stupor. Lashkar followed the Sholite leader into the living room where Josh and Natalie were waiting.

Adrian clapped his hands together just as Nancy walked down the stairs with her large pack strapped over her back. Adrian was distracted for a moment by the creak of the stairs, but then turned his focus back to the Earth people. "There's a lot going on at the new location, and I need to get there more quickly than the ground vehicles would take me. I want you three to take the helicopter ride with Nancy and I, so we can talk along the way." The words finished with the wide, reassuring smile the three of them had become familiar with.

Lashkar, now recovered from his initial shock, blurted, "That will be great!"

"Then grab your bags, and we'll be leaving this place," Adrian confirmed.

Since they'd been told the day before that they'd be leaving, their packed bags were waiting by the door, and they retrieved them after pulling on their boots and thick winter coats. Once they were outside, the air was indeed cold, but helped by the bright sun in the sky. The pilot was doing a pre-flight check, so the co-pilot helped the passengers put their bags in the hold of the aircraft.

The configuration of the helicopter was such that there were 14 seats. At the front, were the pilot and co-pilot seats, leaving four rows of three seats behind them. All seats faced forward except the second row of passenger seats, which faced rearwards. As they boarded the aircraft, this allowed Natalie, Josh and Lashkar to take the third row, facing forward, while Nancy and Adrian were in two of the seats facing them.

Moments later, all doors were closed, and the passengers could tell the speed of the rotors increased, preceding the helicopter's liftoff. The sound differential wasn't huge as the passenger compartment was well insulated, both from the cold air and the noise from the engines and the attached rotor blades slashing through the crisp air.

Adrian said, "Well, we're on our way." The voice was not loud, yet all in the aircraft except the pilot and co-pilot, due to their helmets, could easily hear his words.

A minute later, an electronic voice came over the speaker system. The pilot said, "It's a clear day, so the two-hour flight should be an enjoyable one. We'll be flying at one thousand metres, so enjoy."

This was the first time many of them saw the local landscape from the air. There was a blanket of snow covering the primarily flat terrain, marked by the huge patches of farmland made discernable by the break in the snow at the bounding fence lines. There were smaller forests of evergreens, consisting mainly of pine and fir. As they looked ahead of them, they could see larger patches of green forest off in the distance.

Josh broke the silence. "This is an expensive helicopter as were many of the vehicles back at the farmhouse. I don't mean to be nosy, but how do you raise such large amounts of money?"

Adrian pulled his gaze from the mesmerising landscape and explained, "As Talus 3 hurtles through the vast expanse of space, our scout ships can travel even faster. We mine what we need from planets and asteroids, but we always look for signs of other sentient life. Historically, explorers have supply lines behind them to keep the people fed and afforded the necessities of life. Our supply lines work in reverse. We have scout ships and larger supply ships well ahead of Talus 3. If one of these scout ships would find a habitable planet, our people could leave the constrictions of the asteroid Talus 3 behind."

Josh's face twisted in confusion. "I don't follow you?"

Adrian chuckled. "I don't think you understand how far the supply lines lead Talus 3." He leaned forward to impress the enormity of his next words. "Sholites and Korians, for that matter, have been here for 40 years. "Some of our people were born here and a few are tasked with infiltrating companies and governments to obtain the funds we need."

There was silence for a few moments as they thought of the implications of aliens on Earth for such a long period of time. For many years there were rumours of crashed alien ships and little, grey men with big heads, but now, they were learning these aliens looked much the same as the people of Earth.

Adrian reached over and slapped Lashkar on top of his knee. "Have you heard how well Lashkar is doing on the technical side of our mission. Nancy has told me he's learning our language very quickly."

Lashkar interrupted as he looked at Josh and Natalie. He was excited, evident by his quick-paced words. "The Sholite computer systems are completely different from ours. It's fascinating! But it's based on the Sholite language, so before I can learn their computer programming systems, I have to learn their language."

Nancy added, "Lashkar has progressed quickly. For the device we're making, our computer systems must communicate with already established computer systems here on Earth. Lashkar has helped immensely, and I would estimate he's taken two days off our schedule."

"There's a very peculiar but interesting fact about the Sholite language," Lashkar offered. "Is it okay to tell them?"

"Let me," Adrian interjected. "It took a long time for both the Korians and us to get over this many centuries ago, but the Sholite and Korian languages are, in fact, the same language."

Natalie retorted, "How's that possible? Weren't your worlds millions and millions of kilometres apart?"

"It has to do with our version of the theory of evolution, or perhaps creation," Adrian explained. "In our case and the Korians, the archeological evidence and the scientific evidence says life was left on Kor and Shol by a superior alien race a millennia ago. Our scientists suspect it was some kind of experiment with two similar but still slightly different forms of life. One life form had red blood and the other blue. The superior aliens, who at the time were called gods, came back to check on the progress of their experiment until there came a time when they came back no more. The experiment was lost in time."

"That's amazing," Lashkar uttered as he rubbed the side of his head.

"It certainly is," Adrian agreed. "The Korians and Sholites are like cousins, but nevertheless, there has been an ongoing war for an eternity, it seems. It'll only end when one race is wiped out."

There was a bump as the helicopter hit a burst of turbulent air. The look of distress and anxiety that was forming on Adrian's face, quickly faded, and the reassuring smile replaced it. "I don't have to ask Lashkar," Adrian said, "but are you ready to go the next step on this mission to save your world?"

Natalie brushed the bangs from her forehead. The pink streaks had faded some, but from under them, her eyes considered Adrian and Nancy. "We do have a few questions," she said.

Through a chuckle, Adrian retorted, "Why am I not surprised? Over the past few weeks, both you and Josh have been given assignments of increased responsibility. You've completed supply and surveillance runs, primarily providing support. The reports I hear are exemplary. You've had your guns for quite some time. If you wanted to report us, or even stop us, you could've done so by now. For us to continue on this path, we need to take stock of our allegiances now and see if the trust will go even further, so of course, I will answer your questions."

Natalie thought Adrian's words were always more like prose and brought a soothing calm to those listening. It was no different this time, so her words were formed with her most polite intentions. "Why don't the sophisticated Earth telescopes see Talus 3?"

Adrian whispered to Nancy, "Why don't you answer that?"

Nancy nodded and explained, "Talus 3 has a cloaking system. If you recall, when you saw the asteroid-ship through the telescope, there was a red hue around it. Our telescope has an advanced filter allowing us to see Talus 3, but without it, your telescopes would see nothing."

Adrian added, "Our ships and the Korian ships have the same capability. You see, there's a large black market between the Korian and Sholite ships that inhabit the space for many future years of Talus 3's predicted trajectory. Somewhere along the way, the Korians obtained our science."

"It sounds like a very unusual symbiotic relationship," Josh added.

"We consider it more of a parasitic relationship," Adrian corrected.

Raising an eyebrow, Josh replied, "Indeed."

By now, Natalie knew Josh very well, both physically and mentally. She was curious as there now seemed to be some tension in his voice. To relieve what appeared to be some strain between Adrian and Josh, Natalie offered a joke. "Time is certainly flying by—literally!"

They all chuckled, but Natalie was correct. The terrain below them was more rugged and almost entirely covered by thick forests of northern evergreens. She estimated they had about 30 minutes of flying time left. "Can you tell us where we're going now?"

"We're going to a location just east of a small British Colombia town called Fort Nelson," Adrian revealed.

"Why?" Natalie quickly replied.

Adrian shrugged. "It will be easier to show you when we get there. You have a saying on your world, 'One picture is worth a thousand words.' However, I need to know now, from both you and Josh, are you with us for the duration of the mission? You both know what's at stake." Adrian slouched back in his seat. "As I said earlier, you've done well in the missions you were assigned, but you were always under surveillance. I'm sick of doing that. I want to trust the two of you completely now. Am I wrong in that?" Adrian's light-blue eyes searched Josh's and Natalie's.

Natalie answered first. "No, you can trust me. I'm with you, just as my father is and for the same reasons."

"As am I," Josh added.

"That makes me very happy," Adrian offered. He threw Natalie her cell phone that she hadn't seen for several weeks. "Since we trust each other totally, I trust you'll only use it for mission tasks and emergencies."

Natalie caught the phone and placed it in her coat pocket. She didn't respond to Adrian as none was required. She wasn't sure if she just lied to the man. She had decided to complete this mission with him, but she wasn't sure her trust was complete. Even now, when he gave her back her phone, she questioned his motivation. Quickly, she concluded there was something he needed from her.

The pilot's voice crackled through the speakers. "We'll be landing in five minutes, people."

Natalie tried to look directly ahead of them, but the view was blocked by the plane's fuselage. However, off to the left, about 20 kilometres distant, was a clearing in the trees filled with houses and flat-topped buildings. There was also a single runway airport just east of the small town. She assumed that must be Fort Nelson.

They seemed to be lowering into a forest of trees, but as they cleared the tree line, it was evident they were landing into a clearing between several low buildings. As they neared the ground, a whitewash of snow was thrown into the air. After the landing gear made contact, the engines were idled, and the rotor blades began to slow. Once they were almost stopped, their side door was pulled open by the co-pilot. The passengers jumped out and scurried from the helicopter with their heads hung down until they cleared the rotor blades above them.

Natalie, Josh and Lashkar made a small circle as they gazed around them. Just in front of the helicopter was a hanger large enough for the aircraft. There were three other buildings. One was a long, two-story building that Adrian explained was used as military barracks, many years ago. A second building was two stories as well, but much smaller. Adrian said it housed offices, and the third building, which was one-story, but long, was oriented away from the large snow-covered courtyard formed by the buildings. This long structure was the communications building, and at the far end of it, on a rise of ground was a huge communications array. It was five metres high and seven metres wide.

"What is this place?" Natalie asked.

"It's the Fort Nelson DEW line station," Adrian answered. "Obviously that begs more questions, but I've something to attend to immediately." He saw Jeremy on the other side of the clearing and waved to him, whereby the young man jogged over to their location. "Jeremy, find Lashkar a spot in the barracks with the science team. Natalie and Josh will be in your security group. Get them their own room." Adrian turned to Natalie, Josh and Lashkar. "Meet me in the communications building in one hour for the additional answers you seek."

Natalie nodded, but Adrian and Nancy were already on the move. As they walked towards the barracks, Natalie said, "DEW line station? That rings a bell, but I can't put my finger on it."

Lashkar seemed to know almost everything about anything and he answered, "DEW stands for *distant early warning*. In the '50s and '60s the United States and Canada set up a series of radar stations across the Arctic from Alaska to Greenland. During the cold war this was the early warning system for the supposed attack that would come from Russia."

"This is one of the stations?" Natalie asked.

"Nope. We're too far south. There were literally dozens of these small radar stations across the Arctic, but this station is too big and too far south. I suspect it's a communications base for the DEW line stations," Lashkar elaborated.

Further answers would need to come from Adrian, so they would need to wait. Jeremy led the group into the barracks and gave them a quick tour. Primarily, the building was filled with dorm-type rooms. He showed them the kitchen and mess hall, but when they entered the large lounge area, a voice from across the room yelled, "Natalie!"

Her father strode over to the group and gave Natalie a huge hug while Lashkar and Josh received warm handshakes. Jeremy was anxious to show them to their rooms, so Edward looked at his watch. It was 3:00 p.m. They made an agreement to meet in the mess hall for dinner at 6:30 before Jeremy led them towards a set of stairs at the far end of the room.

Lashkar was led to a large room on the second floor with six beds in it. There was a table in the center of the room and five people were around it playing cards. A young woman saw Lashkar and whooped, "Look who's here! It's Lashkar!" She rose from the small seat and rushed over to him, throwing her arms around him in a huge hug.

Seeing Lashkar literally in good hands, Natalie and Josh were led to their own room at the end of the hallway. Jeremy left them there whereby Josh closed the door as soon as the younger man left. Natalie's face was glowing—a look Josh had come to recognize. He peeled off his boots and coat. The whole time, his eyes stayed locked on hers as he whispered, "We do have an hour…"

It was exactly an hour later when they heard a knock on their door. Natalie and Josh were scurrying to put their clothes back on when they heard Lashkar's voice through the door. "What are you guys doing? We're going to be late!"

When Natalie finally opened the door, fully clothed including her boots and coat, Lashkar raised an eyebrow. He asked, "Are you feeling okay? You look a little flushed."

Natalie pushed him aside as she thought, *maybe Lashkar doesn't know everything about anything, after all.*

Josh followed and the three of them made their way to the communication building, where a guard let them into a large entry area. This building looked much the same as the barracks, with grey walls and a grey floor. There was a hallway down the side of the building, and on one side were windows while on the other was a long wall with doors interrupting its length at several locations. They could hear people talking, but as they walked by open doors, it wasn't until they were at the third one that they found the source. Entering this room, they found Adrian in a chair hunched over some documents as well as eight other technicians, some of whom had clipboards, walking around the multitude of computer stations, while pushing buttons and switches.

Adrian heard the footsteps and saw the visitors. "Ah, you're here. Excellent."

Natalie Josh and Lashkar walked towards the leader of the group who had risen to his feet while offering a warm smile of welcome. Adrian rubbed his hands together and said, "So here we are at the heart of the matter." He half turned and opened his arm towards the far wall, dominated by a map of Canada. As the group looked closer, they could see the map was made of sheet-metal, and across the Arctic were holes filled with little, old-school light bulbs. There were many light bulbs, but as Natalie counted, she found only seven of them lit.

"Why are only some of the DEW line stations lit?" Natalie asked.

Adrian raised an eyebrow in admiration. "Very good Ms. Lowe. There were originally 63 DEW line radar stations built jointly by the Americans and the Canadians. With advancements in radar systems in the '80s, these stations became obsolete. At first, egged on by environmentalists who thought the stations left in nature were an eyesore, the Canadian government began to tear down the facilities. However, soon the financial impact overwhelmed the environmental concern, and the reclamation projects stopped. Half of the DEW line stations still stand as relics of the past, with many filled with ice and snow."

"Except for those seven," Lashkar predicted.

"You are correct again," Adrian agreed. "Those seven stations have been retrofit with alien technology, and over the past month, the ESUs have been installed in all except one last station. That will be completed this week."

Lashkar said, "How will this all work?"

Adrian waggled a finger in front of the curious group. "Excellent question! The modifications we've made to the radar arrays at each of the seven stations will allow a high energy electrical beam to be sent to a position above your north magnetic pole. When the seven beams come together, they'll create a disruption in the earth's electromagnetic field. A large bubble of the field will break off, and if the telemetry of our beams is correct, the bubble will be sent hurtling towards Talus 3."

Josh and Natalie were impressed by what they heard, but Lashkar was scratching his head. Finally, he said, "But the ESUs aren't charged. How are you going to fill them?"

Adrian opened his mouth to answer, but his words were cut off by a shout from down the hallway. "Adrian! Come quickly!"

Adrian's brow furrowed as he recognized Jeremy's voice. He ran out of the room, followed by several others including the trio of Earthlings. Adrian crashed open the front door of the communications building, and a stream of people followed. By now, Jeremy was holding open the door to the barracks, and as Adrian rushed by, Jeremy shouted, "In the mess hall!"

Once they arrived there, a group of people were surrounding one of the tables. Adrian yelled, "Make way! Make way!" Recognizing his voice, the followers parted, and there Adrian found one of the older Canadian scientists, hunched over with his face in a plate of food. Edward stood over him and held a finger to the man's neck, checking for a pulse. When Edward saw Adrian, he shook his head from side to side, confirming, "He's dead."

By now Natalie was beside Adrian. She recognized the face of the dead man. Natalie only knew him as Jarvis. He was over 80 and was one of the people revived from a Canadian nursing home. Her face showed surprise and then a hint of anger as she said, "How can he be dead? The injections are supposed to keep him alive!"

Adrian looked at Natalie while, for the first time, he was at a loss for words, and he looked uncomfortable.

"I'll explain it to her." The soft words came from Natalie's father who saw the awkward situation and interjected his help. He grasped Natalie's arm and pulled her from the crowd. "The injections are not a forever thing," he offered.

She had never considered this. It confused her, but two words spilled out. "How long?"

Edward replied, "All the people who've been revived have only received a temporary reprieve. The injections cure them, but in the end overloads their systems, so they die."

"How long?" Natalie repeated.

"Typically, the injections keep the people revived from three to five months."

Natalie did the mental math, and her eyes welled up with tears as she realized her father's recovery would be very short-lived.

Edward smiled warmly at his daughter. "C'mon, I was worse off than dead in the retirement home. My prognosis was that very soon I would die, drooling and with shit in my diaper." He took a deep breath. "Look at me now. I've been given a second wind!"

Natalie whispered, "But, you will die soon."

Edward shrugged. "Yes, I will, but it'll be quick, just as it was for Jarvis." His own eyes now filled up, but ironically, they were tears of joy. "Now, when I die, it'll be with satisfaction, knowing I helped to save two worlds from obliteration. I will die with pride and dignity. What more could I ask for?"

Chapter 23: Bernard Harbour

Gazing out over the compound, Natalie could see why this location was chosen as a communication site by the Sholites. There were, in fact, three DEW line communications sites at approximately the same latitude within Canada. The Fort Nelson station was selected by the Sholites because of its isolation from civilization, a good 25 kilometres from the town proper.

From her higher vantage point on the hill rolling up behind the site, she could see the only road leading to the station, if one could call the frozen mud track a road. It could only be traversed by four-wheel-drive, and only the most curious and adventurous locals would dare come to this location. For those that did, a large yellow sign had been posted on the mud track and just behind it was a sturdy barricade. The sign read,

DANGER. HAZARDOUS MATERIAL CLEANUP.

Similar but smaller signs had also been posted on one-metre-high posts every 20 metres around the property. Across the other side of the compound, she could see two more guards monitoring their side of the perimeter, and from this distance, they looked exactly as she did.

Natalie and the other guards were dressed in all white, with thick, insulated pants and a matching coat that came down to almost her knees. The bright sunlight glared off the snow and ice with only the dark sunglasses she wore making her vision possible. The only other item breaking up the white camouflaged outfit she wore was the black M16 rifle she carried across the front of her body.

She crouched down on one knee from the 20-metre rise of frozen dirt and rock. Here, on the south side of the station site, tall white pine trees created a tranquil place allowing not only an escape from the wind, but also from the enormity of events having unfolded since they left Toronto.

Sadly, as her gaze panned across the buildings, her eyes caught sight of the small cemetery behind the office building where seven graves were marked by wooden crosses. These were the graves of revived Earthers who had died after the effectiveness of their medical injections had worn off. She realized it was a place her father would lie some time in the near future.

"Natalie!"

The yell broke her attention from the cemetery to a man in similar all-white cold-weather gear, waving his arms above his head at the bottom of the rise of land. Natalie rose to her feet and hurried as best she could down the undulating hillside. She slid the last two metres and almost bumped into the young man. He said, "I'll take over for you. They want you at a meeting in the communications building, right away."

Although the hood kept her warm, her face was numb from the cold, *so it would be good to get inside for a while,* she thought. She jogged the short distance over to the communications building where, once inside, she pulled off the cold weather gear and hung the pants and coat on hooks along the wall.

Once she entered the room she had previously been in with the large map of Canada on the wall, Adrian said, "Sorry for the late notice, but I'm glad you could join us." Of course, as the people around him came to expect, he said the words through a beaming smile.

Natalie took a seat beside Josh. Lashkar was already seated beside Nancy. It had become quite noticeable that there were very few places the science head went, where Lashkar didn't follow. Natalie grinned and wondered if there was more going on there than just scientific calculations.

Jeremy and Rita, along with two other personnel from Jeremy's security group, were also in attendance. Adrian rose to his feet and began the discussion. "It's come to a critical time for our mission and we're a bit behind schedule. I thought it would be a good idea to discuss the objectives for the next few days, so we're clear what must be done to catch us up."

Natalie was confused. She hadn't been involved in planning meetings before, so why were she and Josh here this time?

Adrian continued. "Here, at the communications station, we're 90 per cent complete with our retrofits." He walked over to the wall-size map and pointed to each of the seven DEW line stations in turn. "The first five are 100 per cent complete. The Jenny Lind Island site is 80 per cent complete, so it will make the schedule. Our concern is for the Bernard Harbour site. We're only 50 per cent complete, and the main reason for that is the four ESUs still sitting in our hanger. We're completely out of sartolin."

"What's the plan to recover?" Lashkar asked.

Adrian lowered into his chair and said, "Let's get to the details. We have a De Havilland Buffalo aircraft in our service out of Yellowknife. The plane will come to the Fort Nelson airport where we'll load up the four ESUs, and the plane will then fly to a make-shift runway at Bernard Harbour." He pointed at Natalie, Josh and the two men across the table. "You four will be providing security for the mission, and I'd like you to lead." The last direction was given as he looked squarely at Rita.

Rita nodded her understanding just as Natalie asked, "How far away is Bernard Harbour?"

Adrian turned his gaze. "It's about 1,200 kilometres, meaning a flying time of five hours. Once you're there, you'll receive a delivery of sartolin from space. After that's received, it should take about two days for the remainder of the retrofits to be completed."

"At that point, we'll be flying back to Fort Nelson, right?" Josh asked.

Although, Josh asked the question, Adrian looked squarely at Natalie when he answered. "No. We would like you to fly to Yellowknife."

"Why?" Josh continued the line of questioning, notwithstanding who Adrian looked at.

Still focused on Natalie, Adrian replied, "We need a favour from you, Natalie. At each of the DEW line stations we have generators running on gasoline, but we have a shortage."

Natalie thought, *here it comes. Now I know why you gave me back my phone.*

"It would be very dangerous for us to use our previous suppliers. There's a good chance the Korians are onto them," Adrian explained. "We were hoping you could use your contacts to get the gasoline we need."

"How much?" Natalie asked.

"Forty barrels," came the reply.

"I can try," Natalie offered.

"My apologies, but we need to know now," Adrian urged.

Raising an eyebrow, Natalie realized there was an obsessiveness hidden behind Adrian's warm smile, but she could play that game. Giving her own wide smile, she said, "Sure, Adrian. Just give me a few minutes," after which she rose and relocated herself just outside the office door. She hadn't touched her phone of late, other than to charge it, but now, she pulled it from her pocket and input a speed dial number.

After three electronic rings, a voice answered. "Hello."

"Philip, it's me, Natalie."

"Natalie! Where on Earth have you been?"

"Relax. Everything's fine," Natalie offered.

Instinctively, Philip's voice lowered as if he didn't want someone to hear him. "I've been worried sick. The GPS tracking on your phone just suddenly went off a couple of weeks ago. Even now, it's not tracking. What's going on?"

Natalie figured when the Sholites gave her phone back, it would be modified, and even now, she suspected they were listening. "Everything's fine, and I found my father, so all's well there. However, the situation has turned into a much bigger problem, and I need your help."

"What situation?"

"Philip, you've always had good instincts and knew when to trust me and when to reign me in. Right now, I need you to trust me and do me this favour."

Philip replied, "But…"

"With no questions asked," Natalie qualified. "Trust me. It's not a huge favour. I can tell you it's helping our country, so with a bit of a reach, it falls within our scope."

"What do you need?"

"Today's the 28th of November. In three days, at 3 p.m. I need 40 barrels of high-octane gasoline delivered to the Yellowknife airport."

"Yellowknife!" The exclamation was followed by a few seconds of muffled words as Philip swore vehemently with his hand covering his phone.

"Just please do it. December 1st at 3:00 p.m.—40 barrels of gasoline."

There was a long pause, but finally Philip said, "It'll be there."

Relief swept over her, and she was halfway through saying, "Thank you," when the *click* on the other end indicated Philip had hung up. Her heart sank. She knew Philip had a choice to help her or throw her under the bus with his superiors. With some risk to his own career, she knew he was choosing the more dubious course to help her.

She walked back into the meeting and sank into her chair. "It's done. Forty barrels of gasoline will be at the Yellowknife airport on December 1st at 3:00 p.m."

Rita turned to Adrian and whispered, "We can make that work."

"Excellent!" Adrian exclaimed. "Once you arrive at Yellowknife, the helicopter will be waiting to bring you back to Fort Nelson. The gas barrels will be loaded on the plane for the return trip to Bernard Harbour as well as the other stations needing a top-up of gas."

"I'll need to be there when they deliver the barrels. They won't give the gas to just anyone," Natalie qualified.

"Not a problem," Adrian replied. He sensed Natalie was a little put off by the sequence of events. "Remember, these efforts and sacrifices we're all making are to save millions of lives on Talus 3 and billions of lives here on Earth, so be proud of your efforts."

It didn't take long for the plan to be put in motion. The travellers all packed a light bag and met in the compound 90 minutes later. The four ESUs were put into the white truck, and they slowly plodded down the *excuse-for-a-road* towards the Fort Nelson airport. They arrived and the white De Havilland Buffalo was waiting in front of a yellow hanger, framed by the setting sun. By the time the ESUs were loaded and secured, the passengers loaded, and the engines started, darkness had fallen over Fort Nelson.

The door from the make-shift passenger compartment to the cockpit was open, so the passengers could hear the communications. As the plane picked up speed down the runway, Natalie turned to Rita and asked, "Where is Kugluktuk? I heard the co-pilot tell the tower we're flying there."

Rita chuckled. "It's a secret that we're retrofitting Bernard Harbour, so we tell the tower we're flying to Kugluktuk, an aboriginal and mining support settlement 120 kilometres south of Bernard Harbour."

Josh, who was sitting next to Natalie said, "It's a good five-hour flight to Kugluk...whatever. Try and get some sleep." He put his arm around her far shoulder and pulled her against him. She snuggled her face in, and in no time, she was fast asleep.

There was a slight bump as the wheels hit the runway. Both Natalie and Josh awoke from their slumber, and Josh was about to say, "We're here," when he felt the pilot give the engines full throttle. The plane lifted off the ground and leveled off 50 metres above the snow and ice-covered terrain. Lowering a brow, Josh turned to Rita and asked, "What's going on?"

Rita had to raise her voice to be heard above the engine drone. "We have to make it look good, so we do a touch and go at Kugluktuk. If radar is tracking us, it tracks us all the way here. Now, at a low altitude, we fly the 120 kilometres to Bernard Harbour undetected.

If Josh thought he didn't like finding out information after the fact, he really didn't like the pilot's erratic flying for the next 30 minutes. The ground below was rock, covered with ice and snow, but was primarily flat. However, the night visibility, obscured even more by a light snowfall, made the pilot jittery. The jitteriness translated to his control of the stick, causing them to bank left, then right, then up only to come back down.

Finally, they saw dim lights in the distance defining the frozen, plowed runway. For all his earlier nervousness, the pilot made a perfect landing. If Natalie and Josh thought it was cold before, the blast of frigid air that entered when the rear cargo door was opened, reminded them things could always get worse. The chill air urged them out of the plane, directly into one of the three buildings beside the tiny airstrip. Once inside, they were introduced to three older scientists, each of whom could not be a minute under 80, and several younger men who were both soldiers and the local muscle for any legwork to be done. Several other men were in the process of unloading the ESUs as the pilot shut down the engines.

There was some idle banter for a few minutes, but it was almost midnight. Even though Natalie and Josh had slumbered at least part of the way, the long day had exhausted them. They asked where they would be sleeping and were shown to a room within the thin, metal-walled structure. There was one military-style bed on either side of the small room, and on each was a pillow and a thick sleeping bag.

After they closed the door, as was their ritual, they pushed together the beds. Josh lifted up the narrow sleeping bag, stating, "What the hell?"

Natalie snatched it from his fingers and chirped, "Weren't you ever a kid?" She unzipped his sleeping bag and then hers. She then rezipped them into a double wide sleeping bag big enough for the two of them to snuggle in. The steel walls did little more than keep out the wind. There was a heater in the room, but tonight they would be sleeping with their clothes on for the added warmth they offered.

There was a shout from outside the door, "Lights out in five minutes!"

Natalie was already in the sleeping bag, and before Josh joined her, he retrieved a flashlight. By the time the building lights went off, they were both camped completely within the thick sleeping bag, with the flashlight shining between them, again reminding Natalie—this was just like when they were kids.

It was quiet and would have been silent if not for the wind whistling outside. Natalie began to slide her hand up inside the front of his shirt. It was something she had often done. She enjoyed it because, when her hands were cold, it was a sacrifice he made for her. But this time, he stopped her hand and pushed it away from his skin.

She whispered, "What's up?"

"I've been thinking."

"About me, I hope," she said with a wry smile as she snuggled against him.

He slid away and his brow was furrowed. He seemed perplexed and a little bit angry. Finally, he said, "Here we are well north of the Arctic Circle on a mission to save worlds, and all I can think of is you." She smiled and was about to interrupt, but he interrupted her intended interruption. "We have aliens after us—ones who would kill us, it seems, yet all I can think of is you."

Her smile disappeared. The muscles on her face relaxed. She was melting. In the dim light of the flashlight, his gaze looked into her eyes—but even deeper. In that moment, he saw every minute she had ever lived, every feeling she had ever felt and every hope she ever had. Her lips parted slightly, and a slight breath passed to fall on his own lips. He recognized the familiar sweetness and had to fight the urge to madly press his lips to her. However, in that moment, he knew there was a higher purpose. She saw it now as well, in his eyes. He didn't have to say another word. He would never have to, for she knew them before they left his lips.

"I love you, Natalie," he whispered.

Her lower lip trembled while her cat-like eyes narrowed even more than usual. Her hand came up, and with shaking fingers, she brushed them against his cheek. "And I love you, Josh. I will love you forever."

Then, they kissed. Although they had kissed so many times, this kiss was like a new beginning. It was so because they knew it was not a last kiss, and there would never be a time to fathom such. There would always be another to look forward to.

Natalie's hand slid down his shirt and found his, intertwining her fingers with his, but there was something there. She asked, "What's that?"

With one hand, Josh brought up the flashlight, and with the other, the object Natalie felt. He opened his hand, and in his palm was a beautiful ring. Her lower lip began to quiver again, but Josh's words saved her from the tears that were about to come.

"This ring has been in my family for three generations. With that said, it is a special ring that is to be passed down through future generations. The oldest son gives the ring to the woman he is sure to marry."

He heard a quite audible gasp from Natalie. She didn't hear it due to the heavy thumping of her heart in her chest.

Smiling, Josh said, "Yes, I want to marry you. You already knew that, but this is not the place or time for such a request of you. With a certainty, that day will come, so please accept this ring now as a sign of my intention to never let that day be forgotten as long as there is breath in my body."

She held up her shaking finger as a sign of acceptance, and he slid the ring on it. Now, she had a good look at its beauty. The ring was wider than what a woman would normally wear, and it was midnight-blue. In fact, as Natalie rotated her finger in the light, sometimes the ring looked black and sometimes dark-blue. Around it's circumference there were the thinnest of light-blue lines that, in every way, resembled small tendrils of lightning. She thought it was both unusual and unusually beautiful.

Josh turned off the flashlight, and they were together in the darkness. Their lips met in the softest of kisses. There were many nights when such a kiss led to their romantic love-making, yet tonight, there wasn't a need, for they were betrothed, and that was enough and everything.

When they awoke in the morning, their lips were still very close. As they pulled themselves out of the sleeping bag, Natalie rose to her feet and dramatically leaned back while holding her hand up in the air to admire the ring on her finger.

Josh hadn't yet pulled himself fully out of the coverings and looked up at her. Chuckling, he said, "Nice ring there, Ms. Lowe."

She swept her hand across her brow and continued the dramatics. "Who would have thunk, in the barren Arctic, what trinkets one might find."

By this time, Josh was on his feet and slapped her ass. "Trinkets," he grumbled as he rolled his eyes.

They already heard voices outside their door, and they made their way into the main room. There, thankfully, they found two doors, leading to his and hers bathrooms. Food was next, and then they were ready for their day. Rita gave them directions whereby Josh and Natalie made rounds of the perimeter, but they could only stay outside for 30 minutes at a time, due to the cold, before they needed to warm up inside. Both of them, but especially Josh due to his size, were also asked to help with some of the more laborious tasks.

There was a break for lunch and then more work. Most of the workers were inside the main building, running wires and conduit, while others sat in front of both Sholite and Earthen computers. There was also work going on outside. The main radar receiver from the '50s was in a large ball at the top of a cylindrical building. Workers outside had cut a large opening on one side of the ball and fitted it with doors. Now, they were doing final tests on the opening and closing aspects of the huge panels.

At this northern latitude, at this time of year, the sun had set at 3:00 p.m. Three hours later, when they finished their dinner, Josh and Natalie were ready to relax when Rita interrupted them. "Best you get dressed warmly.

It's cold outside, and we need to get the shipment of sartolin."

Josh frowned. "I thought it was being delivered."

"It is," she responded. "But it would be silly to have it delivered directly to a *secret* location."

Josh rose to his feet and stretched, mumbling, "Why can't it ever be easy?"

Fifteen minutes later, they were in a Japanese made type 10 track-drive vehicle. It was a good seven metres long, white, with a large driver-passenger compartment above the two large tracks, each of which moved around six tracking wheels. One of the young men from Bernard Harbour station drove the vehicle while Rita, Josh, Natalie and two other soldier-types sat in the passenger seats.

The sky was clear, but there was only a quarter moon to light their way. The driver was following a GPS system that gave location, but also terrain. The land they were travelling over was rock formations spotted with small lakes and rivers. All were frozen, but the slight differences of snow over rock or water, required the driver to be especially vigilant.

Twenty kilometres out, the vehicle was brought to an abrupt stop. If there was ever a deserving place for the term, *in the middle of nowhere*, this was it. The rear compartment door of the vehicle was popped open. The driver, who was the first outside, yelled in through the back, "A little help here!"

Now, all the passengers exited and went to the rear of the vehicle where they saw a large, dark-green, metal box. It took four of them to manhandle it out of the vehicle and drop it on a thick piece of level ice.

Rita said, "Rick, you stay here and turn the device on when I give you the signal. We need to move the vehicle at least 50 metres away, and Rick, once you turn the device on, best you run as quickly as possible to our location."

Rick nodded, and then he opened the top panel of the green box. He slid a wide tube out from the box and angled it by using what appeared to be a targeting system within the device. The vehicle was driven the required 50 metre distance, with the remaining passengers jogging along behind it. Both Natalie and Josh carried M16 rifles, but they really wondered, *who else could possibly be out here?*

Rita pulled a satellite phone from her coat, and although the slight wind obscured her words, the others could tell she was talking to someone. She lifted her hand in the air, mimicking Rick, who had his hand in the air above the green device.

Rita was listening to the phone intently. When her eyes widened, she yelled, "Now!" At the same time, her raised hand came flying down to her side.

Logan had fallen asleep in the well-cushioned chair in front of the fireplace, but the alarm woke him instantly. A man came running into the room, with his hand grasping the door jamb. "Logan! The ultraviolet detector has found something. Come quickly!"

Logan jumped to his feet and ran after the man. Once they got to the computer monitor in the back room of the house, they could also see out the window above it. The radar array on the ultraviolet detector was spinning, but the light above it had turned from green to red. Nick was already there with his hand on the shoulder of the Korian computer operator intent on the monitor.

"Quickly, the coordinates!" Logan barked.

The operator changed the screen to show a map of the area. A red blip flashed on the screen. After putting the cursor over the point, coordinates appeared. They were scratched down on a piece of paper, and Logan snatched it even before it was offered. "Let's go, now!"

The group had prepared the same way, night after night. Nick, Logan and 12 other expert Russian fighting men were dressed in black. Two black SUV's were fully fueled and waiting in the driveway at the front of the house. Donning their black winter gear and their assault rifles, the team was on the road in only ten minutes. Nick drove and Logan, sitting in the passenger seat, put the coordinates in the GPS system. Logan gave directions much as the navigator would give in a Rally car. He barked out turns, and he constantly yelled out, "Faster!"

The coordinates took them east along the highway that skirted Grande Prairie. Fortunately, the sun had set long ago, so the speeding vehicles weren't noticed. When they approached the small hamlet of Bezanson, Logan hissed, "North—we need to go north here!"

Both vehicles threw up a wave of slush as they made the corner at a high rate of speed. Where there had been infrequent street lights along the highway, now they were in total darkness except for the headlights of the vehicle. Logan watched the GPS and their position to target. He mumbled, "Slower—slower..."

Nick did slow the lead vehicle. His primary focus was on the road, but he couldn't help but glance at the map on the navigation system.

Suddenly, Logan shouted, "Stop!"

Nick pressed the brakes and the SUV came to a stop while the SUV behind had to veer into the oncoming lane to avoid a collision. Nick squinted his eyes, and to their right, they saw a line of pine trees too thick to see through. There was a mail box on a post, angled at 30-degrees. Just behind it, they could see a driveway winding into the forest of pines, and the tire tracks in the snow indicated it had been recently used.

The two drivers turned off their headlights and carefully drove into the cover of the trees in the forward section of the driveway. After the engines were turned off, the 14 well-armed men, all now with matching black balaclavas and helmets, slowly skulked up the driveway.

Natalie didn't understand the reason for all the theatrics or even Rick who came flying towards them at full speed after he turned the device on. Nothing happened and as they waited, Natalie thought it was all quite anticlimactic. However, ten minutes later, they heard a slight buzz like an insect close to one's ear. Then, the small hairs on the back of their necks stood on end. Although they couldn't see it, they felt the same thing happening to the hairs on their arms. Natalie thought her skin felt strange like there was something tickling her all over. After another few minutes, a burst of snow-laden air came pummeling towards them, but not only towards them, but in every direction from the position of the ultraviolet beam sending unit.

Natalie pulled the goggles down over her eyes, knowing now why they were distributed. With the loose snow now shifted, she looked through the rippling air to see it shimmer until what had been blank space was now dark-grey. A large ship was hovering a metre above the ground. It was like a huge tear drop with the point facing forward and the bottom flattened. The ship was made of many, many square panels, each about a metre square. There were no windows and no doors, until they saw a large section at the bottom of the vessel angle open. A large plastic container, already on skis, was pushed out of the ship.

Only a second later, the door was closed before the ship rotated 180-degrees. As it rose in the air, the air shimmered again, and then the vessel couldn't be seen. Five minutes later, Natalie's mouth was still hung open as she considered the enormity of seeing her first alien ship. As it retraced it's path up the ultraviolet beam, calm came to this little patch of the Arctic with one addition—a large tank of sartolin had been delivered.

The Sholites were thorough and there was a hitch already on the tank. It was connected to the ball at the back of their snow crawler. After the ultraviolet device was loaded back into the vehicle, they started on their return leg back to Bernard Harbour DEW line station.

Nick was the first to see the farmhouse through the trees. He saw the barracks on the right and three barns behind the house. He motioned two men towards each of the buildings. The men were experts. There was no noise—not even the creak of a door. One building at a time, the pairs of men searched, then left the buildings, waving an *all clear* signal with their hands. Nick and Logan moved to the middle of the parking area and met with the returning men. Each pair indicated the buildings were empty. In fact, empty was an understatement as they were picked meticulously clean.

Nick turned to Logan and said in an accusing tone, "What the fuck's going on?"

Logan didn't have a chance to respond or object. One of the Russians, coming back after checking the perimeter, said, "There's something over here you need to see."

The group followed the young Russian to the field near the last barn where he pointed to a green electrical box in the snow. Nick was walking closer when Logan thrust his arm across Nick's body, bringing him to a sudden stop. Logan warned, "There could be some radiation from the device, so don't get too close."

"You know what that is?" Nick replied.

Logan growled, "You have a saying here that fits. That's us getting our stupid asses handed to us on a platter. They have played us for the fools we are."

"Say something that makes sense," Nick said through clenched teeth.

"It's a god damn ultraviolet beam sending unit. They put it here to send us on a wild goose chase," Logan admitted.

Nick glared at Logan, but was distracted by the ringing of his cell phone. He answered it, and Brandon was on the line. His voice had an urgent tone. "The Korian operator who was monitoring the ultraviolet sensing device here says he needs to talk to Logan urgently. I'm giving him the phone."

Putting the phone on speaker, Logan said, "Go ahead Hal. I'm here."

"Commander, I went through the tape of the signal, and there is a second signal."

"Tell me from where." Logan leaned over closer to the phone.

"I'm sorry, but I was focused on the stronger local beam. The second beam is much further away, and without filtering out the interference, point in time, it remains very weak. I can only give a very approximate area."

"What area?" Logan urged.

"Unfortunately, I can only narrow the area to a 400-kilometre circle. The center of the circle would be about 600 kilometres north of Yellowknife, and Yellowknife is about…"

Logan interrupted, having spent hours looking at the Canadian map. "I know where Yellowknife is."

With a sigh, Nick added, "So do I."

Nick hung up the phone. Logan asked, "What does this mean to you?"

"First, it means we need to do much better. These guys are making fools of us," Nick admitted. "We need to do much better, and maybe even change our tactics."

"What tactics?" Logan asked. "You're the infiltration expert."

Nick took a deep breath of the exceptionally cold air. It almost caught his breath, but he managed, "You think this is cold. Wait till we get to the Arctic."

Chapter 24: Yellowknife

The morning after the ruse at the farmhouse near Bezanson, Nick and Logan were standing in front of the fireplace in the living room of the house they were occupying. Gord was on the other side of the room, sleeping in a cozy armchair, so both men were careful with their words even though they were not overly concerned Gord would hear them.

"Let's not even talk about last night," Logan offered. "We were made fools of." He pulled the mug of coffee to his lips, even though he had trouble swallowing after the words of defeat.

"The second ultraviolet beam was likely the one that mattered. The first was just there to fool us," Nick admitted.

"What should we do next?" Logan asked.

"We know they're up to something further north, somewhere north of Yellowknife," Nick added.

"Last night, we had a good look at the map, and the only settlement north of Yellowknife is Kugluktuk. There's a small airport there and about 1,500 people," Logan reminded him.

"We should not overlook that other small hamlet. What's it called?" Nick put his finger to his chin as he tried to remember.

"Wekweeti." Logan provided the name his friend was looking for. "It is a tiny, aboriginal settlement 180 kilometres north of Yellowknife. It is unlikely the Sholites would be there."

"But they do have an airport," Nick reminded Logan.

Logan said, "They only have a population of 150 people, and there is no road access in the winter. You are right. They do have a small airport, but it is the only means of access."

Nick looked into the flames within the fireplace that seemed to be in operation around the clock. He said, "I'm going to fly to Yellowknife, Kugluktuk and, on the way back, to Wekweeti."

Raising an eyebrow, Logan said, "You said 'I' and not *we*."

Nick smiled at Logan. "My friend—what we have been doing has not achieved results. I propose we change our tactics. Let's split up. I'll fly north for a couple of days while you continue to scour this area."

"I am expecting two more Korians tomorrow," Logan admitted. "They are forensic specialists, and I should be here when they inspect the Sholite farmhouse site."

"Then it's settled. I'll go north," Nick reiterated. Scratching his head, he confessed, "I've no idea how to go about this. It's not like I can just phone a local airline."

From behind them, a scratchy voice said, "You guys talk way too loud, especially for intelligence guys."

Nick and Logan turned to see Gord, now wide awake, getting up from the cozy armchair. He stretched upwards, then pushed the tail of his shirt back into the waistband of his pants held up by suspenders.

"Sorry, Gord," Nick said. "We were trying to be quiet, but in our frustration, maybe we were a little too loud."

"Yeah—yeah," Gord muttered as he waved his hand in front of himself. "I can get you to Kugluktuk if you have the money—cash."

Nick turned to Logan and gave him a quizzical look before returning his attention back to the old man. "What're you talking about?"

Gord walked closer to the two agents as he scratched an armpit. "I used to fly all over the north, and although I don't fly much any more, I know people who do."

"You can find someone to fly us from here to Kugluktuk?"

"I figure it'll cost you about two thousand dollars, but you don't want to fly from here to Kugluktuk. I can get you picked up here, and you fly to Yellowknife, but only to refuel. Then, you fly to Kugluktuk. Go to the little restaurant in town. There's only one, so it won't be hard to find. Ask for Uki and tell her I sent you. She can give you a room for the night."

Now it was Logan's turn to look at Gord with a new-found admiration.

Gord continued, "The following morning, my guy will fly you to Yellowknife, and he can make a quick stop at Wekweeti, but Nick is right. There ain't nothing there." Gord yawned before continuing. "You can spend a few hours in Yellowknife, then be flown back here."

Nick, hearing Gord's thorough itinerary, turned to Logan and said, "I'll take Tony with me."

"Three thousand dollars," Gord interrupted.

"What?"

"If you take another person, then the price is three thousand dollars,"

Gord repeated.

Logan and Nick chuckled, but they both thought it would be a good idea to be more careful around the old man whose mind was not as dull as they first might have thought.

The following morning, a yellow bush plane landed on the airstrip behind the Crozier place. Nick and Tony, each with only a backpack, boarded the plane, and it was airborne moments later. Thankfully, it was a clear day, and three and a half hours later, they were landing at Yellowknife. As the plane was refuelled, Nick and Tony had only a few minutes to stretch their legs and find a bathroom. The pilot already had the twin engine propellers turning when the two men re-boarded the aircraft.

The two-and-a-half-hour flight from Yellowknife to Kugluktuk was about as mediocre as their first leg from Grande Prairie. The terrain was beautiful, but eventually, the expanse of white snow and ice, broken by intermittent trees, became repetitive. It was close to 4:00 p.m. when the pilot told them to prepare for their landing. It was a little worrisome to the two agents since, this far north, the sun had set some time ago. Both men tried to peer forward out the small side windows and saw only a few runway lights barely visible in front of them.

Thankfully, the plane landed safely, and the men hastily departed it. There was only one small building beside the runway, and from it, already speeding towards them, was a snowmobile pulling a covered sled. Once it arrived beside the plane, a middle-aged, red-faced man with sparse grey whiskers smiled widely. Through the smile, he said, "You need a ride to town?"

Nick looked in the direction the man was pointing and saw a small collection of shacks, houses and what appeared to be re-purposed cargo containers—lots of them. The settlement was 200 metres away. *They could walk*, Nick thought, but why not take the ride since it was frigid, made even colder by the chill wind. "Sure," Nick said. "Take us to see Uki."

The Inuit man's eyes went wide, first in surprise, then in admiration. "Ah! You know Uki!" He opened the plastic door of the sled and wiped the seat of the small amount of snow that had settled there. "Please, enter and we'll be there in a few minutes."

Nick and Tony boarded the sled, and the local man pulled his hood tight around his face before the snowmobile and sled raced off towards town. Even in the dark, the lack of trees was very obvious. The airport was on slightly higher ground, sloping down to the hamlet, and beyond it was the Coppermine River where it spilled into Coronation Gulf.

As they were driven into the small town, it didn't look any more welcoming than it did from the airstrip. The middle sections of the roads were plowed, leaving a lane wide enough for a single, four-wheel drive vehicle, or the snowmobiles that seemed to be the preference. The snow along the buildings was piled halfway up the outside walls, except where it had been cleared away at the window and door openings.

They stopped at a large, red storage container where a door had been cut into the side of it. Nick gave their driver 20 dollars, and that, once again, brought a wide smile to his face. The local man said, "Anything you need, you tell Uki to send for Pana." For some reason, he saluted before firing the throttle and speeding away.

Strange fellow, Nick thought as he pulled open the heavy door before entering the makeshift building. Once inside, they saw a second and third storage container had been added to the back side of this one. Two passage ways and a long window had been cut between each of them, giving the appearance of a large room. White, painted plywood was screwed to all the walls just as the floor was also covered by plywood, but here, the colour was dark-grey. There were several tables surrounded by chairs, in the triple-cargo container building.

The two men undid their coats as they walked by the large heater sitting on a stone hearth, and continued to the second compartment. They sat down at a small table on two old, wooden chairs. Almost immediately, a tiny woman with obviously bowed legs walked out from the third compartment. She was a local, and for the two men, it was difficult to tell her age. Her face had many wrinkles under the large eyeglasses, but her jet-black hair was long and devoid of even a strand of grey.

She smiled as she walked to the table, and with unusual familiarity, she put her hand on Tony's shoulder. "Welcome guys. Can I get you food, or drinks?"

Nick had removed his coat and pushed it back over the chair back. "Both would be great. What kind of beer do you have?"

"Have you looked outside? Cold, that's the type we have." She was stone-faced as she gave the response, but only for a few seconds before she burst out laughing. "How about a Molson's for both of you?"

Nick had a twisted smile on his face since he was not yet sure what to make of the woman. "Sure. By chance, are you Uki?"

The woman was already walking away when she turned with one raised eyebrow indicating her curiosity. "Who's asking?"

"My name's Nick and this is Tony. We're both from Grande Prairie where a mutual friend, Gord Crozier, said you might be able to help us out."

Her dark eyes lit up. "Gordie! I haven't seen him in forever. How is he?"

"He's doing great," Nick replied. "He's getting older, but he still has a lot of spirit."

Uki flashed her hands in front of her. "Hold on guys. You must be starving, so let me get your drinks, and I'll make you something special to eat. Just trust me on that. Then, you can tell me all about my sweetheart, Gordie."

"Sounds great," Nick yelled, seeing she was already in the next compartment.

As Nick watched, he saw her disappear through a smaller door to what must have been a fourth compartment. A moment later she returned with the two beers. "Sorry for the cans, but we don't recycle glass very well up here."

She was gone in a flash and didn't return until she had two large plates of food, the steam from each indicating it was fresh off the stove. She placed the plates in front of the men, who couldn't decide what was better, the aroma or the beautiful arrangement.

Uki pulled a chair to the table and lowered herself onto it while pointing at Nick's plate. "This is a bit of caribou steak, and this is a nice piece of grilled, arctic char. It's our version of *Surf and Turf*."

Tony pointed to a small mound of light-brown pods covered with a dark-green, leafy plant. "This smells great. What is it?"

"It's grilled, salted seaweed," she proudly replied.

"What's under it?" Tony asked.

She chuckled. "You white guys can be hilarious. It's Uncle Ben's rice!" she said as her chuckle changed to a cackle.

The two men hadn't eaten all day, but even with that, Uki was amazed at how fast they finished their meal. Both men leaned back in their chairs with their bellies fully satisfied.

"So, Gordie's really doing okay?" Uki asked. "We were very close at one time. I think, in our younger years, he asked me to marry him six times."

"He's getting on in years, but he's sharp as a whip," Nick offered. "He told us you might be able to help us out."

"Not sure what an Inuit girl in this little *speck of a place* could possibly help with, but ask away."

Nick leaned forward and clasped his fingers in front of him on the table.

"Tony and I are travel agents who have a very eclectic clientel. We have people who've had enough of summer spa vacations, and even the simple hunting trips don't give them the excitement they search for. We have people who want to hunt for caribou and polar bear, and fish for arctic cod and char. Gord told us this might be a perfect spot for a home base."

Uki confirmed their thoughts. "We have our share of grizzly and polar bears, caribou, seals and beluga. The fishing is also great."

Nick continued the questions. "Is there a lot of competition in this area. I mean, are there white guys like us, coming here to hunt or even visit?" Adding some emphasis, he asked, "Have you seen other strangers lately?"

A cackle erupted from her lips again. "You obviously saw it outside when you arrived." She saw the confusion on both men's faces. "It's dark! It's dark a lot! It's been dark like this for a couple of months."

"So, no one comes here in your dark season?" Nick asked.

She tilted her head to the side, like a dog viewing something it didn't understand. "Not many people come here at the best of times, so why would anyone come here in the dark season? You can't shoot very well if you can't see," she blurted.

While Tony tapped his fingers on the table, Nick said, "You make perfect sense, but from what you tell me, I would assume you have a light season when the hunting and fishing is great. Are there many strangers or hunters around with guides who would give our venture competition?"

The confusion on Uki's face changed to a sympathetic look a loving mother would give to her child when he or she said something really stupid. "There are a few people around in the spring and summer, but guys, I hope you haven't invested a lot in this. Other than the Inuit, who hunt for food, not many others come here. We're not a wealthy people, so our government has licensing fees and export fees, making it very expensive to hunt here."

"Gord said you'd tell us what we needed to know, and I think you have, even if it wasn't what we wanted," Nick admitted.

She smiled sympathetically and said, "You guys must be tired by now. I have another container out back with a heater and two nice warm beds. It's not the Holiday Inn, but for $30.00 each, it'll provide a nice place for you to sleep.

"That sounds like a deal," Nick agreed. He reached into his pocket and gave Uki 200 dollars. "I hope that covers everything and shows our appreciation for the information." He reached into his pocket a second time and pulled out another hundred-dollar bill before pushing it towards Uki.

"This is if you remember any details of other white people who visited, who might be our competition."

With a pointed finger, she pushed Nick's hand away. "Two hundred is very generous. Keep that other bill until I think of anything."

That was the end of their conversation. Uki led them to the cargo container after she obtained two more cold beers for their bedtime snack. She showed them the bathroom and even a shower, before she trained them on the use of the gas heater. Finally, she showed them where extra blankets were piled at the foot of each of the two beds.

They fell asleep quickly, although, their slumber was restless due to the uncomfortable nature of the lumpy mattresses. Considering this, it was not a surprise they were up very early in the morning. Although Uki was very insistent she make them a traditional breakfast of whale blubber, they thought, considering the upcoming plane ride, it would be best to forgo such a meal.

Nick asked Uki if she could contact Pana for a ride back to the airfield. It was 8:00 a.m. so still dark outside: in fact, the sun would not rise until 11:30 a.m. only to set again at 1:30 p.m. Uki picked up a flash light and went outside the front door. She stood facing the airfield and waved the flashlight over her head three times. In the distance, another flashlight was moved in a similar motion.

When she returned into her cargo container, she said, "He'll be here in a minute."

In the small building beside the airfield, Kallik, the keeper of the airfield, and his granddaughter, Sophia, were watching the pilot do a pre-flight check after the refueling. The pilot, who knew a girl in town and slept there, yawned and tried to rub the sleep from his eyes. Kallik and his granddaughter's attentions were drawn away by the sound of a snowmobile engine being fired up. Kallik said, "There goes your father to pick up the two white guys."

The young girl, who was 12, asked, "What did Grandma Uki say about them?"

Kallik squatted down and replied, "She said they are nosy white people who don't belong here."

Sophia put a finger to the corner of her lip and her eyes lit up. "Are these the people the white man with the nice smile told us might come?"

"It seems so," Kallik said. "But remember, the nice man gave us a lot of money to not say a word about them, so we must keep our promise."

"Of course, Grandpa," she replied as she watched her father drive his snowmobile, pulling the sled behind it, in front of their little building.

Nick gave Pana another 20-dollar bill before rushing into the small building, followed by Tony. Nick looked at Kallik and asked, "How much do we owe you for the fuel?"

"It's 800 dollars," Kallik answered.

As Nick counted out the bills, he asked the older man, "Have you seen many strangers land here lately?"

As Kallik closed his fist on the cash, he replied, "No one comes here in the dark season."

Smiling down at the young girl, Nick repeated the same question to her. She gave him a sweet smile and said, "Nope, no one."

Tony and Nick boarded the plane, and moments later, they were airborne, thankfully heading south. An hour and a half later, they landed in Wekweeti, where they quickly realized this stop was even more of a waste of time. Once the two Russian agents left the plane and headed for the recommended local hunting lodge, there were no useful answers. The same answers of not having seen white strangers was affirmed by almost the entire population of 150 people, who were outside the lodge when Nick and Tony walked outside. The native people, who pointed and gawked at them, made it obvious white people had not visited their settlement in a long time.

They only wasted 45 minutes on the ground before lifting off once again, this time towards Yellowknife. When they landed in the capital city of the Northwest Territories, it was noon, and the sun was high in the sky. Their plane was parked beside a hanger, after which the pilot negotiated with an airport worker in the building. Following some arm flailing by both men, their pilot returned to the two Russians standing beside the bush plane.

The pilot held his hand out to Nick and said, "Give me 200 dollars."

"For what?" Nick blurted.

Pointing to a red pick-up truck beside the hanger, the pilot explained, "It's the fee to rent that vehicle for two hours, so you can look around Yellowknife. If you need longer than that, you can rent another vehicle in town."

Seeing there weren't many other options, Nick counted out another 200 dollars. Once the money was transferred, the pilot tossed Nick the keys.

The floorboard in the front passenger compartment was covered with old McDonald's wrappers, but when Nick turned the key in the older model vehicle, it roared to life. It was another cold day, so the two Russians were thankful the heater in the vehicle worked well. They left the airport grounds and took a drive through the town. It didn't take long since there were only 20 thousand people living in Yellowknife, but enough to support a Walmart, Canadian Tire, a Co-op and a couple of independent hardware stores. There was more here to investigate than the two hours would allow them. In addition, Nick had come to realize anyone travelling further north to the Arctic needed to pass through Yellowknife, so he made a decision as he pulled up to the Days Inn.

Tony asked, "Why are we stopping here?"

Nick put the pick-up in *park* and replied, "We stopped here because the sign says they have rent-a-cars."

Tony's eyes went wide. "Hold on! You're not leaving me here!"

With a face showing his irritation, Nick bobbed his head back and forth. "It's only for a few days. You can get a room here and rent a car. I'm going to ask a few questions at the airport and then fly back to Grande Prairie."

Tony's face was red, and it wasn't from the cold he felt as he stepped out of the vehicle. Nick powered down the passenger window and encouraged his comrade. "I'll be back for you soon. Keep your phone on, and keep a close eye on people in and out of the airport."

Ultimately, Tony was a good soldier. He pulled himself up to his full height and answered, "Yes, Sir!"

Nick headed back to the airport where he counted 15 large hangers around the two runways. He went to each in turn, asking questions about flights going north, both ones he might book and ones that might have been undertaken in the last month. Half the people he spoke to were from the native population, so as a white person, they were generally very reluctant with their words to him. Even the more talkative folk didn't give any clues to unusual flights to the north.

There were two hangers left for him to review, and these were the only two on the west side of the airfield. The first hanger was a white, aluminum-sided building, with many streaks of rust along the side walls. When Nick drove up to the building, a man was just about to enter it through the man-door.

Nick stepped out of the vehicle and yelled over, "Excuse me, Sir!"

The man stopped and looked back at Nick who was jogging over. The burly man said, "It's cold out! Hurry up if you want to talk to me!"

Nick increased his pace the last few metres and entered the hanger ahead of the large man. He was easily 300 pounds and six-foot-six-inches tall. Unusually, he had a round, friendly babyface and smiled before he said, "What can I help you with?"

Pulling off his gloves, Nick blew into his cold hands. He peered up at the larger man and said, "I missed my flight to Kugluktuk yesterday, and I need to catch up to my two friends. Any chance you could fly me there?"

The big man blurted, "Now? Really? No one goes to Kugluktuk in the dark season."

Nick sighed. It was the same answer he'd received at every other hanger he checked. He reached in his pocket and pulled out a 100-dollar bill. As he held it out to the man, he asked, "In the last month, have there been any charters flying north? I have my reasons, so I need the information."

Several times, the big man's gaze switched back and forth from the bill to Nick's eyes." He grinned and said, "I wish I could take your money with a made-up story, but I'm not like that. I can't tell you I know of any strange charters of white people going north."

Nick sighed and put the bill back into his pocket. He thanked the man and headed back out to the pick-up truck. As he drove by the last hanger, it looked deserted with the door hanging off its hinges. Consequently, he drove back to the hanger where the yellow bush plane was waiting for him.

The big, baby-faced man watched out the window of the man-door of his hanger. He didn't lose sight of Nick and his red pick-up, and he didn't release his grip on the handgun in his pocket until he saw the yellow plane leave the ground. As he watched it recede in the distance, he heard the engines of a larger plane from the opposite direction. Focusing there, he saw the white De Havilland Buffalo lining up for its final approach. Two minutes later, after landing, the larger airplane was directed towards the hanger he was in. He pressed a button on an electrical box, and the two large hanger doors creaked as they began to slide open. The pilot directed the Buffalo into the hanger, after which the big man pressed the second button on the electrical box, resulting in the doors returning to their closed position.

Once the side door of the plane was opened, Rita, Josh, Natalie and the two security personnel exited the plane. The big man walked over towards Rita where introductions were made. Rita said, "This is Larry. Yellowknife is a critical point in our supply chain, so it was important for us to have a Sholite stationed here."

Josh shook the man's hand, and Natalie gave him a polite nod along with a smile.

Natalie put her hand on Rita's arm and said, "I need to make a call to make sure the gasoline delivery comes to this hanger."

Rita pulled out her phone and saw the time was 2:30 p.m. "My goodness. We arrived just in time."

Natalie was already walking away when she dialed the phone number she'd been told to call with the final directions. A woman on the other end of the connection answered. It sounded like the woman was in a plane, and Natalie gave her the location of their exact hanger. The agent repeated back the instructions in a military manner, verifying her understanding before the line was disconnected.

Twenty-five minutes later, they saw a grey, non-descript Airbus 295 land on the far runway. It taxied over to a position in front of their hanger, and the twin turboprops slowed. A woman exited the plane and was jogging towards the hanger. Natalie met her halfway where the two shook hands. The woman said, "Identification please."

Natalie pulled out her black wallet and opened it before handing it to the woman who then held it up at eye level. Once Natalie's CSE credentials were verified, she handed it back. By the plane, another man in black coveralls, a thick black coat and military boots watched the discussion with his hands on his hips. Once Natalie's contact held her thumb up in the air, the man clapped his hands together. Sound travelled well across the thin, cold air, and they could hear the man yell, "Okay! Let's get this stuff unloaded!" The cargo door of the plane was opened, and barrels were rapidly rolled out onto the snow-covered tarmac.

Thirty minutes later, 40 barrels of gasoline were in the hanger beside the De Havilland Buffalo. The Airbus 295 lifted off just before the Bell 525 helicopter landed in the exact spot previously taken by the covert, military plane.

Natalie was surprised to see Adrian himself pop out of the aircraft. He ran over to the hanger, and once inside, he gave Natalie and Rita huge hugs. He shook Josh's hand as well as the hands of the two security personnel. "I've heard all went very well," Adrian announced. He turned towards the gasoline barrels and added, "I see you've come through as well." He gave Natalie that famously wide smile along with a wink.

Rita interrupted, "Yes, things have gone well. How are things in Fort Nelson?"

"Just as well. We have a few final adjustments to make, but we're ready for phase one of the plan for the day after tomorrow," Adrian explained.

"Phase one?" Josh asked.

Adrian slapped Josh on the back as he said, "Let's get on the helicopter, and I'll explain on the way back."

Once they were on the Bell 525 and they were underway to Fort Nelson, Adrian continued the explanation. "We've finished the control room at Fort Nelson. There are two parts to the plan. The second part we have discussed, where a high-energy electromagnetic beam will be sent from each of the seven DEW line stations, to a point above your north pole. However, Lashkar asked a while ago, 'Where would the energy for the ESUs come from?'"

Recognition came to both Natalie and Josh as they remembered the unanswered question.

Adrian elaborated, "As you're aware, we're very advanced in our knowledge and use of electromagnetic energy. Your sun continually sends out electromagnetic eruptions and, on your world, the larger ones are called solar flares with coronal mass ejections. You have had several huge events of this type, most notably the 1859 solar storm that shut down telegraph lines. There was also the 1972 event that knocked out phone communication across many American states and, more recently, the 1989 event that shut down electricity over a vast part of Canada."

Natalie shook her head. "I don't see what this has to do with the ESUs."

Adrian maintained the smile, but his brow furrowed with irritation. "Isn't it clear? We're going to fill the ESUs by capturing the energy from a solar flare!"

Now it was Josh who shook his head. "Well, you might be waiting a long time for a solar flare, especially one matching the size of the one you need."

Pulling out his phone, Adrian checked the time, and you could tell, as he silently counted, he was performing some mental math. "As you also know, Sholites have been on your Earth for about 40 years in anticipation of this event. We have advanced techniques and equipment which we have utilized to monitor the sun's activities, including sun spots, solar flares and coronal mass ejections. From this, our science allows us to accurately predict these events."

"And?" Natalie asked.

Adrian looked at his phone again and readjusted his calculation. "In a little under two days, or more exactly, 43 hours and 18 minutes from now, a large solar storm from the sun will hit the Earth and we'll be ready to capture the energy to fill our ESUs."

Chapter 25: The Solar Flare

The helicopter, carrying Adrian, Rita, Josh and Natalie, made it back to the Fort Nelson DEW line station just in time. As the rotor blades were winding down, a wall of snow began to fall. It was so thick, the people at the base couldn't see halfway across the compound.

The four travellers had a late meal in the mess hall of the barracks, after which Adrian indicated he was tired. In the morning, he would explain more about the solar flares, and he wanted to show them the control room.

Adrian rose to his feet, and said, "The day after tomorrow we'll capture the energy from the solar storm, and if all goes as planned, I estimate, two days later, we'll fire the EMP. It'll be a great day for the people of Earth and the Sholites on Talus 3 as well."

With a wide yawn, Adrian retreated towards his room, followed by Rita a moment later. Now that she had finished eating, Natalie also realized how tired she was. Her eyelids drooped, and the area beneath her eyes were shaded grey.

Josh also noticed and asked her, "Are you feeling okay?"

Natalie managed a smile. She always managed a smile for him. She replied. "I'm just exhausted. I need my man to take me to bed."

Josh winked at her as he rose to his feet. "I've had worse propositions." He pulled her to her feet and wrapped his arm around her waist as they headed for the stairs.

At the top, they were about to turn right, but a creak from the opposite direction caught their attention. They both turned their heads to see Lashkar, in bare feet, carefully pulling a door closed. He gingerly took a step towards the stairs, but then he lifted his head and saw his two friends watching him. Frozen momentarily, he had the guiltiest look on his face.

Natalie smiled and waved. Lashkar awkwardly waved back, and as much as he would rather go in the other direction, he knew that would make this look even worse. He walked over to his friends and, as calmly as he could, said, "How goes it?"

As Natalie first looked at Lashkar's dishevelled hair, then tilted her gaze around him to the door he just exited, she snickered and said, "Isn't that Nancy's room?"

Lashkar nervously ran his fingers back through his hair and stammered, "Well—yes—she was—uh…"

"Giving you some after-class training," Josh interrupted with a grin.

"Shut up already," Lashkar retorted, his voice loud enough to give his friends fair warning not to pursue the line of teasing he sensed was coming, but low enough to not attract the attention of others in this part of the barracks.

Josh shrugged as Natalie twisted out of his arm. As she walked down the hallway, her fingers waved her goodbyes to the two men. "Goodnight boys," she said.

Josh moved to follow her, but Lashkar grasped his arm. Josh looked at Lashkar's face, and he saw Lashkar wanted him to stay. Josh's gaze followed Natalie and he said, "I'll be along in a minute."

Once Natalie had entered their room, Josh asked Lashkar, "What's up?"

"I was hoping to get you alone for a minute. I see you keeping your distance from a lot of the events around the EMP plan, so I think you might be more objective."

"What's wrong, Lashkar?"

Lashkar shook his head. "There might be nothing wrong, but as you know, I've been helping out on the computer work and calculations. The Sholites leave me alone, and I do a good job. I've been learning their language, and their system of math is a bit different, but it's enough that it slows down my understanding."

"I think you've done very well," Josh offered.

"I think Natalie has told you, and you've seen for yourself by now, I have a hard time keeping my nose out of things," Lashkar confessed. "I've spent some time looking at the restricted Sholite side of the computer systems. I don't think they know I've been poking around there. They don't have firewalls, because, who the hell knows Sholite math?"

"It sounds like you know some," Josh responded.

"Maybe I've learned enough to get myself in trouble. Maybe I'm making something out of nothing…"

"Get to the point, Lashkar," Josh urged.

Lashkar looked nervously down the hall, then up the other side, and with his voice barely above a whisper, he said, "I don't think their math is right. I've looked at the science behind the EMP. This includes the force the EMP will supply and the mass of Talus 3. I'll confess, I only understand bits of their math, but it seems the load they'll be using to nudge Talus 3 off the collision course with Earth, is too much, by a lot."

Josh put his hand on Lashkar's shoulder and looked him straight in the eye. "These are people who say they can predict a solar flare within a 15-minute window. You are the smartest man I know, but if I had to put your suspicion, backed only by a rudimentary knowledge of their language and math, against their experts, I would have to go with the Sholite's knowledge, my friend."

Lashkar began to object, but Josh squeezed his shoulder. Josh said in a tone as quiet as he could, "I've seen their spaceship appear and disappear! They are that far ahead of us."

Lashkar didn't know how to respond to that, so Josh continued, "Keep looking. Don't let them know you are suspicious because it is likely no more than that—a suspicion. Don't tell anyone else about this, especially Natalie. She has enough on her mind right now."

"That makes sense," the younger man replied. "But, if I find out more, I might need your help."

Josh slapped Lashkar on the back. "You can count on me, Lashkar," he said before he headed down the hallway, following Natalie's earlier footsteps.

In the morning, the curtains in Natalie and Josh's room was open just a crack. The sun had just risen, and a narrow beam of bright sunlight cut through the dimness of the room. From their make-shift double bed in the middle of the room, Natalie, lying down, held her hand up in the air. She moved her fingers slowly back and forth through the ray of light. Each time the sunlight passed over her finger, the ring Josh gave her sparkled. At first, she was surprised by the unique ring, but now, she absolutely loved it. The colours seemed to change as she turned her finger, and the light-blue, lightning-like lines fascinated her.

"I'm glad you like it." The sleepy voice came from beside her.

"Josh, I don't just like it. I love it, and I don't think I will ever take it off—at least that's my hope."

"That is the plan," Josh whispered as he pulled her into his arms.

He tried to kiss her, but she brought her fingers up to his chin and held him back. "Things can change quickly. The Russians and the Korians aren't far behind us. You heard what Adrian said about their joint assault squad showing up at the farmhouse near Bezanson. They don't seem like the people who will take prisoners."

Josh wrapped his fingers around her wrist and removed her hand. He was insistent, so he kissed her. It was passionate but quick because he had a few words on the topic to say himself. "I have been doing some thinking as well. I love my home in New York, but this landscape here in Canada is even more beautiful."

She looked at him curiously.

"I know. It's freezing cold, and the last time I looked last night, 30 centimetres of snow had fallen with no end to the white onslaught in sight. To many, they would not see the beauty of this, but I do. I see the snow, and I feel the cold, but it's the kind of cold that makes me feel alive and appreciate the warmth of a fire. I see the grand white pines and the animal life that thrives in this environment. I feel my need for this land as much as they do."

Natalie moved to speak, but Josh put his finger to her lips. He said, "But most important is the knowledge this is the land where we found each other, from our first intimate night in Edmonton, to this past night where, having you curl up to me, gives me the happiest feeling in my life. So, when I see and think of this timeless landscape, it reminds me of us."

Natalie smiled and said, "My, that was quite a speech."

Josh blushed but Natalie quickly added, "Don't get me wrong. I loved it. You're a big man, but inside, you're sensitive, and yes, I'm happy knowing you open your heart to me." Her last words came in a whisper. "It melts me."

Josh chuckled. "I do have an ulterior motive."

"What is that?"

"A request," Josh said.

"I'm listening."

"You mentioned the danger that follows us," Josh reminded her. "If I should be killed here, don't send me back home. I want to be buried here in what I consider my new land."

Natalie turned away from him, so he didn't see the tears that immediately came to her eyes. She waited a few seconds, and after wiping the tears and her nose, she said, "Yes, that makes sense."

Thirty minutes later, they were back in the mess hall. They saw Edward sitting with Lashkar and were about to join them when Josh held his nose up in the air. "Bacon! I smell bacon!"

255

Natalie pushed him playfully. "You go ahead. I'm going to say 'good morning,' to Lashkar and my dad, then I'll join you."

Natalie sat down and did exactly that, resulting in a wide smile on her father's face. However, she looked at his plate and saw very little had been eaten. Immediately her cat-like eyes narrowed with concern and she asked, "Is everything okay?"

Edward chuckled and replied, "I'm fine—just a little tired. I think I overdid it a bit yesterday."

Still having the look of concern on her face, she continued to pester him. "Well, make sure you don't today. Just slow down a bit."

"I will," he agreed.

"Promise?"

"I promise, my dear," he indicated with a look of irritation on his own face to convey the message of, "enough," to her.

Josh interrupted and saved Edward from more pestering. He was carrying two plates, heaped with scrambled eggs and a disproportionate amount of bacon. He pushed one in front of Natalie and sat down in front of the other. After finishing his food in record time, Josh saw Natalie was also finished, but her plate was only half empty. He pointed at it, and she nodded. He smiled and pulled her plate in front of him for *round two*.

After Josh finished, Edward gave his goodbyes, indicating he had work to complete. Natalie warned him again about overwork, then she, Josh and Lashkar headed for the communications building. Looking outside, they saw at least 50 centimetres of snow in the clearing between the buildings. A plow was methodically moving back and forth across the grounds, helped by several younger workers with shovels.

After donning their coats and heavy boots, they walked over to the communications building. There, they removed and hung up their coats. Since they didn't want snow all over the floor, there were disposable *booties* they pulled on before they entered the main communications room they'd been in before. Rita saw them and pointed while saying, "He's in the room next door!"

Josh, Natalie and Lashkar did an about face and were out the door, and they then walked towards the next door down the hallway. Josh poked his face in and knocked on the door jamb.

Adrian, who was sitting on a stool with his face hanging over a book, didn't look up. He said, "C'mon in."

They did so and walked around to the far side of the large work bench Adrian was sitting at. Under the workbench were three computer servers, and there were two computer monitors on the upper surface. They could see one had English writing on it, and the other was filled with the symbols they had learned were Sholite in origin. Both the left wall and the back wall behind Adrian, were filled from one end to the other with floor to ceiling, grey electrical cabinets. On each cabinet was an electrical disconnect, several gauges and many small indicator lights.

When Adrian lifted his face, of course, the wide smile was there. He spread his arms and proudly said, "What do you think?"

Josh didn't say much. In fact, Natalie had noticed Josh didn't ask too many questions, especially when Adrian was explaining things. She knew Josh was no dummy. She'd seen many times, while helping, and most recently at the Bernard Harbour DEW line site, he had an astute aptitude for quite advanced electronics. He picked things up quickly, so when he was quiet, Natalie assumed he just preferred she or Lashkar asked the questions."

"It's very impressive," Lashkar replied.

Adrian rose to his feet and clapped his hands together. "This is where it will start." He pointed to the electrical cabinets. "The electronics are a combination of Sholite and Earthen technology, melded together to achieve our goal." He put his hands on top of the two monitors. "The computers here communicate with all seven DEW line sites, first coordinating the extraction of energy from the solar storm hitting us tomorrow, and then coordinating the firing of the electromagnetic beams that will push a larger pulse towards Talus 3."

"I have a question," Lashkar said.

"Of course," Adrian responded.

"How large is the solar flare, and will it cause damage to the Earth?"

"That's a great question."

Josh frowned at Adrian's words. He had learned it was a response politicians and salesmen learned and used to patronize sheep-like people in their audience.

"This solar flare is nowhere near as large as your last major event in 1989," Adrian explained. "In eastern Canada, the cell phones will likely be out for a few days, and other signals such as cable TV will also be affected. The power will go out in much of Canada, but there won't be enough incoming energy to do permanent damage. Breakers, for the most part, will need to be reset, so the damage will be minimal."

"That's good news," Natalie offered.

"Now, we need to be up and running quickly, so there are precautions we need to take," Adrian added. "First thing in the morning, take the batteries out of your phones, your laptops and anything else electrical. We have electrical disconnects throughout this compound, so we can isolate ourselves. At each DEW line station, we have a similar configuration. We've kept two people at each station who must be ten kilometres clear of the station when the solar storm hits. They'll then return to the stations, reconnect the disconnects and we should be ready to fire the EMP."

Josh frowned again.

Adrian saw this and admitted, "I must apologize again, Josh, but your son was needed to man the Greenland site for this purpose. This has delayed your reunion, but in my estimation, it'll only be another week."

Josh did not reply, just shrugged and gave a slight nod.

"What's that?" Lashkar asked as he pointed to a small, glass screen mounted on one of the electrical panels.

"In fact, that's the *fire* button," the Sholite leader explained. "Once the computer programs are initialized for the EMP, the *fire* command is set in motion by either my palm, or Rita's, being pressed to that sensor."

"It sounds like you're well prepared," Natalie admitted.

"Not, *I*, but *we*, are well prepared. We're in this together," Adrian corrected.

Josh gave a slight smirk and thought, *more leadership training mumbo-jumbo.*

The rest of their day was relaxed. Lashkar left the group to work on some calculations with Nancy who, by all appearances, was his science trainer with benefits. Natalie went to check on her father and then returned to Josh. Although tomorrow's solar storm was easily diluted down by Adrian's smooth words, Natalie and Josh couldn't help but think there was some element of risk. That thought resulted in the two lovers being curled up naked in their bed. Their lovemaking was intense with an urgency that left them both out of breath several times.

In the morning, things were different. There was a flurry of activity around the compound, but it was organized. Everyone seemed to know where to go and what to do. Natalie, as instructed, removed the batteries from their electrical devices, and they put them in an isolation bag they'd been given. They moved to the communication room which was filled with people. Adrian sat at the head of the large table, monitoring everything from a management level. Rita, in fact, was the one who was barking out orders and held a phone to her ear every few seconds.

There was a LED timer on the table in the middle of the room, and it was counting down. At that specific moment when Josh and Natalie sat down, the timer read, *62 minutes*.

When the timer hit *60*, Rita yelled out, "Quiet!"

The room fell silent, and Rita put her cell phone on speaker. One at a time, she called for each DEW line station to call out the disconnection of their specific stations. A voice from each station in turn, verified with a single word, "Disconnected."

Once all the stations were verified, Rita told the personnel at each station to clear their area. The timer read, *40 minutes*.

Rita now disconnected her phone, put it down and picked up a two-way radio. She pressed the button and said, "Nancy. Come in Nancy."

"Nancy here," came the response.

"Disconnect Fort Nelson power," Rita said.

"Roger. Disconnecting now," Nancy replied.

As Rita pulled the battery from the back of the two-way radio, the overhead lights in the room shut off. Now, there was something no one would've noticed until now. When the power went off, generators were shut down as were the heaters and furnaces. What they thought was quiet before, was now complete and utter silence in the barren, cold landscape of northern British Columbia. The timer read, *26 minutes*.

Now, everyone waited. Some of the people in the room began to feel the cold. Others, notwithstanding this, began to nervously sweat. Natalie could see many were going over their calculations in their head, hoping they hadn't made mistakes and hoping the people who checked their calculations, did so thoroughly. It was the first time Natalie saw Adrian without the wide smile on his face. Each time the timer in the center of the table clicked down one minute, the tension in the room increased. The timer read, *9 minutes*.

It seemed to take forever, but minute by minute, the timer counted down. When the timer hit *1 minute,* Natalie tensed up and clenched Josh's hand tightly in hers. When the timer hit zero, everyone held their breath, but the anticipation of the unknown was unnecessarily melodramatic since nothing happened.

In the silence, Adrian held a finger in the air, indicating, *wait*.

Beside the timer on the table that was now counting down in negative numbers, there was a small gauge. It was simple and white-faced with a red indicator arm on it. The timer continued to count down and when it read, *11 minutes*, the red indicator arm jumped to the far right of the gauge, hitting the end stop.

Adrian lowered his hand and, finally, there was his wide smile. He said, "Congratulations, people."

There were whoops around the table, and there were hugs while others shook hands. Natalie just sat there and thought, *that was it?*

Adrian clapped his hands together until he had everyone's attention. "In two hours, we'll start the reconnection process. Everyone, keep warm until then. We'll let you know when the station power is on, and when it's safe to turn on your smaller electrical devices. We're all going to meet back here at 4:30 p.m. to evaluate the success of the ESU charging operation." Adrian gave a final clap, indicating the group was dismissed.

Natalie admired Adrian. He seemed to have the charisma to be a born leader. People easily came to trust and follow him. Josh hung back as Natalie and then Lashkar both shook his hand, then Rita's. There were smiles all around.

Lashkar apologized and said he needed to check his equipment, but Natalie and Josh knew he was off to find Nancy. Josh and Natalie went to the mess hall where a second group of people had been waiting, including her father, Edward, who was in a deep conversation with two senior engineers about the amazing, but invisible solar storm.

By 4:30 p.m. the sun had set, and now they saw the effect of the solar storm. Fort Nelson was far enough north so that the workers at the DEW line station had seen the Northern Lights often, but now, due to the charging from the solar storm, the greenish, flowing glow was so intense, it broke the darkness they were used to. It was beautiful, intense, and as they discovered when they met in the communications room, very effective.

Cell phone communications weren't working yet, but the radar connection between the Fort Nelson station and the seven radar stations was. As they watched, they saw each light on the map of Canada on the wall, change from red to green.

Adrian announced, "The ESUs are all successfully charged!"

Once again, there was loud, exuberant clapping, and Adrian had to motion with his hands to regain the quiet in the room. Adrian said, "Rita, please follow up on the check list."

For the next 45 minutes, Rita barked out requests for updates. Workers reported operational computer systems, servers, electrical cabinets, heaters and furnaces. It seemed every piece of equipment had been reviewed and verified. There were only two electrical disconnects that were burned out, but these had already been replaced.

The next order of business was for Nancy to give a report on the impact the solar flare had on the world. She went through several countries and their state of repairs coming out of the event. Of particular importance was the impact on Canada and their present remote location. The affected infrastructure in Eastern Canada was coming back on line quickly. The recovery work in Western Canada was slower, but the storm intensity was less in this area. Nancy concluded her report by saying, "We have electricity to all our systems now, through our generators. We expect regular electrical power, communications, including cell phones, will be back in operation by noon tomorrow."

For a third time, there was a thunderous ovation in the communications room. Adrian yelled over the noise, "There are drinks available in the mess hall for everyone!"

There was a final loud whoop. The meeting didn't need an official adjournment after that. The people piled out of the room, but Natalie and Josh went over to Adrian, once again, to offer their congratulations. Natalie was excited, but Josh not so much. He watched the throng of people exiting the door, and curiously, a young guard, with arms swimming, was trying to make his way into the room against the grain of people. He finally cleared the people and ran over to Adrian.

There was concern on the young man's face, causing Adrian to quickly ask, "What is it?"

Out of breath, the young man said his words through panting breaths. "Come—to the mess hall. It's Edward—collapsed."

Natalie and Josh turned immediately and raced out the door. They pushed people aside and barged their way into the mess hall. Edward was already on a stretcher and was being carried to their infirmary. Natalie sucked in a deep breath when she saw her father was so white, but thankfully, he was conscious and smiling. She grasped his hand and went with the doctor to the medical area.

Josh followed Natalie but kept a respectable distance back. Adrian and Rita met them a few minutes later, where the Sholite leader asked for an update. The Sholite doctor, as he had done many times now as revived people passed away, gave his head a slight shake. Natalie saw the motion and screamed out, "No!"

Josh did not say a word, but put an arm around her. Natalie's face was livid and wild as she yelled, "Give him more medication! Give him more time!"

Edward, now lying in a bed, gripped his daughter's hand and drew her attention. "It's fine Nat. I've had a really good life, and Adrian gave me more time—more quality time."

Natalie was sobbing, and Adrian came in front of her and whispered, "We'll give you and your father some privacy now. There's nothing else we can do. Just know your father was a great man, and he provided critical help in saving our worlds."

Natalie's eyes narrowed. "*Is* a great man."

"Of course," Adrian corrected. He looked at Edward and put his hand on the older man's shoulder. "Thank you for your service."

Each, in turn, put their hand on Edward's shoulder, likely to feel the life in him for the last time. Finally, Josh did the same. Edward whispered, "I know I don't have to tell you to look after her. I've seen your love for her since I met you. All I can say is, thank you."

Josh smiled and then he looked to Natalie, searching.

Natalie clenched Josh's offered hand, but then released it. "Please wait for me outside. I'd like to be alone with my father now."

"I will be in the hallway. Call if you need me," Josh replied.

As Josh left, he closed the door. There were awkward looks between he, Adrian and Rita. Finally, he told them, "You don't have to wait here."

Adrian put his hand on Josh's shoulder and said, "You're a good man, my friend."

There was a chair in the hallway, so Josh sat down as he watched Adrian and Rita walk away. He didn't move from that spot throughout the night. Through the door, he heard Natalie and her father having constant conversations and even some laughter. Josh couldn't make out the words, and he didn't want to. This was a time for the two of them to say goodbye.

Adrian and Rita came back every hour to see if Josh needed anything since, it was obvious, they could do nothing for Edward or Natalie. They even brought Josh a coffee and a sandwich in the early hours of the morning. It was 10:00 in the morning, just as Adrian and Rita came to again check on things, when they heard the click of the door knob. Natalie opened the door. She didn't have to say any words since the message was written on her face. Her father was dead.

Josh jumped to his feet, then slowed as he moved closer to the woman he loved. Once he was within reach, her arms flung around him and a gasping scream came from her throat. Her knees buckled as she fell into his arms. Now, there were only deep sobs and Josh half-carried her away from her father's body, back to their room.

Adrian and Rita stood in the hallway, looking through the door at Edward's body.

Rita mumbled, "Is this all worth it?"

The smile was missing from Adrian's face. "Of course, it is. We know that, so we stay the course."

There was a long pause until Rita added, "You didn't tell him."

"How could I," Adrian blurted. "You saw how badly Natalie took this. We're so close to our goal. We don't need complications."

"But you lied to him."

Adrian let out a deep sigh. "Yes, I did." He looked Rita square in the eyes and whispered, "In two days this will all be over. We can't take unnecessary risks, so how could I tell Josh his son died in this same manner four days ago?"

Chapter 26: The Revelation

It was just after 8:00 a.m. when Logan interrupted Nick's breakfast with a request. Logan told him they needed to go into Grande Prairie for something important. Nick filled his mouth with the last half piece of toast, thankful for the opportunity to leave the farmhouse. The last two days had been a loss with the solar flare event and the subsequent repairs the day after. Their power and all communications were restored now, including the local cell phone towers.

Nick was driving the gold Subaru SUV south down the slush-covered sideroad from Crozier's farmhouse to highway 43. He made a left turn onto the highway and asked, "What business do you have in town?"

"We're going to visit Rick Jensen at Jensen Electric," Logan revealed.

Nick pressed his foot to the brakes and brought the SUV to a stop on the shoulder of the road. "Are you crazy. He doesn't know who we are. That was the plan."

Tilting his face towards his Russian friend, Logan replied, "He knows who we are now. Remember, we have very few leads, so while you were in the north, I contacted Jensen. I told him the same thing we told Gord Crozier. Jensen now firmly believes he was duped by Russian agents who he unwittingly helped. As far as he knows, there is a national emergency he helped create, and we are the Canadian intelligence agents sent to clean up the mess."

Nick looked behind him before easing the vehicle back onto the highway. "Does he have some new information?"

"Not as far as I am aware, "Logan responded. "I sent my two forensic Korians there two days ago to review all his dealings with the Sholites along with their purchase orders over the past few months. They contacted me this morning, indicating they were ready to provide a report."

"I thought your forensic guys were at the Sholite farmhouse?"

"They were, but they finished there, so I sent them to see Jensen," Logan explained.

Nick asked, "Did they find anything at the farmhouse?"

"The place was pretty clean, but they found one crucial piece of information. In one of the barns, they found residual traces of a chemical called sartolin. You wouldn't know it since it does not exist on Earth, but it is a fluid used in an electrical storage unit. These ESU's, as we call them, are very powerful sources of electrical energy, and are proof they are creating a large device to destroy your world."

They were now driving slowly through town until Nick brought the SUV to a stop across the road from Jensen Electric. Once inside the building, Jensen greeted them with a suspicious smile, and he was introduced to Nick.

Logan asked, "Where are Simon and Shane?"

With a slight rearwards flick of his head, Jensen said, "They're in the back."

Jensen led the two men into his back office where the two fellow agents were seated beside the desk. When they saw Logan, they jumped to their feet and gave their greetings.

Logan smiled and looked at the younger of the two men. "Shane, you called earlier and said you have a final report."

"Yes, Sir," came the reply from the tall, blonde, young man. He straightened himself and said, "We've gone through the last three months of purchases Jensen says were made by the Sholites...err...Russians." He smiled before continuing. "Here are the important facts. The purchases of tantalum and mica would indicate they're not making one large device. Rather, they're making several smaller charging stations."

"How do you know this?" Nick interrupted.

The smile on Shane's face fell to a frown for a moment before he answered. "They purchased seven high power electrical emitter assemblies. That's a strong indication there are seven stations in play."

"What else?" Logan asked.

"The ESU's they're building are also smaller—about two cubic metres each. There are 24 in total." He knew the question Logan was about to ask and interjected, "We know there are 24 because they purchased 48 high voltage electrodes—two per cell."

Logan nodded. "So, we aren't looking for one large building, but seven small buildings."

"Yes, Sir," Shane replied, "but not that small. The size of the housed assembly would still be significant."

"Larger than this building?" Nick asked.

"Yes."

Nick followed up the first question. "Bigger than the farmhouse we're staying at?"

"No. It's likely a bit smaller, but not much," Shane clarified.

Logan said, "Good report Shane. We'll meet you two back at the farmhouse."

Logan and Nick walked by Jensen who'd been waiting at the doorway to his office. As the two men entered the main shop, Jensen ran after them yelling, "Guys! Hold up a minute."

Logan and Nick turned as Jensen made his way to them. Jensen asked, "Who are the Sholites?"

Logan lowered an eyebrow and grimaced while Nick reached into his coat pocket, fingering the trigger of his gun. Logan realized Jensen must have been listening carefully by the door and heard the slip Shane made in his report. Logan thought quickly and offered, "The Sholites are a group of people from the city of Shol in northern Russia." He chuckled. "It's probably colder there than it is here."

Jensen had a blank look on his face. You could tell he was reviewing a map of Russia in his mind. Then, he broke out in laughter. "Of course— Shol!"

Logan slapped Jensen on the shoulder and offered, "We won't let those Russians from Shol continue to be a problem. We're scouring Alberta, and we are very close to finding them."

The smile on Jensen's face faded as he said, "Alberta? Why Alberta?"

Nick saw the confusion and interjected, "Why *not* Alberta?"

Rubbing his chin, Jensen admitted, "I never really thought about it, but seeing as you guys had a sack over my head, and you didn't ask, in my panic, I guess I forgot to tell you."

"Tell us what," Logan urged.

"Well, when Nancy came in her truck to pick up supplies, the license plate on the truck was a British Columbia plate, not Albertan."

Both Logan and Nick had the same look on their face. It was a *what the hell* look mixed with a bit of embarrassment at the oversight. Nick, curtly stated, "Thanks. We gotta go," and the two men were out the door.

When they got back to Crozier's farmhouse, neither man was in a good mood. They asked Gord if he had a map of British Columbia, which he did.

There were four of them at the kitchen table looking at the map: Nick, Logan, Gord and Brandon, the Russian agent from Calgary. They scoured for highways that went from Grande Prairie to any part of British Columbia. In fact, because of the towering Rocky Mountains, there were very few.

Gord slammed his finger down on the map and stated, "You can look at the map as long as you want, but I'm telling you there are only two roads from Grande Prairie into British Columbia. Either you go highway 97 south, and you get to Prince George, or you take the same highway north, and you arrive at Fort Nelson."

Brandon leaned forward and urged, "Let's keep our heads. What do we know, and what are we looking for?"

Nick summarized what they knew. "We know the bulk of the enemy force was staying at Bezanson, just east of here for quite some time. They all left there a week ago, and we don't know where they went. We've checked the Yellowknife area and they aren't there, but now we have a lead that indicates they might be in British Columbia."

"Didn't you take a trip further north?" Brandon asked. "What's it called, Kugluk…"

"Kugluktuk." Nick finished the name for him. "We know the enemy was doing something up in the Arctic, and somehow, that's supposed to have a connection to British Columbia."

Logan interrupted. "Not only that, but we are looking for a series of seven buildings, not small, yet not overly large. Each would be a bit smaller than this house."

"There was nothing like that in Kugluktuk," Nick elaborated.

"You're wrong," Gord said in his high-pitched voice.

"I was there," Nick retorted.

Gord rose to his feet and stretched his back before saying, "I need to get another map to prove you're wrong." The old man shuffled away, and a few minutes later, he returned with a metre-long roll of paper. He unrolled it on the table and used the salt and pepper shakers to hold it open. The map they all saw was yellowed with the ripped edges showing its age. It was a map of Canada, but in the bottom title block, stamped, were the words, *Classified. Property of the Royal Canadian Army*.

Logan pulled open the curled edge of the map nearest him and said, "What's this, Gord?"

"It's a map showing the locations of the old DEW line stations across the Arctic Circle," Gord explained.

All three other men leaned in as Nick asked, "What are DEW line stations?"

"Back in the '50s, we were afraid of missile attacks coming over the Arctic from the Commies. The Americans, with our help, built a series of 63 radar stations to watch for this. DEW stands for *distant early warning*, so that should make it self explanatory," Gord indicated.

"Are these stations still active?" Nick asked.

"Hell no!" Gord hissed. "I said, 'in the '50s.' They're obsolete now. Some have been torn down, and some are still there in ruins, filled with snow and ice."

"How large are these radar stations?" Logan asked.

Reaching into the pocket of his housecoat, Gord retrieved a black and white polaroid picture and tossed it to the center of the table. "That's me in front of a typical station in 1956. You can see the two-story building and the radar and communication towers in the background. Most of the stations also had a runway. I know because I used to deliver supplies to them."

Nick leaned over the map and traced a finger along the northern coast near Kugluktuk. "There are three DEW line stations right here."

"I guess it's possible," Logan added. "These sites are remote and would be perfect for the enemy to set up their equipment. All they would have to do would be to retrofit seven of them."

Brandon scratched his head. "I'm lost. What connection does this have to British Columbia?"

Gord had a smirk on his face. "The stations across the Arctic Circle go from Alaska all the way to Greenland, but these are only the radar sites. There were also bases whose sole purpose was to communicate with the radar stations, processing their data and requests. These three communication bases were further south."

"So?" Nick said.

Gord thrust his finger downwards and pushed it into the map. His eyes were narrow slits as he said, "One of the communication bases was right here." The other three men looked, and the old man's finger was pressed on Fort Nelson.

"You have to be kidding!" Nick uttered.

Logan rose to his feet and waited a moment as he looked at the old, *but not so dull* man. "You said you could still fly that Chinook helicopter."

"Yup."

"How long to fly to Fort Nelson?" Logan asked.

"A little under three hours. I've done it many times," Gord stated.

Logan took a deep breath. He looked at each of the men surrounding the table. "At 8:00 tomorrow morning, we're going to the Fort Nelson DEW line station—all of us." He turned to Brandon. "You make sure everyone is prepared and armed. Also grab the fellow who came from Vancouver who said he knew helicopters. Get him to check out the Chinook with Gord and take it for a test flight. I don't want any surprises in the morning." Logan turned to his friend, Nick and put his hand on Nick's shoulder. "I think we've finally caught up with them. With any luck, tomorrow, this will all be over."

Chapter 27: The Battle

Lashkar was lying on the bed in Nancy's room. He had a restless night, just as many of the people at the Fort Nelson DEW line site, Sholites and Earthers alike, would've had. It was 6:00 a.m. and the room was dark except for the light shining through the open bathroom door. In fact, this time of year in early December, it was dark for most of the day. On this particular day when the electromagnetic pulse was to be shot out towards Talus 3, the sun was set to rise at 9:21 a.m. Adrian thought it would be apropos for the EMP blast to be initiated at that same moment.

However, Lashkar's concern for the blast calculations had grown. He slung himself up to a sitting position with his legs slung over the side of the bed. He said, "Nancy, there's something we need to talk about that's been bothering me."

Nancy came out from the bathroom wearing a pretty burgundy pair of work coveralls. She smiled at Lashkar and turned on the light in the main room. "Have you seen my cell phone?"

Holding his arm up over his eyes to deflect the sudden onslaught of light, Lashkar replied, "How am I supposed to see anything?"

Nancy chuckled as she reminded him, "You did pretty well in the dark last night, Loverboy." She pointed to the bundled-up blanket and urged, "Check for my phone in there."

Lashkar lowered his arm and searched, but he returned to his original thought. "Nancy, listen to me for a minute. I know more about your mathematics than you think, and the power of the blast is incorrect."

By now, Nancy had searched the small table in front of Lashkar, and made her way to the dresser on the wall behind him. "You know we're pretty good at math, Lashkar."

Lashkar wrung his hands in front of him as he continued. "I know, that's why I'm having a hard time believing the math offset is an accident."

Nancy slid the top drawer open and muttered, "Where's that phone?"

Focusing on the door across the room, Lashkar raised his voice. "Seriously! Tell me what's going on with the EMP."

Nancy scooted onto the narrow bed behind Lashkar and cuddled into his back. She kissed his ear and purred, "You're too suspicious—" Nancy pressed the sharp needle from the syringe into the opposite side of his neck

"—for your own good."

Immediately, Lashkar's eyeballs rolled up and then his eyelids closed. He slumped back against Nancy who redirected him down into the bed. She made him more comfortable by placing the pillow under his head. She caressed his face as she whispered, "We don't need any distractions this morning, so you'll be asleep for about 24 hours." Her eyes warmed for a moment as she added, "When you wake up, I hope you'll understand."

She pushed off the bed to her feet, and pushed her feet into the thick boots. She picked her coat off the hook on the wall before pausing for a moment. She took one last look at Lashkar who looked so content, and as she closed the door behind her, she thought, *maybe I left my phone in the communications room.*

Natalie heard heavy footsteps in the hallway, and her eyelids fluttered open. Their room was completely dark except for a thin beam of light through their window from a lamppost outside. She turned towards the edge of the bed, and the small, metal table there. The LED numerals on the clock told her it was 6:20 a.m. She turned back and stretched with her hand, reaching out towards the far side of the bed where Josh should have been.

Instantly, her eyes opened wide with concern, and her hand searched around until her fingers contacted a piece of paper. She pulled it in front of her eyes but couldn't read anything in the darkness. Sitting up, she moved the small note in front of the narrow beam from the window until the words were visible to her. The note read,

> *Natalie,*
>
> *With all the anticipation, I couldn't sleep. I went to get something to eat and take a short walk. I'll be back before you know it.*
>
> *Remember how much I love you.*
>
> *Josh*

As she fell back into her soft pillow, she yawned. Her night had also been restless, but apparently, not as restless as Josh's had been. Adrian had requested that everyone meet in the center clearing at 9:00 a.m. From there, she assumed Adrian would provide a heartwarming speech, right after he mesmerised everyone with that hypnotic smile of his. Her eyes began to close as she thought, *I still have some more time to sleep before Josh is back.*

In the main control room, Adrian and Rita were making last minute finalizations. Adrian was looking intently at the Sholite monitor, watching lines of script fly by. Intermittently, his fingers would flash across the keyboard, followed by another onslaught of script.

Rita stood beside him with her butt leaning back against the edge of the heavy workbench. She had her phone pressed to her ear. "Okay, you're clear." There was a slight pause, and then she added, "Great! Thanks for your help, and make your way to the rendezvous point."

She disconnected the call and said to Adrian, "That was the last of the DEW line stations. Everything is on automatic at all seven stations, and all the personnel are clear."

Adrian replied, "Wonderful. This is going strangely well, with no hiccups at all." He tilted his face to look up at his second in command. His finger hovered over a key on the keyboard as he added, "This is it, Rita. When I press this key, the palm scanner will be activated, and we'll be only one step away from our goal and the goal of the Sholite people." He waited until the smile on Rita's face matched his own, and his finger came down on the key.

There was a staccato of clicks from relays engaging in the electrical cabinets around the room. Lights on them went from red to green, and finally, the palm scanner lit up bright-yellow. They both looked for a few moments at the end result of years of effort from the Sholites and, more recently, from their revived Earthers.

Their silent gloating was interrupted by a barely audible beep. Rita frowned and looked nervously at the electrical cabinets. Then, she heard the beep again, but this time she looked down at her jacket pocket. Pulling her phone from it, she saw the flashing, blue light in the upper corner, after which she engaged her text message screen. After a moment, she said to Adrian, "I have a text from Nancy. She needs my help for a few minutes in the generator room."

One eyebrow on Adrian's face lowered in irritation. "Best you take care of it. Now that the hand scanner is engaged, I can't leave the room."

"No problem," she replied. She placed her hand on Adrian's shoulder for a moment and mumbled, "No hiccups."

Rita walked out the door at the front of the communications building and reversed her direction down the narrow, plowed laneway to the back of the long building. The generator *room* was actually its own *building* between the communications building and the communications tower. There was an overhead flood light overtop the man-door to the generator building, and oddly, Rita noticed the guard, who would normally have been posted there, wasn't. Her brow creased with irritation as she stomped to the door. Some of the revived Earth soldiers weren't as strict as others. She would have to remember to get the name of the delinquent soldier who probably, at this moment, was drinking hot coffee in the mess hall.

She opened the door and entered the huge room filled with six large gas generators. The room was lit by a single overhead emergency light bulb. Reaching for the main light switch to power the bank of overhead fluorescent lights, she flicked it on, but there was no reaction. She flicked it off and on several times. She thought, *I hope our electrical geniuses did a better job on the blast emitters.* Walking towards the center of the room between the tightly packed generators, she said, "Nancy! Are you in here?"

She turned her face to the left, searching with her narrowed eyes through the dim light, and then she turned her gaze to the right. When she did so, a gloved hand from behind her, covered her mouth. The other gloved hand pushed the short blade into the side of her neck. Within three seconds, her eyes were lifeless, and her body was dragged back between the generators. There was a small space between one of the generators and the outside metal wall where her body was dumped on top of the guard who, apparently, wasn't drinking coffee in the mess hall.

There was a loud shrill beeping causing Natalie to bolt upright in her bed. Her first thought was to look down beside her. She saw the bed was still empty, so she turned to the clock on the table, and her eyes widened as she saw it was 8:45 a.m. She jumped to her feet, and now that the sun was just creeping over the horizon, she saw her phone doing a small vibrating dance on the metal table.

She thought, *who the hell would be calling me?* She picked up the phone and connected the caller. "Hello," she said.

"Natalie! Thank god. It's Philip. I've been trying to get a hold of you for days."

Natalie fell back onto the bed and rubbed her tired eyes. "It's been busy. The solar flare made a mess of communications for a while."

Philip interrupted her, "I'm getting really nervous. I don't know what you're up to, but I don't really want to. I probably shouldn't even be making this call, but I came across something that was boggling my mind."

"I'm at a loss concerning what could possibly boggle your mind," Natalie sarcastically replied.

"Smartass!" Philip chirped. "Seriously though, remember a couple of months ago, you asked me to check up on a fellow named Josh Harris?"

"Sure," Natalie responded.

"I kept that search algorithm open for no reason in particular. In fact, it was more because I forgot to close it," he admitted.

"Get to the point," Natalie urged.

"Something confusing came across my desk a few days ago. You see, Josh Harris of Upstate New York is dead."

"What!" Natalie blurted.

"Two weeks ago, a couple of hunters found a decomposed body in a shallow grave in the woods near his mountain home. Forensics have positively identified the man as Josh Harris."

Natalie was shaking uncontrollably as she disconnected the phone. Her shaking fingers pushed back the bangs off her forehead as the multitude of thoughts put quite a quandary in her mind. *The man she new as Josh, was not Josh! The man she loved was not Josh! He had lied to her all this time, but why?* It didn't take her long to get her thoughts lined up, and then, they only led to one conclusion. *The man she knew as Josh, must be a Russian spy!* She looked at the clock one more time and saw it was 8:50 a.m.

To save time, she pulled on a pair of work coveralls and a long-sleeved thermal t-shirt. The socks and boots were next, and before she left the room, she pulled on her shoulder holster along with her hand gun. Rushing out the door, she took the stairs down, three at a time and, moments later, was in the clearing between the buildings. Her fellow Earthers and Sholites were already beginning to gather in the central clearing, watching to the north where Adrian told them they would see a colourful display once the blast was released.

Natalie ran through the growing group, knocking people aside as they uttered their protests. She didn't stop until she reached the double doors to the communications building, and even there, it was only momentary. She rushed down the hallway and glanced in the first doorway to the main communications room, but as expected, it was empty. She didn't pause as she ran for the second doorway. She was sweating. She knew what she would find. Her mind was awash with confusion. She loved Josh or, at least, the man who portrayed himself as Josh Harris. Yet, at the same time, she was feeling anger and even hatred towards him as her concern for her planet grew.

She reached the doorway of the control room and banged into the far door jamb. In the room, she saw Adrian with his back to her and his hands in the air. Josh was on the far side of the room with his back against an electrical cabinet. His shirt was splattered with red blood and he held his handgun up, pointed at Adrian.

Instinctively, Natalie pulled out her own handgun and pointed it at Josh. "What the hell are you doing!" she screamed.

Adrian half turned and saw it was Natalie. The now familiar smile was replaced with a sneer. "Kill him, now, before it's too late!"

Josh shouted, "Don't move Adrian! Tell her the truth!"

"What truth?" Natalie blurted.

Josh's eyes, which had been cold as steel, turned softer. He said, "Adrian has been lying to you and I and all of us. Remember, I love you, so give me the benefit of the doubt. Things aren't as they appear. I could explain to you, but you will only believe the real story if he tells you." Josh flicked the barrel of the handgun at Adrian.

Adrian turned to Natalie and attempted his signature smile, but his lips were shaking and only one side curled up. "Remember, your world and mine are at stake. Kill him before it's too late."

Natalie was at an impasse. She didn't know what to do, and that's when things played out, taking the decision from her.

They heard the sound of an approaching helicopter. They'd become accustomed to the sound of their smaller Bell 525 machine, but this sound was deeper, and as the sound came closer, they could distinguish two rotors playing off each other. Moments later, there were loud bangs as flash grenades went off outside the building. There were yells and screams, followed by the sound of gunfire. The sound of single shot pistols was overpowered by the louder automatic machinegun fire of AK 47 and M16 assault rifles.

Adrian realized they were under attack. It was now or never. He lunged for the palm scanner. There were two shots, one a fraction of a second after the other. Adrian's palm was about 20 mm from the scanner when the bullet hit his stomach, throwing him back into the corner of the room. He was leaning against an electrical panel as he looked down and saw the blood pulsing from the wound. He put his hands over it, delaying the inevitable outcome.

Josh's eyebrows rose in surprise. He turned his gaze towards Natalie and saw the wisp of smoke from the barrel of her handgun. He faltered, pushing back against the control panel behind him. Slowly, he slid down to a sitting position, leaving a streak of blood against the green, metal door of the cabinet.

There was more and more screaming and gunfire from outside the building. There was even the occasional blast from what must have been a rocket launcher. Natalie ignored all this, and in her shock, she threw her gun aside. She ran to Josh and slid the last metre on her knees. She was surprised by the streak of blue blood on the panel behind him, but it didn't matter. She just shot the man she loved. Her life was turned upside down, but as far as she knew, her planet was about to be destroyed. She was angry, yet now, she was disgusted at herself in that she didn't care about her world. She just wanted Josh to live. Lifting his chin, she looked into his eyes. He half smiled, and she saw his teeth were coated with blue blood.

Tears were rolling down Natalie's cheeks in a nonstop torrent. She said, "Why did you do this? I love you..." Her indistinguishable words trailed off in the sobs that overtook her.

Josh knew he only had time for a few words, so best make them the important ones. He knew he was looking into those cat-like eyes under the pink streaks of hair for the last time. He whispered. "I love you. That's why I did this. I did this to save us." He coughed and a trickle of blue blood appeared at the corner of his mouth. "I'm not the bad guy." His head tilted slightly to the side, and there was a last deep exhale of breath. Natalie waited for the intake of air, but it didn't come. There was nothing. She screamed and put her arms around Josh's lifeless body.

Crying uncontrollably, she didn't hear the gunfire lessening. She was at a point where she didn't care about her world or her life. She just wanted to hold Josh. She heard footsteps behind her and then a yell. There was a second yell, but she still didn't respond. She felt her neck being grabbed, and she was pulled roughly to her feet, after which her body was slammed against the wall.

When the tears blurring her vision cleared enough for her to see, she was shocked. She thought her mind was playing tricks on her, for in front of her was a handsome face. If the face was not topped with black hair and the mouth not surrounded by a thin black moustache and beard, she would have thought she was looking at Josh.

Seeing she didn't have a weapon, Logan let her go and sidestepped backwards. He saw Adrian gurgling with the last minutes of his life in the far corner, and then he saw the palm scanner. Logan lifted his automatic rifle and put a burst of bullets into it.

The sound of running footsteps could be heard. Nick, dressed in black military gear and carrying his own rifle, poked his head in the doorway. "The site is secure. The enemy is either dead or captured. Do you need any help?"

Logan was looking at Josh's dead body, and his voice was subdued. "No, continue with the cleanup and I will be with you in a few minutes."

Once Nick had left, Logan flicked the muzzle at Josh and said, "Did you kill him?"

Natalie instantly began to sob. Through it, in an angry voice, she exclaimed, "Yes, I killed him! I love Josh and he gave me no choice! I had to kill him to save our world and the Sholite people on Talus 3!"

Logan's face turned red with anger. "Is that the bullshit the Sholites have been feeding you?" He lifted his gun and pointed it at Natalie. Natalie knew what was coming, but still, she threw up her hand instinctively. She waited, but the burst of bullets she expected to end her life didn't come. She lowered her hand and looked at Logan. The gun was shaking in his hand and the red began to ease from his face.

Logan asked, "Where did you get that ring?"

"What?" Natalie muttered. She looked at her hand covered in blue blood that was already turning clear. She saw the ring. "Josh gave it to me. We are—" She choked on a sob "—or were deeply in love. He told me this ring represented the day we would be married."

Logan wavered and then lowered the gun. He sighed and his demeanor completely changed. His voice was soft as he said, "The ring on your finger is an ancient heirloom from his family. It wouldn't be on your finger unless, as you have said, he gave it to you, and he would have only given it to you if you shared a deep love."

Looking at the ring again and then back to Logan, she asked, "How would you know all this?"

Logan looked sadly at the lifeless body. "The man you call Josh is a Korian, and he's my brother."

Natalie expelled an audible gasp.

Logan continued. "Both of us came to Earth many years ago. My task was to obtain help from the people of Earth and stop the firing of the EMP device. Josh's mission was more difficult. He was to infiltrate the Sholites and be the last resort in case I failed. It seems I was a few minutes too late."

Shock was setting in, but Natalie managed to keep her head. "But the EMP was to nudge the Sholite asteroid out of a collision course with Earth. Now we're all doomed."

Blurting out a guffaw, Logan retorted, "That's what they told you?"

Logan didn't wait for a reply. He moved over Adrian's form, and dragged him up to a sitting position at the workbench. He had to hold him upright as the Sholite leader gurgled from the wound to his gut. Logan looked at it and told Adrian, "You don't have long. Tell her the truth."

With a great effort, Adrian lifted his head and looked at Natalie. There was no smile as he said, "The EMP was to save both our worlds, but especially my people on Talus 3."

Logan roughly shook Adrian. "Tell her the truth! Go to your death with a clear conscience!"

After that, Adrian did actually manage a slight smile. "Natalie, I'm sorry, but this is war. Talus 3 is actually a Korian world. The story I told you about Shol and Kor is correct, just the positions are reversed. The blast we would have sent would have been very powerful, resulting in the Korian asteroid, Talus 3, being obliterated."

Adrian's head slumped over, but Logan shook him again. "What damage would the EMP have done to the people of Earth?"

After a few seconds and another shake from Logan, Adrian said, "One percent of the northern ice cap would have instantly melted. Your magnetic axis would have shifted ten degrees, resulting in earthquakes. It wouldn't have been an extinction event, but many millions on Earth would have died." He lifted his head for the last time and managed a shrug. "Acceptable collateral damage." Then his eyes went blank and Logan released him to slip to the floor, dead.

Natalie let all of Adrian's words sink in. She deserved to die. She felt grief, but she felt stupid and she was embarrassed. "Please kill me now," was all she could say.

Logan walked over to her. His words were filled with genuine concern. "I couldn't kill you now. You see, that ring on your finger makes you not only Korian, but also part of my family. I'm now sworn to protect you by my family oath."

Natalie didn't feel it was appropriate to say anything. Thanking him, or begging him further to kill her, would both be disrespectful to Josh and his brother.

Logan put his hand on her shoulder and offered, "Your Earth is safe, as is my home of Talus 3. Unfortunately, the war does have casualties. The Sholites are experts in coercion and turning people to their selfish purposes. You're not the first to fall prey to them." He gave a squeeze to Natalie's shoulder, hoping it would give her some assurance. "Adrian and the Sholites are the bad guys. They would've wreaked havoc on both our worlds. We Korians and our Russian friends are the good guys." For a moment, he looked sadly at his dead brother. "The man you called Josh, was a good guy. You just wound up on the wrong side."

Chapter 28: Saying Goodbye

Logan stood on the rise of snow-covered land south of the Fort Nelson DEW line communications station. It had been two days since the battle. Looking to his left down into the compound, it did indeed look like a battle had been fought. During the fight with the Sholites, the hanger had caught fire, and the helicopter inside exploded. Now, there was only a twisted metal frame visible through the metal roof that had collapsed. There were still some smoldering embers providing small wisps of smoke into the air.

Thankfully, the Sholites had an ingenious device that could dig and crumble frozen rock and soil, allowing for the mass grave in the center of the compound. There was a roar as a plow let off a blast from the diesel exhaust as the front scraper smoothed out the crushed material over the grave holding 12 Sholite bodies, including Adrian and Rita.

In front of Logan, two Korian men were just finishing the cover of crumbled, frozen soil and rock over his brother's body. A similar but smaller machine, with some difficulty, had been hauled up to this vantage point at the insistence of Natalie. The machine cut a one metre wide by three metre long grave. Thirty minutes ago, Josh, wrapped in a white, Korian blanket, was placed within it. Silently, Logan and Natalie who stood beside him, said their goodbyes, as did Nick and Lashkar, who stood to the right of the grave.

Nick felt awkward from the beginning of the burial since he never met Josh, but he stayed out of respect for his friend, Logan. However, now, it was time to give the others some time on their own. He quietly said, "I'll catch up with you later. I have some things to attend to." With that said, he walked around the top of the unmarked grave and made his way down the hill.

Lashkar also thought it better to leave Natalie and Logan alone in the last moments they would spend with Josh. "I'll take my leave also."

As he walked by Logan, Logan grasped Lashkar's arm and asked, "Are you sure you will be coming with us?"

Lashkar awoke the day after the battle and found the world turned upside down. Adrian, Rita and Josh were dead, and Nancy, who he'd become close to, was a prisoner of the Korians. He talked to her, but her interest in their relationship had faded quickly. He justified this with the thought, the failure of their mission and the death of her leaders was in the forefront of her mind. Lashkar made up his mind, at that time, to continue to learn the advanced math and science of the aliens, and if that meant he would continue with the Korians, so be it. "I'm very sure, Logan. I'd like to learn more, and I think I can help you."

Natalie asked Lashkar, "Where are you going now?"

Lashkar made a sad effort at a grin. "I won't see my father again. I need to call him, and then I'm going to send him 5 million dollars."

"How are you going to do that," Logan blurted.

"I wrote a program," Lashkar explained. "I have added two cents to the power bill of everyone in New York State, for the next three months. The program will divert the accumulation to my father's account." He winked at Natalie before following Nick's boot prints down the hill.

Shrugging, Logan said, "He certainly seems a clever fellow."

Natalie added, "You won't be disappointed."

The two Korian men finished with the grave and left Natalie and Logan alone in the small clearing between the white pine trees. It was just past noon, and even though there was a slight breeze, the sun was bright and warmed them.

Natalie's mood was sad and lacklustre. To a degree, she was still in shock, having lost her father first and now, Josh, the only man she had ever truly loved. She had very little sleep since whenever her eyes would close, she would relive the moment she shot him. She knew the vision would never leave her, but perhaps the day would come when it wasn't there every single moment.

Without taking her eyes off the grave, she said, "I've made the biggest mistake of my life, and I am a fool."

"You told me Lashkar was one of the smartest people on your entire planet," Logan replied.

"What does that have to do with me and the fool I am?"

Logan offered, "Lashkar was fooled by the Sholites as well. It seems you are in good company. It shows the deception had less to do with how smart you are or aren't, and more to do with the Sholites expertise at such duplicity."

Natalie's fingers had been clenched in her coat pockets, but now they relaxed somewhat. She played with the ring on her finger, and it reminded her how lucky she was. Logan had every right to kill her, but he didn't. In fact, since the battle, he had made every effort to comfort her. Even though

Josh was dead, she couldn't stop loving him—she never would, but she could see much of Josh in Logan. Just being with him was helping her heal.

A gust of cool wind tussled Logan's black hair, and he brought his hands up to his lips and blew into them. He had also come to like Natalie. Even though the events that occurred had her in shock, Logan appreciated how well she handled herself. He could see what attracted his brother to this woman. That's why it was difficult for him to tell her what he had to say. "My work here is done, and I will be returning to Talus 3. Since you know too much about the Sholites and now us, you must come with me."

"I've been thinking about that, and knew it was coming." Natalie pointed to the graveyard behind the barracks and said, "My father is buried there, and Josh is here. I've no one else on Earth, so I'll gladly come, but it'll probably be more difficult for you than for me."

Logan smiled. "You will come to see the Korian people are not very complicated. In many ways, they are more like people from the Russian culture where logic is more prevalent than emotion. Things are more black or white, and there are less shades of grey."

"They will see me as the woman who killed your brother."

"To a small degree, yes," Logan agreed. "But my brother will be seen as a state hero. More than you being seen as the person who killed him, you will be seen as the wife of a hero. Korians love a good story, especially if romance is involved. The history of your relationship with the man you knew as Josh, will be written this way."

Natalie's cheeks filled with air and she gave a long exhale. At the same time her hand moved to her stomach.

Logan saw this and raised an eyebrow. "You are with child."

"Yes," she whispered.

"Did he know?"

"No," she answered. "I was going to tell him after the EMP blast."

Logan nodded. "Now, you definitely have to come with me. A select group of Korians have been on your world for 40 years, so it might be a surprise that your baby will not be the first as a result of a joining between an Earthling and a Korian. However, for your baby to survive, you will need to be under the strict care of a Korian doctor."

"As I said, even if I wasn't pregnant, I'd want to come with you," Natalie repeated. "This spot for Josh's burial was not by chance. He came to love this land and the wilderness. He wanted to be buried here, if something should happen to him."

Logan reached up and put his hand on Natalie's nearest shoulder, but only for a moment. He quickly slid his hand across to rest on her far shoulder. "When I first saw the pink streaks in your bangs, I thought it was quite odd. But it's grown on me, and I think you should keep them when we go to Talus 3."

A few days ago, she would have snickered at his comment. "On Talus 3, I hope to make amends for what I did to Josh and to your family. I want to prove myself to be worthy of your faith in me. Hopefully, when I die, I'll be buried on his world, just as he is buried on mine. It would be apropos, don't you think?"

Logan gave her shoulder a reassuring squeeze as he smiled. He did not respond or add to her words, for he could not have said them any better.

Natalie felt the squeeze and she leaned in just a bit closer to him. She felt guilty at how she enjoyed the familiarity of his touch. It provided a small ray of hope that, one day, she would smile again.

The story continues in Galactic Illusions, book two of the Talus 3 series.

Dear Reader:

Reviews are important to every author. We are thankful that many readers take a few moments to return to the purchasing website, in this case, Amazon, and leave a rating and a review.

If you could do so for this story, it would be much appreciated. Keep in mind, a Hollywood style review is not needed. Even a few simple words would be great.

Thanks again, and I hope you enjoyed the story.

Peter Sandor

www.ingramcontent.com/pod-product-compliance
Lightning Source LLC
Chambersburg PA
CBHW021335250626
47155CB00002B/711